...Real world ...at...... .... of the entries in this gathering of supernaturally charged dating adventures end more than well enough to satisfy. As theme anthologies go, this one is unusually successful."
—*Publishers Weekly,* for *Mystery Date*

"A winning treat . . . this low-key pub crawl is surprisingly consistent, delivering a punchy blend of shocks, laughs and otherworldly action."
—*Publishers Weekly,* for *Cosmic Cocktails*

"Denise Little has put together some really nice collections in the past few years, and it's gotten to the point where, if I see her name as editor I know I'm in for a worthwhile read."
—*Chronicle,* for *The Magic Shop*

"Given the career of an English boy named Harry, the creation of an American school for magic-workers was inevitable. Not inevitable was that the place be a fount of intelligent entertainment. Editor Little's judgment helps make it such, and the comprehensive folkloric expertise she displays."
—*Booklist,* for *The Sorcerer's Academy*

"Exceedingly well done."
—*Booklist,* for The Valedemar Companion

"*Familiars* is a load of fun to read for the fantasy fan or anyone who wants a good escape. Little has gathered fifteen highly original short stories that deal with magical companions."
—Kliatt, for *Familiars*

"After finishing this anthology, readers will never look at magic shops and new age/metaphysical bookstores the same way again. Little aptly describes the anthology as a 'collection of stories of the changed fates and challenged minds of the amazed consumers—both mundane and magical—who dared to shop at a Magic Shop.' Buyer beware!"
—*The Barnes and Noble Review* for *The Magic Shop*

Also Available from DAW Books:

Swordplay, **edited by Denise Little**
Swords—at one time they were the quintessential weapons, and even today there are true sword masters practicing their craft around the world. Certainly, swords are essential tools of the trade in fantasy novels. From a dwarf-crafted blade meant to slay a dragon to a cursed sword that once belonged to D'Artagnan, from Arthur's legendary Excalibur to the Sword of Solomon, from a sword bespelled to crave blood to cold steel that magicks its wielder into a video game, here are seventeen imaginative stories that cut right to the heart of fantasy adventure. From Kristine Kathryn Rusch, Nina Kiriki Hoffman, Peter Orullian, Laura Resnick, Loren L. Coleman, Janna Silverstein, J. Steven York, Jean Rabe and others.

Intelligent Design, **edited by Denise Little**
Even though evolution has long been accepted as scientific fact, there are still many who believe everything that exists in our modern-day world is part of a divine plan. And despite the proof offered by fossils on our own world, and the discovery of other inhabitable planets scattered across the galaxy, many people still believe that the Bible should be taken literally. But even among those who believe religion trumps science, there are many who seek to integrate these two ways of perceiving the universe into a larger, meaningful pattern. Now eleven intrepid explorers of this controversy—Kristine Kathryn Rusch, Brendan DuBois, Jean Rabe, Jody Lynn Nye, Sarah A. Hoyt, Janny Wurts, Dean Wesley Smith, Laura Resnick and others—bring their own unique perspectives to the debate in tales that range from a look at life on Earth as an out of control science project to a story that reveals which species will actually inherit the planet to the investigation of a scientist determined to discover the truth about God.

Witch High, **edited by Denise Little**
High school can often be the most influential period in a teenager's life. Enduring friendships are formed and possible directions for the future are explored. For some it is a time to shine, for others just four years to be gotten through. The fourteen original tales, by Diane Duane, Sarah Zettel, Esther M. Friesner, Sarah A. Hoyt, Jody Lynn Nye, Kristine Kathryn Rusch, Laura Resnick and others included in *Witch High* explore the challenges that students of the magical arts may face in a high school of their very own. If you think chemistry is difficult, try studying alchemy. If you ever fell victim to a school bully, how would you deal with a bully gifted with powerful magic? If you ever wished for extra time to study for those exams, could the right spell give you all the time you could possibly need?

The Trouble with Heroes

edited by
Denise Little

DAW BOOKS, INC.
DONALD A. WOLLHEIM, FOUNDER
375 Hudson Street, New York, NY 10014

ELIZABETH R. WOLLHEIM
SHEILA E. GILBERT
PUBLISHERS
http://www.dawbooks.com

First Printing, November 2009

1 2 3 4 5 6 7 8 9

DAW TRADEMARK REGISTERED
U.S. PAT. AND TM. OFF. AND FOREIGN COUNTRIES
—MARCA REGISTRADA
HECHO EN U.S.A.

PRINTED IN THE U.S.A.

ACKNOWLEDGMENTS

Introduction copyright © 2009 by Denise Little

"Geeks Bearing Gifts" copyright © 2009 by Kristine Grayson

"The Horror in the Living Room," copyright © 2009 by Adrian Nikolas Phoenix.

"Take My Word for It: Bad Idea," copyright © 2009 by Mike Moscoe.

"Merry Maid," copyright © 2009 by Jean Rabe.

"The Problem with Dating Shapeshifters," copyright © 2009 by Nina Kiriki Hoffman.

"Reclaiming His Inner Ape," copyright © 2009 by Terry Hayman.

"For a Few Lattes More," copyright © 2009 by Annie Reed.

"Beloved," copyright © 2009 by David H. Hendrickson.

"Inspiration," copyright © 2009 by Phaedra M. Weldon.

"Honey, I'm Home," copyright © 2009 by Pauline J. Alama.

"Ballad of the Groupie Everlasting," copyright © 2009 by Robert T. Jeschonek.

"The Quin Quart," copyright © 2009 by Laura Resnick.

"How Jack Got His Self a Wife," copyright © 2009 by John Alvin Pitts.

"If The Shoe Fits," copyright © 2009 by Dayle A. Dermatis.

"Big Man's Little Woman," copyright © 2009 by Dory Crowe.

"Boldly Reimagined," copyright © 2009 by J. Steven York.

"Roxane," copyright © 2009 by Peter Orullian.

"A Long Night in Jabbok (or, Who, Exactly, Is in Charge Here?)," copyright © 2009 by Janna Silverstein.

"Love in the Time of Car Alarms," copyright © 2009 by Ken Scholes.

"The Problem with Metaphors," copyright © 2009 by Steven Mohan, Jr.

"If I Did It," copyright © 2009 by Allan Rousselle.

"Clay Feet," copyright © 2009 by Kristine Kathryn Rusch.

TABLE OF CONTENTS

INTRODUCTION

Denise Little

All actual heroes are essential men.
And all men are possible heroes.
—Elizabeth Barrett Browning (1806-1861)

Heroes are much the same, the point's agreed,
From Macedonia's madman to the Swede;
The whole strange purpose of their lives to find,
Or make, an enemy of all mankind!
—Alexander Pope (1688-1744)

Everybody loves a hero. We extol them in folk tales, legends, comic books, movies, genre fiction, and live newscasts. We love nothing better than seeing an ordinary man raised to the level of hero by making an impossible rescue, or foiling a terrible crime. We like heroes so much that we invent them, many too much larger than life to ever be believable—heroes like Paul Bunyan or Jack the Giant Killer. We've founded a whole genre around impossible heroes—comic books exist to tell the tales of bizarre but useful citizens like Batman and Supermen. In real life, I'd run screaming from a guy in tights who was trying to interfere in my adventures.

1

But I still love to read about heroes, and I never miss a good hero movie.

But there's a big problem with heroes. No matter how wonderful they might be in fantasy or reality, at the end of the day after they've worked their heroic deeds, they're stuck with the problems of ordinary living. They have to go home, rest up, kick back, and get ready for the next heroic deed. So if a hero enters a woman's life in a nonheroic way, and she gets involved with him, she's still left with all the usual problems of housekeeping, cooking, scheduling, and otherwise working around the life of a man who can be called away on a moment's notice to save the world. Words like "irritating" and "disruptive" don't even begin to cover the feelings engendered by dealing with a hero on an everyday basis.

The Trouble with Heroes is all about the other side of heroism. From what it's like to be Hercules' wife (complete with an appearance by Hercules in drag), to the trials of H. P. Lovecraft's housekeeper, to the perils of being a giant ape's girlfriend, to the downside of dating a shapeshifter, this anthology takes the reader voyaging into an advanced course on heroism, concentrating on the behind-the-scenes trauma, not the glorious rescues. Which not only turns heroism on its head, it also frequently leads to belly laughs. Even more intriguing to me, these stories show the delicate dance it takes for a superhuman to function—and not very many can function well without a good support staff. So the conceit of this book is to shine a light on the true heroes: the people who enable and put up with heroes. More power to them, and God forbid I ever become one of them.

I have a feeling I'd be terrible at it.

But I sure enjoyed reading about the problem.

I hope you do, too.

GEEKS BEARING GIFTS

Kristine Grayson

Kristine Grayson is the author of several award-winning humorous fantasy romance novels, including *Absolutely Captivated* and *Totally Spellbound*. *Publisher's Weekly* calls the series "delightful." Her short fiction has also appeared in many anthologies, including *Time After Time*.

Bethanne Dupree did not know a lot about mythology. In fact, what she knew, prior to what she later called The Event, her employees called The Incident, and her customers called The Class Action Suit, was a handful of names. Venus, Jupiter, and Zeus were the ones she could recite, not realizing that two were different names for the same guy.

On the day that the Event/Incident/Class Action Suit started, she had no idea that gods existed outside of musty textbooks and yummy Brad Pitt movies. She didn't know that gods got bored. And she had no idea that bored gods used humans.

She certainly didn't expect to be the victim of those gods.

And when she found out that she was, she knew she didn't have a defense that would stand up in court.

In fact, she didn't have a defense at all.

The whole mess started on an ordinary day at Eros. com. All days were ordinary at Eros.com. Eros.com wasn't the largest internet dating service, nor was it the smallest. It wasn't the oldest nor the most famous.

But it had started back in the days when the internet was young. Bethanne's then-boyfriend, Larry, wrote a program to help his geek friends find the perfect mate.

Larry named the service Eros.com, figuring anyone who didn't know the name Eros wasn't smart enough to find a mate on Eros.com. Bethanne never told him that she didn't know who Eros was. She just quietly—and unobtrusively—looked up Eros in the dictionary. And found that Eros was what the Greeks called that cherubic half-naked boy with the bow and arrows, whom most of the known world called Cupid.

She never liked the name Eros.com, and she wasn't that fond of the business, but by the time Larry's friends had all hooked up with potential mates (and Larry realized that the girl of his dreams was actually a guy), Eros. com did $2.5 million a year, had sixteen employees, and a web network of over ten million lovelorn souls.

Whatever Bethanne was (and she'd been called a lot of things), she wasn't the kind of woman to walk away from millions, no matter how bogus she thought the company actually was.

There were a lot of desperate people out there, all willing to pay $25 per month for a standard subscription to Eros, whose best promotional campaign had claimed that you could actually trust Geeks Bearing Gifts.

Bethanne paid Larry $200,000 for the whole company with a promise that he'd get an extra 20K every time he upgraded the program—money she earned back in the first month alone. Fortunately for her, Larry, for all his brilliance, cared less about money than he did about code.

Fast forward ten years, through the dotcom crisis (which she weathered by never trying to go public) into the Bush era and beyond. Eros.com still wasn't the big gun or even, really, a small gun. It was just a bet-hedger for the desperate daters, the ones who didn't care if their date weighed three hundred fifty pounds, so long as he could carry on a decent conversation and earn a pretty good living.

Which was why the Greek God's arrival at the office was so very stunning.

First of all, he wasn't calling himself a Greek God. The staff started calling him a Greek God from the moment they saw him. He called himself Ray.

He came to the office's front door. Some clients did that. The website did say that clients could come to the office to make their initial video blog if they so chose. Most did not so choose. After all, Eros.com had been designed for and still catered to the geek, and most geeks figured they could make a better v-log than some random employee at an internet dating service.

What the geeks didn't know—and probably didn't care about—was that Bethanne kept some makeup artists on hand. These people were supposed to make even the ugliest client look passable. Sometimes that was easier said than done. But she did keep before and after pictures, just to prove that an improvement had been made.

The office's front door opened onto a side street near the company parking lot. Bethanne had installed a lot of security, since occasionally Eros.com had to protect itself from dissatisfied clients.

Dissatisfied clients weren't really upset with the service—they were upset with the date. They hadn't read the fine print, which said that Eros.com wasn't responsible for the experience or, really, the match. It just facilitated a meeting while—to the best of its ability—trying to screen out anyone with a criminal record.

But that didn't stop dissatisfied customers from occasionally pounding on the door. Some hated their dates. Some hated the marriages born of the dates. And some just plain hated everything and needed someone to blame.

So, Bethanne had installed a state-of-the-art security system, complete with cameras. The cameras showed a 360-degree view of the person at the door as well as scanned for weaponry, using (although she'd never admit it to the cops) a scanning system that was similar to (but more sophisticated than) the ones airports used to see bombmaking material hidden under clothes.

All of this meant that the moment the Greek God knocked, someone got to see a 360-degree (mostly naked) view of one of the handsomest men of all time.

What did one of the handsomest men of all time look like? Well, he was Greek after all, which meant he had a slight accent—although no one noticed that for a good half hour. His eyes were the startling blue of a sun-dappled sea, his skin a Mediterranean olive that accented his black-black hair.

He had broad shoulders and narrow hips (and, Bethanne thought privately as she reviewed the footage later, the best ass she'd seen on a man in her entire life). His lashes were long, his lips delicate, and his cheekbones high.

His eyes sparkled with an intelligence that might have seemed higher than normal simply because it was attached to such an astonishing face.

He—quite literally—glowed. The glow was an amazing special effect, almost as if he were lit from the inside.

"What's *he* doing here?" Rachel Vadder, who was monitoring the door that day, asked no one in particular. But her question brought Anna Cummings, the security chief, and Stuart Robinson, the IT guy in charge of facial recognition, over to Rachel's screen at a run.

"I'm sorry," she said as they crowded around her,

wanting to know what the problem was. "I didn't mean 'What's he doing here?' as in 'Oh, no! Not that guy again!' but as in 'What the hell is *he* doing here?' As in 'What's wrong with him that he feels he needs us?' I mean, really. I'll go out with him now, and he hasn't said a word to me."

"With that body, he doesn't have to," Anna said, leaning closer to the monitor.

"He can stand there for hours," Stuart said. Stuart was another of Larry's love-'em-and-leave-'em conquests who stayed at Eros.com. "I really won't mind."

"You're supposed to be looking at his face," Rachel said tightly, even though she was the one who had just implied that this man didn't need to be vetted.

"I . . . am . . . did . . . am . . . looking at his face," Stuart stammered.

"I certainly am," said Anna. "Not to mention the rest of him."

"I don't think we should mention the rest of him." Bethanne spoke from behind the group.

They jumped as a unit, but they didn't turn away from the screen.

Bethanne had come to see what the commotion was all about and had found three of her most trusted employees drooling over a man standing outside the office door. A man who appeared mostly naked, at least on the computer screen. A man who appeared mostly naked on that screen *without his permission*.

"In fact," Bethanne said as calmly as she could, "I think we should let him in before we violate his privacy even farther."

"Yeah, right, sure," Rachel said, and was about to press the enter button when Bethanne leaned forward and caught her hand.

"Follow procedure, Rachel," Bethanne said.

"Oh, yeah, right," Rachel said, her cheeks turning bright red. "I . . . I . . . I'm . . ."

She was probably trying to say she was sorry, but

she couldn't seem to finish the sentence. So Bethanne swept her employees aside and slipped into a nearby chair.

As she scooted that chair closer to the screen, she finally saw the man who would soon identify himself as Ray Greco, and her breath literally caught in her throat. Her heart sped up and her hand started to shake.

A man had never ever made her forget what she was about to do next, but this guy did. Finally, she understood all the romance novel clichés—*love at first sight, so beautiful that it was impossible to see anything but him, so appealing that all she wanted to do was* . . .

She got a grip on herself and her mental processes. Then she pressed the intercom button.

"Sorry to keep you waiting, sir," she said. "This is Eros.com. Please state your business."

He looked around until he saw one of the tiny cameras. Then he smiled at it.

Bethanne was stunned that the camera didn't explode from the sheer wattage behind that smile. She'd never seen anything quite that powerful before.

She heard herself gasp audibly, glad she hadn't kept the intercom button pressed, so that the only people who heard her indiscreet little reaction to that unbelievably handsome man were her three employees.

"Hi," the Greek God said. "Your website says that I can make a video blog here if, um, you know, I want to be a client. And I do want to be a client."

Bethanne had to replay his words in her head twice before she understood them. Because, when she first heard them, she simply reacted to the timbre of his voice. Then she thought about it and found herself distracted by the word "timbre." Was his voice like Gregory Peck's? Or like Hugh Jackman's? Both had that rich baritone that could delve into bass or rise to tenor if need be. But each had a slightly different quality, a different take on that theatrical warmth—

She had to shake off that thought too before she

could replay the words one final time in her head. He wanted to be a client. He wanted to do a v-log.

If he liked making v-logs, he could come to the office every week and update. She could look on his beautiful face *every week*.

"I'm sorry to keep you waiting, Mr.—?"

"Greco," he said.

"Mr. Greco." Bethanne prided herself on her professional tone. Only she knew how hard-won it was. "Of course you can make a v-log here. If you wait near the entrance, one of our employees will get you and take you to processing, where you'll fill out the information forms and make your first v-log."

"Okay," he said, but she cut off the word midway through the "O" and the "K."

Her hand was still shaking.

"See?" Rachel asked, still clinging to her chair. "Why is *he* here? Shouldn't he be—I don't know—dating a supermodel or something?"

"Maybe he's so deep in the closet that his dates with women never go well," said Stuart in a wistful tone that Bethanne had never heard before. "Maybe he needs to find a man who—"

"Or," Bethanne said, not wanting to hear the extent of Stuart's fantasies, "maybe he's shy."

"Oh," Anna breathed. "Imagine if he's shy. I do so love shy men."

"Especially if they look like Greek Gods," Stuart said.

Bethanne rolled her eyes. Before she dealt with this crew—and the still naked-appearing man outside—she had to think of someone in processing who was male and straight. Very, very straight. So straight that he might not notice a good-looking man unless the man bit him in the ass. And then he'd punch said good-looking man without a single qualm.

No one in this room would ever punch Mr. Greco, even if he deserved it. After all, they wouldn't want to mar his lovely skin.

She pressed a different button on the intercom.

"Craig," she said to the straightest, most macho man who worked at Eros.com, a manly man who made the Marlboro Man seem like a gun-toting wimp. "Get down to the main entrance pronto. We have a potential client who has been waiting much too long to go to processing."

"Got it," Craig growled and signed off.

She trusted Craig to get Greco to the right department. What happened after the man arrived would be anyone's guess. She might have to supervise that as well, given everyone's reaction to the man (including hers).

But she would think about that in a minute. First, she had another matter to take care of.

"Your behavior," she said to the three beside her, "was extremely unprofessional. And if Mr. Greco ever finds out about our security scanning—which is supposed to take place in less than twenty seconds—you could open us up for a lawsuit. What do you have to say for yourselves?"

Anna bowed her head. "I'm sorry."

"I *was* looking at his face," Stuart said, in a tone so defensive that he probably never really saw the man's face at all.

"C'mon, Bethanne," Rachel said. She'd been at Eros. com for nearly fifteen years, through ups, downs, and Bethanne's rather ugly break-up with Larry. "You saw him. We've never had a great beauty from either gender. He was worth staring at."

"He's a client," Bethanne said. "We're professionals. Let's act that way."

Then she stomped back to her office, hoping that she could remain professional along the way.

Professional was hard. Professional was very hard when you were single, pushing forty, and concentrating on helping not-so-attractive people find their soulmates each and every day.

Bethanne's office had become her refuge. She had created it during a particularly bad stretch in her life. She had broken up with Larry (over, of all people, Stuart), had bought the business, and then had been sued by six different clients who all alleged failures in the Eros. com system. One client believed her new boyfriend was a stalker, another's new boyfriend got arrested (and later convicted!) for rape, and a third had married a man who had four other wives. The remaining three cases were simple cases of buyer's remorse—the three men claimed that the women they dated weren't the same as the way the women had been presented on Eros.com's website.

So Bethanne had hired a big-name law firm which made all of the cases go away, and then redesigned the company's disclosure forms to better protect Eros.com, its owners, and its employees. Bethanne soon realized it was cheaper to hire an in-house counsel and pay an exorbitant salary for prevention than it was to keep the big-name law firm on retainer.

But in the course of winning these cases, preventing future cases, and figuring out how to save herself some money, Bethanne nearly had a nervous breakdown. The shrink she'd hired (and later fired) recommended a bit of feng shui at the office, just to help Bethanne calm down.

Bethanne didn't want to spend another fortune redesigning the Eros.com offices, which, in those days, were in a dying strip mall on the outskirts of town. So, she bought the warehouse that became Eros.com's current offices and built a loft on the top floor.

That loft became her office. Actually, it was her office suite. The kind of office suite that most people in corporate America could only dream of. It had three sections: the reception area, where she greeted her guests and often met with them; her private working office, with her files, her various computers, and her various desks; and the apartment, complete with built-in kitchen, full-size bathroom (with a shower built for five—not that she had ever shared it with anyone), a full-size closet with enough clothes that she wouldn't have to go home for the rest of her life, and a bedroom with a queen-sized bed and a wide-screen television hooked up to every single cable channel her provider had.

She didn't live at the office, but she could. Mostly, she used that queen-sized bed for baby-sized naps, guaranteed to calm her and help her through very long days.

After her confrontation with her staff and her own unprofessional behavior, Bethanne would normally have fled to the bedroom of her office suite, flopped on the bed, turned on the Cooking Channel, and gotten a few moments of shut-eye.

But she couldn't look at the bed at the moment. Because if she did, she wouldn't think of sleeping. She would think of how wonderful Mr. Greco had looked without his clothes, and she would . . .

She shook that not-so-tender thought from her brain and went into the office part of her office suite. Really, what she needed to do was go to the shower of her office suite, set the water temperature on frigid, and hoped that it cooled her down. But the shower was built for five, so it could easily accommodate two . . .

She had to shake that thought out of her head too, and several other thoughts that came in rapid succession. Mr. Greco, whoever he was, was not just the most beautiful man she had ever seen but he was also the only man who had ever inspired this kind of uncontrollable lust in her.

If asked—even two hours ago—she would have said that women didn't feel the same kind of uncontrollable lust that men felt. She would have said that women never thought with their gonads, while men always did.

But she would have been wrong. Because her gonads— or her hormones—or her (sadly neglected) sexual self— had controlled every thought she had since she first saw Mr. Greco (naked).

And she was somehow going to have to get over that.

* * *

Staying in her office obviously wasn't calming her down, so Bethanne decided to supervise Mr. Greco's intake exam. She wasn't the only person who had found her way to receiving. So had every woman in the place and about half the men.

As she pushed her way through the crowd, she saw Mr. Greco lounging in front of Craig's desk, answering questions as if the response really didn't matter.

The crowd didn't seem to matter to him either. He was clearly the kind of man who received attention wherever he went.

Which begged the question: What the hell *was* he doing here?

Bethanne almost pulled him aside and asked, but she got wrapped up in watching the way his hands moved as he made a point. His fingers were long and tapered, his movements graceful, and that voice—she still couldn't decide if it was more Hugh Jackman or Gregory Peck.

She completely lost her opportunity to talk to Mr. Greco during intake because she found herself wondering if his hands indicated the size (and elegance) of other parts.

And while she wondered, Craig led Mr. Greco to the small video section of the warehouse.

Craig also had the foresight to order everyone else back to work.

They went, reluctantly, not because Craig told them to but because Bethanne was there. And the young geeks all believed that Bethanne was too old and dried up to be interested in Mr. Greco. She clearly had to be in the intake area to supervise Craig (and the rest of them). She certainly wouldn't be interested in a man as gorgeous, luscious, and just plain amazing as Mr. Greco.

Still, she was glad they left. She trailed her employee and his beautiful charge to the video wing and settled on a chair to watch.

The video wing was small but state-of-the-art.

Bethanne could have produced an independent film in that little section of the warehouse—if the independent filmmaker wanted a choice of three sets (a bedroom, a comfortable kitchen, and an outdoorsy scene that varied depending on what the interviewee wanted, thanks to a more-expensive-than-she-wanted-to-think-about blue screen).

Mr. Greco chose a sun-dappled Mediterranean scene—lots of white with marble stairs and columns and an unbelievably blue sea sparkling in the distance. The image, viewed through a monitor, made his eyes bluer and his hair a richer black. It also brought out his glow, as if that sun-dappled whiteness had reflected on his own incredibly lovely olive-colored skin.

Craig gave him the option of doing one, two, or five v-logs. "You won't have to return as often if you do the first five right now," Craig said, admirably repeating the pitch, "and you get a price break." Mr. Greco smiled at him. "Everyone loves a price break," he said.

Bethanne watched, listened, absorbed, and didn't remember a word the man said. When he finished, she turned to one of the lab techs (whose name escaped her—damn near everything was escaping her at the moment, including her usual level of perfection) and said they needed someone like Craig to do the edit.

Of course, she had to whack the lab tech twice before she even got the woman's attention. And then the woman asked, "Who the hell else will be as oblivious as Craig?"

It took five minutes to remember who Bethanne's macho employees were and another two minutes to confirm that a couple of those macho, macho men weren't simply compensating.

Then she excused herself, went into the corridor, and took several deep breaths. Crazy, crazy, crazy.

A single man shouldn't make a sensible woman crazy. He shouldn't make an entire business crazy, yet he had done that with hers.

She finally got a grip on herself—or could at least pretend to have a grip—when she headed down the corridor to the intake area, determined to read his profile.

Instead, she ran into him.

Literally.

The man smelled of sunshine. She noticed that first. He wore no cologne, and none of that damn bodyspray so many geeky men thought improved their chances with the opposite sex. He put his very firm hands on her shoulders and helped settle her.

Instead, shivers ran through her. His touch was quite *un*settling.

She wanted to melt into him, but that would be unprofessional. More than unprofessional. It would be embarrassing.

And the idea of embarrassing herself in front of this man made her untangle herself from his grasp.

She extended her hand. "Bethanne Dupree. I own Eros.com."

His smile was slow and sexy, not the full wattage thing he'd done outside, but something infinitely more effective. "Ray Greco."

He took her hand, but didn't shake it. He just held it, as if it were the most precious thing in the world.

Her cheeks heated. Her whole body heated. She had a full-on major hot flash, even though she hadn't reached that time of life yet.

She made herself shake his hand once and let go. His fingers released hers a little slowly, almost reluctantly it seemed.

She blinked. Each breath was a struggle for control. She held onto her brain like a woman under anesthesia trying to remain conscious.

"I must say, Mr. Greco, you're not our usual client."

He raised a single eyebrow. The movement was elegant, simple, and not affected at all. Had any other man done it, it would have seemed affected.

He didn't seem to know how to be affected.

"Really?" he asked, and she couldn't tell if the tone was sarcastic or not. (Hell, she couldn't tell if his voice was more Gregory Peck or Hugh Jackman, so how was she going to hear *nuance*?) "What is your usual kind of client?"

She bit her lower lip. Mr. Greco hadn't been vetted yet. For all she knew, he was a representative of the competition, with a teeny tiny webcam attached somewhere on his person. If she spoke the truth about her clients, she might see a video of that truth on YouTube, and that video might make its way to *20/20*. She could almost see the teaser: *Internet Dating Services—what they really think of their clients,* followed by her own voice-over saying, *Well, usually, Mr. Greco, they're fat, pimply, socially awkward men who make more money than should be allowed . . .*

But she didn't exactly know how to answer Mr. Greco without insulting him too. Because she couldn't say, *Our usual client is a high-achieving male with an IQ off the charts* since that would imply that Mr. Greco a) wasn't high achieving or b) had an IQ off the charts.

(Although she did think that. Why did she think that? Because he was so pretty? Pretty men could be smart, couldn't they? *Couldn't they?*)

"It just seems," she said, "that a man like you wouldn't need a service to get a date."

"Ah," he said, as if he just understood the secrets of the universe. "You're right. I don't need a—what do you call it?—service to get a date. I'm hoping that Eros.com will help me find the *right* date."

"The right date," Bethanne repeated. Why hadn't she thought of that before? The *right* date. Not any date. Not just a date. But the *right* date.

Already she could picture the advertising. Of course, Ray Greco would be front and center, saying in that delightfully deep voice, *Eros.com helped me find the* right *date. It's so hard to find the perfect person on your own . . .*

"You know, Mr. Greco," she said, "this would make a spectacular marketing campaign. I'm just heading to dinner. Would you like to join me? We could talk about the difference between a date and the right date."

His eyes narrowed, and for a moment she thought she had made a mistake.

Then he smiled that multimegawatt smile.

"Of course," he said. "Dinner would be absolutely lovely."

And dinner *was* absolutely lovely, and so was dessert, and so was the long, incredibly aerobic sleepless night that followed, along with the wonderful breakfast, and the too-soon parting. Ray—and he was Ray now, not Mr. Greco—promised he'd pick her up after work for another dinner and, she hoped, another sleepless night, and maybe an even better breakfast.

Bethanne was whistling as she came into work.

Only to find her staff running around in tight circles, everyone with an air of complete panic because, as Stuart finally informed her, the server crashed.

"Why didn't someone call me?" Bethanne asked.

"Why didn't you answer your phone?" Stuart snapped in response.

She flushed, but he was too distracted to notice. He and the other IT guys were trying to bring the server back on line, but every time they did, the damn thing crashed again. Stuart was making mumbly noises about calling Larry, which was something he hadn't done since their awful break-up—Larry and Stuart's, not Bethanne and Larry's—nearly a dozen years before.

"Why is the server crashing?" Bethanne asked.

"Why is the sky blue?" Stuart snapped at her. "No one knows."

"Actually," one of the IT guys said from behind a stack of microprocessing equipment, "they do know why the sky is blue . . ."

"And we know why the server is crashing," Stuart said,

still using that awful tone. "*You* should know why the server is crashing. Everyone else on the planet does."

Then he disappeared into the bowels of the IT department, choosing not to answer her question. So she peered around that stack of microprocessing equipment at the IT guy who actually knew why the sky was blue.

This IT guy—who called himself BloggerBoy and whose real name she couldn't remember—looked like a typical Eros.com client, the kind she couldn't describe to Ray yesterday.

(Was it only yesterday? Her entire life had changed since then. Surely it must have been weeks, maybe even months ago. So many things shouldn't have happened within twenty-four hours . . .)

"The sky is blue," he said, "because of the way light—"

"I know why the sky is blue," she lied. "I want to know why the server is crashing."

"Oh," he said and somehow managed to sound like a man who just realized his boss didn't know how to add two plus two. "Because of the v-log."

"The v-log?" she asked.

"You know," he said, "of the really pretty guy."

He said that with such disinterest that she realized BloggerBoy was one of her extremely straight employees. He could note the attractiveness of another male, but only in a disinterested, just-the-facts kinda way.

For some reason, that little detail about BloggerBoy surprised her.

It took her a moment to get past the surprise and realize what he was talking about. "Someone put up Ray Greco's profile?"

"And his v-log. He paid for everything. And Rachel said to get it onsite as soon as possible because we'd get so many new subscribers that we'd probably make this year's nut in a single day. Which, I suppose, we would have, if everyone who *tried* to log onto the site had been *able* to log onto the site. But we're not set up for this kind of volume, and it's not going away. *Everyone* wants a piece of this guy, and if they don't want a piece of this guy, we want to know how to become this guy . . ."

His voice trailed off as he noticed his own slip.

"I mean," he said, "you know, *they* want to know how to become this guy."

"I know what you mean," Bethanne said. She had gotten a piece of this guy and enjoyed every single bit of it. "Do what you must to get us back on line."

"Aye, aye, Capitan," he said in a really strange accent—probably some film reference that she didn't recognize. Then he buried his face in the electronics again.

The server was down for the first time in their history. Ray's beautiful self had brought down the business, creating the first real crisis since the early lawsuits.

Somehow that didn't bother her as much as his profile did. Not what was in it, but the fact of it. The fact that her staff had put it up, when it was clear she and Ray were involved.

Only it wasn't clear. It couldn't be clear. Even though it felt like she had known him all her life, she had known him less than twenty-four hours, and in those twenty-four hours she had done things she hadn't even imagined possible . . .

She took a deep breath, trying to get the slow-motion replay out of her head.

She had a crisis to solve and a dinner to have and an all night-aerobic session to look forward to and then of course breakfast, and what had Scarlett O'Hara said? *Tomorrow is another day*.

Bethanne whistled all the way to her office—which, she would admit later, wasn't her normal crisis response.

It wasn't normal at all.

But then again, dinner followed by aerobics followed by breakfast wasn't normal for her either. Although it could become normal and she wouldn't complain. Even if she collapsed from lack of sleep.

The server came up on day three, Eros.com got hit with more subscribers than it had gotten on its most successful four subscription drives combined, and all of the newcomers—every last one of them—wanted a date with Ray.

Who seemed just tickled pink about it.

Well, tickled gorgeous, anyway.

When that man smiled, he was not just the prettiest man Bethanne had ever seen, but he was the prettiest man in the entire universe.

She would swear to it.

And so, she thought, would everyone else in the office.

Somehow Ray had arrived at the office right at the moment the server came back on line. Bethanne wasn't notified of his presence for several hours.

In fact, she wasn't notified of his presence at all. She saw him as she walked to the lunchroom for yet another cup of coffee.

He was sitting on a desk in reception, staring at Stuart's laptop. Stuart was sitting on a chair beside him, looking up at him worshipfully. Several members of the staff sat in a circle around him, offering comments.

"I do hope this is work," she snapped as she stepped into the room.

A dozen people got up and ran to their desks. Stuart and the receptionist remained.

"He's scrolling through the responses so far," Stuart said to Bethanne, proudly or so it seemed.

"I never expected so much information." Ray didn't lift his head from the screen. He barely acknowledged her. "How am I supposed to pick the right date from this much information?"

"There's a program embedded into your account," Stuart said. "You can sort potentials by whatever means you deem necessary."

"Hmmm," Ray said, and pressed a few keys. "Like this?"

Stuart leaned toward him, brushing against his thigh. Bethanne's lips tightened. She wasn't going to say anything. She had no right to say anything. After all, Stuart hadn't done anything wrong, just flirted with a man who seemed oblivious to him.

And Ray . . . Ray had paid for the dating service. He had the right to look through the responses.

Hell, she would have looked through the responses if she had gotten that many. Which she hadn't. Not that she had ever posted her own profile on the site. (She wasn't, she kept telling herself, that desperate.)

"By Olympus in all her majesty," Ray said, "who knew that so many sour-faced women described themselves as intelligent?"

"Maybe they are," Bethanne said.

Ray finally looked up at her. And smiled. That multimegawatt smile warmed her just as it had the first time—every part of her except the little chill forming in her heart.

"This is going to take me all night," he said.

"I certainly hope not," she said. "We have reservations."

Stuart looked up at her in surprise. So did the receptionist. Bethanne smiled, even though she really didn't feel like smiling at all. She wasn't one of those sourfaced women, was she? What was wrong with her that her staff seemed surprised she would go to dinner with the handsomest man to ever walk into Eros.com?

"Yes, dinner," Ray said. He didn't seem to notice the harshness (and hint of panic) in her tone. "One always needs to eat. Especially with all of this facing him."

"You can borrow the laptop," Stuart said a bit too eagerly.

Ray turned that smile on Stuart, who almost fell out of his chair.

"Thank you," Ray said.

"Any time," Stuart said. "It's my pleasure. Really. To have you touch—"

"Stuart," Bethanne said, "don't you need that laptop for work?"

"No, not if I'm at my desk." Then he flushed. "Which is where I'm going right now."

The receptionist looked at Ray, then at Bethanne, and finally she stood. "I should probably get some Post-Its from supply."

Bethanne could see the Post-Its on her desk from across the room. "Stay," she said. "I'm sure Ray'll be busy until we leave for dinner."

"And after," he said distractedly, tapping a key as he scanned the material.

And after. Bethanne would normally have been heartened by those words, but not now. Because she knew he wasn't speaking about dessert or aerobics. He was talking about the profiles on the screen.

She sighed and walked back to her office, reminding herself all the way that he had come here to find the right date. Not any date. The *right* date. And what man, when faced with a willing applicant pool, took the very first volunteer?

Except that he had taken the very first volunteer. The question wasn't taking her. It was whether or not she was right applicant, not just the first available one.

And he was clearly going to go through each and every one of those profiles to make sure he hadn't made a mistake.

She was able to keep it all in perspective—Ray, the aerobics, the profiles, the crashed server, the drooling women (and some men)—until the maitre d' at the restaurant Ray had chosen let his arm brush Ray's shoulder as he put the menu into Ray's hands.

The restaurant was exclusive, the interior dark and romantic, the table a private one in the back. They had been taking turns paying for dinner. On this night, it was Ray's turn. He had chosen the restaurant, and if she hadn't been so on edge, she would have loved the choice. The tablecloth was long enough that she could slip off her shoe and slide her bare foot along his thigh without anyone else noticing.

But the moment the maitre d' left, Ray brought out the stupid laptop and opened it.

Bethanne slammed the damn thing shut. "What do you think you're doing?"

"I'm looking over the applicants," he said, frowning slightly in confusion. "I'm a bit overwhelmed at the sheer volume."

She stared at him. His eyes widened. He was clearly puzzled, dammit.

"I suppose we should be talking about what to order," he said slowly. "My mistake."

"What do you think we're doing here?" she asked.

"Dinner?" he said slowly as if he were no longer sure.

"The last few nights we've had lovely dinners," she said.

He nodded and looked a little relieved.

"And lovely desserts," she said.

He relaxed against the chair.

"And even lovelier after-dinner . . . celebrations," she said.

He smiled.

"So why are you now trolling for a date?" she asked.

He put a hand protectively over the laptop, as if she were going to take it from him. "I . . . um . . . paid for it?"

"So?" she asked.

"I'm . . . curious?"

"Clearly," she said.

"I . . . um . . . didn't realize we had a commitment," he said.

She rolled her eyes. "The least you could do is not look at that crap in front of me."

"Why?" he asked. "You generated the crap."

"You did," she said. "With your lovely face, and your

'I like to spend as much time in the sunshine as I can' profile. I had nothing to do with it."

"Except designing the whole system," he said.

"I didn't design it," she said. "I bought it, and I run it, and I didn't think you needed it any more."

The light left his face. The room became noticeably darker.

"I'm sorry," he said. "I'm here on a fact-finding mission."

She knew it. He was too good to be true. He worked for the competition, and he wanted to see how well Eros. com functioned. Well, clearly the place didn't function well in the presence of beautiful men.

"Fact finding," she said flatly. "So tell me, who are you really?"

"Um," he glanced around as if expecting someone to save him. But apparently the maitre d' or the waiter or whoever was supposed to come over next had the sense to stay away. "My real name is Phoebus Apollo, but it's not inaccurate to call myself Ray since I am the God of Light nor is it wrong to call me Greco, which is just a word for Greek, which I am—"

"Phoebus," Bethanne said, ignoring everything else he just said (mostly because she didn't understand it). "Who the hell names a kid Phoebus?"

"My dad." That was a whole new voice. It sounded like a trumpet blaring and it came from the chair to Bethanne's left.

A man was sitting there, a man she hadn't noticed before. He was attractive in a he-man kind of way—broad forehead, high cheekbones, cruel lips. The romance novels she used to read (before Larry) would have called him an alpha male.

Now she just thought of men like that as dangerous.

"Who the hell are you?" she snapped.

"I'm—ah—Phoebus' brother, Ares, although I prefer to be called Mars, even if they did name a red planet after me. The Romans knew how to respect manly men instead of—"

She slammed her palms on the table, shutting him up. "What is this all about?"

"Ah, my fault actually." Ares looked at Ray—Phoebus or Apollo or whatever his name was—and then shrugged. "I found your little website, and thought Eros.com had something to do with the Greek Gods. I was hoping someone set up a dating service that catered to us."

"He thought it was a porn site at first," said Ray. (She couldn't think of him as Phoebus. That was just wrong. No man that attractive should be called Phoebus.)

"But I scrolled around," Ares said, "and I thought maybe it might actually help us find, you know, someone to pass the time with."

"Actually," Ray said, "he bet me that the site couldn't handle people like us."

"And," Ares said, "it turns out that I'm right."

"What?" Bethanne asked.

"Look," Ray said, taking her hand. She snatched it back. He raised his eyebrows in surprise. "Our father slept with everything that moved, pretty much from the time he dethroned our grandfather—"

"Father Time," Ares said, making Bethanne wonder if he was all there.

"—actually, our grandfather was named Chronus, but that's neither here nor there. The important thing is that Dad slept with anything female and fathered—what, Ares, maybe a thousand children?"

"Who counts?" Ares said.

"And we decided long ago that we don't want to be like him, but it does lead to a lonely life, especially in a family as long lived as ours, and we were hoping when we saw your site—"

"*He* was hoping when he saw your site," Ares said.

"That you could help us all find the right person for

right now. That way we wouldn't have to come down from the mountain very often, and we wouldn't have to interrupt our real work and we wouldn't have to—"

"Real work," Bethanne said.

"He likes to tell people that he pulls the sun across the sky with his chariot," Ares said, "but really he just controls the light as it filters through the atmosphere. No one has believed that chariot thing since, what, 'Pollo, Copernicus?"

Ray glared at his brother. "We don't discuss Copernicus."

Bethanne had never discussed Copernicus, mostly because she had no idea who he was. And she wasn't going to ask.

"You came to my office as a *bet*?" she asked Ray.

He shrugged a single shoulder.

"You *used* us?" she asked.

"It turned out better than I'd hoped," Ray said.

"Idiot," Ares said. "She really wants to know if you used her."

The man with the cruel mouth was right, but she didn't want to give him the satisfaction of saying so. Still, she didn't add anything because she really wanted to hear Ray's answer.

Ray glanced at his brother, then back at her, then back at his brother again. "You know," Ray said under his breath, "I'd almost believe your kids were here."

Ares grinned at Bethanne. "I call the little buggers Terror, Trembling, Panic, and Fear. Although it's not fair to call them little any more. They've taken over so much of the world."

She blinked at him, not certain if he was joking. He didn't seem like a man who was joking, and yet every word out of his mouth was unbelievable. And where did he come from? She hadn't seen him arrive on his own.

"I'm sure 'Pollo mentioned them because he's feeling all of those lovely emotions. My sister Eris should have shown up. You know her as Discord. She would have *loved* this conversation." Ares' grin wasn't a kind one. His eyes were as cruel as that mouth of his.

"I didn't use you, Bethanne, seriously," Ray said. "When I arrived, I was hoping I'd find a woman to keep me company for the next sun cycle."

"I was keeping you company," she snapped.

"I know," he said, "and I appreciate it. But I'm not all that great with English, and when you said that we would talk about dates and marketing and mentioned dinner, I thought you meant dates and marketing and work, not a relationship."

"Then what was that all night stuff?" she asked.

He shrugged again. "A delightful work experience?"

"Oh, for gods sake," she said.

"Which god?" Ares asked.

"I hadn't had time to see if any of the women are appropriate," Ray said to Ares. "I just started looking through the files . . ."

"And that's all the looking you're going to get." Bethanne snatched the laptop away from him. "You perpetrated a fraud. Both of you. I'm going to fire whoever checked out your background."

"Don't do that," Ray said. "I got one of the muses to write me something pretty. Really, it's mostly true. I am a well known poet and musician. I *invented* the flute and the lyre—"

"I doubt that," Bethanne said. "You didn't invent the liar, but you certainly are an adept one. Either that or you're both stone-cold crazy. Which comes back to fraud again. And fraud negates our contract, which no longer gives you the right to look at these profiles or anything else to do with our site. Got that, Ray?"

"Apollo," he said softly. "I hurt your feelings. I didn't mean to. I was just—"

"Save it," she said. "And don't ever bother us again."

Ares sighed. "You know, for someone who doesn't want to be like Dad," he said to his brother, "you sure know how to piss off women."

"Stop," Ray said to Ares. Then Ray stood. Somehow a spotlight illuminated him, making him the brightest (most beautiful, astounding, gorgeous and spectacular) thing in the room.

Bethanne worked at ignoring him.

"You want me to take care of her?" Ares asked. "We could go for a tiny little interpersonal war or something larger—like a conflict between internet agencies—or something even large, maybe on the scale of Iraq."

"I said shut up," Ray said. Then he reached out a hand to Bethanne. "Bethanne, please. I'm apologizing."

"That's not going to make things better," she said. Although she was having trouble walking away from him.

"What can I do to make things better?" he asked.

How many men had asked her that question before? How many of them had asked her that question after screwing up her life?

"Just leave me alone," she said tiredly, and walked away.

She resisted the urge to look back at him. She really didn't need to. The mirrors in the hallway leading to the kitchen reflected his afterglow.

The man did seem to have control of the light somehow. Or maybe handsome men just figured out how to use light to their advantage.

She had no idea. It was safer to believe he and his brother were crazy. They used Eros.com, and now she would pay for it.

Halfway back to the business, she remembered she hadn't eaten dinner. She ordered a pizza—extra thick, extra cheese and extra pepperoni—and made sure it would arrive shortly after she did.

Which it did.

She ate the entire thing alone, while she composed the letter she had to send to all the new subscribers. Before she sent it, she called her investigative team, her legal advisor, and Rachel into the office.

She fired the investigative team for failing to do their

job. ("Pretty men do *not* get a pass at Eros.com," she said, but even she knew she was speaking about the future, not the quite recent past.) She put Rachel on probation for making the decision that Bethanne herself might have made if she had been in the office that night.

And she listened to her lawyer's doom-and-gloom predictions, most of which came true. Like the class action lawsuit, not just from the new subscribers (all of whom got their money back—if they asked for it, of course), but from some old ones claiming fraud as well.

Bethanne's lawyer had to meet with some ambulance-chasing class-action attorney and show him that Eros. com was a victim of fraud as well. Which wasn't hard when someone actually investigated the information that Ray Greco had provided the company.

Why hadn't they investigated that properly? The class action ambulance chaser had asked.

Fortunately, that particular ambulance chaser had been female (as had the arbitrator overseeing everything), and Bethanne's attorney took the risky option of showing them the security tapes.

The naked security tapes.

Of Ray Greco a.k.a Phoebus Apollo a.k.a. the Greek God waiting outside Eros.com.

No one questioned the security procedures. Both women asked for the recording to be replayed more than once, and later the ambulance chaser asked for a copy, which she did not get.

The class action suit evaporated. Unfortunately, the memory of Ray Greco did not.

Bethanne herself spent too much time on the internet reading translations of Homer and Ovid. She bought Edith Hamilton's mythology books and got angry every single time she saw Apollo presented as the God of Truth.

That alone should have made her Apollo a fake Apollo. But he looked a lot like the statues she saw reproduced online (and some in touring shows when they

hit the local museum). And then there was that glow of
his . . .

In the end, it didn't matter. Pretty men, men who
used, simply didn't belong at Eros.com. She had a few
fun nights with a con artist. That's how she ended up fil-
ing the Event in her mind.

And she did get a new slogan out of it for Eros.com.
Not "We find you the *right* date," but a twist on Geeks
Bearing Gifts. Now Eros.com's slogan read: We *Prefer*
Geeks Bearing Gifts.

Because she did. She really and truly did.

THE HORROR IN
THE LIVING ROOM

Adrian Nikolas Phoenix

Adrian Nikolas Phoenix has had stories published
in several magazines and anthologies. Her debut
novel, *A Rush of Wings*, was released by Pocket
in 2008, and the second book, *In the Blood*, will
be released in 2009, with more novels to follow.
She currently resides in Oregon (with three cats,
of course).

Peeking through the small window inset in the front
door, Augusta Howard regarded the slimy blob pul-
sating on the front step. It rang the bell again with a
delicate poke of a tentacle. Augusta sighed as the chime
echoed through the house.

"It's another tentacled horror from beyond, sir," she
called.

From deep within the living room's darkened interior, Lovecraft said, "Honestly, Mrs. Howard, I'm in the
middle of something! Ask it to return later, please."

She waited a moment, expecting—

"Or does it want an autograph?"

Augusta eyed the heaving mass in front of the door.
"I do not see a pen, sir."

"Ah. Well, then ask it to return at a more convenient time."

"As you wish, Mr. Lovecraft." Augusta smoothed her hands over her apron. "After supper, then?"

"No, I believe a Thing Beyond Description is due after supper. Perhaps later in the evening, but before midnight." The stink of sulfur wafted from the living room, chased down the hall by Lovecraft's muttered, "Blast!"

The bell chimed again. Augusta unlatched the peek-through window and a tentacle shot up and presented the yellowed eye at its center. An eager yellowed eye.

"Thank you for your patience," she said, managing a polite smile. "Mr. Lovecraft is booked this evening, but he would be willing to see you later, before midnight."

A second tentacle joined the first and both yellowed eyes narrowed. The mass below the tentacles emitted a series of belches.

Augusta frowned. "Mr. Lovecraft is a *very* busy man," she said. "He's graciously agreed to see you even though you've arrived without an appointment."

The horror roared and belched. A tentacle smacked against the window's screen.

"I will *not* have that kind of language," Augusta said. "I don't give one fig about the distance you've traveled, the colors you've seen or lost in space, or that you desire to rend and absorb Mr. Lovecraft. You need to win *me* over in order to get through that door. So I suggest you conduct yourself like a gentlething."

Augusta closed the window and relatched it. Beyond the door, darkness shuddered and writhed and pouted, unable to bypass her employer's wards. She heard slurping, sucking sounds as the horror oozed down the steps and away.

As well it should, impertinent creature.

Several shrieks came from the street outside.

But perhaps it *was* time Mr. Lovecraft employed a secretary.

Angela strode down the portrait-lined hall, her steps muffled by the thick Persian carpet. The stench from the living room grew worse with each stride. Augusta's eyes stung and watered. She pulled her handkerchief from her apron pocket, but before she could blot up the tears, she halted at the living room's mouth and stared. The handkerchief fell from her fingers.

A sigil or Elder sign or some other damned thing that would require lots of elbow grease and scrubbing to clean had been etched into the carpet with what she suspected was the last of her flour. Candles positioned along the sigil's edges dribbled wax onto the flour, adding the scent of beeswax to the sulfur stench curling through the room like a ghastly yellow fog.

Lovecraft sat in his overstuffed easy chair, a notebook in his lap, a pen in his gloved hand. A leather raincoat protected his shirt and trousers from ichor, goggles his eyes. But nothing protected the room. The walls, ceiling, plush velvet sofa, and carpet were spattered with a greenish-black spray of gore. And so, of course, was the easy chair.

"Dear God," Augusta whispered.

Ichor trickled down Lovecraft's thin cheeks, dripped from his chin. He pushed the goggles to the top of his head and smiled. "I am fine, Mrs. Howard," he said. "I managed to transcribe the creature's story before consigning it to oblivion."

"I *just* cleaned in here!"

Lovecraft pushed up from the easy chair and stripped off his gloves. Dropped them onto the carpet. "Is supper nearly ready? I've worked up quite an appetite."

Augusta could only nod.

"Then I shall wash up," Lovecraft said, combing his fingers through his hair. "I would appreciate it if you could tidy things a bit before the Thing Beyond Description arrives." His warm smile was so genuine and boyish, Augusta could only nod once again. "Mrs. Howard, you're a gem!" He peeled off his raincoat and then bounded away toward the bathroom.

Bending, Augusta picked up her handkerchief, then blew out the candles. She straightened and regarded the mess. She had asked Mr. Lovecraft several times to confine his work to a room dedicated to that purpose. He'd nodded, then swept a hand through the air.

"I have," he said. "My work encompasses my life, so everything in my life is a part of my work."

Since then, Augusta had decided that Lovecraft's wife had fled to a sanitarium in order to *keep* her sanity, not because she had lost it. Sweeping up spare tentacles and the odd eyelid tended to make one's sanity a tad loose.

Lovecraft's work was necessary, yes; he was quietly saving mankind from tentacled doom. But, really, how hard was it to pick up after oneself?

Augusta walked into the kitchen, breathing in the rich, meaty smell of roasting beef and vegetables. She pulled a pan from the cupboard and clattered it onto the stove. She opened the canister of flour and found it empty. She sighed. Nothing to be done but to buy more flour. And perhaps a padlock for the canister.

Augusta adjusted the oven temperature, then went to the hall cupboard and fetched her purse, sweater, and hat. "I'm going to the market. I shall be back in a few moments," she shouted, pinning her hat to her hair.

"Fine! Oh! Could you please purchase a handful of chicken hearts?"

Augusta bit back the reply trying to edge past her lips: *I could, but I shan't.* Instead, she shouted, "One handful or two, sir?"

"One should do it!"

Unlocking the front door, Augusta stepped outside and into something that squished. A fetid outhouse stink assailed her nostrils. She jumped back just as tentacles whipped out of the quivering blob. She tried to slam the door shut again, but the returned horror snaked a tentacle inside the house, its yellowed eye blinking in excitement.

The insidious tentacle looped around Augusta's ankle

and yanked. She toppled over backward. She grabbed at the hall table, but her fingers skittered off its well-polished surface. She and the table hit the floor. The Persian carpet absorbed some of the impact, but the fall knocked the air from her lungs.

Augusta made a quick mental note to never wax that table again.

"Mrs. Howard? Is everything all right?"

A cold tentacle slithered around Augusta's other ankle.

"Yes, quite!" she yelled, pulling the hat pin free of her hair and stabbing it at the gloating yellowed eye.

The tentacle bobbed and weaved, danced like a cobra, eye wide. She poked and thrust with the pin, but the unnatural blob from beyond time and space refused to hold still. "You can forget about seeing Mr. Lovecraft tonight or any other night," she said, still breathless, as she parried tentacle jabs with feints from her hat pin.

The wretched horror barked a series of rapid belches that sounded like an auto backfire. Augusta sucked in a sharp breath of air. "How dare you?" She kicked free of one tentacle and needled another with her hat pin. "I'll have you know that I am a housekeeper!"

Greenish ichor leaked from the punctured tentacle, and the heaving gray mass hiccupped, whirling its mass of tentacles overhead like a rodeo cowboy about to rope a heifer. And spattering walls, ceiling, and carpet with green ooze in the process.

Of course.

Augusta blew the hair out of her eyes and stepped forward into battle, blocking tentacles with her spinning purse while she stabbed yellowed eyes with her hatpin.

More blinking. More hiccupping. More ichor spray. More mess.

Oozing-step by oozing-step, the horror backed up, and something inside Augusta lifted, buoyant with victory.

Unexpected darkness blotted out the light from outside.

Something seized the twitching and ichoring mass and yanked it outside. A ripping sound, followed by a splat suggested that the horror was now the least of Augusta's worries.

She stared into a black and endless maw. A maw like a starless sky. A frosted gate into the Void. Wait, maybe not a maw, exactly, or even a gate ... it was a Thing Beyond Description.

Her green-slimed hat pin was worthless against ... *that*.

"I'm afraid you're early," Augusta said, voice steady, despite her dry mouth. "You will need to return in an hour, after Mr. Lovecraft has dined. Then you may join him for ... uh ... brandy and ... uh ... cigars." She realized it would need to be a very *big* cigar.

The TBD didn't move, didn't blink or belch or hiccup, didn't utter a sound. It simply breathed frost into the air and something else, something Augusta caught from the corners of her eyes—a capering darkness, edging against her thoughts.

Augusta pulled her vision back to center. It seemed to her that, like a fine bottle of wine, this thing brought its host ice and madness.

And how *does* one serve madness? Chilled with ice? Or should it be saved for those special occasions?

"Oh, my," Augusta murmured. "This won't do. I haven't time to go mad." She stooped and picked up her hat and pinned it back onto her hair. "You really must leave now. I have shopping to do—chicken hearts, you know, and flour—and you need to return later."

But the TBD did nothing. Except ...

Was she drawing *nearer* to it? Frowning, Augusta looked down at her feet in their sturdy black shoes. Although she was relieved to see that she hadn't taken a single step, she was being reeled in along with the carpet into the maw or void or well, really, did it matter *what* it was? She was being reeled in.

Augusta tried to step off the carpet, tried to back up,

but discovered she couldn't move. She stood on the carpet as the TBD reeled her in like a good-monster treat.

"I am quite serious," she said, amazed that her voice remained level. "You must leave and return later. Mr. Lovecraft will be most unhappy if you persist in your attempt to devour me."

No blinks. No belches. Nothing but frost and madness.

Oh, really, you shouldn't have! We have more madness than we know what to do with as it is!

Augusta saw colors swirling in the dark maw ... void ... thing, fevered and vivid shades. Unnatural color. "It's not sporting to refuse to at least give me a chance to escape," she chided. "Not sporting at all."

"I agree," a calm voice said behind her.

Augusta's heart leaped into her throat. Lovecraft stepped around, then in front of her. His leather raincoat creaked as he passed her, his goggles perched on top of his head, his thin face cleaned of ichor. He held a book in his hands, a black book marked with sigils.

"I believe the roast needs attention, Mrs. Howard," he said.

"I feel confident the roast can wait a few more moments, sir." Augusta unpinned her hat and handed him the slimed pin. "You may consider it my favor, Mr. Lovecraft."

"I am honored to be your knight, Mrs. Howard." Slipping the pin between his gloved fingers, Lovecraft offered her a grim smile. He slid the goggles over his eyes. "Once more into the breach, eh?"

"Indeed, once more," she said. "But perhaps you might slay your guest outside?"

"Only after I've collected its story."

The Thing Beyond Description blew a blast of frozen air into the hall. Ice sheeted the walls, crackled across the ceiling, and hung in icicles from Lovecraft's goggles, nose, and sleeves. His breath plumed white.

Augusta shivered. Her teeth chattered. "Do you need any assistance, sir?"

"No, Mrs. Howard. I will tend to this. You tend to the roast. I'm afraid I shall be quite ravenous since my supper is being delayed."

"Of course," Augusta agreed. She started to turn away, then paused. "Will your guest be joining you for brandy and cigars after supper?"

The Thing Beyond Description huffed another winter gale into the hall. The glass covering the family portraits hanging on the wall cracked. Augusta thought she caught the distant glimmer of stars within the TBD's gaping maw.

"Due to my guest's appalling lack of etiquette, I'm afraid not, Mrs. Howard."

"Well said, sir."

Lovecraft lifted the black book, opened it, and began to read aloud from it in a language Augusta didn't know, but the words sounded exotic and a little chilling.

The Thing Beyond Description roared.

Appalling manners, indeed.

Patting her hair back into place, Augusta left the hall and walked into the warm and fragrant kitchen. She tied on her apron, her gaze on the empty flour canister. She thought of the mess she still needed to clean in the living room and mourned the loss of her flour. Well, she would simply have to make do. A bit of cornstarch to the roast drippings and she'd have a fine gravy.

Grabbing a couple of hot pads, Augusta pulled the browned roast from the oven. From the hall she heard a sudden wet POP. She sighed. Lovecraft was a hero to the human race, no doubt in her mind. But he'd be living in ichor-smeared squalor, knee-deep in flour sigils and tentacle bits and eyelids if not for her. Men were often quite helpless about domestic matters.

"Mrs. Howard?" Lovecraft called. "Do we have any large scoops?"

Smiling, Augusta shook her head and wiped her hands on her apron. Yes, quite helpless. "How many do you need?" she asked.

"As many as we have."

The doorbell chimed.

Augusta swerved from the closet and its stack of scoops and beelined for the dripping hallway. "I'm not in," Lovecraft whispered as he passed her on his way to the living room.

"Very good, sir," Augusta murmured. "Please put your gear in the wash tub and not on the carpet." Unlatching the peek-through window, she drew in a deep breath.

Once more into the breach.

TAKE MY WORD FOR IT: BAD IDEA!

Mike Moscoe

Mike Moscoe is a multifaceted writer. As Mike Moscoe, his short stories are frequently nominated for the Nebula Awards by the Science Fiction Writers of America. As Mike Shepherd, he has five books out in the *Kris Longknife* science fiction saga, with the most recent volume, *Intrepid*, released in October of '08. Three have made national bestseller lists. Look for *Kris Longknife—Audacious* and *Kris Longknife—Intrepid* at your local bookstore.

Harken to my words,
You women of Greece. The poets love to spin tales of the heroes, but they never had to live with one. The lies they spin are but half the tale. Trust me. I married the greatest hero of them all, Heracles himself. And unlike his other two wives, he neither slaughtered me, nor did I kill him.
Harken to my words.

The first time I saw Heracles, he sported a full set of slave chains. Not caring much for the sight, I turned to my steward. "Agron, what business have I with a slave?"

"Normally none, my Queen. But after I had bought him for the silver mines, his seller took me aside and enlightened me."

"I assume you will enlighten *me* before too long."

"Yes, my Queen. This is the hero Heracles."

My throne room suddenly became very quiet as my ladies ceased their chatter and my generals their plotting.

"And, pray, what brings such a great man before me in chains?"

"It concerns the matter of him throwing his best friend, Iphitos, from the walls of Tiryns when Hera sent a sudden rage upon him."

"Like the sudden rage Hera put him in when he murdered his three children," I said dryly. Why do we girls always get blamed for the trouble these guys get into?

"Yes, ah, yes, my Queen," Agron said, happy to agree with me. Then my steward saw the error of his way and blushed red before adding quickly, "Or so I was told."

"So tell me, what does this matter to the Queen of Lydia?" This was not the first time that a neighbor's problem had suddenly become my problem. My neighbor kings do love dropping hot rocks in my lap. Usually the ones that were far too hot for them to handle.

"The Oracle decreed that Heracles be sold into slavery for three years and the money paid be handed over to Eurytus as the blood price for his son's death. The king to whom he was sold could set him to any labor he wished."

"King," I said, dry as any south wind.

"Yes, my Queen. However, no king would allow him to be sold in his kingdom. There was the matter of King Eurystheus."

Yes, that might worry my local brother kings. King Eurystheus of Tiryns had happily tasked Heracles with twelve near impossible and deadly labors for murdering his wife and children in that rage. Some of the poets claimed Heracles then killed King Eurystheus and most of his court. No doubt, my neighborly kings might be reluctant to take on the job of punishing Heracles for killing his own best friend.

But that did not mean that I had to like this hot rock in my lap. Nor did that give me any idea what to do with this challenge.

"Agron," I said dryly, "you must be more careful in the future to get the full story before you buy me a new slave."

"Most assuredly, my Queen."

So I found myself leaning back on my throne and studying this man the poets called a hero and the son of Zeus.

No question he was beautiful in all those ways that a man can be. He towered above the men who guarded him . . . from a comfortable distance. His shoulders were broad enough for any two of my soldiers. His skin was tanned but unblemished by scar or imperfection.

And every bit of it was revealed for us to look at . . . and, no doubt, admire. The lion skin he wore covered his head and not much else.

Then he grinned. It wasn't a smile he gave my court, but the boyish grin of a six-year-old who knew that mommy would never really punish him. Not while he fixed her with that twisted, white-toothed grin.

The man seemed insufferably sure every female heart would melt after one glance from him. And every man would buy him a cup of wine.

If I didn't do something about him, and quickly, my court would be his plaything for the next three years . . . or however long he chose to stay.

"Take off the lion skin," I ordered.

The smile vanished from his lips. If I surprised him, he didn't show it. Indeed, he didn't show anything. If I were to guess what was going through his mind, I would bet he was of half a mind to laugh me off.

Our eyes locked. I did not blink.

Slowly, he reached for the ties at his neck and undid them. The lion skin puddled at his feet.

"Arete," I said to my chief lady in waiting, "bring me the skin."

Arete was the one woman in my court I could count on to obey me without stint or pause. This time, she shot me a glance, but she hurried to do as I said. When she brought the skin to me, I said. "Put it on me."

Her nostrils flared, but she obeyed.

The skin was well tanned; it still held the smell of warm sun and open fields . . . and the manly scent of the hero. I had to fight the urge to run my fingers through the tawny lion pelt and the hero's curly hair. Distractions both lewd and delightful flooded my mind. I struggled to keep my thoughts on the plan rapidly taking shape in my mind.

"Oh, dear," I said, "It seems our champion has nothing to wear. Arete, have you torn up and remade your grandmother's chitons?"

"Not yet, my Queen," my lady said, a small smile nibbling at the edges of her mouth. My generals might still look puzzled, but at least my closest woman confidant was beginning to see where I was going.

"Bring me one of her larger size robes," and my lady was off, her sandaled feet slapping rapidly against the stone hallways of my palace. She returned in only a moment, the dress thrown over her arm but billowing out like a sail, threatening to engulf her trim figure.

"Give it to our new slave."

She did.

"Put it on," I told him.

He shook out the chiton. Grandmother had grown very large in her old age. I expected his shoulders would be well covered. I doubted, however, that it would be long enough.

"How do I put this on?" he asked, giving me another one of those bent boyish grins.

"The same way you take it off a woman. I'm sure you must have done that once or twice, if the poets can be trusted at all. You do the same steps, only in reverse order." Around my throne room, there were several chuckles. Well disguised chuckles. Someone had slapped irons onto his legs and arms. That same someone had either forgotten to or not dared try to take away his olive-wood club.

I was not the first to find conflict and confusion in the need to punish a half-god.

Heracles cleared his throat and the room became full silent. "I have helped a woman or two undress, Queen Omphale . . . but not while chained," he said, raising an arm, then a leg. The thick irons rattled.

"A good point," I said, "Agron, have the chains removed."

"My Queen, is it safe?"

I have to love my steward for his sincere concern for me . . . after he had gotten me into this mess. It was left to me to enlighten him.

"Agron, if Heracles does not wish to be here, there is nothing any one of us, or all of us together, can do to make him stay. If he does not wish to be in chains, Lydia has none that will hold him." After a moment's thoughtful pause, dawn seemed to come up slowly behind Agron's eyes.

"Have the chains removed," I repeated.

A smith arrived at a run only a few moments later. While he knocked the irons from Heracles's ankles, the hero himself pulled the wrist restraints apart. It was no surprise to me, but several of my guards looked very pale.

With a lopsided grin, Heracles tossed aside the irons and pulled on the chiton. He modeled it like a young girl might, spinning in her own very first woman's wear. "It will need to be let out in the back, and it is way too short," he said. The chiton failed to reach the top of his knees.

"It will do for now," I said, and stood. "Heracles, I now

set my first labor for you. My banqueting table requires a new tablecloth. Go, join my chief weaver, Momma Doris, and ask her what you may do to help her and her spinners and weavers."

"That is to be my first labor, my Queen?" he asked with an expressive raising of one eyebrow.

"That is the one I have set for you."

"My kingly brother set rather higher standards for labors in his service."

"You may have noticed that I am a queen."

"It would be impossible for a man not to notice," Heracles said, sweeping me a low bow.

In the meantime, the corner of my throne room that my generals occupied exploded with whispers that fell little short of shouts.

As our half-god hero departed, I signaled for the leaders of my army to walk with me in my garden.

We were hardly among the olive trees before my chief general blurted out, "My Queen, this man is a hero among lesser men. He slew a half-dozen men with a single swipe of his club. We should make use of him."

"Filippos," I said, resting a restraining hand on his shoulder, "Heracles was sent here to be punished, was he not?"

My soldiers nodded.

"And the last time he was put to punishment, the fool king who did it sent him off on errands that would have left any lesser man dead, is that not so?"

"Precisely, my Queen," my general said.

"And when Heracles finished his last labor, did our hero not thank the king by slaying him and half his court?"

Filippos rubbed his chin. "So the poets say. But they say many things."

"I would prefer not to risk my life on that. While Heracles resides at my court, I will ask him to do nothing that *he* might consider an effort on my part to have him end up dead. Do you all understand me?"

No one made to answer me, but I could almost smell their brains burning as they slashed their way into unfamiliar thoughts.

"Besides," I added, "how much silver and wine will men pay a poet to sing the tale of Heracles's manly work among the spinners and weavers?"

That got several laughs. But only after a brief pause so my generals could look around to make sure the butt of their laugh was not in sight to object to their humor.

"One more thought, my generals. While I have every intention of surviving the next three years, I also have no desire to make enemies of our neighbors or give them grudges that will unite them against us once our slave has taken his strong arm elsewhere. Because as sure as poets sing songs, Heracles will tire of our company and head on down the road. Are we in agreement?"

Again, no one made answer to me. Clearly, my bronze hats were lost in thought. I hope my generals found it an interesting change for once.

Me, I was very happy about my labors for that day. I had given that man-child a punishment that would surely give him pause. And it would give him no cause to kill me or mine. Nor could Homer himself spin these deeds into something to buy him lodging, even on a warm night.

Yes, I was very proud of myself.

I checked in late the next morning with Mother Doris to see how my idea was working. "Is my new slave of any use to you?"

"He'd be of more profit to you and Lydia in the silver mine," she said with a sour look.

"Is he that bad?"

"I figured he had a good right arm, so I set him to scutching the long strands to break the woody core. In no time he was pounding away, whipping the retted stems of the flax on the boards. He beat that flax so hard against the boards, there was no telling the fibers from the chaff. The girls had a good laugh."

"I expected him to find woman's work no easier than killing the hydra. But different. Requiring a more thoughtful touch," I told Doris. "Don't let him off easily."

"We didn't. I sent him off with Rena to bring back some bundles of flax for retting. They were gone a good hourglass, but when they came back, Heracles had enough to keep us busy for a week."

I should have noticed the sidewise glance Doris cast me, but I was so intent on what she did with Heracles next that I missed asking a question of my own.

"I've tried using him to spin the yarn, but he keeps turning it into a tug-of-war and pulling the yarn until it breaks. If you wanted to teach him that brute strength is not the answer to everything, he's in the right place."

We both laughed at that, and again I went away very proud of myself.

It was two or three months before it started to dawn on me just how much I'd been outfoxed. That was when the younger ladies-in-waiting began petitioning me for permission to marry. Their childhood sweethearts. The sooner the better.

I, of course, granted their wishes. And then those sweet, maybe not so blushing, brides, began showing baby bulges well before a matronly woman would.

Now, it is a well-known fact that a young bride can often produce in six months what an experienced wife always seems to takes nine months to do. Suddenly, we had plenty of evidence of the difference between an eager bride and matronly diligence. It seemed that every woman in my court was sprouting a baby bump!

Even Momma Doris was proudly showing off a bulge.

When I caught my very own advisor, Arete, standing between me and the setting sun, her belly lit up as if by a bonfire, I could delude myself no more.

Dressing Heracles in women's clothing might not have been as good an idea as I thought. Having him sit

among the woman may not have been quite the punishment I intended. Clearly, not all of Heracles's labor
had been devoted to spinning and weaving me a great
tablecloth.

"Arete, walk with me in the garden," I said as the sun
slipped below the portico and the evening cool came
on.

"Yes, my Queen," she answered, eyes cast low like a
modest matron.

So we walked while I tried to find the right words
to say to the woman who knew my deepest thoughts ...
and, apparently, some things about my court that I was
not fully aware of.

Under the eves of the buildings, the doves cooed softly.
High above, a hawk still circled, looking for dinner. Had
I put the hungry hawk among my turtledoves?

The silence between us dragged on until Arete, not
I, broke it.

"Are you troubled, my Queen?"

"Are you with child, my counselor?" I shot back.

"Oh, is that what bothers you, my Queen?"

"Of course not," I lied. "If General Filippos is de-
lighted with this late-in-life gift from his wife, who am I
to raise a question. Come to think about it, of late there
has been little squabbling among the men and women of
my court," I said, eyeing Arete in the deepening dusk.

"Maybe it is because we are all well satisfied and
looking forward to raising these gifts from the gods."

"Or one half-god in particular?" I asked dryly.

In the dim light, I suspected she gave herself over to
a modest blush. I was wrong.

She turned on me. "What would you have us do, my
Queen? You have Heracles's strong right arm at your
bidding and you think only to teach him to spin. Lydia is
small, My Queen. Every night my Filippos goes to sleep
worrying about when our 'beloved' neighbors will move
against us next. You make no war, my Queen, but kings
always do. It is their sport."

She patted her belly. "So, if my son, born from a god's son, can make it safer for my other three children, so be it. Filippos will gladly foster a son that is none of his seed if that is the price for a strong Lydia."

She paused then, and in the deepening dusk, I saw her smile. "And besides, being the bride of Heracles, if only for a night, is hardly a labor at all. He is quite pleasant to lie with, my Queen. You should take advantage of the chance you have."

I snorted bitterly. "How am I to give him punishment when he cómes to me in the morning if I have withered in passion under him the night before?"

"You worry too much, my Queen. You have always done so. Look at Heracles. He does not worry about tomorrow. He takes it as it comes." Now Arete did laugh, a clear and happy sound like clear water over rocks. "We all could learn something from him."

"I will not have my slave teaching me," I said, knowing my voice was tight and low. "I must master this slave, not be his slave."

She glanced at me, but in the dark, I could make out no expression. "Suit yourself, my Queen, but I would seek a way if I were you."

I swallowed any retort. Arete made him sound so desirable. Had she forgotten so quickly that this godman-child had killed his first wife and slaughtered their children! How could I bring such a man to my bed?

We walked along in quiet for a great while after that. It was Arete who finally broke the silence. "My Queen, if you can agree with me that placing Heracles among the ladies was not as much of a punishment as you intended, is it possible that you might see your way to letting him do a few more strenuous labors?"

"Putting that child in your belly was not strenuous for him?" I said.

"Pleasant, yes, but strenuous, my Queen? You have heard the story of the Thirteenth Labor of Heracles?"

"Why? Did he brag about it?"

"Oh, no, my Queen. You can say many things of Heracles, but he is no braggart. The truth about him is quite enough."

"And he does have the poets to exaggerate, doesn't he?" I said. The story of the thirteenth labor, was of one undertaken with enthusiasm, not as punishment for the murder of his wife and children. According to the story, King Thespios was so impressed with my man-child slave that he offered him his fifty daughters. Heracles is supposed to have visited all of them on one night and left the whole brood pregnant. I'd often wondered what kind of man would ill use his daughters so, but now, I was standing beside a woman likewise pregnant by that self same nocturnal visitor.

Maybe silence would be the best policy.

"Okay, I will spit it out," Arete said. "Heracles would like some tougher work. Something that would take him outside. He's itching to get his hands on something that would work up a sweat." She paused. "Other than a woman, I mean."

I sighed. "That was what I was trying to avoid. Any ideas, O Counselor of Mine?"

"We do have that boar up near Calydonia. It's been stealing more sheep than usual. We could let him have a go at it."

I sighed. Yes, it would be nice to be rid of that sheep-killing pig. But it was not yet fall. Heracles would think nothing of chasing after a razor-tusked boar in the green-leafed thicket just now, but I'd rather not bury two or three of my soldiers if they took off into the woods after Heracles and didn't prove so unkillable.

"You may tell your Heracles that I will let him chase after our boar come autumn. With luck, the thought of that will keep him happy. And there are still a few un-pregnant bellies in my kingdom, aren't there?"

"One or two," my previously ever-supportive counselor said. I think it was followed by a chuckle, but in the gloom I could not be sure.

So, once the weather turned crisp and the leaves began to turn, I called for the men to go hunting, and I suggested that the Calydonia mountains might provide good game. I rode out with them, being one of the few women not with child. I took along a few new serving girls as well as my three best huntresses. Diana the Huntress had blessed Elena, Ioanna, and Iris with eyes that could spot a spiderweb at two hundred paces and bows that could take down the spider in that web. If the boys went chasing off after this or that, my huntresses would see that I was safe.

It was good that I had them beside me.

We chanced upon a gutted sheep carcass, still bleeding, in the middle of the trail. The huntsman released the hounds into a deer run into the thicket. They were baying in no time.

With a shout, my eager slave leaped from his horse. One of my guards tossed him a short spear and Heracles was off at a run. And I found myself staring at General Filippos, an unasked question on his glowing cheeks.

"Go, go. All of you men, go." I said. "I will not keep you."

In a blink of an eye, I, my three huntresses, and two young grooms, whose mothers had extracted promises from me that they were yet too young for the hunt, were left to struggle with a dozen abandoned horses and pack mules.

It took but a little while to hobble them all. "Do you think he's hunting in his chiton?" Elena asked as we pushed the mares away from where we'd put out the stallions to browse.

"I'd lay you tomorrow's chores he ditched the dress as soon as he was out of sight of her." Ioanna said, throwing me a quick glance.

"Iris, you are best at tracking," I said. "Go collect the dress once all is settled here. And take a long spear. That old boar may have tired of sheep and be thinking of pretty young women as a good change of diet."

They laughed at my good humor, but Iris took a spear when she slipped up the animal track, and Elena strung her bow and laid three arrows down at her side. The young boys equipped themselves with spears and handed me one before joining us on a rug in the shade of a wild olive tree.

Iris returned with a huge chiton thrown over her shoulder. "I could not see your camp from where I found it," she said, in answer to my upraised eyebrow, then she shrugged. "But the bushes had grown quite thick. In truth, it was not far."

Ioanna took the dress from Iris and laid it out. Heracles may not have worn it far, but it was torn along sleeves and hem. In one place a length of hawthorn stuck out of a rip. "Give it to me," I sighed. "If I intend to put him back in this, I'll need to mend it."

"The ladies of the court are always having to mend his clothes," Ioanna said.

"He is very hard on chitons," Elena said. That got a giggle from the three of them . . . and blank stares from the two grooms. They were quite young.

So we four each took an edge of the chiton and began to mend it.

And to tell stories of other hunts that alternately frightened our two young listeners and made them look at their toes in discomfort. Boys come to that awkward age later than girls. The one where they are so curious about what it is between boys and girls . . . and are more than half afraid of the answers. We took terrible advantage of our two listeners.

Almost so much that we did not hear the shouts of the hunt as it drew near again to our road.

A huge blur of darkness and fury broke from the woods not ten paces from where we sat. I would like to say that we leaped immediately to our own defense, but in truth, we all froze for a second, taken in by the small, beady eyes taking us in with rage.

But if we stood, one moment, transfixed with surprise,

I think the beast was just as much surprised to find us on his road.

Whatever it was, the boar took a moment to stomp its feet and to roar its defiance at us. And my three hunt-resses put that moment to good use. Iris and Ioanna stood, bringing their spears points up between us and the beast. Elaine brought an arrow to the string and edged out to my left, pulling back the bow and taking aim. Both boys shook with terror, but they stood their ground, spears out, taking their place between that roaring death and their queen.

It is at moments like that that I realize how much I am loved by my people. They will do anything for me. And I for them. Why do the poets never sing of such love?

Death roared its defiance and charged us. Elaine's bow twanged and an arrow buried itself in the boar's side.

And a man fully as terrifying in his own power as the boar shot from the thicket. In one jab he transfixed the beast with his spear.

The boar squealed in pain—and whirled to face this new attacker. Any man would want a long boar-spear between himself and those razor-sharp tusks. Heracles stood with his arms spread, dancing first right, then left. Daring the pig to charge.

"He needs a knife," I said.

"He can have mine," Iris half-whispered.

"Toss it handle first, to the ground beside him," I whispered back.

She did. Heracles seemed unaware of our help, or had no room in his killing eyes for anything but the pig.

The boar charged. Heracles grabbed it by its gaping jaws. They rolled, thrashing on the leaf strewn ground as if the very Earth Goddess herself was lost in a passion-ate embrace.

And just as suddenly as it had started . . . it was over. Iris' knife stood up in the boar's chest as it heaved its last and its lifeblood pumped out onto the ground.

My heart pumped as if I myself had fought the boar.

My knees trembled as if all my muscles were but water. But I could not collapse, not so long as my slave stood.

I would not give him that satisfaction.

"You have done well, my hunter." I said with all the dignity of my station.

"I am glad that I could be of some service," he said between gasps for air.

"Come, sit with my ladies, refresh yourself while they tend to your scratches." Some of those scratches would have laid another man in his bed for a week.

"Boys, bring wine and fruit, bread and cheese." They fell all over themselves as they loosened a pack and brought its contents to us.

Heracles finally sat down beside me ... and I collapsed with as much nobility as I could preserve. Elaine and Ioanna put their sewing kits to better use now stitching up the skin of the man who wore the chiton they had mended not half an hourglass before. Iris came back from the nearest stream with a bowl of water. Heracles half-drunk it dry before allowing that the rest might be needed to wash his scrapes.

So it was that Heracles was in fine fettle when my generals, soldiers, and huntsmen began to struggle back to us. He was also back in his chiton, relaxing with me and my ladies.

Filippos took in the drying blood around the huge boar and the rest of us and shook his head. "There must be quite a story here," he said as the men gathered around him.

Heracles said nothing.

The two boys took in the growing silence as men and women exchanged only silence. It broke them. One of them blurted out "Heracles killed the boar."

"With Iris' knife."

"Elena put an arrow into the beast."

And so the story tumbled out of the two boys, in little order and with even less rhythm. I suspect neither of them would ever be a poet.

And all the time, Heracles sat beside me, combing my hair.

Arete was right, Heracles might have many vices, but bragging was not one of them. Not once did he stop to correct the boys, not even when one of them seemed to give Iris the credit for the knife blow that slew the beast.

All the time he just kept combing my hair.

His hands were fire up and down my back. His breath was sweet, and my lips begged for his. My body ached at his touch and pleaded for more. Not since my husband died had I felt such an urgency to slip away and give a man all that I was.

But I was the queen, and he was a slave.

He combed my hair, and I sat there hoping my men would not see past my robe to the trembling flesh beneath.

Lydia is a small kingdom with little to draw strangers. Now, merchants who had passed us by stopped to trade for a day or two. Apparently, Heracles in a chiton and me in his lion skin was quite the scandal. They came to see, but they also did business with us. My people profited, and there was a small increase in the royal coffers.

Those three years were pleasing and profitable . . . and peaceful.

That was good since there were so many babes at breasts. Heracles apparently had gone through all the women of my court about the time he killed the boar and was starting on the serving wenches in town. Even the good wives of Lydia's artisans and farmers seemed unusually fecund.

The man was shameless.

But for three full years, we were also at peace with our neighbors.

Which makes it hard to understand why the Itones invaded us. It might have been a difference in the calendars our priests used. Heracles would be free of my

labors on the first day of the next month. Their army
marched against us the first day of the month before.

It was disgusting to see the delight among my generals and soldiers as they hastily mobilized to march out to
meet the foe. And my god-man-boy was no better.

"I knew you wouldn't let me go without showing me
at least one good fight," he said, settling onto his horse.
He was still in a chiton, but now he seemed to hardly
notice.

My general did and cleared his throat beside me.
"You will give him back his lion skin? Intimidating the
other poor bastard is half the battle won."

I tossed up the lion skin to Heracles, and, while he
donned it with a laugh of pure joy, I signaled Iris to bring
me my horse. Iris led the mare forward, herself carrying
a suckling baby at her hip. My three huntresses had been
late succumbing. Now, their too-long-defended honor
put them needed at home while I and the army marched
light and quick.

Arete would ride with me, having recently weaned
her Titos. I would need all the help I could muster if I
was not to be left with embittered Itones on my border
when Heracles walked away.

We marched hard for two days, and I slept out under
the stars like my men. On the afternoon of the third day,
we marched into the valley the Itones had suddenly laid
claim to.

Their army, no larger than ours, was already arrayed
in ranks.

As was the custom, they stood there, in the hot sun,
and waited while we finished our march up and the men
found their places in ranks.

I took the time to send forward a herald to ask for
parley.

Filippos smiled at my efforts; he at least understood
my wish for peace even if he disagreed with me. He and
his wife Arete rode out to call for the parley. Him to call.

She to make sure he didn't do anything to make productive talks impossible.

I knew I was putting her in a hard place with her husband, but if not her, who else would do what had to be done?

They trotted back less than half of an hourglass later. "Their king will talk with us," Arete said.

"I suggest we keep Heracles back in a tent," Filippos said. "Let him come as a surprise."

"Heracles, you come with me," I said.

For the first time in three years, I think the god-man-child was ready to balk. "Your general is right. If they don't know I am here," he said, "I can slay dozens and dozens."

"And many women will weep and many sons will swear vengeance for their father's blood. No, mighty Heracles, you *will* ride with me."

We locked eyes, as we had not done since before I had the chains cut off him. He glanced at Filippos. Had the two of them already been planning the slaughter? Composing the poetry?

Filippos looked angry and deadly and defeated. The way a man might look whose wife had just told him she would never come to his bed again. He threw a glance Arete's way that said maybe this *was* the look a man cast at just such a wife.

We rode out together, Heracles and me, Filippos and Arete. It was a silent ride.

The look on King Nireus' face was well worth the ride. "What is he doing here?" he demanded once he had gotten control of his horse. The poor beast seemed to have suddenly taken on a strong desire to run.

"I am Heracles, and I go where I will," was the only answer he got.

The three generals behind him looked no more eager now to cross their spears with Heracles's club. Heracles rode with the sturdy wood settled comfortably in the

crook of his arm. Ahead of me, the entire ranks of Nireus' army went silent as they recalculated the odds of
easy victory into what their chances were of surviving
the run home. Most looked none too happy with their
chances.

There is a certain amount of fun, watching an army of
men suddenly drinking terror to the dregs. But I had not
come out here for my own fun but for the lasting peace
of my people.

"I am of the opinion that we can settle this matter by
a challenge between champions," I shouted.

A collective sigh escaped the Itones battle array.

"Where could we find a champion to go up against
yours?" King Nireus said, his voice almost but not quite
breaking. "Heracles will be your champion, won't he?"

I allowed the question to hang there for a moment
before I posed a question of my own. "Does Itones have
no wrestling champion?"

"Wrestling champion?"

"Yes. I propose that we settle your claims against this
valley by a wrestling match. Your champion, or whoever might wish to chance his luck against the mighty
Heracles."

"As many as may wish?" The astonishment in King
Nireus' voice was purest gold.

I turned back to my slave for one more month. "Only
one contest, or as many as may find the courage to come
against you?"

No boy of five or six was ever so happy. "No more
than five at once," he said, "and I get a break after every
five contests to refresh myself."

The deal was done, and the next day, you hardly
dared approach the Itones camp for fear of flying losers.
I think every man in their army took a go at Heracles.
And once all comers from there had done their best, our
own men asked for a chance. Everyone wanted to boast
that he had wrestled Heracles. That they lost usually was
not mentioned.

And so it was that I brought my army back, drunk, stuffed, and very happy at its great victory. "No doubt the poets will have Heracles slaughtering the Itones army and massacring the town." Arete and I shared the laugh.

But the victory was not bloodless. Even at play, Heracles did not know his own strength. Two Itones and one Lydian died of broken backs or necks.

A month later, Heracles stood tall before my throne in my great hall. He bowed.

"I have served you three years as slave," he said.

"For three years you have done all that I asked," I agreed, talking to a full hall.

He shimmed out of his chiton, wadded it up, and threw it toward where my ladies in waiting stood by their spindles. They cheered as three of them ran to catch it and began to cut it up into fragments for each of them. Thank Hera, the chiton was plenty large.

He turned again to me. "I would ask for what is mine to be returned to me."

I handed the lion skin to Arete, his olive-wood club to Filippos and together they took them to him. Filippos helped settle the skin around him, though it left the sight of most of him to delight every eye.

He was now free to go, and I expected him to make his way through the cheering crowd of my court. Instead, he leaned on his club and stared at me.

For so long he had been my slave and I had been his master that I forgot that a proper maiden should break from such a stare. Even a widowed queen should not lock eyes with a demigod, hero, and man.

But I had been the master, with only my eyes to secure obedience. For one last time, I gave as much as I got. The warmth of our locked eyes brought silence to my court and those strange feelings that I had denied since my husband's death. Those feelings that a queen could not afford, not if she was to keep her head about her and the safety of her kingdom first.

"Now, my Queen, I ask you for what you have never given me," Heracles said.

I swallowed hard the dryness in my throat, the yearning in my belly. Were we once more to cross those swords that the gods and goddesses had given every man and woman?

"You may approach our throne," I said, then turned to those around me. "Leave us to talk."

Arete and Filippos failed to suppress grins as they ushered my inner court away.

Before me, Heracles went to bended knee. The hardness of his male need was before my eyes, impossible to ignore. Yet he knelt in supplication.

"What is it you want?" I hissed. "To raise the only chitin in all Lydia that has not been tossed aside at your first wink?"

"I know what lies beneath your hem. I know where you bathe." He said with his innocent grin.

I knew that he knew my place by the river. I had lingered there more than once when I thought he was looking. "Then state your intent clearly, man. I am a queen, not a tavern wench."

"I want to marry you." He said the words so simply, so softly, that I almost asked him to repeat them.

"You want to marry me?"

"Yes."

A "yes" of my own leaped to my lips, but I denied it. "You who slew your wife and slaughtered your children ask for my hand in marriage. It is a poor deal you offer." And one no wise woman would leap at. Certainly not without the appearance of dickering.

"Yes, my Queen, there is that. Hera sent a rage upon me, and when I knew myself again there was only blood and death around me."

The boy-child looked so repentant, so heavy with sorrow that I longed to hold his head on my breast, run my hands through those curls. Make him forget.

"Why should I risk the love of one so hated by the goddess?" was my only defense.

"Because he loves you truly. He will care for you, and," here he grinned, "I have never known anyone, man or woman, who can keep the peace like you. Maybe some of your peace will wear off on me."

I looked at him, so eager for me. Yet I knew that I could not hold him like a trapped bird in a cage. Sooner or later he would leave me for other sights and labors that the poets would tell their lies about. Still, for a little while, I could have him, enjoy him. Live each day in his arms.

I will never regret my choice I swore to the goddess. "Yes," was on my lips as I reached for him and drew him to my throne, my bed, my everything.

Three years later, I refused to taste regret as I stood on Lydia's walls with my baby. "Wave good-bye to Daddy," I said, raising Agelaus' pudgy hand to wave to Heracles as he walked down the road to the south. Not once did he look back.

Agelaus twisted in my arms, intent on getting at my breasts. Pounding with his fists, he demanded I lower my chitin and let him at them. Ladies, you may think that you know what it is to have the darlings of your life treat harshly your own delicate portions, but until you've had your breasts pummeled by a son of Heracles, you've had it easy.

I sat him down on the wall's walkway and signaled a waiting youth to see that Agelaus didn't try leaping off it. There was nothing in my breasts for him; they'd gone dry. His father had left me a parting gift.

I wonder, if I'd mentioned that would he have stayed longer? Or would my punishment for holding too tight be one of "Hera's rages?" No, it was only too obvious that Heracles' feet were itching for the good spring roads and the adventure over the next hill.

For three years he served me as slave. For another three years he had been as faithful a husband as he knew how to be. For six long years I had kept Lydia safe from the vultures who pass as our neighbors.

The plan did not come to me the exact moment Agron presented me with this "slave." I should have asked the old fellow before he died if he truly didn't recognize the lion skin and the olive-wood club. I know he was hard of hearing, but he must have heard the poets yammering.

I thought I solved the problem of Heracles in my court brilliantly. Dress him in a chiton and put him to work among the women! Why was I surprised when the women themselves came up with their own plan to strengthen our poor Lydia? They opened their wombs to Heracles; the results now shouted in the training yard behind me.

A five-year-old son of Heracles could throw any ten-year-olds, so we let them wrestle only among themselves. Hopefully, the gods will grant one of them some brains. If the lying poets spread the story of Heracles and Omphale far and wide, Lydia's army will need a general.

Sweet Hera had already noticed us. Heracles should have warned me about the snakes. That part of his tale didn't make it to Lydia until after I got the fright of my life. I walked into the nursery to find my eight-month-old baby boy with snakes wrapped around his pudgy arms up to the elbows. I thought they were swallowing him.

But no, Agelaus had grabbed them by their throats and smashed them against the walls of his crib so often and so hard that they were little more than pulverized meat. Heracles was so proud of his giggling little boy and his new playthings. I wanted to throttle them both. So he explained how Hera had done the same to him in his crib. I wondered if all his cute little bastards got the same birth gift. But no, it seems that Hera saved that one for just him and my little boy.

The sons of Heracles meant plenty of adjustments for

Lydia. Each now wears a red wool string on his right hand. One six-year-old lost his life tussling with his three-year-old brother. And the wise women of Lydia had to come up with something to toughen a nursing mother's breast. You really haven't had a baby suckle at your breast until you've had one of them pulling. Of course, once the first tooth starts showing, it's solid food for them.

But what soldiers these men will make for Lydia even if they are growing up in a quiet town where a god-man-boy kept the peace for six wonderful years.

Good years, when a hero named Heracles let his wife dress him in a chitin, and she was known to prance around in her old man's lion skin.

I wonder what the poets will make of that. Strange, in the last six years, not one line of new poetry has reached Lydia. I knew my time with Heracles would not last much longer the night he commented on that . . . and wondered if he'd been forgotten.

I turned my eyes back to the road, but I turned too late. Heracles was gone. Gone from Lydia. Gone from my life. I refused to regret his going, but I will long treasure the six years that were ours. Three of fussing and fighting. Three of loving . . . and fussing.

> *Harken to my words*
> *You women of Greece. The poets are liars and never to be trusted. They will tell your men any tale they want for a bit of silver or drop of wine. But the truth is that we women and men are greater than the poets ever will find words for. Celebrate you who live each day with open eyes, and joy clasp firmly to your bosoms.*
> *And never look back*
> *with regret.*

MERRY MAID

Jean Rabe

Jean Rabe is the author of twenty-six novels and twice that many short stories. In her spare time, she edits anthologies and newsletters and tugs fiercely on old socks with her three dogs. She spends idle moments at the edge of her goldfish pond ... unfortunately, she doesn't have nearly enough idle moments. Visit her website at: *www.jeanrabe.com.*

The green of the meadow was so bright it hurt Marian's eyes. So she tipped her head up and focused on the tops of the trees that marked the beginning of the blessed forest she ran toward.

Damn the dress, she thought, nearly catching her legs in it as she tried to increase her pace. At least she'd loosened the corset a few minutes past, else she'd not have been able to manage anything more strenuous than a Maltese Bransle in this fluffery. Her shoes were little more than fancy slippers, the soles so thin she felt every clump of dirt bite at the bottoms of her feet. She slammed her teeth together when a rock—as sharp as an arrowhead she swore—jabbed into her heel.

Faster, she demanded. *Don't let him catch me ...*

She heard voices calling to the man who chased her—encouraging and taunting him.

Faster! Almost there!

She held her right arm against her side, as if that gesture might lessen the ache that had started there, and she sucked in one great gulp of hot summer air after another. The scent of Sherwood was so strong she could taste it. She lowered her gaze, seeing now only patches of the hurtful bright grass between the shadow lances of the massive trunks and the smeared colors of wildflowers.

The tall hardwoods seemed to stretch toward her, their branches like crooked fingers beckoning her to escape into their ancient embrace.

Then she was beyond the meadow and into the woods. The light was softer here, the canopy high and thick and keeping the sun at bay, the air noticeably cooler. Still she ran, though not quite as swiftly now because of the closeness of the trunks. Her braids slapped against her back.

In spurts she darted between oaks and chestnuts. She leaped a stump and slipped on a patch of slick ground; it had rained hours ago, and this fiery July day had not yet chased all the moisture away from the woods. Her arms flailed as she pitched forward, and her hands caught at a low-hanging branch. She dropped to her knees, and she heard her overskirt rip, snagged on something she didn't take time to look for. She gave the material a vicious yank as she regained her feet and plowed ahead.

Marian heard him, her pursuer; he'd reached Sherwood too and was thrashing through the underbrush, sounding clumsy in his haste.

Don't let him catch me . . .

She darted headfirst through wide-spreading ferns and bushes. Twigs and thorny vines clawed at her, but she pushed them away and thrust the pain to the back of her mind as she continued her maddened dash. The snort of a startled wild pig cut through the clearing ahead, followed by the flutter of wings from ground-nesting partridges.

The thrashing behind her grew louder.

Faster! Faster!

She closed her eyes for just an instant, seeing flashing motes against the black. Then she opened them and with more determination grabbed up her skirts and picked up her knees as she charged across the clearing and to the cluster of birches on the other side. He might know these woods better than she, but she spied something familiar up ahead, a tall limbless ash bright white with death. She raced toward it.

Not much farther, she told herself. *Don't let him win this time. He can't win. Not again.*

The greens of Sherwood blurred around her, like an artist's watercolor left in the rain. She felt lightheaded from the exertion, yet at the same time she felt invigorated and was lifted by the prospect of success. Marian ignored the constant jabs of twigs and rocks against her thin soles, the scrapes of branches, the ache in her side—much worse now—and the burning that centered in her chest.

She focused on victory.

And victory was hers as she barreled into the Merry Men's camp and thudded to a stop.

"I won," she gasped. She bent over, hands on her knees, sucking in air that smelled of the forest and of men and of extinguished cook fires. Then she straightened and thrust her chin out proudly. "This day is mine, Robin. I won."

"Maid Marian!" The voice was clear and strong that came from behind her. "Well done, my love! This race indeed is yours."

She glanced over her shoulder to see the outlaw leader grinning at her, his eyes sparkling with mischief.

Marian spun and faced him. "You let me win, didn't you, Robin?" She noted that despite the summer heat and the distance of their run, he wasn't winded. He'd clearly not put as much effort into this race as she had.

"Let you?" He raised an eyebrow. Then in two long

strides he was on her, hands wrapping around her small waist and lifting her above his head, twirling both of them so that the shades of the forest and of the clothes of he and his Merry Men—who'd just now joined them— became a swirl of green that made her dizzy.

Robin brought her down and held her close, nuzzling his face into her neck and giving her a gentle kiss.

Marian practically gagged.

Robin stunk of sweat, of going too many days— perhaps weeks—without a bath. The scent of greasy venison clung to a tunic and leggings he hadn't changed out of for God-knew-how-long. The oily pong of his tangled hair hung in her nostrils and threatened to bring up the meager breakfast she'd enjoyed a few hours ago. The bits of food that had dried in his beard scratched against her cheek.

"Aye, Maid Marian, I must confess that I let you win this race," he said finally. "But only because you'd already won my heart." He shifted and brought his lips against hers, and she sagged against him because the odor of his breath was so foul it nearly made her pass out.

After a moment, she found the strength to push him an arm's distance away. He gave her a lopsided look and gestured to the center of the camp where the Merry Men had drifted.

A Norman noblewoman, daughter of the late Lord Fitzwalter, Marian wondered how she had allowed herself to fall so hopelessly in love with this filthy, striking rogue. Handsome, Robin was that and more, even in his disheveled state. So handsome she never tired of staring at his face.

"A rest shall we take, Maid Marian?" He extended his arm the way a gentleman would at court, and she lightly placed her hand on it. He guided her to a blanket that Friar Tuck had laid out for them and flopped down on it. He looked up at her and smiled broadly. "You need to rest after that race."

"A rest, yes, dear Robin, gladly. But first I must change out of this ruined dress and these shredded shoes. I was a fool to suggest such a romp wearing this." She crossed the camp to a small thatch hut that practically blended into the foliage. It was one of a half-dozen one-room homes that the Merry Men had constructed and slept in during inclement weather. She had a few changes of more practical clothes there, along with some other personal possessions, and a large jug of water and a cake of perfumed soap that she was quick to wash with.

"Do not be too long, my love!" he called. "I've the prospect of wealth to share."

"Aye, Dear Robin, I'll not tarry," she cheerily returned.

Marian had met Robin Hood a little more than a year ago, when he entered an archery competition in Nottinghamshire. It was those flashing brown eyes that had first caught her attention, large and inviting and oh-so-easy to lose herself in. She couldn't remember how long she'd gazed into those eyes that first day, though she knew it was much longer than proper. When she had finally forced herself to look away, she took in the rest of the man. His face was all angles and planes, as if sculpted by an artist, his skin tanned and smooth and soft against her fingertips. His curly russet locks shone warmly in the sun; the slight breeze teased the strands over his forehead, while his rakish wink tugged at her heart.

She'd never seen a more perfect-looking man.

Of course, Robin had bathed before the event, and had washed his green tunic and leggings, and perhaps had found a place to press them, as not a wrinkle could be seen. He had smelled of sweet musk, she recalled, and his teeth glistened like wet pearls. And when he drew her close and kissed her that first time after she presented him the trophy, his breath tasted of honeyed mead and wholly intoxicated her.

That night when he scaled the castle wall and precariously perched outside her window, he kissed her again and wooed her with poetry. A few days later she went riding and "accidentally" found herself in Sherwood. Now she practically lived there, appearing just often enough in court to satisfy the Sheriff of Nottingham- shire, her legal guardian.

Despite all of Robin's odious faults, Marian dearly loved him. And despite the insects and the night-hooting owls, the naps on hard ground and the hunting and for- aging for her own sustenance, she adored this massive, beautiful, seemingly endless forest.

Changed into a tunic, leggings, and knee-high boots, she emerged looking every bit like one of the Merry Men. Marian joined Robin on the blanket and stuffed her hair under a hat he offered. A bowl of fruit had been placed near them, filled with cherries and blueberries, raspberries and early peaches. Robin bit into a peach and let the juice run down his lips and mingle with an assortment of crumbs that had collected in his beard.

Tuck was a few yards away, sitting on a felled log and stuffing his fleshy face with bread that must have come from one of the nearby villages. Marian was fond of the friar. Though far from refined, and terribly overweight, lecherous, and an alcoholic, Tuck bathed more often than the rest of them. Too, he was the most devout of the lot—generous, courteous, and deceptively danger- ous with a sword.

Tuck had told her once that he hailed from Foun- tains Abbey in Yorkshire, that his given name was Mi- chael, and that until five years ago he was the Sheriff of Nottinghamshire's chaplain; that was just before she came to live in the castle. Then he'd fallen in with Robin Hood, and he began preaching to the outlaws of Sher- wood instead. He promised to preside over her upcom- ing wedding to Robin, an event Marian looked forward to with an equal measure of delight and foreboding.

Robin had proposed to Marian that first night, when he'd climbed the castle wall and clung outside her win- dow. She'd thought he was teasing her then, but he asked her again a week later, and a week after that; he'd

not yet begun to reek. Marian accepted on the third occasion, giddy with the prospect of marrying the most
dashing, muscular man she'd ever seen—the man whose
name was on the lips of everyone in Nottinghamshire
and beyond. Robin was the most famous and infamous
man in practically all of England.

He was even royalty, in a fashion, her Robin Hood—
Robin of Locksley, the Earl of Huntington. So she had
assuredly selected a mate that would place her in the
history books on multiple counts . . . if she could stomach this continued closeness.

She did love him, didn't she?

To buy her time to make that decision she had ar-
gued that they should wait to wed until the outlaws were
pardoned and Richard the Lionheart had returned from
the Crusades and could bless the union. Then she could
have an elaborate wedding in the castle, in a dress decorated with yards and yards of lace and precious seed
pearls. Perhaps she could get Robin to bathe and shave
before the ceremony and put on something . . . cleaner.

Robin had agreed to wait, and hence she was still
Maid Marian, rather than Lady. Merry Maid, he affec-
tionately called her.

Robin interrupted her thoughts. "Marian, I've learned
that taxes are being collected in Eaton in three days."
He finished his peach and reached for another.

"And we shall collect from the tax collectors!" This
came from the peddler, Gamble Gold, cousin to Little
John and one of the several tradesmen who were part of
the Merry Men.

"Aye, collect in full!" echoed George Green, the pin-
der of Wakefield in Yorkshire. Marian remembered his
voice as being the loudest in urging Robin to catch her
during their race.

Arthur Bland nodded in agreement. He sat on the
ground next to Green, staring into a mug of what she
suspected was ale. Bland shared Tuck's love of spirits.

"Eaton's a poor place, for the most part," Gamble

Gold said, "but it's been a while since the taxman's been there. They'll have some coin saved up."

"Coin and sheep and fine, wool blankets. Eaton has weavers," Tuck added.

"I could do with a new blanket," Robin mused.

"A thick one for me," George Green said. "I don't take the cold well, and that'll set in come a few months."

"Eaton won't be the only place the taxman'll be stopping." Bland finally said something. "Should be some heavy purses ripe for plucking from him, eh Robin?"

More Merry Men filtered into the clearing, drawn by the talk of gold and goods. Most all of them were yeomen, carrying swords rather than a peasant's quarterstaff. Some said Robin's band numbered a hundred, but Marian knew it to be half that. She also knew that Robin wanted to increase his force so they could cover more roads coming into Nottinghamshire.

"Marian, greetings!" called Much, the Miller's son. With him was Little John, who towered over all of them; David of Doncaster; Gilbert, who for a reason Marian had never deduced was called Gilbert with the White Hand, and who was nearly as good as she and Robin with a bow; Wat o' the Crabstaff; Will Stutly; and Will Scathlock, or Will Scarlet as he preferred to be called. The latter Will rivaled Robin for looks, Marian judged, perhaps even surpassed him. But Will Scarlet didn't seem to favor women, neither was he at all fastidious, and so Marian's eyes had not strayed.

Robin continued to talk about the tax collector's route, which would take the reviled man through Milton, West Drayton, and Gamston before reaching Eaton. Marian stretched a delicate hand forward and plucked several ripe blueberries from the bowl, eating them whole and careful not to stain her lips or fingers.

Robin started talking tactics.

Robin and the Merry Men were said to "rob from the rich and give to the poor," but that wasn't precisely true. He was known to waylay poor men, such as tinkers, as easily as he'd go after men known to have good coin. No matter his mark, he planned each attack meticulously and cleverly.

Marian interrupted him. "That's three days from now, the taxman." She rubbed at a spot of dirt on her leggings. "I know of something happening tomorrow, a good distance north of Sherwood. Something better."

Friar Tuck's eyes widened, and he thumped one fist on his knee and raised the hunk of bread high with his other hand. "Something without as many guards as the taxman will have?" Tuck was always worried about the guards.

"Coming south from Barnsdale and Pontefract, this something is," Marian tempted. "Coming from the large abbey in Yorkshire."

Tucks eyes widened further.

"Tell us more, fair maid," Robin leaned against her and brushed her with his lips, getting peach nectar on her cheek. "If this 'something' is tomorrow, we can strike it *and* then the taxman two days later. Richer, we shall all be." Robin's expression grew dark. "It has been some time since we've had a significant haul."

She reached for another handful of blueberries and popped them in her mouth, chewing slowly and noting that all eyes were on her, waiting. The blueberries were sweet, and their taste helped cut the stench of her beloved. Oh, if only he would give in to her request that he occasionally take a dip in one of Sherwood's many ponds, she thought.

"I mentioned the abbey," she said finally. "For decades gold crosses and goblets, jewels and more, have been in storage in the cellar. Not enough room in the chapel proper to put them all on display, I guess."

Tuck set down his loaf of bread and leaned forward. The friar was well aware of the large abbey's resources.

"When I was in court yesterday, putting in an appearance to satisfy the sheriff, I accidentally overheard that the abbot had ordered some of those trinkets brought to the castle in Nottingham, an offering of sorts to help fund the Crusades."

"They'll be funding the sheriff's next endeavor instead, I reckon," Little John said. "That despot cares not a whit about the Crusades. He'll see that only a smidgen reaches King Richard, if that much, and he'll take the best of the gold for himself."

"The best gold should be for us," Robin whispered.

"The sheriff cares only about persecuting the poor and demanding more taxes." Will Scarlet's voice was rich and melodic, and Marian liked listening to it. "Guy of Gisbourne will get his share of the abbey's gold, too, I'm certain." Scarlet spat at the notion of Gisbourne, who had sent another outlaw, Richard the Divine, to hunt the Merry Men two months past.

Scarlet and Robin had killed Divine—with the aid of Marian, who dispatched Divine's lackeys with her precise bow shots.

"What about guards?" Tuck persisted. "Marian, did you hear anything about guards?"

"None from what I gathered," Marian said. "Guards draw attention, good friar, I heard the sheriff say. A lone carriage carrying a priest or two does not."

Robin kissed Marian again and rose, dropping what was left of his peach and setting his sticky hands against his hips.

"Gisbourne and the sheriff will get none of that abbey's riches," Robin proclaimed. "Neither will King Richard get a whiff of it. He has enough for his Crusades."

Marian wrinkled her nose at the word 'whiff' and stared at Robin's leggings, smudged with dirt and stained with grass and grease from the game Tuck had cooked for them. Robin had a bad habit of wiping his hands on his clothes. She looked to the bowl of fruit, studying the play of light across the berries.

"Once more, our Merry Maid has found a worthy target for us," Robin continued. "Once more, Marian has used her presence in the castle to our advantage."

"And this time we shall give some of the gold away, aye?" This from Tuck. "This time we share some of it with those less fortunate and not bury it in the heart of Sherwood for ourselves. Rob from the rich to give to the poor, as some local folk think we do."

Robin's growing legend claimed that he was a champion of the people and fought against corrupt officials and stood up for the common man. But in truth, Marian knew he was instead self-indulgent, and that the gains from their raids padded his own treasury. Occasionally, he would help peasants. But when he did it was to improve his image and to drum up a few more Merry Men from the villages where he sprinkled the coins.

That was the trouble with heroes, Marian thought, they're only heroic when it suits them. And it didn't suit Robin Hood often.

"Aye, Tuck, if this haul is as good as Maid Marian hints," Robin said, "we'll help the fine folk of Markham Moor with some of it. Fire took a handful of their homes two weeks past. A sack or two of gold should more than set things right." So softly only Marian could hear, he added: "And gain me some needed accolades in that part of the shire where my favor is waning."

Marian stood and stretched. "I'll get my bow and sword, Robin. We should leave soon."

"Aye, Merry Maid," he returned. "We've some miles to go before we can entrench ourselves for a proper ambush for the abbey carriage."

She lay on her belly on one side of the road, face pressed against the sweet earth, and her senses filled with the fragrance of grass and stonecrop and newly bloomed motherwort. Tuck was beside her, concealed only because he lay in a depression that swallowed his belly. Robin and Little John were on the opposite side, and a dozen Merry Men were perched in the trees, their green clothing helping to hide them amid the leaves.

Marian felt alive.

She relished these escapades, delighting in the danger and the dangling promise of ill-gotten wealth. No courtly dance, no matter how spirited, could set her heart to racing so. She could hear it pound now in her ears, practically in time with the beat of the approaching horses' hooves.

"Here comes the abbot's gold," she whispered to Tuck. "Delivered like a roasted goose on a platter."

"Just as you promised, Merry Maid," Tuck returned. He snaked his arm down to his side, his doughy fingers closing on the pommel of his sword.

The outlaws waited until the lead horse was in sight of Much on the highest limb, then on a signal from him, Robin, she, Tuck, and Little John dashed to the center of the narrow road. Marian drew her sword and pointed it forward. The sunlight made her Spanish-forged blade gleam.

Robin was in front, hands on his hips, head thrown back, and voice booming.

"Halt now, men of the abbey! Share your gold with the men of Sherwood!"

The carriage driver pulled hard on the reins, and the lead horse reared back, hooves flailing a mere yard from Robin's head. The outlaw didn't flinch. Instead, he doffed his feathered hat and bowed, just as the carriage stopped. He stepped to the side and replaced his hat, and waved his hand as a signal to his archers. A dozen arrows thudded into the ground in a perfect crescent around the lead horse, causing it to rear again.

"Out, out of the carriage, my good sirs!" Robin impatiently tapped his foot.

Marian loved it when Robin became theatric. No man was more charismatic than he, she believed, more arrogant and playful, so risk-taking and sure of himself. Robin was at his best when he was after gold. And at this distance and with the wind in her favor, Marian couldn't smell him.

But she could see the dark sweat stains beneath his

arms and the sheen on his face, the backs of his hands streaked with dirt.

Perhaps it would rain soon, she thought; the clouds to the south were swollen thick and tinged with gray. A good downpour would clean him up a little—clean up all the Merry Men, for that matter, and chase away some of this summer heat.

The carriage door creaked open, and soft leather boots in pale gray leggings extended beneath it. A moment more and the rest of the man came out. He wasn't *the* abbot, Marian had seen Abbot Carswell on more than one occasion. But he was one of the abbot's favored priests. Thin and pasty faced—a scholar's complexion, she corrected herself—Father Dorsay adjusted his robe so that it fell down in neat folds to his ankles. He puffed himself up, as much as his frame allowed, squared his shoulders, and met Robin Hood's gaze. Marian detected the faintest quiver in the priest's lower lip.

"I say, priest, hand over your treasures to Robin Hood and his Merry Men!" Robin continued his theatrics. "Else I will order another volley of arrows, and this time they'll strike more than the road."

Dorsay opened his mouth as if to say something, but his words were cut off by the thundering of more hooves. Four horses charged from the north, their riders in chain mail and wearing Abbott Carswell's colors, an escort that had kept a distance.

"Look lively!" Robin called. "We've company." On another signal, more arrows 'thwupped' down from the trees; one struck the carriage driver, who'd been going for his sword.

Marian dashed forward, meeting the armored man who had emerged from the other side of the carriage. "I'd not expected this, Robin! There was no talk of guards. This one, yes, I'd expect, but the others—"

She was at the same time frightened and thrilled. Marian loved a good fight. "Try not to kill them!" she hollered so loud the Merry Men in the trees could hear her. "They're Carswell's. They're men of God!"

She brought up her sword to parry the blow of her armored foe. Through the open doors of the carriage, she spied Robin grabbing Dorsay on the other side. Then she had to concentrate on her opponent as he brought down his sword again and again, caring not that she was a woman and treating her as he would any of Robin's men. He was a practiced swordsman, and his blows fell with great force, taking all of her strength to deflect them.

"You don't want to fight me," Marian hissed. "I'm better than you, second only to Robin Hood. Keep your life and drop your sword."

"Thief," he cut back. "Brigand! She-devil."

"Aye." She couldn't help but smile. "I am happily all of that." She went on the offensive now, sweeping her blade behind her and bringing it around with all her force to meet his broadsword. His was the heavier sword. It was difficult to maneuver so close to the carriage, and so Marian stepped back, the armored man following as she again parried his swing.

"We told Abbot Carswell to expect trouble," the man said. "That Robin's men might learn of this somehow."

"No *man* learned of it," she countered. "But you were right to worry about Robin Hood." Away from the carriage she could sweep her blade in a wider arc. She dropped in a crouch when next he darted in, feeling the air stir above her head from the strength of his swing. Then she jumped up and turned her blade so the flat of it struck his side. She registered the surprise on his face.

"That could've killed you," she said. "Drop your sword now."

Instead, the man gritted his teeth and lunged. Marian sidestepped him and this time came around behind him. Then she kicked him hard in the rear, sending him off balance and flying forward. She pursued him, again ducking behind him as he awkwardly turned, sword leading.

He wasn't a challenging opponent, and so Marian listened to the fight around her. She registered the 'thwup' and 'thwunk' of arrows being shot and landing in the ground and in the wood of the carriage; she was grateful the Merry Men were not trying to kill Carswell's small force, though she knew the carriage driver was lost. She heard the frightened whinnies of the horses, Robin hollering. She couldn't make out his words at first, as there was a sudden clanging of swords, someone shouting: "Death to the forest brigands!" and the angry curses of the man facing her. She effortlessly parried his swing this time.

"I truly do not want to kill you," she said. "But if it's my life or yours, I'll be the one to keep breathing."

Marian thought she heard him call her "bitch" and something else less complimentary. He raised his blade above his head, meaning to bring it down on her in a death stroke.

"Fool," she whispered. Then she surged forward, her sword arm driving with all the strength she could summon and forcing the tip of the blade through his tabard and the links of the chain shirt beneath it. She registered the look of surprise on his face and saw blood trickle from his mouth as he dropped his sword and she raised her foot, planting her boot in his stomach and pushing him back and off her sword.

"Surrender!"

She heard Robin clearly now, as the fighting was dying down. A heartbeat later he repeated the command, and the clanging of steel and 'thwupping' of arrows stopped. Wiping her sword on the dead man's tabard, she sheathed the blade and came around the front of the carriage to see Robin holding his own sword against the priest's throat.

One other of Carswell's men lay dead, his head bashed in by Little John. Another had been wounded by Tuck.

The two remaining held their hands at their sides, and Much, who'd come down from the tree without Marian noticing, was collecting their swords.

"I shall kill him," Robin warned the men, "I'm not above slaying a man of God." Marian came to Robin's side, seeing his eyes narrow and knowing he wasn't bluffing.

"Hands higher!" Marian said. "Now." Then she went from one man to the next, removing knives from sheaths on their belts, and checking their boots for more blades. Tuck joined her, his sword out protectively.

When she was satisfied all the weapons were collected, she searched them for coin purses; Much searched the dead men. "They carry considerable coin for men of God," she said.

"Carried," Robin corrected. "It's ours now."

Marian looked to him, just in time to see him push the priest away. Father Dorsay fell to his knees, crossed himself, and began praying.

"Ours along with whatever treasures they were taking from the abbey to Nottingham." He gestured to Little John and Marian. "Watch this pair and the priest." Though the men were disarmed, Robin was still wary; being careful was how he'd managed to live this long, Marian knew.

Then Robin turned his attention to the coach, rummaging beneath the seats inside and pulling out two chests and a leather sack. Not bothering to open them, he returned to his search, slicing open side panels and cushions and retrieving two more pouches.

"There's a box on top," Marian told him. "Beneath the carriage driver's seat."

Robin was quick to retrieve it, then searched the carriage once more to make certain they'd found everything. A waggle of his fingers and Much and a half-dozen more Merry Men came to his side.

"We'll take the carriage and horses," Robin told them, "just for a bit, to carry our gains back to camp."

"And then—" Much looked to the carriage. Red and yellow, Abbot Carswell's colors, it was too bright for the forest.

Softly, Robin answered: "We'll break up the carriage for firewood and give the horses to the farmers in Eaton."

Much was pleased with the latter bit of charity and ordered the booty returned to the carriage for transport back to Sherwood. He gathered the reins of the four loose horses and tied them to the back of the carriage, and then he tossed the men's coin purses inside.

"Your boots," Robin told the men. "You, too, priest. All of you, take off your boots."

The men protested only slightly, and Much threw their boots inside the carriage. "So you won't be walking anywhere too quickly," Much explained. "And those chain shirts, they're worth good coin."

The men grudgingly doffed their armor.

"Time to leave," Robin announced. He extended a hand to Marian and helped her into the carriage, Tuck following and causing the wooden step to creak in protest. "Thank you for contributing to the welfare of the men of Sherwood," he directed to the still-kneeling priest, again doffing his hat and bowing. Then he sprang onto the carriage seat and grabbed the reins in a single motion.

The Merry Men seemed to melt into the greenery surrounding the road, and Robin drove the carriage, the horses kicking up dust and clods of dirt as they thundered toward Sherwood.

They waited until they were well into the forest before stopping to look into the chests and sacks. Robin never examined his prizes in front of his victims, a quirk Marian found odd but endearing. She was the sort who wanted to know at this moment what the prize was. As a child, she never could wait until the morning of her birthday to open her packages; she would always search through the manor days in advance when her parents were occupied.

The chests were filled with cold coins, jeweled crosses, and gem-encrusted goblets, some bearing the marks of long-dead abbots. The sacks contained old coins and prayer beads made of pearls and precious stones.

"Impressive," Robin pronounced. "I'll take that chest there." He pointed to a polished mahogany chest inlaid in silver with the crest of Abbot Carswell. It was the smallest of the three, but it contained the most gems. "The rest . . . Little John, see that it's divided among the Merry Men."

Tuck cleared his throat.

"Oh, yes, the villagers of Markham Moor." Robin pointed to the pouches taken from the men and the priest. "See that a few of those are given to the people who lost their homes in the fire. And see if there are any young men there who want to join our band."

Tuck sighed, nodded, and scooped up the coin pouches.

Marian scowled and opened her mouth to protest the meager amount, but she changed her mind. She knew the villagers would be grateful and that it wouldn't be a small amount of coins as far as they were concerned. But Robin could have contributed so much more.

"Merry Maid—"

Marian looked up. Robin had been talking to her, but she'd not been paying attention. "Sorry. What?"

"I said perhaps we should not wait for that pardon. Perhaps you and I should wed with the coming of August."

Marian sucked in a surprised breath. "But Robin—"

"That fine dress you talked about, with all the pearls and lace . . . one small bauble from this haul would buy you that and more. The good Friar Tuck has already agreed to perform the ceremony."

Marian felt lightheaded and fought for air. It was as if she'd run yesterday's race all over again. "I need to think, Robin."

He flashed an amazing smile at her, and his eyes sparkled so warmly she worried she would drown in them. So handsome, her Robin, and so famous and infamous, royalty of sorts. She did love him, didn't she?

"Think about it, Merry Maid, on the way back to our camp."

"Aye, Robin. I will marry you with the coming of August," she said as the familiar dead white ash came into view. After all, she told herself, he was the most striking man in all of Notinghamshire. He would put her in the history books.

Marian had never looked more beautiful. Her dress was ivory, silk imported from the east and acquired one week past when the Merry Men absconded with a large merchant wagon. It was sewn by the women of Markham Moor, in exchange for the coins Robin had bestowed upon the village. It was decorated with pearls from one of the strings of prayer beads taken from the abbot's treasure and with lace that had been stolen personally by Robin from a shop in Nottingham.

Robin looked even more dashing than usual. He'd bathed before donning a new tunic and leggings that Marian knew had also been stolen. And he'd shaved.

He sat with her at the edge of a pond, well south of the Merry Men's camp. They watched the setting sun tinge the surface of the water a molten gold.

"Wife," he said. "I like the sound of that."

She gave him a coy smile and drew in a deep breath. He smelled of something sweet and musky, and when he leaned close and kissed her, she tasted the heady flavor of mulled cider.

"I like the sound of that, too," she admitted.

"My Merry Maid . . . I won't be able to call you that after this evening." His voice was easy on the ear, and the words came slow. "Lady Marian, you shall be." He kissed her again, and when he finally pulled away he noticed the sad look on her face. "Marian, I—"

"Merry Maid," she said, as she pulled him close again, the fingers of one hand tugging at the top of his tunic, the fingers of the other clenched firmly around a fist-sized rock. She hit him once, hard, on the back of his head. He tried to pull away, but was too stunned. She hit him again—not on his face that was all angles and planes and peaceful-looking now—and he slumped against her. And when she pushed him away, she struck him three more times, again on the back of the head . . . just to be certain he was dead.

Then she rose and turned away to stare at the water, shimmering like the coins and jewelry in Robin's hidden treasury—which he had shown her minutes past. Tears filled her eyes, but she wiped them away with her lacy sleeve.

"You looked so fine for our wedding," she said. "But it wouldn't have lasted, the smell of soap."

Marian knew it would have been a long time before he might chance to bathe again, perhaps even longer before he would have washed his new tunic and leggings. He would have reeked again soon, of sweat and venison grease and the blood of men he would kill.

Better that her last memories of him be of his clean, handsome self, she thought.

Had he kept living and leading the Merry Men, Marian was certain he would have kept yet more gold for himself—from all those future capers, giving only a little to the poor to help his reputation and make the common folk think him a hero.

"I'm sorry, Robin. I really had no choice."

She vowed that she would give more to the people, much more—while still tucking enough away for herself and the rest of the Merry Men.

She had loved him, hadn't she?

Friar Tuck would be here soon, to help her bury Robin beneath that death-white ash. He'd earlier helped her concoct a fine tale that she would tearfully relate to Little John and all the rest. It was an accident, Robin's death, they'd decided. He fell and hit his head on the rim of rocks by the pond.

Then after a short, suitable period of mourning she would set herself up as their leader, rightful successor to Robin Hood's band.

The Merry Maid and her Merry Men.

She liked the sound of that. It would give her a more prominent place in those history books, and a chance to be a better hero than Robin was.

She really had loved him.

THE PROBLEM WITH
DATING SHAPESHIFTERS

Nina Kiriki Hoffman

Over the past twenty-some years, Nina Kiriki Hoffman has sold adult and YA novels and more than 250 short stories. Her works have been finalists for the Nebula, World Fantasy, Mythopoeic, Sturgeon, Philip K. Dick, and Endeavour awards. Her first novel won a Stoker award. Nina's young adult novel *Spirits That Walk in Shadow* and short sf novel *Catalyst* came out in 2006. *Fall of Light* is due from Ace in May 2009. She does production work for the *Magazine of Fantasy & Science Fiction* and teaches writing through her local community college. She also works with teen writers. She lives in Eugene, Oregon, with several cats and many strange toys.

You know how it is. Your father's a river god, your mother's the naiad of a nearby spring, you figure you'll marry some feature of the landscape and give birth to baby boulders or, who knows, something from the plant kingdom, when along comes a honey-mouthed stranger with fingers soft as feathers, and before you know it, you've let him into yourself, and then he turns you into a cow because his wife has been spying on you and this is the stupid way he covers up his mistakes.

You've heard the stories. He turns himself into a swan, a shower of gold, the girl you love, a white bull that smells of flowers, a perfect imitation of someone's husband so she thinks she's doing the right thing by bedding him; he turns his girlfriend into a mosquito and swallows her and she ends up in his head, he does this, he does that, all in a vain attempt to keep his wife in the dark. He's got all this power of change. Why doesn't he just turn his sister-wife into something helpless and get on with his amours like a normal person?

But no, not Zeus. Maybe it's because the only mother he knew was the goat Amalthea, a very giving sort of mother, but not a human shape; perhaps that's why he turns his mistresses or himself into animals. Maybe Hera won't play those kinds of games.

He came to my father's country disguised as a beardless youth, and at first all he wanted to do was debate philosophy with me. I loved a man I could match wits with, and the gods knew I didn't meet many such wandering through the countryside. That was why I so often snuck into the city at the mouth of my father's river, to listen to the philosophers arguing all afternoon in the square—that, and to buy figs and honey and olives.

I don't know how Zeus knew this argumentative boy was the guise that would work on me, but, then, he's all about courtship and getting under as many women's chitons as he can. We all have our strengths.

Mine was, I suppose, that I was a pretty, girl-shaped nymph, and I spent lots of time wandering near my father's river and rarely visited my mother's spring. Mother might have warned me not to talk to Zeus. She was always warning me about things like that, which was why I stayed far from her. She hadn't wanted me to learn whittling or knife-fighting or card playing or any of the other things city boys had taught me.

Father, on the other hand, only paid attention if I

called for him to help me, which was why I considered
Father my favorite parent. He never noticed the beardless boy who came to court me.

In my rambles beside my father's river, I sometimes
teased the shepherd boys until they kissed me, and I enjoyed inspiring them with hopeless longing without ever
letting them press more on me than a kiss. I knew this
boy was different, though I didn't know how.

Zeus knew how to look as inoffensive and ineffectual
as those boys, though he was handsomer and cleaner.
His golden hair gleamed in the sharp spring sunlight,
and his chiton was green as new leaves, but he carried
nothing I feared—no knife at his belt, no shepherd's
staff in his hand. If my father were watching, he might
have thought nothing of seeing me with yet another cal-
low youth.

In the course of my spirited discussion with the boy,
an amphora of sweet red wine and two handle cups
painted with scenes of satyrs and manaeds appeared.
The boy poured, and we both drank from the cups. The
wine was not watered the way men drank it when they
held their discussions long into the night. (A city boy I'd
met had snuck me into his master's household while the
family was away and let me taste the wine, hoping for
favors. I let him listen to my laugh, though I found the
drink weaker than water from my mother's spring).

This boy-disguised Zeus and I went from a clash
about how often the gods should meddle in the lives of
mortals (he: often; I: leave the mortals alone; aren't they
cursed enough already?) to a kiss.

Perhaps Zeus noticed a stray drop of wine at the corner of my mouth. Perhaps he leaned forward to lick it.
Perhaps I turned my head to catch his lips with mine,
and his breath was sweet, redolent of apples and honey,
with none of the scents of garlic and onions so often on
the breath of shepherds that wandered the Argolis hills.

His kiss was pleasant, and the spirits in the cup he
offered worked through me. The boy and the sun were

warm against me, and I was sleepy with wine and content with his caresses. In drowsiness I did not at first notice when he moved past caresses to push into me, but then the red pain came, and I woke. I tried to shove him away, but he held me tight and finished pleasuring himself despite my struggles. How sweet my afternoon had started, and how bitter the taste on my tongue now.

When he had finished, the boy drew back. He stroked away my tears with his thumbs, and kissed me again, and said, "That wasn't so bad, was it? Next time will be better. I will teach you joy."

I didn't believe him; my tears flowed.

He gathered me against him, gentle this time, and he smelled of new grasses and the first flowers of spring, and even though I feared him, I felt comforted.

Then we heard a thing, though I was not sure what it was. A bird call I had never heard before, or a footstep on the air. The boy sat up and waved his arms, and clouds covered the bright summer sky, and that's when I felt an even deeper apprehension. I had thought him a clumsy and half-kind boy. Now I knew he was more, a meddling immortal, the kind who gave gods a bad name.

"She's coming," he said, "and I need you to be something else." He hugged me again, and I changed. My fingers fused to become hooves; my arms bunched into spindly legs, and I fell forward on my new front hooves; my legs shifted and my feet bent double as though to make fists, my toenails spreading into hooves; my eyes grew, and my nose and mouth stretched; my dark hair fell out. White hair covered all of my skin. My ears lengthened, horns thrust from my forehead, and at the base of my spine, out stretched a tail tasseled at the end with snowy hair. I grew large and strange to myself. I could no longer see in front, only to both sides. I could not stand upright. I opened my throat to protest, and the voice that came out of me spoke only a long, nasal groan unlike anything I had ever uttered before.

The boy, standing beside me, grew in stature and

musculature and sprouted a full, curly beard. The golden
hair he had worn darkened to bronze. His face matured
into a man's face, handsome and hard-edged and cruel.
He stood with one hand on my back as the clouds he
had conjured cleared, and a glowing, matronly woman
stepped down from the sky. "Zeus!" she said. "What are
you doing down here?"

"Just admiring this heifer," he said.

"Is that all?" She came to him and thrust a hand into
his chiton below the waist, grasped the part of him he
had thrust into me. "Hmm," she said. "Perhaps you've
already finished, or perhaps not begun. Well, what a
beautiful animal you have here." She touched me between the eyes. Now that I knew who my seducer was, I
feared the worst, for Hera's jealousy was legendary, but
her touch was gentle, not poisonous. "She is so sweet, so
pretty and clean. Cows are sacred to me. You got her for
me, didn't you? So thoughtful!"

Zeus smiled and shrugged and kicked at the dirt.
"Your pleasure is my pleasure," he said.

That's the problem with dating shapeshifters. They
can look like your dream come true. You only find out
later that when their wife asks them to give you to her,
they go ahead and do it, instead of saying, "Oh, she's not
mine to give, I was just watching her for a friend," or,
"Wait, I have to go to the bathroom," and while the wife
looks the other way, turn you into something small she
can't find so easily, or something so horrid she wouldn't
want it.

"Come with me, sweet thing," Hera murmured. She
grasped one of my ears and tugged. It hurt. I stepped
toward her and the pain eased. She led me up into the
sky, and we walked with air beneath us until we came to
a slope of Mount Olympus, where thick grass and fruit
trees grew. We had left Zeus behind on Earth.

Hera sat down on a tuft of grass and said, "I wonder
what you looked like before. I always wonder when I
rescue those he's mistreated, but he is the king of the

gods, and I gave up some of my power when I married him, so I can't change you back. But I can keep you safe from him, poor child. Would you like that?"

The great mother goddess would keep me safe from the god who had taken my virginity without asking me and then changed me into a beast? The idiot who had betrayed me into her hands?

I lowed, and she stroked my nose and summoned her servant, Argus, who had eyes in the front of his head, the back of his head, the sides of his head, and speckled elsewhere on his body. I tried to imagine what it must be like to see in so many directions at once—he had eyes in the palms of his hands, on his knees, on his shoulders—but I couldn't, even though I now knew what it was like to see two directions at once without being able to see in front of me.

"Argus, keep that bully Zeus from bothering this child," said Hera. She ran her hand along my spine, dropped a kiss on my brow, and left me alone with this odd all-seeing giant.

Argus was not much of a conversationalist. His vocabulary consisted of grunts. I wasn't much better. I could low. We had a few exchanges of grunts and moos and gave it up.

He did as Hera had asked and followed me everywhere. I ate grass on Olympus and hated it. I wandered in search of something that tasted better, but everything I bit was bitter, and I couldn't even complain to my many-eyed companion.

I was sick with longing for a proper conversation, or even an improper one, but the other cattle Argus and I encountered couldn't speak to me in anything other than moos and bellows. Sheep and goats made more sounds but even less sense. I would have cursed Zeus if I could have formed words.

We came down off the mountain and wandered through fields and forests for an age, until I finally drank

from a river whose water tasted sweeter to me than anything else had since I had changed. I was confused by
this, until I realized I had finally found my father's river
again.

Then I cried. Argus, who with his club had driven off
suspicious golden-haired shepherd boys, a white bull,
and even a persistent eagle, shook his hands in distress
and grunted loudly. Eventually, my father came to see
what was making such a horrible sound on his shore.

When my father stood before me, my frustration with
my form and my diet erupted into fresh tears. Father
stroked me, offered a handful of grass, and asked Argus
what was going on. Of course, Argus had no words. Finally, I realized I could write what I couldn't say, and
I scratched my story into the damp dirt at the river's
edge.

My father was reduced to grunts and mutters, too, as
he read my account. The occasional phrase snuck out
of him, tortures he'd like to try on unnamed beings of
celestial might, a vow to sacrifice a white heifer to Hera
in thanks for her help, an exclamation of dismay as he
realized what he had just said and apologized to me and
to Argus and to the sky and the earth and any other
nearby deity he might have offended. Argus had heard
enough. He twined a rope around my neck and led me
away from my dangerous father.

I was so tired of my existence I wished Zeus would
come so I could kick him in the ass and maybe receive
a sizzling thunderbolt in response. Then another fair-
haired boy arrived, bearing a strange flute he claimed
he had made from reeds taken from the final form of
another girl pursued by a god she wasn't interested in—
she turned into a plant to get away from him, like that
ever worked! It only meant she could no longer run, and
he could do whatever he liked with her. I wondered if
this was another disguise for Zeus.

Whatever he was, he was wily. I had no idea anyone so
full of vocabulary could produce such a string of boring

sentences. I thought I had been longing to hear anyone say anything. I was wrong! Trying to follow this man's perambulating sentences put me to sleep.

Unfortunately, they put my guardian to sleep as well. When I woke up because something thudded past and spattered me, I discovered the stranger had struck off Argus's head.

So he hadn't been a witty conversationalist, or even good-looking (though he looked well), Argus had still been a faithful and helpful companion who had kept me safe. Hermes, another god in disguise, was the one who had killed him; he seemed to expect gratitude for his deed, but I was too heartsick at the loss of my friend. It was a gift that I couldn't speak then, for surely I would have gotten myself into worse trouble if I had spoken my mind to him.

Instead, I ran away.

I was helped in my escape by a gadfly. I didn't know which god or goddess sent it; its bite stung me, and it would not let me be, so I suspected it was Zeus again, taken with me in my new form, The gadfly chased me wherever I went; it would not give me peace. I took to plunging into rivers, rolling in mud so I had armor against its sting, and then, sometimes, I could sleep.

Between the stings of the gadfly, I discovered that I liked running. I wore myself out with it, so I didn't notice how horrible grass tasted everywhere I went and how even nectar-rich flowers didn't satisfy my hunger.

I traveled through lands like none I had ever seen before and tasted water from different rivers, sensing the gods and naiads in them, sometimes being greeted by these cousins, uncles, aunts, though they did not know me.

Pursued by the gadfly, I encountered people who spoke languages I didn't recognize and who wore garments strange to me. I traveled through mountains where rain fell as hard crystals whiter than my coat. I met a tribe of warrior women who led me to the edge of a sea and showed me a ship-killing rock in it. I crossed a river that tasted of copper and swam in a sea no one had named until I immersed myself in it.

I came to a land where people had dark skin and the sun shone so hot very little grew, and finally I came to a wide flat river I could wade in, with lush black mud that gave me a lovely coat. I followed the river's flow down to where it turned into many little rivers embracing tiny islands, the streams braiding around and through each other, and there I stopped, for I felt something strange. My world had changed, and at first I did not know how.

I had lost the gadfly somewhere along the river. The air tasted hot, sandy, and spicy, but there was a flavor missing, though I wasn't sure when it had faded. Gone were the scents of olives and grapes. The river's water, when I dipped my nose into it, carried an earthen flavor with none of the mud of home, I could not taste anything of my father's river, my mother's spring, or even sense any relatives of theirs in this wide, wide water. The very plants looked different and strange: feather-topped trees and reeds.

I stood with my hooves in the water and felt the prickle of change shiver along my skin. All the cow-hair fell off of me, and my limbs shortened; my hooves split into toes and fingers, the hardness retreating to nails; my snout shortened, and my ears pulled back against my head, as hair spilled from the top of it.

Under the hot summer sun, I stood up, human once more, and realized that the gods I knew had limits, and I had passed beyond them. All-father Zeus could not touch me here. All-mother Hera could no longer protect or attack me.

I put my hand on my belly and realized I still carried something of the old country within me, a final gift of Zeus. Like so many of his other women, I had his child inside me. It had not quickened while I wore the shape of the cow, but I felt a flutter of movement now.

Damn him. Well, my child would be born here, where Zeus could no longer find me, and I would raise the child here, where gods didn't drop out of the sky or wander over a hillside, converse with you, seduce you, and screw up your future.

Then again, I didn't know anything about the gods of this country. Maybe they were as capricious as those of mine.

I stood in the flowing water with the sun shining on the crown of my head and hugged myself and the seed child inside, staring toward a sea I could smell but not see in the reed-wrack of the shimmering little islands around me.

I turned to look upriver. I saw a group of copper-skinned, black-haired people staring at me. One had a javelin in his hand, poised point toward me, but at my glance, he dropped it into the river, which carried it away. I wondered if the god of this river was my friend.

The people dropped to their knees before me and lowered their foreheads to touch the water. Only then did I realize they must have seen me change from heifer to human. Perhaps that would startle anyone, especially those not acquainted with the behavior of my gods.

I felt a tide of something strange in my chest, the taste of delicious nourishment on my tongue, the best flavor in my mouth since my last visit to the city. Honey? No, better. This must be ambrosia, the food of the gods.

I was the daughter of a water god and a naiad, but I had never been worshiped before. This was what fed me: the people's awe and wonder. It warmed me all through. Power glowed on the tips of my fingers, sang along my skin.

No wonder Zeus got so excited.

I realized I was a shapeshifter myself, whether I had effected the change or not.

I took a step toward my new people. The rustle of power flowed over my skin, clothing me in gold, colored beads, and the feathers of a bird I had never seen. On my head, the weight of a domed crown settled. I smiled at my worshipers. I did not understand their muttered chants and prayers, but I felt the delicious power flowing into me. Oh, yes. I could get used to this.

I would be a good god, I decided. They would be glad they had chosen me. I would help them, not hurt them.

You know, you can tell yourself things like that before you know what you're getting into, and even believe it. This power is heady stuff, though. I'm not sure I'm going to wield it well.

I can only hope.

RECLAIMING HIS INNER APE

Terry Hayman

Terry's a former Toronto lawyer, actor, and writer of corporate videos, who now lives much more happily in North Vancouver, BC, with his wife, kids, lazy cat, and hyper dog. His stories have appeared in a wide range of magazines such as *Woman's World*, *Dreams of Decadence*, *Aeon*, *Grain*, and *Boys' Life* and in anthologies such as *Mota 3: Courage*, or DAW's own *Mystery Date* and *Hags, Sirens & Other Bad Girls of Fantasy*.

"Hey, sailor," Mary said over the rumble of morning traffic outside their second floor Brooklyn walk-up. "What's a girl gotta do to get laid around here?"

Given they both had to leave for work in the next ten minutes or so, she was only half serious. But she still undid the top four buttons of the dress she was going to wear to the rehearsal, slid it off her left shoulder, and leaned back against the bedroom door, watching him tie his tie in the mirror over their battered old dresser.

And you know what? If he did decide for the first time in . . . too long . . . to throw prudence to the wind and take her up on the offer, well, maybe she would just go along with it. Maybe they'd even rediscover some of the thrill they'd had on the good ship *Avast* and the absolutely insane terror and heart-pounding excitement that had followed that, which had brought her and Sam together.

Escaping from Ape.

The Big Ape.

If Sam could just be as he had been then, Mary would let him throw her down on the bed here, paw her as Ape had pawed her, sniff and smell her, *touch* her, make her blood pound. And then Sam would . . .

The subway went rumbling past their second-floor apartment en route to the bridge, and the shuddering of the floor and walls covered up her shivers of want.

Sam finished straightening his tie for his job at the museum and barely glanced at her. "We're going to be late," he muttered. It was barely audible over the continuing traffic noise.

"Let's be late, Sam," she said. "I can be late."

"Sure you can. 'Cause you're a damn writer, and they always are, right?"

Whoah. Mary blinked at the verbal slap. She slid her dress back up her shoulder. "You . . . want to . . . um . . . clarify that?"

He snorted. "Just saying. Bridge traffic's gonna be bad. And the job I got might be nothing special, but I got to be on time. Not like they couldn't get someone else to replace me quick as a blink."

With a third of New Yorkers out of work, that was probably true, but . . . George would never fire him, would he? He owed Sam too much.

Sam gave his tie a last vicious downward tug to straighten it and ran his fingers over his Brylcreemed hair.

Mary's heart squeezed. Sam was so goddamned handsome and sometimes still knew it, all vee-shaped torso and nice round behind. And she didn't really care that all his taut edges had softened a bit over the last two years. She didn't even mind the bit of a gut he was developing. It was just his general attitude, the self-conscious frown, the slumping shoulders, the bitterness like this morning, that worried Mary. They weren't Sam. None of that was Sam.

She knew it was because he was no longer out on the ocean, in the fresh air and doing the work he loved, but he'd said he was fine with leaving that. He'd assured her. Promised her.

"You want to meet for lunch or something?" she chirped. "Raoul's giving me most of the afternoon off. He's focusing on the scenes with the mayor and his advisers. Slapstick stuff."

Sam had turned from the mirror to grab his suit jacket—worn old brown thing with high, skinny lapels, but he wouldn't let her buy him a more fashionable new one—and paused just long enough as he shrugged it on to mutter something under his breath.

"What was that?" she said.

He raised his face and finally looked at her. "I thought George Waring was going to turn all your stories into movies."

"When the museum makes enough money or he gets some more financial backers, I'm sure he will."

"Yeah, sure. *I'd* be rushing in to throw some money at him. He's so reliable. Shows such good judgement."

Mary's face flushed. "He's your boss now! And he saved your life, Sam. Don't forget it. And mine. And—"

"Oh, shut up, Mary! He just about got us all killed a hundred times over with his craziness! And how many people *did* die, hunh? When his goddamned giant monkey got loose and crushed that Wimpy's? When he smashed cars and ripped up Central Park? Stepped on people. *Ate* them! Even when he finally took that header from the bridge. You know he took out two cops on that boat when he landed? You think *their* families were all jumping happy about this great 'Marvelous Horror from the Ends of the Earth' that we helped George Waring drag back from . . . Jesus . . . from the ends of the earth? You only get Waring's version in the Big Ape Memorial museum, and the papers never told half the truth!"

He shook his head and grabbed the car keys off the dresser top.

"Well, it was exciting," Mary said weakly.

"Exciting! *Exciting!* The man's a raving idiot. Captain Cathcart should have thrown him overboard the second we found out where he wanted us to go."

"And then steamed back to port?"

"Exactly!"

"So we never would have met Ape. Never would have had any of those adventures?"

"Yes!"

"And you'd still be out navigating the ocean."

"*Yes!*"

"Without me holding you back."

He opened his mouth then shut it and pursed his lips until they turned white.

"You know the only one holding you back from doing great things, being great, is you, Sam. It doesn't have to be out on the ocean. It could be right here. The two of us. Come in here."

She backed out of the bedroom to the one other room in their place, not counting the bathroom, and he slouched after her. Though they'd lived here for almost nine months now, ever since their wedding, the room sat mostly empty. It held a kitchen table near the middle of the room, across from the kitchenette. And it gripped a couch with a second-hand lamp near the window.

Not much, but it was more than so many people had these days. Even just having their own place, their both having jobs . . . Particularly when they'd both started with next to nothing. Goodness, Mary had literally been raving at a theatrical producer's door when Waring rescued her, offered her a job chronicling his venture on the good ship *Avast*. But that had been fate, because that's where she'd met Sam Halloran.

"Now, Sam, I want you to close your eyes and picture what this room should be like. What would it take to make it special for you? To make this home special for you?"

He said nothing, staring at her, his face unreadable.

"Sam?"

He finally just brushed past her to reach the front door and yank it open for her. "Are you ready to go?"

Crossing the bridge, it was as though he took up all the oxygen in the car. Mary looked out over midtown to pick out the Chrysler building and all the other skyscrapers, then her eyes drifted further southwest to the towers of the Brooklyn Bridge. Right there. She couldn't breathe. She couldn't speak. Her heart was pumping hard and high in her chest as though she might be having a panic attack.

Was that because she remembered what it had been like when Ape took her up there, swung her about like a toy until she had whiplash on her whiplash? Or was it because she *missed* it?

Yes! Because somehow she'd known that Ape didn't want to hurt her then. And that Sam was coming for her. Sam would always come. He'd always find her. Always be there. Always love her. Never leave her.

"Let me . . . let me out at Times Square," she choked as he steered them toward Broadway. "I need some more of that special hair coloring."

Sam just grunted. A minute later she was out of the Packard, and he was off to Park and 73rd.

And that was that. That was her life right now. She'd deal with it. Survive. Cope. She'd always been able to do that before.

Somehow.

With a deep breath, she tried to throw off the morning's gloom. She had a *rehearsal* to get to. A rehearsal of her first professionally produced play!

"Taxi!" she called and reflexively showed a little leg.

The cabbie who pulled over had trumpeter Louis Armstrong's "Body and Soul" playing out the cab's open windows. When the cabbie saw Mary, he gave her the kind of silly grin that told her she still had it.

Just not with Sam.

"Hey, lady," he snorted from the front seat as they pulled away from the curb, "I heard this good one at the garage. You know how everybody's eating these hamburger things now, right? Wimpy's ten-cent burgers? Buy 'em anywhere? You know why? Think about it. *What did they do with Big Ape's body?* Hunh? Hunh? You know, because—"

Mary gave a hollow laugh. "Please just drive."

The theater rehearsing Mary's play was called the Grand Rio, one of the few remaining big ones on the Great White Way since the great Shubert brothers had declared bankruptcy. It held four private balconies near the front and an enormous red-velvet curtain with a colossal braided-rope hem. Gold and red damask layered the walls as if all the wealth that had fallen out of the stock market had splash-landed here.

The play was *The Mayor Is Blue.*

Emilio Hernandez, producer and brother to Raoul Hernandez, the director of Mary's play, believed, and had convinced a lot of financial backers, that Mary's play was one for the ages. Or at least one that people would think referred to Mayor Fiorello La Guardia and therefore keep running for a few months or so.

Actually, thought Mary as she sat in the overstuffed audience seats and munched the egg-salad sandwich Sam had packed for her, the play wasn't that bad. Waring had suggested she write it because Mary's notoriety post-Big Ape made people gossip that she'd had an affair with La Guardia, and scandal had a way of boosting ticket sales.

But the play stood on its own merits.

It made Mary want to rush out and spend her big

paychecks to live large with Sam. Because the play really could become a hit and run on and on. And lead to more shows. And maybe even, as Waring suggested, to Hollywood and writing movies.

But she also agreed with Sam that it might not last. And she'd actually been warmed by the responsible way he'd invested it in government backed bonds that couldn't fall like common stocks. Those savings would let them move to a house someday, Sam said, out of the city. Which he thought meant the water. And Mary thought . . . well, okay. He'd given up sailing; she could give up the city.

Maybe.

And keep house.

And even have babies. If only Sam would help her make them.

"I've seen happier faces on a starving cat," said George Waring, suddenly at her elbow.

Mary shrieked.

Raoul et al., rehearsing the slapstick that goosed up the second act, stopped dead and looked into the seats at her.

"It's okay!" Mary called to them, waving. Then added quietly to George Waring, "I think?"

"You tell me, baby. What's eating you? What's got you down? What's grabbed hold of that irrepressible spark you once had and snuffed it down to nothing but a barely glimmering spot of pained loveliness? No, wait. Let me guess. It's Mr. Muscles. It's Mr. I-can-take-on-all-fantastic-menaces-of-a-lost-world-and-rescue-the-fair-damsel Halloran."

"Sam."

"That's what I said."

"I think he's desperately unhappy."

"Yes. And why wouldn't he be?" said George Waring.

"What?"

"Sure! He rescues the prettiest, smartest screenwriter I've ever seen, marries her, gets a good job at the museum I set up to commemorate our adventure. Of course he's miserable."

"Because I'm making more money than him, and he had to give up his career as a sailor."

"As a navigator. Sure, sure. But that's not really it, baby. You know what it really is, don't you?"

"No."

"You don't need rescuing anymore."

"Oh!" Her hand flew to her mouth and she wiped off the last bits of egg salad there. "So what am I supposed to do? Make up some sort of crisis? Act all scared and helpless again?"

"You do good scared and helpless."

"Sure. When I'm getting swung all over the place by a giant hairy monster! How likely is that to happen again any time soon?"

"Well, let me tell you about this little project I've been looking into . . ."

"You're kidding, right? Tell me you're kidding, George Waring."

"I'm kidding, baby. But some of that scared and helpless and 'ooh, I need you' is something you might want to try. I'm not saying this as a member of the male species who needs this. But neither am I the one who chased Ape into his very seat of power to rescue you."

"Miss Piper?" called Raoul from the stage, flicking his nose in the air as if he could smell Waring from there. "I think you and your . . . ape-promoter-slash-movie-director might take this outside? I've told you I don't need you this afternoon."

"Miss Piper?" said Waring, not moving but lowering his voice. "You're using your maiden name?"

Mary bit her lip and whispered too. "Sam said I should. He said that's what the public knows me by. He said I could change it once I'm well-established. But I'm wondering if maybe it's because . . . Because . . ."

"Sam is an idiot with more brawn than brains."

"Who works for you! And I love him!"

"Do you, baby? Do you really?"

"I do! He's sweet and gentle and kind. He's much deeper than he looks. He thinks about things a lot. And he cares for me! He risked his life for me!"

"No. Now that's where you're wrong, baby. Take it from me. He risked his life for the adventure. You were just the excuse. He barely knew you. I bet he still probably doesn't know you."

Mary opened her mouth. Closed it.

"No answer to that, hunh. Well, don't take it so hard. Half the men in this country don't know their wives. They just want them to cook for them, clean the house, raise the kids, give them a little physical companionship when the mood strikes . . ."

"I wish."

"Hm. I don't think I'll explore that one right now."

"Which shows you're smarter than you look."

"Why, thank you. But listen, baby, the reason I'm here is actually about Sam. He's not coming to pick you up after work today."

A shard of pure ice shot down Mary's spine. "Wh-why not?"

"See, baby? The scared and helpless terror thing. You do it so well."

"George!"

He smiled like a favorite uncle, quickly checked his pocket watch, then patted her hand where she'd gripped the polished wooden frames of the theater chairs in front of her. "I'm sure it's okay. He knew you had the afternoon off, and he said there was something he needed to do after work, someone he needed to see. And I, as a museum-owning impresario, have no fixed schedule, so here I am, escorting you around. Just like old times."

The shard of ice just got bigger, spreading into Mary's stomach.

Just like old times? What? Like when she was alone and starving? And Sam was single and out on the open seas? What was it he needed to do?

"So, are you ready to go?" Waring asked.

"Why is everyone always pushing me around!" Mary cried. But she stood and grabbed her bag from down between the seats.

And if Sam tried to leave her tonight, she decided, she would scream louder than she'd ever screamed in Big Ape's arms. She'd scream and scream and scream and . . .

"Mary?"

Mary stiffened. Sam had barely cracked open the door to their apartment where she waited, and he wasn't coming in.

On the other hand, he'd growled low, firm, and commanding like the first time he'd told her that women shouldn't be hanging around guys like George Waring. And that sent a shiver through Mary almost as serious as the ice-caused ones she'd been feeling all afternoon.

Her fingernails were nibbled raw. Her hair was a mess. She wanted to jump up and grab onto him, drag him into the room, tell him she'd do anything—quit writing plays, move out to the country, become a deck hand on any ship he found work on—if only he'd stay with her.

But she didn't go to him. Instead, using all the control she'd struggled so hard to learn as an independent woman, she drew her knees up on their couch where she'd been waiting. The skirt rode up over her knees and she let it. Make him remember. Just a glimpse. A hint.

She'd also dabbed on the last of his favorite perfume, a lilies-of-the-valley scent she'd worn for the first time aboard the *Avast*. (It had, ironically, been a gift from Captain Cathcart. She'd never told Sam that and never would.)

"Come in!" she called.

He did. But his entrance was odd, bum first, hunched over. He lugged something heavy under his arm and was dragging something man-sized behind him. Mary gasped as she saw the larger item.

"It's . . . it's Ape," she gasped.

Once inside, Sam kicked the door closed with a grunt and carefully let the box he carried slide to the floor with a clank. Then he rocked the stuffed imitation ape upright on the flat pedestal that was attached to its bottom. It actually reared larger than man-size now. Nothing like the monstrous impossibility that Ape had been, but still impressive.

As Sam hunched beside it, breathing heavily, Mary cocked her head. The two of them standing side by side, Sam and Ape, looked almost like . . . brothers?

"What's in the box?" she asked, biting her upper lip and pointing to the heavy object Sam had slid to the floor by his feet.

"New deal," he panted, always the one for long speeches. "I'll show you."

He bent and hefted it up and onto the kitchen table. With a few fumbling flicks of cleverly concealed latches around the box's bottom, the entire upper shell lifted up and off to reveal a complete surprise.

"A typewriter?" Mary frowned. It was a very thick-looking, heavy typewriter. Her old aunt had owned a typewriter, but it had been all spindly, with sticking keys. Which is why Mary had refused to ever use one. They had secretaries for that.

But this machine was different.

Sam gave a toothy smile, and even not knowing why, Mary's heart skipped a few beats. It had been so long since she'd seen him smile. She raised her eyebrows and wanted to leap off the couch at him, but Sam shook his head. He clearly wanted to play this for all it was worth.

"You remember this morning," he said, "when I said nobody out there had got the full story about Ape, about Waring and us and all the people who died. The whole damned thing for true? And then you showed me this room and said I could make something of it, and maybe make something of myself?"

"Oh, Sam! I didn't mean that you weren't already something! I only—"

He held up a hand to stop her with some of his old braggadocio, something she couldn't believed she'd actually missed.

"You were right, Mary. I've let this promise to give up the sea drag me down as if I were a little boy. There *are* many things I can do. The sort of things I did as a navigator are going to be needed everywhere as we rebuild this city, this country. And I'm not rightly sure which industry or company I'll end up in, but I can tell you that I'll be rising fast in it whichever it is. Either here, if you become big on Broadway, or out in California if Waring ever gets his act together enough to get you out there."

"Or both!" said Mary, swept up in his enthusiasm. Overcome by the emotion rising up in her. It was heat, melting the ice that had been freezing her insides, flushing her cheeks, going to her head.

"Sure. Both maybe," Sam said and laughed. "But first we're going to use this here typewriter, this *electric* typewriter they've just made that they say makes you go twice as fast, to co-write a book of everything that really happened with us, with the *Avast*, with Ape, with all the people he killed and their families. It's like, working at Waring's museum all these months, I got this thing stuck in my craw that's just got to come out."

Sam raised up his hands in his excitement, baring his teeth. And at that very moment the 7:10 subway roared by, shaking the entire room, and Mary swore she could see Ape standing right there inside Sam, roaring at the lip of his cave, telling the whole world he was back, he was home.

Mary felt that flush in her face shoot everywhere inside her at once and drive her up to her feet. She walked toward him, her eyes locked on his.

"Oh, Sam," she said.

"I know. I'm sorry I been gone so long and . . . Aw,

hell." He looked around. "I forgot to pick up any paper to use in the typewriter."

"Do you even know how to type, Sam? I don't. I write everything longhand."

He rolled his head back and forth in that cocksure way of his. Just as Ape had done when he had her, when he *knew* he had her. "We'll learn what we need to."

She lowered her eyes and looked up at him through her lashes. "I need rescuing, Sam Halloran."

He grinned in that way he had. Then he rescued her.

Over and over.

All night long.

FOR A FEW LATTES MORE

Annie Reed

Annie Reed is an award-winning fiction writer
who lives in Northern Nevada with her husband
and daughter, a varying number of high mainte-
nance cats, and a few kamikaze quail just to make
life interesting. Her short fiction has appeared in
Ellery Queen and numerous DAW anthologies,
including *Cosmic Cocktails* and *Hags, Sirens, and
Other Bad Girls of Fantasy*.

The cowboy parked his horse in the handicap spot in
front of Starbucks.

Terri almost dropped the Halloween coffee mug
she'd just tagged with a second red clearance sticker.
Ten minutes to closing. Of course. The strangest people
always came in right before closing.

"You see that?" she asked Leon, who was sweeping
the floor on the other side of the clearance display.

Leon craned his neck around a shelf full of travel
mugs decorated with glow in the dark ghosts and gob-
lins to look out the plate glass storefront. "Huh," he said.
"That's a new one."

Terri watched as the cowboy in the battered hat and

leather duster got off his horse and wrapped the reins around the freebie community newspaper stand in front of the handicap spot. The cowboy was tall and thin and wore his hat low over his face. Thanks to the overhead lights in the strip mall parking lot, he was little more than a silhouette and totally out of place riding his horse in the middle of town.

"He's really going to leave his horse right there," Terri said.

"I'm not cleaning up after it," Leon said. "No way. Cleaning the bathrooms is bad enough."

He had a point. Picking up horse poo wasn't in either of their job descriptions.

Terri and Leon saw a lot in the way of weird walk through the doors of this particular Starbucks. Three blocks from the casinos, liquor stores, tattoo parlors, and pawn shops of downtown Reno and a block away from the biggest dorm on the University of Nevada campus, it wasn't all that unusual to see frat pledges in penguin suits chilling in line next to black leather-wearing bikers. Terri got propositioned by the frat boys on a weekly basis. The bikers went straight to offering Terri a free peek at tattoos on body parts she didn't want to think about, much less see. And that was on a slow night. Throw in a holiday, like Halloween or New Years Eve or the anniversary of Elvis's death, and anything at all might walk through the door.

Like a cowboy straight out of one of the spaghetti westerns her dad used to watch when she was a kid.

"Just wait," Leon said. "He'll want a latte."

Terri shook her head. "Coffee, black."

"Quarter?" Leon asked. A quarter was their standard bet. They went as high as fifty cents when they were feeling lucky and flush.

"A dollar," Terri said.

Leon grinned. "You're on." He put the broom away and wiped off the nozzle on the steamer. Terri logged back on to the register as the cowboy opened the door.

His boot heels clicked on the tile floor and his spurs made jangling noises in time to his strides. He had something that looked like a small cigar shoved in one corner of his mouth. The tip glowed beneath the ash as he sucked in a breath. If the lit cigar wasn't bad enough— the front door clearly had a no smoking sign in not only English but also the universal You Can't Do That symbol of a circle with a slash—more than just a whiff of the barnyard surrounded him like a toxic cloud.

When she was little, Terri used to crush over the cowboys her dad watched on television. They all seemed so ruggedly handsome. Independent. Heroic. Whenever there was a damsel in distress—or an entire town in need of someone who could kick some serious ass—the lone cowboy would ride in and save the day. Back then, Terri never thought about what these guys must actually smell like. She was pretty sure she could have lived without knowing.

"I'm sorry, but you can't smoke in here," Terri told the cowboy when he stopped in front of her register.

Piercing blue eyes peered at her from beneath a pretty dirty hat. "Coffee," he said around the cigar still clenched between his teeth. "Black."

Jeez. Dense much?

"Seriously," Terri said. "You can't smoke in here. We'll get fined."

Well, probably not, but she wasn't going to tell him that. Just because he looked like the crushes of her childhood, with his blue eyes and strong jaw and just enough stubble to be manly, not sloppy, didn't mean he could get away with smoking in her store. Even bikers didn't smoke in her store, and most of them looked like they could bench press a Harley.

Two freshman-age girls who'd camped out for the last half hour on the easy chairs near the front windows, gossiping over their skinny mochas, took one look at the cowboy and giggled. He ignored them.

"Coffee. Black," he said again.

"Smoking. Not allowed," Terri said. "Please?"

He took the cigar out of his mouth and put it in the pocket of his duster.

Okay. That wouldn't have been her first choice, but at least he wasn't smoking anymore. Technically. She wasn't too sure about his duster.

"What size?" she asked.

He stared at her.

"Your coffee. Tall, grande, or venti?"

He still stared at her.

She pointed at the display of empty cups they used to show drink sizes. "Small, medium, or large."

"Medium," he said.

"Any particular blend? Tonight we have our house blend, Columbia Supremo, and Tanzania. Unless you want decaf."

He stared at her again. He was really taking this strong, silent thing a bit too far.

"How about we just go with the house blend," she said.

He didn't say no, so Terri called it good enough. Starbucks was all about pleasing the customer, but she didn't think the training materials anticipated customers like this.

The cowboy paid for his coffee with dollar bills that definitely looked as though they'd seen better days. Terri tried not to think about where that money might have been.

Leon had the coffee poured and the lid on the grande house blend before Terri finished making change. Leon wasn't just fast at making coffee. He also broke the land speed record for cleaning up. He had a theater major girlfriend waiting for him at home who made extra money as a cocktail waitress. A very shapely cocktail waitress, by all accounts. Leon was motivated.

The cowboy stuffed his change in another pocket of his duster. He headed back out the door but stopped just inside. At first, Terri thought he might say something to the girls who'd giggled at him. Instead, he stared at a blue 8x10 flyer in the front window for a long minute before he went out the door.

Most flyers posted in Terri's Starbucks advertised concerts at the events center on the north side of campus or poetry readings in the fine arts building. This particular blue flyer featured a picture of a smiling eighteen year old girl who'd disappeared after a party a few months ago. Initially, the blue flyers had been posted everywhere on campus. Now only a few remained, which made a sad situation feel even sadder. It was like everyone had forgotten all about the missing girl.

Everyone except a weird guy who rode his horse to Starbucks for a late night coffee fix.

Terri watched through the front window as the cowboy fetched the cigar out of his pocket and stuck it back between his teeth. He hauled himself up on his horse and headed out of the parking lot.

Whoever he was, he was the real deal. A weirdo with a great costume and a rented—or stolen—horse couldn't have pulled that off without dumping his coffee in the parking lot. The cowboy looked like he hadn't spilled a drop.

Leon pressed a dollar bill in her hand. "Should have gone with the obvious."

Good advice. Maybe the cowboy was just that—a cowboy who preferred his horse to a car.

In a pig's eye.

The cowboy came back every night for a week, always ten minutes before closing, and always on horseback. He wasn't Terri's most talkative customer, but he was rapidly becoming her steadiest. Every night he bought a grande coffee, black, and he always paid for it with rumpled dollar bills. Not that he called it a grande coffee. After the second night when they went through the same routine when it came time to figure out how much coffee he wanted, Terri figured grande was his size and house blend his drink of choice. It fit.

At least he didn't smoke in the store anymore. As the week went on, Terri almost missed the cigar when the guy started to smell a little ripe. The cigar smelled a heck of a lot better than the cowboy did.

"Where are you staying?" she asked him on the seventh night, hoping it would lead to a conversation about nice warm showers and motel-provided soap.

"Manzanita."

"Hall?" she asked.

Manzanita Hall was the second largest dorm on campus. A few dorm residents were students in the undergraduate class Terri taught as a graduate teaching assistant. If this was just some prank to see how long she'd put up with a smelly cowboy customer, her students were going to be in for a whole different kind of lesson.

"Park," the cowboy said.

Manzanita Park was the greenbelt at the front of the campus. Thick with ponderosa pines and cedars and oaks and, strangely enough, not a single manzanita bush, the park wrapped around a small lake that was home to a pair of cranky swans. The park had some pretty dense undergrowth here and there, but enough to hide a man and his horse?

Terri glanced at the bedroll on the back of his saddle. "You sleep in the park."

She was pretty sure the campus had rules against that.

"Don't sleep much," he said. "Park's as good as anywhere else."

Except for the whole no shower thing.

"I hear the pond's good for swimming," she said. "That's what some of the frat boys tell me."

"Don't swim much," he said. "Not in winter."

Right. Because chilly water is too cold for a guy who sleeps outside in the winter.

She handed him his coffee, and he nodded at her from beneath his hat. It occurred to her that this had been the longest conversation they'd had.

"Nice talking to you," she said and gave him a smile.

He nodded again and touched the brim of his hat this time. His blue-eyed stare looked a little less severe.

"You like him," Leon said after the cowboy got on his horse and rode away, coffee in one hand, reins in the other.

"Do not," Terri said automatically.

"So if I smelled like that, you'd spend as much time talking to me?"

"I don't talk to you now."

"Liar," Leon said with a smile.

Just because she tried to be polite didn't mean she liked the guy. He was just strange enough to be intriguing. Like talking to a character out of a movie. Really. That was all.

The last two customers of the night were two harried-looking girls with book-laden backpacks almost bigger than they were. Finals started in a couple of weeks. The undergrads in Terri's class were panicking already. Freshmen always panicked. Terri refused to freak about her own finals. She still had a week and a half to study. It just took a little discipline. And focus. And not spending too much time thinking about a mysterious cowboy who slept in the park.

"Have you heard?" one of the girls asked her. She was a semiregular and someone Terri knew from around campus.

"Heard what?" Terri said as she rang up their order.

"Some guy tried to grab this girl after she got off the shuttle. Cops have the stadium parking lot all cordoned off. They've been there for hours."

"She got away," the other girl said. "So did the guy."

"Yeah, they announced it in class. We're all supposed to walk in pairs now. Or call the escort service to go to our cars."

"Like that's going to help. They don't have enough escorts, and how do we know it's not one of them doing this?"

"In the movies it's always the guy you don't suspect," the first girl said. "I bet it's one of the escorts." Her eyes grew wide. "Or maybe it's the shuttle driver. No one would suspect him."

"Too many witnesses," Terri said. "Unless you're the last person on the shuttle getting off at the last stop for the night."

Terri had said it as a joke. Sometimes she had a pretty odd sense of humor that seemed to work well with nervous freshman. Not tonight though. These two looked like they wanted to take notes.

Parking was a nightmare on campus. The university provided a shuttle service to the far-flung parking lots at the north end of campus, nearly a half mile away from any actual classroom building. The shuttles were nothing more than half-size city buses and packed to overflowing during the day. Not great, but something. Except the shuttles stopped running at eight every night. Evening classes got out at eight-thirty. Seven o'clock classes didn't get out until ten, and by that time the classroom buildings were mostly deserted.

When the girl on the blue flyer first disappeared, Terri started carrying pepper spray in her bag. She still carried it, but mostly because she didn't clean out her bag too often.

"Look," she said, handling the two girls back their change. "Just be smart about it. Don't go walking around campus by yourself at night. You'll be fine."

She hoped they took notes on that.

An hour later, Terri thought maybe she should have been the one taking notes.

"Just be smart," she said in an angry parody of her own voice with more than a hint of her mother's thrown in for good measure. "You'll be fine."

Right.

Driving through a construction zone on the way to work when you haven't checked the air in your spare tire in forever isn't smart.

She must have picked up a nail. Or ten. When she got back to her car after she and Leon locked up the store for the night, the right rear tire on her old Toyota was flat as a board and Leon was long gone, headed home to his girlfriend and whatever they did that Terri didn't want to think about.

Terri had parked her car three blocks away in a service station lot. The service station closed at six. The guy who owned the place let her park there in exchange for tutoring his sixteen-year-old son so the kid could keep his grades high enough to play on his high school football team.

Okay. So she had a flat. No problem. She was a capable woman. If a guy could change a tire, so could she.

Unless the spare was also flat.

Terri stared at the dark and locked service station. Of course she'd have a flat at one of the few service stations in a 24/7 town that actually closed before midnight.

She could have called a tow service. Or a taxi. Or even Leon, since she had his number and he swore he never turned his cell off, even while his girlfriend was entertaining him. She could have done any one of those things—if she'd actually plugged her cell phone in the charger last night instead of burying herself in schoolwork until two in the morning before pouring herself into bed.

She looked around the outside of the station for a pay phone. The place was pretty dark, only a streetlight on the corner and the occasional headlights from a car driving by. She had to concentrate on her feet to keep from tripping on the uneven asphalt. Wouldn't that just be the perfect end to a perfect evening.

She found an empty half-booth, one of those things with two sides and a shelf for a phone book but no privacy for Superman to change clothes. The cord that used to hold a phone book ended in a ragged stump. A faded outline of a phone marred the formerly white wall, and the empty screw holes from where the phone had been stared at her like dead eyes. All very atmospheric in a creepy kind of way, but the one thing she really needed—a phone—was missing.

"Great," she said. "Just great."

Her voice scared her a little. It sounded small and frightened. She dug into her bag until her fingers wrapped around the canister of pepper spray. She was a modern, capable woman, fully able to handle life's little emergencies without falling apart.

She could go to her office on campus and call someone to tow her car. Except this was Thursday night and no one in her department taught class on Thursday nights. Terri had a sneaking suspicion they scheduled it that way deliberately because no one taught classes on Friday nights either. After working the night shift at Starbucks for over a year, four nights off in a row was Terri's idea of heaven. The building would be locked up tight. While she had a key to her office, as a lowly teaching assistant slash grad student, she didn't have a key to the building. Scratch that idea.

She couldn't go back to Starbucks. The place was locked up tight, the security alarm set. The store manager was strict about not opening the store back up at night unless it was a matter of life and death. Terri didn't think a flat tire qualified. The other businesses in the strip mall were closed for the night too.

She tried to remember if she'd seen a phone booth anywhere on campus besides the student union. Which was across campus on the far side of the stadium.

Where police might still be investigating a crime scene.

And where, if she remembered right, there was a semienclosed and well-lit bus stop. She'd never taken the bus before, but even if she rode this one to city center, she'd be able to figure out how to get home from there.

Terri mapped the route in her head. She could walk around the outside of campus, stay on the sidewalks next to traffic. That would add about twenty minutes to her walk and a lot of hill climbing. This was November in Reno. Ice liked to masquerade as clear pavement. The last thing she needed was to fall and break an ankle, or even sprain her ankle, when she didn't have a working cell phone to call for help.

The faster route was through the center of campus. Less hills, more stairs that the university actually treated with deicer. More lights along the walkways. More chance of running into other people who weren't going to attack her. The police would have scared the guy away for the night, right? No criminal in his right mind would try to attack two women on the same campus in the same night. Besides, she had her trusty pepper spray.

Five minutes later it occurred to her that she'd never actually used her pepper spray. Did pepper spray have an expiration date?

The English building was on her right, the Engineering building dead ahead, and the School of Mines, the oldest building on campus, off to the left across an expanse of lawn. Each building was surrounded by thick shrubs and tall trees, way too many places for a determined person to hide.

Maybe this hadn't been such a good idea. She was cold and tired and annoyed with herself, and she hadn't seen another person during her entire walk. She'd feel better if she actually had her pepper spray in her hand.

Except she couldn't find it.

This was ridiculous. She'd just had the thing not that long ago, but now she couldn't put her fingers on the little can. It was like her bag had eaten it.

Terri held her bag open and peered inside. The light along the walkways wasn't the best, but she thought she saw—

The blow caught her totally off guard. One minute she was looking inside her bag, and the next instant half a galaxy of stars seemed to explode on the inside of her eyelids. The world canted to the side, and she was falling. Falling.

Terri barely got her hands out in front of herself in time to keep from planting her face on the concrete sidewalk. She still hit the ground hard, jarring her entire body and stealing her breath. Her bag skidded away from her, contents scattering into the bushes where her attacker must have been hiding. The can of pepper spray rolled across the concrete, out of reach.

She scrambled after it. She got to her knees before the guy hit her again. This blow struck her in the side of the ribs. New pain exploded through her entire body, and she collapsed on the ground. He hit her again.

Where was the cowboy when she needed him? If anyone needed rescuing at that minute, she was it, but the strong, silent cowboy was nowhere around.

She was in serious trouble. Terri knew it even as she wanted to deny it. Something like this couldn't happen to her. She'd been prepared, dammit.

Her attacker had been silent throughout the assault. She hadn't heard him come out from behind the bushes, and he hadn't made a sound, even a grunt, when he hit her. She wanted to yell at him, ask him why her, but she couldn't draw in enough breath to whimper, let alone scream.

Get to the spray. That's all she had to do. She could still see the can just inches away from her outstretched fingers. If she could reach that, everything would be all right. It had to be.

A new sound reached her, a rhythmic, muffled thumping. Her brains were so scrambled, it took her longer than it should have to realize the sound was hoofbeats across grass.

The cowboy.

Just like in the movies, the hero was coming to rescue the damsel in distress. Finally!

Except now this damsel didn't need rescuing.

Terri closed her fingers around the can of pepper spray. She rolled over and pressed the button on top of the can just as her attacker saw the cowboy, leather coat billowing out around him, barrel across the lawn in front of the School of Mines.

It wasn't the best aimed shot of pepper spray in the world. Terri's hands shook too badly to hold the can steady. Still, enough of the gas must have gotten in her attacker's face because he yelled and started clawing at his eyes even as he turned and tried to run away from the cowboy.

The chase was short. Terri got to her feet and backed away from the cloud of pepper spray about the same time the cowboy threw a lasso around her attacker and jerked him off his feet. By the time Terri had her heartbeat under control, the cowboy had the guy hogtied.

"You're safe now, miss," the cowboy said as he gave the rope wrapped around her attacker's hands a final tug. "Wouldn't be walking around in the dark like this if I were you."

Tell me something I don't know, Terri thought.

"My car had a flat, and my cell phone's dead," she said. She made herself look away from the guy who'd attacked her. She'd been well on her way to saving herself, but the cowboy did try to rescue the damsel. Might as well be polite. "Thank you," she said.

He touched the brim of his hat and nodded at her.

She heard the first siren wail on the night air. Someone must have seen what happened and called it in.

The cowboy got on his horse. "You need a ride?" he asked.

Terri thought about it for all of a half second before she said no.

He rode off before she could say another word.

That was the trouble with heroes. In movie westerns, the lone cowboy who rode in to rescue the town or the damsel was always cool and collected, handsome and enigmatic. He rescued the damsel before the bad guy barely laid a hand on her. At the end of the movie, the damsel always rode off with the cowboy into a nice sunset, and everyone looked like they just got out of a long, hot bath. That wasn't reality.

Reality was smelly and dirty.

Reality was a cowboy hero who didn't get there on time, and even if he did, he treated the poor damsel who'd been fighting for her life—and doing a pretty good job of it, if she did say so herself—like she didn't have a brain in her head. When all along he'd been the one who was so out of step with the world that he didn't even know how to order coffee or that he couldn't smoke in a restaurant, and on top of all that, he slept in a park. A park!

And he left before the dirty details, like police reports, were taken care of.

The last thing Terri was about to do was get behind the cowboy on his horse. No, thank you.

Terri realized she didn't even know the cowboy's name. Good thing the guy on the ground had seen him too. Otherwise, the police might not believe Terri when she told them about the guy who'd hogtied her attacker.

She could just make out her attacker's face in the dim light from the walkways. Even with his eyes scrunched up and watering, and his face red and blotchy, she could tell he had the kind of features some guys have who never seem to age. He could have been in his twenties or his late thirties, a customer or someone she saw around campus or a total stranger. He was unremarkable and unmemorable and the last person a woman would feel threatened by.

Forget carrying the pepper spray in her bag. A pocket would be good. A holster would be even better. Did they make holsters for pepper spray? She'd have to look that up.

She didn't want her picture to be on the next missing girl flyer around campus. From now on, she'd really be prepared. You could never tell who might stop in at Starbucks for a latte ten minutes before closing. A hero, a frat boy in a penguin outfit, or a villain hiding behind a smooth baby face. Movie heroes should stay in the movies. The only hero Terri wanted to rely on from here on out was herself.

BELOVED

David H. Hendrickson

David H. Hendrickson has published over eight hundred works of nonfiction ranging from humor and essays to scientific research and sports journalism. Recognized as one of the nation's top college hockey writers, he has been honored with the Joe Concannon and Scarlet Quill awards. His short stories have appeared in magazines, literary journals, and the anthologies *Swordplay* and *Food and Other Enemies*. He is a graduate of Odyssey, the fantasy writing workshop. Born and raised in New England, he lives north of Boston.

There's nothing like a man holding the severed head of a giant to get a woman in the mood.

It did nothing for me, but my younger sister, Michal, looked to be in heat. Her pretty little face flushed. Her bosom, more ample than mine, heaved. Her breath came in short, quick gasps.

"He's *so* handsome," she said.

Atop a platform that overlooked the palace court-yard, David lifted Goliath's head and shook it. The crowd roared. Women danced and beat upon their tambourines. Men still decked out in their battlefield attire raised their spears and shouted. Clouds of dust rose up to us on the royal balcony beside the platform.

"Look at those eyes," Michal gushed.

She was becoming insufferable. "What if the stone had missed the giant?" I asked. "Would he still be so handsome? What if he had run from the fight, so terrified he soiled his loincloth? Would his eyes still be so pretty?"

A pout formed on Michal's lips. "You're such a cynic, Merab. There's not a man in Israel that could impress you." She finally tore her eyes away from David. "If Father expects to marry you away first, I might die a virgin."

Father would have no trouble marrying me off; he was the king. But Michal would be the prize. She was the pretty one. I was plain. Serviceable. Like a healthy donkey.

"Maybe I don't want to marry," I said.

She shook her head in that way that said she'd never understand me. "Well, I do." Her cheeks burned red. "David, son of Jesse," she said. "I'm going to marry him some day."

I raised my eyebrows. "Does he know?"

"You can be so—"

She gasped and touched my arm. "He's coming this way!"

David strode to our side of the platform, his eyes fixed on Michal. Following behind him were my father, King Saul, and my brother, Jonathan. I'd heard David had been a humble shepherd, but those days were no more. He looked drunk with the glory being showered upon him.

Michal gripped my arm tighter. I thought she might fall over into a dead faint.

David bent one knee and bowed his head. "King Saul's daughters are as fair as this day is great."

A smooth talker. As if Michal weren't already smitten.

"Tell us of your feat, O Champion," she said.

David beamed. "The Lord God Jehovah slew the giant. I was but his instrument."

Clever, I thought. The obligatory deference followed by a proud retelling.

Her voice quivering, Michal asked, "Will you deny the king's daughter your story?"

"Of course not." David smiled. "The giant threatened all of Israel, commanding us to send one man who would fight him. Your father, the king, offered me his armor, helmet, and coat of mail, but I took them off. Instead, I chose five smooth stones from a brook and put one within my sling. The first one struck the giant in the head and he toppled to the ground. I fell upon him and, using his own sword, cut off his head."

David shook the giant's head again, setting off another roar from the crowd.

"This was your first time in battle?" Michal asked.

David flushed.

My sweet, pretty sister had not the sense of the flies buzzing about the giant's head.

"Yes," David said, "but while tending my father's sheep, I defended the flock by killing a lion and a bear with my own hands."

"*A lion?*" Michal gasped. "And a bear? With your own hands?"

So much, I thought, for deference to the Lord God Jehovah.

"I caught the creature by its beard, struck it, and killed it."

"Such bravery!" Michal said.

I stifled a laugh. *If* there had been a lion or bear, I was pretty sure that what had protected the flock was a rock within David's sling. There'd been no wrestling the beast to the ground, much less beating it to death with David's bare hands. It was a nice tale to charm the young women of the kingdom, but I didn't believe it.

The way his chest swelled with pride, though, I suspected he'd come to believe the tale himself. Vanity at its worst.

"Your mother, the queen, awaits our appearance inside the palace," David said. He looked at Michal. "Perhaps we shall meet again."

"Yes," she said, looking as though she might throw herself off the balcony to him.

David bowed and turned away.

For the next few days, every time I spotted Michal with that lovestruck look in her eyes, I said, "He's beating another lion to death right now. With his bare hands!" I'd gasp and add, "Such bravery!"

She'd glare or perhaps throw something at me as I burst into laughter, but eventually she began to laugh too.

"He was trying to impress me, that's all," she said. "There's no harm in a little embellishment. He can't be *perfect*."

"Of course," I said. "Just trying to impress. I'm sure he's as smitten with you as you are with him." Then I mimicked her dreamy-eyed look.

"That's not funny," she said.

"You should see yourself."

A pout came over her lips. "Will you speak to Father about David for me? He listens to you. He treats me as if I'm still a child."

I gave her the look. "I wonder why."

"I'm a woman now," she said defensively. "Just because you're the eldest doesn't make me any less a woman."

She waited. "Will you?"

I didn't respond right away. I thought the one person David was most smitten by was himself. Drunk with the chants of the crowd.

Or was I just being jealous, upset that the good-looking hero favored Michal with his attention while ignoring me?

"Don't help me," she finally said, bitterness in her voice. "Forget I asked. You're as evil as you pretend to be."

"Oh, stop," I said and agreed to help her.

I got my chance sooner than I expected.

Father summoned me to his side in one of his chambers. We sat at a table and Father dismissed his guards, telling them to wait outside. He drank deeply from a cup and sighed. Mother sat beside him, looking pleased.

He got right to the point. "Merab, it is time that you be wed," he said. "You have become a woman, and it is right that, as God provided Adam and Eve for each other, you should have a mate."

If Michal had made reference to Adam and Eve during one of her endless discussions about true love, I'd have asked how well that one had worked out. But that didn't seem to be the right thing to say now.

I wanted to beg for more time. A year. Two years. Ten years. A lifetime. I wasn't ready for a man. I doubted that I'd ever be ready.

But I said, "Yes, Father."

He nodded. "Adriel, the son of Barzillai the Meholathite, has offered a dowry fitting for a king's daughter."

Father ran through a list of all of the man's virtues, chiefly being that he was rich enough to afford my dowry, but I barely listened.

Why couldn't I be like Michal, enthused about marriage? Most girls were like her. Or at least they were more accepting of the prospect than I was.

I cringed at the thought of a foul-smelling brute climbing atop me and inserting something repulsive into my most private place, all so I could get a baby inside me. A baby that would then hurt so much coming out that, by comparison, I wouldn't think the act that got it there in the first place was so awful.

Maybe I talked to the servant girls too much. Or to the wrong ones. Still, I didn't understand why anyone would look forward to that.

But I knew my place, so when Father finished, I said, "It would please me greatly to marry the man you have chosen. I hope that God will bless me with many male children."

Father and Mother nodded and smiled.

I felt like running from the room, but I remembered my promise, so I asked, "When will Michal marry? She, too, is a woman now."

They both were taken aback.

"After your marriage," Father said. "You are the eldest. Why do you ask?"

"Have you considered joining our house to David, son of Jesse?"

Father's face clouded over. He gripped the sides of his chair so tightly, his hands shook. "Must I hear his name from you too? Will even my own household speak of him?"

His eyes blazed and he began to shout. "Have you heard the chants when we return from battle? 'Saul has killed his thousands. David has killed his ten thousands.' What else is left for him? To take away my kingdom?"

I bowed my head, hoping that the madness would not overtake him. "Father, I meant no harm. Forgive my tongue, for I speak when I should be quiet." I took a chance. "Though not as often as Michal."

He glared at me for a time, his face red, but then burst into laughter. "Not as often as Michal." He roared. "On that you are right. That girl is never quiet."

I took one more chance. "Father, you are the king, the first one given by God to Israel. You need fear no poor shepherd's son. But if David's popularity becomes a danger, marry him to one of your daughters. Then he becomes an ally."

Father stared in wonderment. Mother looked on with confused fear, her gaze moving back between Father and me.

"He is but the youngest son of a poor shepherd,"

Father said. "How could he pay a dowry fitting a king's daughter?"

I drew in a deep breath. "Is not an ally worth more than any dowry a richer man could pay?"

Silence filled the room for a long time.

Then Father nodded, a smile forming upon his lips. "You have wisdom greater than all my advisors." He glanced at Mother and said, "So it shall be."

Michal shrieked with delight and hugged me, begging forgiveness for all the times she'd called me evil. Over and over, she pried me for details I might have forgotten.

Days later, we were summoned before the throne. We wore jewels and our finest tunics, covering our heads even though that wasn't required until the actual wedding ceremony.

As the eldest, I went first while Michal remained in a rear antechamber. Mother and I stood behind Father's throne as the guards stepped outside. Flowers adored the walls. A musician played the lute and sang. I awaited Adriel the Meholathite.

In walked David.

I froze. What was he doing here? I glanced at Mother. She beamed.

When the lute player finished, Father began. "David, son of Jesse, you have become the greatest warrior in the kingdom," he said. "I have summoned you today to repay you. I offer my daughter's hand in marriage. Merab will make you a good wife and bear you many male children. I require only that you be valiant for me and fight the Lord's battles."

David ruddy complexion turned pale. He looked to me. I averted my eyes.

"Oh, great king," he finally said. "Who am I? I am the least of all men, the youngest son of a poor shepherd from the least of the tribes. Who am I to be a son-in-law to the king?"

Heavy silence fell over the court.

He had rejected me? I wanted none of this man. I wanted none of any man. But to be offered to *a poor shepherd* and then scorned made me want to cover my head in shame. I had never felt such humiliation. I might not be pleasing to the eye, but I was the king's daughter.

"But . . . the people love you," Father said. "You are not the least of all men." Appearing unable to comprehend David's rejection, Father said, "I require no dowry but that you serve me in battle."

David bowed his head. "It is a great and kind offer, O King, but I cannot accept. Please offer Merab's hand to a man more worthy than I."

More worthy? His vanity knew no bounds, his chest swelling with pride when the people chanted of the king killing his thousands and David his ten thousands. He claimed not to be worthy?

I knew who he considered unworthy. Me!

Not that I wanted him, but had ever there been a king's daughter offered with no dowry but loyalty? That would be shame enough. But for such a woman to be considered so repugnant that even such an offer was refused was beyond the pale.

I ran from all these witnesses to my shame, and burst into the antechamber where Michal waited, almost knocking her over.

Mother followed behind. Her face ashen, she said, "Michal, go to your father. He awaits you."

Startled and confused, she left.

I buried my face in my hands. This was the problem with heroes. They became so filled with pride that even the lowliest of them—a poor shepherd!—could reject the hand of a king's daughter.

Michal flew back into the room in a cold rage. "You said you talked to Father!"

"I did, but he—"

"You stole David away from me! You don't love him. You only speak of him with scorn. How could you have done this?"

"I spoke for you, Michal, but Father heard what he wanted to hear."

"But—"

"Michal!" I said. "David rejected me."

She blinked. "*Neither* of us is getting married?"

I nodded.

"Because of the dowry?"

In a voice barely above a whisper, I said, "There was no dowry. David had to only pledge his loyalty."

Michal's eyes widened and for a time she said no more. Finally, she asked, "Do you think . . . he loves me?"

So I married Adriel the Meholathite.

Marriage hasn't been as bad as I imagined. Only on the six days leading up to the Sabbath do I pray that the Lord God strike me dead.

Father offered Michal's hand to David, though this time with a dowry to be earned on the battlefield. With me out of the way, David no longer felt unworthy of being the king's son-in-law.

What a surprise.

I still believe that David's vanity will one day cause Michal pain, as it does for so many who love heroes, but I've come to believe that he loves her too.

Perhaps it is one of those lies we tell ourselves often enough until we believe it—like David's killing of the lion and bear with his own hands—but I now accept that David's refusal was not a rejection of me but rather that he loved Michal and could accept no other.

That I can forgive.

For I cannot question his devotion.

You know a man is in love when he pays a dowry of two hundred Philistine foreskins.

INSPIRATION

Phaedra M. Weldon

Phaedra Weldon is the author of the Zoë Marti-
nique Investigation Series about an astrally travel-
ing heroine. *Wraith* and *Spectre*, are available now
in bookstores. Book 3, *Phantasm*, will be available
in June of 2009. Her first *Shadowrun* book, *Dark
Resonance*, will be available April of 2009. She has
published in such shared universes as *Star Trek* as
well as several Tekno/DAW anthologies. She lives
in Atlanta, Georgia.

Heroes.
 They come in all shapes and sizes.
 Human, as well as . . . well . . . not-human.
 At first, I wasn't sure if the mugger had knocked the
sense out of me, or maybe I'd finally gone one step up
that corporate ladder of disconnectedness.
 'Cause the events on my run that fine spring morn-
ing outdid the rest of the day as well as the presenta-
tion I was supposed to deliver to the company's top
executives.
 Who knew Fairy Kings were real?
 It all happened so fast—me running, pumping

muscles, breathing deep, going over my speech and my figures, building up my confidence with mantras I'd long ago created for myself as the only female executive in a Fortune Five Hundred corporation, burning off the nervous tension that had refused to let me sleep the night before—and then I was on my butt.

Correction—my back. I was on my back, looking up. And my head *hurt*.

The morning was cool, though the day would warm up nicely in the early spring. The sky was blue with little fluffy white clouds. I could just see all of it through the opening in the trees. I'd been running every morning through this park for over two years, and I'd never looked up.

Which was what I'd been doing wrong—not looking up—and had not seen the dark figure in the hood and baggy jeans hiding just to the right of the tree. He'd jumped out, knocked me across my face, and dragged me into a little glade just on the other side of the running path.

But that wasn't the real problem at the moment. No, my attacker hadn't had time enough to do any serious damage, except maybe rip my tee-shirt enough to expose my sports bra.

No, the problem was the big, naked guy standing in front of me—the one who'd, like, popped out of nowhere and decked the jerk attacking me with one blow.

And as I lay there looking up at the tightest, smoothest naked behind I'd ever seen, the more rational part of my brain—the one with the MBA in finance—screamed at me to run. Because in reality, it looked as if one normal rapist had been replaced by a crazy, naked rapist.

The sun filtered through the trees at that moment as he turned. His skin glowed golden, much as ripples moved by a soft breeze on a calm river. His neck muscles flexed as he turned, and his hair shimmered with the color and incandescence of a raven's feathers as he turned and looked down at me.

But even as I prepared to scramble and scream out of his way, his smile twinkled in that filtering light and his eyes—a brilliant garnet red—shone bright. "Are you okay?" he asked in a rich, accented voice.

I blinked. I hadn't expected him to speak. The man had the type of body that spoke of primordial fighting and ritual mating. The rational part of my brain now paused and tried to identify the accent.

He turned around fully to look at me and then knelt, and with a shock of surprise, I realized he wore a leaf over his crotch. I pushed myself up on my elbows, my white bra visible in the sunshine that now seemed to bounce off him and into my eyes.

I winced. "Hey, turn down the shine, dude." I held up my left hand to protect my eyes.

"I am sorry," the voice said.

The light vanished.

And I mean *all* the light vanished.

When I opened my eyes, the sky was dark, with twinkling stars, which was nuts because the stars were never visible in the city. But the small area of the park we were in was well lit as tiny pricks of light floated up from the ground, illuminating everything.

It was pretty—and I was sure at that point that my brain had gone bye-bye.

I felt his hand in mine, and he was pulling. I moved with him, letting him hold my weight until I was standing. And as I absently readjusted my tee-shirt, I looked up between the trees again and stared open-mouthed at the stars.

"Are you all right?" he asked me again. "You didn't say before."

The accent shifted and rolled as if he were looking for the right channel.

I looked at him. And I mean *really* looked at the naked man in front of me. Something fluttered behind him, and I narrowed my eyes at it before taking a step back. I held out my hands, flattened, and bent my knees, centering my body for defense. Just as Mr. Takeshi had taught us to do in my weekly karate class.

"Look, you freak," I said in a very solid voice. I was proud of myself—I'd been afraid I wouldn't be able to keep the quiver out of my throat. "I don't know who you are, or why the hell you think you have to march around here naked, but I'm warning you—I have been trained to defend myself."

The attacker lay on the ground to my right—he wasn't moving. The fact that naked guy had laid him out with one punch wasn't lost on me.

At all.

Naked Guy smiled. It was a nice smile—but it also looked condescending.

Which just drove me bug-nuts.

"I am Oberon, King of the Fairies. And I am at your service." He held out his right hand and bowed.

And that's when I saw them. Right there, growing out of the center of his back—a pair of tiny, purple fairy wings.

He straightened and smiled.

I giggled. I really tried not too.

And then it sort of bubbled up inside of me—and before I knew it, my defensive karate stance had turned into a full-on belly laugh.

After a few seconds of deep laughing like I hadn't experienced in years, I looked at him. Mr. Oberon looked a little put out. "Why . . . why are you laughing?" he said.

I leaned forward and braced my hands on my knees as I tried to take in a few deep breaths. A few more and then I was able to stand and keep a straight face. "You have . . . you have these little like . . . baby butterfly wings on your back. Did you forget the rest of your costume?"

"Costume? My wings?" he glanced back. "Is there something on them?"

"No, no. It's just that . . ." Oh, god, it was hard keeping a straight face. "It's just that my life usually isn't this—

well—crazy. I mean, I'm in the middle of the woods talking to a big, naked fairy." I gestured to the sky. "And it's like nighttime, and there are fireflies all over the place."

"Does this make you uncomfortable?"

I looked around. "It's weird. But I figure I'll wake up in a hospital at some point and make an appointment with my shrink real soon."

Oberon gave me a sardonic smile and snapped his fingers. It was morning again, the birds twittering, the breeze blowing, exactly as it had been minutes ago.

Oh—kay.

I was beginning to think this wasn't a hallucination. "Nice trick. Okay . . . look, time for me to go," I glanced at my watch. It was already past seven, and my meeting was at nine. I needed to get home and get changed into my power suit.

Oberon took a step forward. I didn't sense anything menacing from him—actually, he just looked really confused. "I'm sorry—but I don't understand. I just rescued you. I saved you from violation."

I nodded. "Yeah, and I think I'm grateful for that, but you'll have to excuse me."

I'd intended to just run off, back to my car.

But even as I turned, Oberon was abruptly in front of me. Still naked, I might add. "I'm . . . confused," he held up his right hand. "I just saved you . . . and you do not wish to reward me with a kiss?"

A kiss?

I looked him up and down. Given the fact he was naked—and he had the body to be naked if he wanted too—I wasn't all that hip on kissing a crazy, naked fairy.

I didn't really believe he was a fairy. I mean, those things just don't exist. The wings were a prop, and he was really one of those wackos you read about in the papers all the time. The ones that dress up like superheroes and try to save people.

But as far as I was concerned, heroes usually just made the situation worse.

"So you think," I held up my right index finger in his face. "That since you rescued me, I owe you something?"

Now he looked even more confused. "Well, of course. I am Oberon, and you are a damsel in distress. I have saved you."

"So," I put my hands on my hips. "That's what's in it for you? The glory and my undying gratitude? This kiss you think I owe you? What, so you think I should paw over you now?"

"Well, not paw, exactly." The accent suddenly vanished and Mr King of the Fairies sounded strangely . . . New York. "But yeah, I'd think you'd show a little gratitude."

Uh huh. "So what's your schtick? You just hang around out here in the woods till some idiot tries to mug or rape some girl? And then you swoop in all naked, surprise them, and then bask in your own glory?"

"You were a beautiful damsel in distress—it was my duty as a hero to rescue you from the evils of this world."

And there it was—the truth on his face. And in his words.

I frowned. "How many rapes or muggings have you actually just let happen because you didn't think the victim was a beautiful damsel?"

He bowed his head.

"Oh, geez," I sighed. "So you've just let poor innocent women get attacked in this forest so you can pick and choose?"

Oberon crossed his arms over his chest. "You sound like my wife."

I started. Wife? I took a step closer. "You have a wife?"

"Yeah," he nodded to the woods. "Tatania. Real shrew. That's how we met, you know? I saved her, she fell instantly in love with me, and then we ruled the land of fairy together. Only . . ." he shrugged. "She lost interest."

"So . . . you're in the forest playing hero so you can make her jealous?"

He pursed his lips. "Maybe. I just needed a boost." The New York accent was gone now, replaced by something she recognized as midwestern.

"Boost of ego?"

"No, that boost of knowing we're needed. You know? Part of being a hero is knowing you're protecting something even greater." He lowered his arms. "Look, I'm sorry. I just—" he held out his hands. "You just looked like you needed help, okay? So yeah, I wanted some gratification. I wanted a little adoration." He turned away. "So sue me."

I watched him a few minutes. This guy, this naked fairy guy with the fluttering wings on his back, was both confusing and intriguing. Not to mention the way he talked was weird. "So . . . why do you come out here naked?"

He kept his face turned away. "I'm a fairy. We don't have need of clothing."

I pursed my lips. "How many damsels have you actually saved out here?"

There was a very long pause. "Two."

"Am I number two?"

"No, you're number three. If you ran screaming from me I was just gonna tuck it in and go home."

"It's the being naked part."

He half-turned toward me. "You think that's scary?"

"I think it is. Look, you've got a killer body, and it's very nice to look at, but the tiny little fairy wings," I shook my head. "Not cutting it."

"So I should wear clothes?"

I nodded. "Yeah, for now I would."

"Thanks." He paused. "So . . . you're leaving now?"

"You bet," I turned to look for my water bottle. I'd dropped it when the first guy attacked me. I didn't see it.

I didn't see the first attacker either. He wasn't on the

ground anymore, and I had no memory of him getting up and running off. Which meant he was still nearby.

As I turned to ask Oberon if he'd seen the guy in the hood and jeans, I caught a movement out of the corner of my eye. The attacker moved in behind Oberon, whose attention was lost on some thought rolling about in his head.

I saw the flash of a blade and I realized I was no longer the kid's target.

Oberon was.

My body acted on trained instinct now—I was paying attention, unlike before. My mind was going off in several directions, but it was in the here and now. And I was running quick at Oberon. The Fairy King noticed my movements and sensed something behind him. He crouched as the kid lunged at him.

Oberon's crouch was low enough so that I could jump over him and tackle the kid—but not before he was able to drive his small knife into the Fairy King's back. I landed on the attacker's head, knocking him backward. Two well-driven kicks and he lay still.

I turned to Oberon.

He was on his stomach, the knife protruding from between the wings. They were fluttering madly as if trying to escape. I knelt down beside him, unsure if I should remove the knife or not. There wasn't any blood—or none that I could see.

"Well," came Oberon's voice low and unsure from beneath the pile of raven hair. "Apparently I wasn't—diligent enough in dispatching your attacker." Again his speech cadence changed.

"Hold still," I said as I leaned in closer to the knife.

The wings crumpled like singed silk and vanished in a wisp of smoke.

Oberon cried out and grabbed at the leaves and grass beneath him. "Oh, great mother, that hurts," he muttered.

"What—what just happened?" I sat back as blood welled up from the wound and ran over his back in streams of crimson. Well, it was definitely human blood in my opinion. I reached into my back pocket and pulled out my cell.

"No . . ." he said in a soft voice. "Don't. I'm not . . . human."

"You're bleeding, and that knife is lodged in your spine."

"Just pull it out—"

"No, you'll bleed faster." I dialed 911.

"Please . . . take it out . . . quickly . . . I'll be fine . . ."

The phone was wrenched from my hand as leaves and refuse spun upward into a funnel the size and shape of a man. I moved closer to Oberon and shielded his wound from the flying dirt, putting my own hand up to keep the stuff out of my eyes.

"Well, well, well," came a deep, rich voice.

I looked up to see another man—long blond hair and a thin face, dressed in loose jeans, a white, long-sleeved hooded sweater, and worn sneakers. His features reminded me of a wolf—a white wolf.

"Pull it out . . ." Oberon hissed.

I hesitated—I knew if I pulled it out he would bleed faster.

"Please . . ." he pleaded with me.

I reached for the knife's hilt—

And the wolf-man was there, kneeling beside me, and he struck me with the back of his right hand. I fell back, totally unprepared for that move, my cheek stinging. The wolf-man had moved too fast—no human could move that fast.

As he moved back from me and from Oberon, I could see his back as well.

Small, black gossamer wings fluttered on his back. They made the sound of a bumblebee.

I put a hand to my burning cheek. Man, I needed to get out more often if seeing winged men was the way my mind decided to express its dementia. Wolf-man stood up straight and looked own at Oberon.

"You are now just as I had always imagined you. Helpless. Paralyzed."

"This is your doing, Puck," Oberon said through tight jaws. I knew he was in pain. The wound continued to bleed. "You sent the man after this woman."

"I knew you couldn't resist being the hero," Puck said as he shoved his hands deep into the pockets of his jeans. "And it's so hard to be a hero in these times. Hell, it's hard for us to even exist. Why do you think Tatania retreated into the Carn so quickly? She knew that memory was the only place for us to live. This world doesn't need heroes."

I watched this guy—and decided I didn't like him. Forget the fact that he'd slapped me—he was also just not particularly nice, and he was totally wrong about this world not needing heroes.

"You're wrong..." Oberon said. He tried to push himself up but couldn't seem to gather the strength. And each time he tried, more blood welled up from the wound and flowed onto the ground.

Mushrooms popped up where his blood landed. Bright red toadstools with large white polka dots on them.

"No, I'm not wrong, Oberon. You're only a dreamer. Which is why we've all left you. You're the last to remain here. A pitiful creature that lingers in hopes of being a hero in some fashion. A hero does mighty deeds, Oberon." Puck moved closer, his hands still in his pockets and leaned over Oberon. "What have you ever done that was great, oh fairy king?"

Oberon remained still.

I felt a little bad for him then—especially when I realized how sincere he'd been—and how disappointed when I didn't appear to show him the *ooh* and *aah* he expected.

The reaction he seemed to need.

"That blade in your back," Puck was saying. "It was forged from the blade of the Elven King—I've read the old text, Oberon. This is your death in this realm! When you wake again, you will be within the true Realm, and we can leave this bleak and unfeeling world behind."

Now, I wasn't sure I knew what was happening or what they were talking about. What I did know was that this poor naked man had saved me, whether or not it was a setup. And I felt he honestly believed he had done a service.

And maybe it was an ego thing. As long as his heart was in the right place.

I didn't know what the knife being forged from some elf's blade meant—I was just a finance wizard. What I did know was that my morning in that meeting wasn't going to happen unless I got these two to calm down.

Voices from the other side of the cropping of trees caught Puck's attention and mine. The running path was just over that embankment, and there were people close by. So when he turned, I made my move.

I scrambled back to Oberon, grabbed the hilt of the knife, and yanked it out with a yell.

The ground shook at that moment, and I heard someone scream nearby. When I'd pulled the knife out, the strength of my pull had sent me head over heels backwards, so that when I came up to a seated position—

Oberon was on his knees, fully clothed in black jeans, black top, and—

A large man-sized set of black and gray gossamer wings. They were bigger than Puck's, and the blond fairy was looking a little frightened. Oberon had a sword in his hand and moved purposefully toward the now much smaller man.

"You think you can defeat me? For me, me— Oberon—to retreat into the Carn?"

Puck had his hands up, his wings fluttering frantically. "It wasn't my idea, my liege. It was really Tatania's idea—she wants you home."

"Home?" He stopped a few inches in front of Puck. "This is my home. Please tell my queen that I have work still to do in this place."

"Work," Puck's bravado returned and he moved out from Oberon's path. He pointed at me and stared hard. "You—human woman—do you need a hero?"

I opened my mouth and then shut it. I looked at Oberon. He still faced away from me, his expression hidden, his head bent.

I had to think hard about that question. Do I need a hero, or did the world need one? I took a few steps toward Puck. He looked less menacing now, and his wings no longer fluttered behind his back but were still. "Do I need one? No."

Puck smiled.

I saw Oberon's shoulders drop.

"But I want one."

Puck paused.

I prepared myself to speak, gathering my thoughts. I wasn't talking to a board room table of men who believed they knew more than me—but to a creature of imagination.

Same thing as far as I could tell.

"Do I as a mortal in this world need a hero, or a champion? No. I have to learn to fight my own battles, win or lose. And it's me who has to make my own decisions. There isn't anyone else out there who can do that.

"The world doesn't need a hero either—not in the way I think you and Oberon believe. I think what it needs is a symbol of hope. You'll never be able to heal every heartache, or rescue every cat from a tree, or even save every woman from a brutal attack. But you can inspire," I smiled and looked at Oberon's back just then. "Because inspiration can lead to action, and in that end," I shrugged, "well, we can all be heroes."

Oberon turned then and looked at me. I'd thought he was nice to look at nude, but he was even more attractive clothed as he was. A dark, mysterious figure that did not paint the image of the hero on the shining horse riding in to save the day but more of the reality of life's grays. That good and bad weren't as clear-cut as they were a decade ago.

Hell, even a week ago.

Puck moved back then and vanished into the woods. The tension in the tiny wooded area eased, and I could hear the birds chirping again, though I hadn't noticed they weren't there to begin with.

Oberon took several steps toward me and stood before me. His face was even more handsome than before—ethereal. His wings no longer appeared a comical extension but more a part of him. A distinction between reality and the imagination.

"You're welcome," he said in a low voice. And then bent down and touched his lips to my forehead.

The tingle that traveled down to my toes was real enough that I shivered involuntarily, but I was also filled with a renewed sense of joy. And of confidence. "Thank you."

He smiled at me. "Do you mind if I rescue you again some time?"

I returned his smile. "Not at all, King of the Fairies."

Oberon turned and moved to the woods. His image shifted and he became a cop in uniform. The city's finest. "Now if you'll excuse me, I have a criminal to arrest," he nodded to the now stirring attacker, his cuffs out and his voice stern. And his accent? Perfect. "You have the right to remain silent . . ."

Heroes.

They come in all shapes and sizes.

HONEY, I'M HOME

Pauline J. Alama

Pauline J. Alama author of the fantasy novel, *The Eye of Night*, has published stories in the anthologies *Witch High*, *Mystery Date*, *Rotten Relations*, and *Sword & Sorceress XXIII*. Her next novel will be *The Ghost-Bearers*. Although graduate studies in medieval literature made her fairly intimate with Beowulf, she has since settled down to a quiet life with few epic battles, except between her cats. She lives in northeastern New Jersey where the sacking of cities is a vice only practiced by developers.

Sing, Muse, the tale proud Homer would not tell: how resourceful Odysseus, man of many travels, sacker of cities, scourge of Troy's citadel, returned home after twenty years' absence and moped outside his bedroom door, pleading with his wife, circumspect Penelope, to let him in.

As the disgraced dog, having broken the precious amphora with his romping, whimpers disconsolately in the yard, yearning for the warm fireside and the master's caress, so did the illustrious king of Ithaka wail, "Penelope of the shining visage, how can you fail to know me, your husband? Have I not rescued you from your pernicious suitors? Have I not answered the riddle you set me, recalling that our marriage-bed is rooted to the ground, its post a living tree? Who else could I be but Odysseus? What other man has gone where I have gone and knows what I know?"

"No man, perhaps, but the immortal gods sometimes toy with human women, taking on the semblance of their husbands."

As Dawn treads softly across the waking world, lending rosy color to hill and dale, so a flush of pleasure, of pride, perhaps of relief, stole across the seafaring hero's face. "Ah, so you take me for some god?"

"Some god, perhaps, with a low estimate of human intelligence, impersonates my husband imprecisely. It may be that after twenty years' separation, my memory has begun to fail me, but I distinctly recall that when I married resourceful Odysseus, man of many stratagems, I believed my husband had a brain. Thus is your impersonation inexact, whichever of men or gods you may be."

"Prudent Penelope, august queen, what have I done that you should think me less cunning than I once was?"

"Resourceful Odysseus, sacker of cities, loser of the way home, can you wonder at the coolness of my welcome, when you come home twenty years late for supper?"

"War detained me, my queen. For ten years we besieged Troy's proud citadel."

"Insult not my understanding. I know the difference between ten and twenty. Where have you been these ten years since Troy fell?"

"Wandering on the wine-dark seas, home of fierce Poseidon."

"And not once in those ten years did you think to ask directions, Mr. Athena-is-my-copilot? Odysseus' *dog* could find the way home from Troy in less time. I'm sorry, but I *refuse* to believe you're the man I married."

Then spoke far-traveled Odysseus, man of many hardships: "When immortals set their wills in wrath against a mortal man, he strives in vain for his homecoming."

As the frosty wind of Boreas sweeps down from the north, withers blossoms, freezes limpid pools, and makes the trees of the greenwood tremble, so did the glance of gray-eyed Penelope freeze the very summer air. "Some say not all your striving with immortals was born of wrath, oh, guileful Odysseus, man of many-sided words, boy-toy of goddesses."

"Oh, bright-shining Penelope, most excellent of queens, if by 'goddesses' you mean the nymph Kalypso, hear me out. I was held against my will, a prisoner on her inaccessible island."

"Doing *hard* time, I'm sure," snarled faithful Penelope.

"Circumspect Penelope, most understanding of women, consider my plight. You know how touchy these immortals can be. When one of the blissful gods, drinkers of nectar and eaters of ambrosia, requires one's attendance at the sacred rites of the bedchamber, one can't just plead a headache. For all the nights that she held me—a wretched captive—I thought only of you."

"Of me? Oh, crafty Odysseus, master of many lies, why then did you come home, make your landing on Ithaka's coast, and reveal your counsels to our impetuous young son, and even to the pigherd, rather than to me?"

"Queenly Penelope, fearsome in your splendor, I deemed it undignified to reveal myself to you, confess my true identity, until I could show myself properly victorious over the vicious gang of suitors, ungodly freeloaders, breakers of the sacred guest code, who plagued you in my absence."

"Sacker of cities, terror of Trojans, what piece of Troy's wall landed on your head that you could devise no better way to rid yourself of unwanted houseguests than gory massacre in our feasting hall? One of your interminable tales of woe would have cleared the hall much more cleanly. Now the great palace of Ithaka stinks like a slaughterhouse—and who's to clean it, when half the serving maids lie dead with the suitors?"

As the proud tomcat, challenged by another mouser in the hunting-ground he has marked with urine, arches his back, fur bristling, and yeowls his defiance, so too did godlike Odysseus bristle at his wife's complaint. "Can you be so ungrateful that I rescued you from these vipers? Or did you secretly long for one of them, to take pleasure in the heat of his lustful body?"

"Faithless Odysseus, most tardy husband, those suitors were worthless boors, and if you'd returned sooner, they'd have left sooner. But I had them under control."

Like the thunder Father Zeus sends down from the mountaintops, Odysseus raged, "Under control! They were feasting here at their pleasure, eating up our flocks and herds, our grain and oil and wine."

Circumspect Penelope, most prudent queen, spoke calmly. "And if they had indeed been living off our bounty all these years, giving nothing in return, there would now be nothing here to interest them: neither feast for them to eat nor estate for them to covet. But I have made them serve me while they thought to serve only themselves. I would tell one of them, 'All real men are gone from Ithaka since the dark ships left for Troy. If only Odysseus were here, the olives would have been harvested by now.' And shame and greed would move him where decency would not, and the suitor would pick olives—or rather, the lazy lout would bring slaves from his estate to do the job, leaving his own olives to rot while they harvested ours. You've gotten more work done for me in your absence than you might have in person—"

"That's not fair!"

"—because there were many of them, and once I had set one of them to work, I could say to the rest, 'What favor do you expect of me, layabouts, while Eurymachos is harvesting my olives?' "

"You are indeed crafty, my queen," conceded wily Odysseus, maker of the Trojan Horse. "But has your strategy considered all the wickedness of these suitors? I heard them murmur among themselves of a plot to kill our dear son, Telemachus."

"Yet they could never do more than murmur, their thoughts bound and confused as I worked on the great loom."

"Peerless craftswoman, disciple of Athena, I fail to see what your handiwork on the loom, however fine, has to do with the danger that faced our son."

"On the *great* loom. Athena's wedding gift."

"Oh. *That* great loom."

"I told the suitors I could marry none of them till I had finished weaving a shroud for your esteemed father against his death day. And so, in sight of them all, I wove on the great loom day by day. Yet none of them knew what I wove in that web: their thoughts, their hopes, their desires, their murderous plots. And night by night, I unraveled it, till they forgot all they had plotted, all they had done, all they had thought. Their plots against young Telemachus could never be sprung, for they were forgotten as soon as they were made. Each time they conceived the foul plan of murder, they thought it the first time. Yet Telemachus' thoughts were not unraveled, and he was aware of their enmity."

"Indeed, wise Penelope, most excellent weaver, you work subtly," said Odysseus. "Such ingenious weaving might be put to more than one use."

"So it was, wily Odysseus, deviser of deceptions. I often told the forgetful suitors that never in their whole supposed courtship had they given me gifts, precious treasures, as a suitor should give his desired bride. And each time they vied to give the richest presents, dazzling jewels, marvelous works of the goldsmith's craft, exotic ornaments gained in journeys of trade or piracy. Whatever they gave, I hoarded away unseen so that our son will have fine merchandise to sell when he ventures out trading in the dark-prowed ships, seaworthy vessels, to increase his fortune; or fine gifts to present when he turns suitor himself, seeking some highborn maidcn as his bride."

"All this was shrewdly plotted, prudent Penelope, most cunning of queens. Nonetheless, do you not agree that the shameless suitors who connived at our son's death, however vainly, deserved to die?"

"Surely they deserved it, raging Odysseus, drawer of the great bow. Yet consider well: Had you merely revealed yourself, the suitors would have scattered like chaff to the four winds, knowing it vain to court the wife of a living warrior, a victor of many battles. But now they lie dead, pierced by your swift arrows or slashed by your sword edge. And when this day's work is known throughout the islands, how many kindreds will rush here like wolves to a carcass, seeking vengeance? And how will we buy peace with all these families, when half our treasury is filled with suitors' gifts that they would recognize as drawn from their own treasurc troves?"

Resourceful Odysseus, sacker of cities, dropped his head in his hands. "Wise Penelope, resplendent queen, all you say is true. Now I rely upon you, most guileful of women, to help me devise a stratagem to disarm all our enemies."

Circumspect Penelope, most excellent of wives, chewed her fingernail, considering. "Tomorrow will be a long, weary day at the loom, and a subtle piece of work it shall be, indeed."

"And I know you shall weave it as no other pupil of Athena can—in the morning, when our wits are fresh. But for now, would you be pleased to rest in a pair of once familiar arms and see if I can recover, in your embrace, the cunning I once knew?"

Then did godlike Odysseus kneel like a suppliant and embrace his wife's knees; yet still she stood hesitating. Slowly, like the slow progress of spring, his embrace inched higher. And as the subtle fingers of Dawn creep wondrously into every part of the land, caressing leaf and bud, dancing across the face of the waters, filling vale and glade with a thousand unexpected glories of light and color, so did the subtle fingers and lips of Odysseus creep wondrously over the surface of his wife's body, filling her with unexpected glories of joy and desire.

When she could speak again, shining Penelope sighed. "Ah, yes. Now I remember why I called you 'resourceful Odysseus.' Come to bed."

BALLAD OF THE GROUPIE EVERLASTING

Robert T. Jeschonek

Robert T. Jeschonek wrote "Acirema the Rellik" for DAW's *Future Americas*. His collection of fantasy and science fiction, *Mad Scientist Meets Cannibal,* is now available from PS Publishing. Robert's stories have also appeared in *Postscripts, Helix, PodCastle,* and *Abyss & Apex*, among others. He has written *Doctor Who* and *Star Trek* fiction, including "Our Million-Year Mission," which won the grand prize in the nationwide *Strange New Worlds VI* contest. Visit him online at *www. robertjeschonek.com*.

So here I am, in the year of your Lord 2009, lying beside the corpse of yet another dead musician, a rock star flamed out on heroin, and I make the promise one more time.

"This is the last one." That's the promise. "No more musicians for me."

How many times have I said those words over the centuries? Over how many musicians' corpses? And how many times have I broken that promise? Again and again and again.

But maybe this time, it will take.

After all, this guy was special. As I stroke his long, blond hair, I'm filled with regret over the dead potential of him, the lost opportunities. He could have changed the world, honest and truly . . . could have healed it with the music I inspired in him. I felt it in my bones this time, I *believed* it with every iota of my essence.

Maybe that's my flaw. I want too badly to believe in these people. These children of music. After all, I *created* music. I *am* a muse.

Not "muse" in a general sense, like every dumbass bar band numbskull calls his underage cutie to get into her pants. I'm *a* muse, *the* muse, plain and pure and simple. The one and only original Terpsichore. Ta-da.

So I've got a thing for musicians, which sucks, because they *always* let me down, just like this guy. But I always come back for more, because you just never know. Maybe the next one will light up the world for good and true and teach the world to sing in perfect harmony and all that happy horseshit.

I lean down and kiss my latest flameout on the forehead. Give him my blessing. Speed him to my special corner of the Underworld.

And tears roll from my eyes. More tears than I've cried in ages. This guy's the biggest letdown to come along in centuries. My biggest failure since the fourteenth freakin' century and that Gottfried guy back in Germany.

In that craphole town called Hamelin.

Here's how the Pied Piper got his name: He sucked so bad, people used to throw pies at him.

That was back when he was starting out, of course. Before I helped him turn things around.

In fact, the first time I saw the Piper, whose name was Gottfried Hazenstab, he was taking a rotten pot pie square in the face at the Oberammergau town fair. He was only two songs into his first set, too.

And he was lucky. Europe was full of tough crowds in those days; life was short and harsh, and people didn't have much patience. Gottfried was lucky they didn't just kill him.

And luckier still that I was in town that day.

See, I had an eye for raw talent, and I spotted it in Gottfried before the pie hit. The way he played his flute, I could tell he had that certain something.

Which is the whole reason I got into this business in the first place. To find that rare musical flair. That special magic.

And set it free.

"Hello there." I handed him a rag after the show. "My name is Terpsie."

Gottfried wiped the gravy from his face. His bright blue eyes flashed like sapphires, framed by pure gold streamers of hair that touched the tops of his shoulders. "I am Gottfried. Thank you for this." He held up the rag.

"When is your next show?" Smiling, I produced another rag from a pocket of my dress and dabbed at his cheeks.

"Never," said Gottfried. "I quit."

Power flowed out from my fingertips and wafted from my breath, fanning the sparks of talent within him into crackling flames. "I think you should do one more."

"No more." Gottfried shook his head. He sounded like he might be ready to cry. "I'm done."

"One more." Gazing deep within his eyes, I nodded slowly, exerting my influence.

Gottfried's headshaking turned to headnodding. "One more."

This time, when Gottfried played, he took a custard pie in the face. This was an improvement over the rotten pot pie ... but who cared what the people thought. I was paying more attention to a different audience altogether.

A nonhuman one.

While the people jeered and hooted and stomped away, another audience listened with rapt attention. An audience much lower to the ground.

Along the base of a nearby tent, a group of rats and mice lined up and watched until Gottfried stopped playing. There were seven of them, sitting up on hind legs, snouts quivering in the air of the fair.

They scattered as soon as the pie cut the show short, but I'd seen enough. Now I knew for sure.

"Come with me, Gottfried." I handed him a fresh rag for his face. "We're going to make beautiful music together."

He looked at me as if I were insane. "Beautiful? Are you sure you don't mean *awful*?"

"Awfully successful." I took him by the shoulders and stared him in the eye. "Forget about the masses. Your kind of talent has real niche appeal."

"'Itch appeal?'" said Gottfried.

"You're perfectly positioned for the changing marketplace," I told him.

"What are you talking about?" said Gottfried.

"Trust me," I said. "I've got inside information."

It was wonderful watching Gottie come alive in the months that followed. Watching as his career took off just as I'd known it would.

All because of a little something called the Black Plague.

Mystical farseeing wonder-muse that I am, I'd seen the plague coming, spreading across Europe with terrible swiftness. And I'd known exactly what would cause it.

Namely, disease-infested fleas carried by rats.

So now you see where Gottie came in. I singled him out as the savior of Europe, leader-away of rats and all things plagueish.

Not just the savior of Europe. Maybe the savior of all humanity before he was done.

And the savior of one thing more in the bargain: the savior of me.

Right after Gottie's first big success, clearing the rats from the town of Babenscham, we spent our first night together as lovers.

We lay naked in each others' arms in a room at an inn, basking in the aftermath of our lovemaking. Gottie had been the perfect lover, just as I'd known he would be.

And I had been well pleased.

"How did you know?" he asked, softly stroking my auburn hair. "What made you believe in me when no one else did?"

"Vision," I told him. "And feeling."

He smiled, his bright blue eyes shining upon me. "You mean love, Terpsie?"

I considered lying, but couldn't do it. I never could, not with any of them over the centuries. "Yes. Love," I said. "I loved you at first sight."

He frowned then, brows crinkling in the candlelight. "You did something to me, didn't you? Changed me somehow?"

"Only gave you a push." I shrugged. "The true power was always within you."

"You're amazing." He ran a finger along the length of my nose and tapped it on the tip. "You really are my muse, aren't you?"

"Yes," I said, snuggling against him, relishing the heat of his body.

Just then, he tipped his head to one side and gave me a funny look. "And I'm your *first*, aren't I?"

That was when I made a mistake, though I didn't realize it at the time. I told the truth.

"No," I said. "Not the first."

His look went dark in a flash. "There've been others before me?"

"Yes," I said. "But you're my only one right now."

The dark look lingered a moment, then dispersed. "All right." He smiled and kissed me. "That's a wonderful thing."

"I know." I whispered the words. He was starting to make love to me again. "Wonderful it is."

I wish you could have seen Gottie in action. It was truly amazing the way he cleared a town of vermin.

Eyes closed, he blew his breath out through the flute in great scintillating bursts. His fingers flew along the length of the instrument, hopping like bees over the holes, scampering from end to end and back again.

He danced with abandon, free and wild as his music. Hair flying, he leaped and spun and twisted, feet spending as much time in the air as on the cobblestones or dirt. His moves would put any modern rock star to shame; if he were alive today, I'm convinced he'd be bigger than any star on Earth.

And then came the rats, pouring out of every building and burrow and crack . . . not just running, either, but dancing themselves, bounding and whirling. Watch them for a moment, and you realized—they were coming as close as they could to copying Gottie's own moves. In their hundreds, their thousands, their millions, they were aping him, riding the music with eyes closed and whiskers twitching like wheat stalks in a cyclone.

And then the lot of them would dance right out of town. He would lead them, dancing and leaping, down the street and across the fields, weaving in a squealing, stinking parade that trampled grass and flushed game from the undergrowth in its path.

It was truly amazing to behold. My heart pounded every time I saw it happen, absolutely every time.

And I was filled with the joy of being a part of it. Helping him to blossom as a piper, and in so doing, helping him to save Europe and all mankind.

At least that was how it was until he started leading more than rats.

*   *   *

The first ones showed up around Lindelhof, dressed in colorful tatters with flowers in their hair. They came out to watch Gottie perform, clapping and dancing in time with his flute ... staying well clear of the rats but taking pains to stay in Gottie's line of sight.

I'd seen their like before, wherever musicians plied their trade down through the centuries. We didn't call them groupies back then, but that was exactly what they were.

When Gottie finished and strolled back to town, they mobbed him, giggling and touching and gazing adoringly at him. Pushing each other out of the way to get close to him.

And when Gottie and I left town, they followed us. A dozen of them, without explaining or asking our permission, fell in line behind us.

By the time we'd finished the next job, in Dusseldorf, eight more had joined us. Six more came along after Bitburg. Pretty soon, we had a real entourage. Think Deadheads, only smellier and more likely to hurt you.

I should've stopped it right there. Sent them all packing before it was too late ... but I didn't. I kept thinking they'd go away on their own, or their families would come looking for them.

How stupid could I get?

Next thing I knew, the groupies—or Pipettes as they called themselves—were washing Gottie's clothes and cooking his meals. They were tending his horse and carrying his things. They were doing everything short of tucking him in at night.

Which of course went straight to his head. It was the same old story, though I'd been hoping for better this time.

I watched as the change came upon him ... as he went from being sure of himself to being full of himself. All the girls, all the victories, all the praise and rewards built him up to legend-in-his-own-mind status.

Worst of all, he started to drift away from me. He stopped acting so attentive and affectionate. He didn't look at me the same way anymore.

I soon realized it was time for a wakeup call.

I decided to go with honey instead of vinegar for Gottie's wakeup call. One night, I sneaked him away from camp and took him to a spring in the forest. We skinny-dipped and made love by moonlight while frogs croaked and katydids buzzed around us.

It was a perfect night, just like before the Pipettes came along. I gazed into his bright blue eyes, and things felt back to normal for a while.

"You're doing wonderful work, you know," I told him. "Your music is saving so many lives."

Gottie held me close in the water of the spring-fed pool and smiled. "I could never have done any of it without you, Terpsie."

I was glad he remembered that part. "Thank you," I said. "We make a great team."

Gottie frowned then and tipped his head to one side. "Why don't you ever do it? Why don't you play music yourself?"

I looked down at the moon's reflection in the rippling dark water. "I wish I could."

"You can't?" said Gottie.

I shrugged. "My job is to bring the music out in others."

"But is there a rule that says you can't play it, too?" said Gottie.

"Not that I know of," I said.

"Then why not try?" said Gottie.

"A muse is not a musician." I looked back into his sapphire eyes. "And a musician is what it takes to save the world."

Gottie gave me an odd look then. "Save the world?"

"The world of mankind." I leaned forward and kissed his lips. "All of mankind is depending on you."

Gottie kissed me back like a wild man and snapped his head away at the end of it. "I never imagined music could take me this far," he said.

"You should see how much farther it can take you." My voice was like a purr as we moved against each other. "Stick with me and find out."

"Don't mind if I do," said Gottie.

But of course he didn't.

I never caught him having sex with his Pipettes, but it wasn't hard to guess it was happening. When the Pipettes started showing up pregnant, with no other men but Gottie in our camp, I got the picture.

"Well, *I* wasn't *your* first and only, was I?" That was what he said when I called him on it. He didn't even try to deny it. "So I guess it's okay for me to be with more than one person, too."

As if it wasn't bad enough that he was banging the groupies he had, he kept gathering up new ones wherever we went. He played for them three times a day, different songs than for the rats, and the music seemed to bond them to the group. Instead of fighting over Gottie, they worked together to make him happy.

And before I knew it, making him happy took on a terrible new meaning.

"We haven't done enough," he told the assembled Pipettes one morning. "It's time to save the world!"

By this point, there were at least three hundred Pipettes in his entourage . . . and they all roared with excited approval.

"The best way to do that . . . the only way I see . . . is to *take over*." Gottfried looked in my direction and winked. "It is the only way we can save mankind the world over."

Again, the crowd went wild.

"Let us begin a new march now to save the world!" Gottfried pumped his flute overhead, and the women and girls in the crowd pumped fists and weapons. "Music will show the way to the dawning of a bold new age!"

The crowd howled and danced. Even the pregnant Pipettes joined in, bellies bouncing like basketballs under their frocks.

At that moment, I finally realized just how far gone Gottfried was and how bad things had gotten. Finally, as I looked out over the cheering, gyrating crowd, I saw what he had built with the groupies he'd gathered.

I had underestimated him. My world-saving Gottie had built himself an army.

"Please stop this." That was what I said to him after the big rally. "You can't save the world this way."

Gottfried kept marching through camp with his back to me. "I think it's the *best* way. Who better than the Pied Piper—a true natural born *leader*—to guide mankind through these dark times?"

"You're going to send an army of untrained women against the knights and soldiers of Europe?" I said. "How do you think *that'll* go?"

"We'll find out tomorrow when we reach our first target," said Gottfried. "A town called Hamelin."

The next day, just like always, we marched up to another dismal Dark Ages town in the German countryside, and Gottie pulled out his flute. This time, though, he changed the tune he played.

Instead of luring all the rats out of town, Gottie made them scurry in every direction through the streets, terrorizing the citizens.

Then, he made an announcement.

"Attention, people of Hamelin," said Gottie. "Acknowledge me as your new ruler, or I will order the creatures at my command to devour you all!"

"*Why*?" asked one of the townspeople as she tried to flee across the town limits. "Why are you *doing* this?"

"To *save* you, of course." Gottie gestured, and his private army stepped forward, stopping the woman from leaving Hamelin. "To save the entire world."

At that moment, I took action. I had waited as long as I could, giving my once beloved Gottie every chance to reverse his course . . . but now I knew. The Pied Piper was a lost cause.

It was time to put a stop to this insanity before it went any further.

Glaring, I stepped in front of Gottie. "That's enough!" I said. "Call off your rats."

Gottie played the flute more wildly than ever, shaking his head for my benefit. The rats danced in the streets, and so did his army as they drove back the people of Hamelin.

"I said *stop it*!" Even as the words left my lips, I knew they weren't enough. So strong was the spell Gottie had woven, it would take more than language to break it.

Perhaps I knew just what could do it.

Closing my eyes, I reached deep into the timeless realm that existed inside me and drew out a metal object . . . a flute. I had never played one before, though I instinctively knew how; after all, I'm the one who *invented* music in the first place.

Perhaps, if I could play it well enough, I could overpower Gottie's commands and change the course of what was happening to Hamelin.

Raising the mouthpiece to my lips, I hesitated. Never before had I allowed myself the luxury of trying to make my own music. Never before had I really believed in myself enough to stand up and do it.

But now, at last, I had the chance. And the stakes were high. People's lives were at stake in Hamelin if I couldn't override Gottie's song.

So I started to play.

The music came slowly at first, then picked up speed. It came naturally to me, perfectly—swirling and skirling as I blew and spun and danced.

And with each note, I felt more liberated. More at peace. More the way I was meant to be.

But it wasn't enough. Gottie continued to leap and charge and wail like always, weaving a wild skein of sound that beast and groupie alike were compelled to respond to.

As hard as I fought to match and outdo him, I couldn't manage it. The son of a bitch had gotten too good to be beaten . . . at least on his instrument of choice.

So maybe that was the key to it. Maybe I needed something new. Something brand new, conjured from dreams of a future yet to come.

Throwing aside my flute, I reached back inside my realm and drew out something else. Another instrument, also metal, also played with breath and fingers on keys and holes.

I rested the long, curved shape of it against my body. The smooth brass gleamed in the afternoon haze.

I adjusted the strap across my back, which held the instrument in place. Then, I eased my lips forward, fitting the mouthpiece between them.

And I blew. I played.

For the first time in the history of the world, the sounds of a saxophone rang out across the land.

I played with the same abandon Gottie used when playing the flute—running off streams of rapid-fire notes and chords in maniacal, tuneful sequences. Hurling out one blast of sound after another, screaming and singing and shouting with joy and sorrow and love and anger through my instrument.

Taking my solo and running with it. Hitting it hard.

And damn it if I didn't run Gottie right down. Damn it if I didn't turn those rats and Pipettes away and run them right off.

Damn it if I didn't play with such fever and fury that I burned all the musical magic right the hell out of Gottie. Every last bit of his fabulous power rushed out of him like water down a drain.

Leaving the Pied Piper a shadow of his superstar self, cursed to wander the Earth all the rest of his days, playing his flute for anyone who would listen.

Playing it off-key.

Centuries later, I walk into a club on 14th Street in the Village. This is six months after the death of my latest rock star lover, vintage 2008.

And I see him. A new candidate.

He sits on a stool on the tiny stage in the corner, singing and playing guitar. His long black hair falls over his face, hiding his eyes from the spotlight.

Then he looks up and shakes the hair back, and I meet his gaze. His eyes are glittering emerald green, bright as moonstones or new-mown grass. Full of possibilities. Full of raw talent.

I feel the pull of him like the drag of a chain wrapped around my waist, my heart, irresistible. Almost.

If I go to him, and awaken him, I know he will be great. He will do great things with me as his muse, as his lover, just as so many thousands before him have done.

And in the end, I know, he will let me down. They all do. He will let the life of glory go to his head, like the Pie-in-the-Face Piper, and he'll screw me over and maybe kill himself like the last guy, O.D.-ing on drugs. The story's *always* the same.

Unless *he's* different. There's always that chance. It's what I live for, after all—the hope that the next one will be better than all the rest.

Or is that really all I live for?

In all the years since the Piper, I'd let it slip my mind—that one more thing that made me happy. That one thing other than seeking talent and love in the heart of feckless musicians throughout history.

It slipped my mind. How happy I felt that day in Hamelin.

So for once, for once in my life, I resist the pull. I turn

right away from it, away from the man in the spotlight, and I head for the door.

I push it open and march out into the night. Heading for a corner to call my own, alone. Where I will put down a case on the sidewalk, red velvet lined to catch the quarters of passersby.

And I will play my own music.

THE QUIN QUART

Laura Resnick

Laura Resnick is the author of such fantasy novels as *Disappearing Nightly*, *In Legend Born*, *The Destroyer Goddess*, and *The White Dragon*, which made the "Year's Best" lists of *Publishers Weekly* and *Voya*. You can find her on the Web at *www. LauraResnick.com*.

"The queen is not popular," King Arthur lamented to his trusted advisor, Merlin the Magician.

"Well, what did you expect?" Merlin said. "I *told* you that marrying a Welsh woman wasn't the shrewdest idea you'd ever had."

"But the marriage was politically expedient at the time," Arthur reminded him irritably. "Besides, she brought that excellent round table with her as dowry. Who in all the land besides me has such an impressive piece of furniture?"

"I have no idea what you see in that table," Merlin muttered. "We barely managed to get the damn thing through the main gates of Camelot, and now we're spending a fortune building a special hall just to hold it! Why couldn't your bride have brought something

167

practical with her as dowry? Such as—oh, for example—gold and riches?"

"What a very unoriginal notion," Arthur said dismissively.

"Oh? Well, then, do let me know when you come up with an *original* way that table can inspire your vassals to fight by your side, in lieu of something as unoriginal as riches."

"That tone is quite unnecessary," Arthur said with a scowl.

"It's not even as if we can eat at that table! What on earth is a person to do if someone on the other side of that massive thing asks him to pass the salt?"

"Obviously, we won't use it for dining," Arthur said. "The new hall we're building for it is too far from the kitchens. Our guests would die of starvation between courses."

"So, basically, we're emptying the coffers to build a new hall just to keep the queen's dowry out of the rain."

"Nonsense! We'll find a use for it." Arthur's face brightened with a new idea. "Card playing!"

"It won't work unless the dealer has arms the length of a well-fed python."

"What's a python?" Arthur asked.

"Never mind. Something from an ancient scroll I was perusing the other day while trying to lift my spirits about the sorry state of the treasury."

"Perhaps we could use Guinevere's dowry for table tennis?"

"A *round* table?" Merlin shook his head.

"An innovative theatrical stage?"

"Theatre ... in the round?" Merlin thought it over. "No, it'll never catch on. The backside of most actors is not a thing to be gazed upon at length."

"A dance floor, then?"

"The first person to fall off the edge while doing a lively gavotte would sue us. And we have enough financial problems without adding that to the list."

"A cockfighting ring?"

"Sure, that's right," said Merlin. "Take sport out of the village square and put it in an enclosed hall inside the castle walls. That'll make you *really* popular."

"Hmph. Which brings me back to the subject of my woes: the queen's ratings."

"Ah, yes. I listened to the morning herald. I gather Her Majesty is at an all-time low in the polls."

"Welsh, sallow, blunt, still childless after two years of marriage, literate, good at math, an excellent rider, a skilled archer, and an expert at self-defense . . ." Arthur sighed. "She's everything my beloved people most despise in a woman!"

"Yes, as royal wives go, you really did pick a doozy," said Merlin.

"And it's killing me in public opinion," Arthur said. "Oh, Merlin, Merlin . . . My wise teacher, my trusted friend! What am I to do?"

"I'd start by selling the table."

"Oh, who'd buy it?" Arthur snapped. "Even *we* didn't have a hall big enough to house it."

"Good point." Merlin stroked his long white beard as he mulled over the problem. "In truth, sire, the queen isn't a bad person."

"Of course not! She's my lady wife. And Queen of England. She is, by definition, an exceptionally fine person."

"What I meant," Merlin said, "is that she doesn't cause trouble around the castle."

"When would she find time to cause trouble? She's always reading. Or writing letters. Or working on math problems. Or practicing her archery, horsemanship, and combat techniques."

"Yes," Merlin mused. "It's not as if she overspends, or drinks, or beats the servants excessively, or goes into hysterics every time a mouse runs through the castle. Overall, she's a pretty reasonable woman, despite being Welsh, sallow, blunt, and childless." He added generously,

"And, of course, it's not as if she can help being Welsh and sallow."

"I don't think she can help being childless, either," Arthur pointed out.

"Without wishing to be too inquisitive, sire, er . . ." When Arthur just looked at him blankly, Merlin continued, "Might one inquire whether your conjugal bed is, um, an active place?"

"Oh, good God! Yes, man, I do my duty as a husband, a king, and a prospective father," Arthur said impatiently. "It's not as if it's *my* fault that the queen is childless."

"Just checking," Merlin said.

"And I assume Guinevere's ratings would go up—I mean, surely they must!—if she delivered me a son. Or preferably a half dozen sons. But until such time as that happy event occurs . . . Well, frankly, I fear the effects of the encroaching propaganda of that motherless swine, Mordred."

"Mordred . . . Ah! That upstart who claims to be your illegitimate son and the deserving heir to your crown?"

"And who doesn't seem inclined to wait for the crown until I die of old age, either," Arthur said darkly. "I do wish that slimy toad would go back to wherever he came from."

"Er, is there any chance he might actually *be* your son?"

Arthur's face grew red. "I know what you *really* want to ask, so why don't you just ask it? You want to ask if the *other* thing they say about his parentage is true, don't you? Who his mother is? The woman they say I supposedly sired him with? As if I would *ever* have . . . um, you know."

"I have no idea what you mean, sire." Merlin's reputation for wisdom wasn't just spin; he quickly changed the subject. "But to return to the matter of the queen's low ratings, Your Majesty, I do agree with you that positive public opinion about the Pendragons is crucial for the stability of the kingdom. Although the queen herself is not an entirely objectionable monarch with whom to share a castle, there is certainly a serious problem with the British public's perception of her."

"Agreed! So what shall we do, Merlin?"

"I shall have to dwell upon the matter," the magician replied.

"They're called the *what*?" Queen Guinevere said to her husband and his elderly advisor.

"The Quintessential Quartet," Merlin replied.

Arthur added helpfully, "There are four of them."

"Four? A quartet? Really?" The Queen glanced at her spouse. "You surprise me."

"Welsh, sallow, blunt, educated, accomplished, *and* sarcastic," Arthur said to Merlin. "Can the Quartet really help us?"

"Farfetched though it may seem," replied the sage, "I believe it's possible. They have an impressive résumé of image makeovers."

The queen set aside the trigonometry problem she'd been working on for fun, when interrupted in her study (which, for the sake of cultural sensibilities, everyone called her "solarium"). She said, "So you believe these four fellows can bring stability to the kingdom and security to the monarchy by making me seem more suitable to the mainstream sensibilities of the British public and appealing to traditional cultural constructs of aristocratic womanhood?"

"Huh?" said Arthur.

Merlin gestured to the queen and said to Arthur, "I believe that's exactly the sort of thing the Quintessential Quartet can fix."

"Fix?" Guinevere said ominously.

"Er, *modify*, Your Majesty. At least, when we're in public."

"The queen continues sinking in the opinion polls," Arthur said, "dragging me along with her. I'm ready to try anything!"

Guinevere sighed and said to Merlin, "Very well. If His Majesty wishes it, and if you believe it's in the best interests of the kingdom, I accede."

"You what?" Arthur said.

"I'll meet with the Quintessential Quartet and cooperate with their advice."

"Ah! Thank you!" cried Arthur. "God save the Queen!"

"I'm convinced this is for the best, my lady."

"Whatever," said Guinevere.

"The sons of Lot are waiting in the main hall," said Merlin.

"Who?" said Guinevere.

"The Quintessential Quartet."

"They're King Lot's sons?" Arthur said in surprise. "That old reprobate?"

"I'll have a page fetch them," said Merlin.

"I suppose you must," Guinevere said in resignation.

A short time later, four young men entered the queen's study. Two of them were dark, and two were fair. All were dressed in the latest mode of courtly fashion. One of them daringly sported a faintly Moorish look in his ensemble. Another had long golden hair that any maiden would envy.

"Good knights," Merlin said, "I present you to Their Majesties, the King and Queen."

The fellow with long golden hair bowed with a flourish. "My humble obeisance, sire! And my lady Queen, it is a great privilege to meet you. I am Sir Gawain, your new fashion consultant."

The other blond man bowed next and introduced himself as Sir Gaheris, in charge of comportment and composure.

"I'm Sir Agravain," said the Moorishly dressed brother. "I instruct our clients on culture and class consciousness."

And the final brother, Sir Gareth, identified himself as a decorator. "And your Majesty, we can't get started soon enough. If I may be frank, my lady, this solarium—"

"It's my study, actually."

"—is a *disaster*. It almost looks like ... like a *study!*" Gareth shivered with distaste.

"It *is* a study," said the Queen.

"I can see I *totally* have my work cut out for me," said Gareth, looking around at the chamber.

"Ohmigawd, me too!" said Sir Gawain. "That *gown* you're wearing, Your Majesty! Tsk, tsk tsk!"

Guinevere looked down in puzzlement at the respectable gown she wore. "Is it unacceptable?"

"You're the q*ueen*," Gawain said, flipping his long golden hair. "'Acceptable' is totally *un*acceptable! You need to make a *statement* with your ensemble. To lead fashion. To *wow* the eye and dazzle the masses!"

"Oh."

"And look at the way Her Majesty slouches," said Gaheris, shaking his head sadly. "I have come not a moment too soon!"

"I read a lot," said Guinevere. "I guess I get into the habit of rounding my shoulders when I'm absorbed in my r—"

"You *read* a lot?" said Agravain in horror. "Oh, dear! Oh, no, no, no. That won't do, it won't do at *all*. You must cut back on that immediately, Your Majesty!"

"I must? But—"

"A little reading of your prayer book each morning. Perhaps a love verse now and then, in the afternoons. That's what is appropriate for a gentlewoman," said Agravain. "Anything more than that is excessive and unbecoming."

"Love verses?" the queen said lifting one brow. "I really don't think—"

"Thinking should also be kept to a minimum," instructed Sir Agravain.

"Heaven preserve us!" said Gareth, prowling around the Queen's study. "Where did that wall tapestry come from? It is *so* last century."

"It was part of the queen's dowry," said Merlin.

"Ah!" Gareth and Gawain exchanged an eye roll. "From Wales. Well, that explains it."

"If you please—" the queen began, raising her arm to order them out of the chamber.

"Oh, Your Majesty!" Gaheris seized her hand. "What harsh gestures you have! Loosen the wrist, my lady. *Curve* the arm. *Soften* the elbow. Like so." He moved her hand and arm around as if she were a string puppet.

"Oh, my," said Arthur approvingly. "My goodness. That small, simple touch is already a distinct improvement, young man! Merlin, do you see how much more womanly the queen suddenly looks?"

"Womanly?" Guinevere repeated as Gaheris pushed and prodded her shoulders into a straighter position, then took her other arm and started shaking it into quivering limpness. "Surely I currently look more like a rag doll than like a woman?"

"Not a 'woman,'" said Agravain, holding up an admonishing finger.

"No, indeed!" said Gawain.

"A *woman*?" said Gaheris. "Egad!"

"You are not a woman, Your Majesty," said Gawain. "You are a *lady*."

"Oh, Merlin!" Arthur embraced the old wizard. "You have once again set me on the correct path to destiny. These young knights are brilliant!"

"Indeed," said Merlin, sounding rather pleased. "I think we may be onto something here."

"Are you sure . . ." Guinevere ceased speaking for a moment when Gaheris took her chin in his hand and waggled it.

"Show *delicacy* in the set of your jaw, my lady, not resolve," he said. "And always be sure to hesitate before you speak, as if not sure your thoughts are worthy of being voiced."

"Are you sure these gentle knights know what they're doing?" Guinevere asked Arthur and Merlin, failing miserably to hesitate before voicing her thought.

Gaheris sighed and said, "We'll work on it."

"Have faith, Your Majesty!" cried Sir Gareth.

"Be of good cheer," said Sir Gawain. "The Quin Quart are on the job!"

Arthur blinked. "The who?"

"It's what they call us up north ever since we turned around Beowulf's image," said Gaheris.

Arthur's face brightened. "You worked with Beowulf?"

Merlin said, "I told you they came highly recommended, sire."

"Worked with Beowulf?" repeated Gareth. "I think it's fair to say we *made* Beowulf."

"At the risk of bragging," said Agravain, "he was just another uncouth warlord with a man-eating monster on his hands when *we* met him."

"Living in that garish wreck of a castle," said Gareth with distaste.

"Spitting on the floor of his own dining hall," said Gaheris fastidiously.

"And the fabrics he wore," said Gawain. "*Tragic.*"

"He was loathed by his own men in those days," added Agravain. "Also by the villagers, his wife, his children, and the other local warlords. Even his mother thought he was a loser."

"In short," said Gareth, "he was reviled and ridiculed."

"Ignored and overlooked," said Gaheris.

"And *so* badly dressed," said Gawain.

Agravain prompted, "And *now* what is he?"

"A *hero*!" cried Lot's four sons in unison.

"Beloved of the masses!" said Gaheris.

"The most envied and emulated fashion plate of the northern lords," said Gawain.

"And the featured star of a major epic poem!" said Gareth.

"Oh, Merlin!" cried Arthur. "Camelot is truly saved!"

"The queen has gone out riding?" said Arthur to the Quin Quart. "*Alone*?"

"Yes, sire," said Sir Gareth, supervising the hanging of new French tapestries in the Queen's solarium.

"But I thought you were going to put a stop to that sort of thing!"

"Becoming fabulous is a *process*, Your Majesty," Agravain said soothingly. "It's not possible to change all of a client's flaws at once. It takes some time."

Arthur nodded. "Well, all right. Given the miracles you've already accomplished with the queen, I'm sure you know best."

In the month since the Quin Quart had arrived at Camelot, the queen had become graceful, fashionable, and demure in her public appearances. The noble-women of Camelot were already starting to imitate her new mode of dress, new way of gesturing, and new style of speaking. Even her sallow complexion, previously abhorred, was now becoming all the rage.

Gaheris shook his head. "But we're not quite the miracle workers you'd hoped for, sire. Not yet."

"Oh, indeed you are!"

"No," Gawain said modestly, "we've fallen short of our goals so far."

"But the queen is a much improved woman!" said Arthur. "Er, lady."

"And yet," said Gareth, "the latest opinion polls that Merlin shared with us this morning show that there is still considerable room for growth in her popularity."

"At the moment," Gaheris said, "one clumsy gesture or sarcastic comment, and the polls could dip."

"Even nosedive," said Gawain.

"Hmmm. So what do you propose to do next?" said Arthur.

"We're still thinking about ..." Agravain paused as they heard someone approaching the solarium. "Hark! Could that be the queen I hear returning?"

Gaheris frowned. "I certainly hope not. Listen to those clumping footsteps!"

There was a brief moment of dismay when it was indeed Guinevere who appeared at the entrance to the chamber. But then Gaheris exhaled a sigh of relief when they saw that she was accompanied by a large young man whose sturdy boots accounted for the footsteps they'd heard.

Both the queen and her companion were quite disheveled, however, which condition caused cries of anguish among Lot's sons.

"Of *course* I'm damn well disheveled," said the queen, pushing past the fluttering knights to fling herself into a chair.

"*Language*, my lady," admonished Agravain.

"And posture!" cried Gaheris.

"I have today engaged in mortal combat with half a dozen young swain—or perhaps I should say *swine*," the queen snapped. "Don't nag me right now."

"Combat?" exclaimed Gaheris. "Oh, no!"

"Even worse," scolded Agravain, "a clever play on words? *What* did we agree about that, madam?"

"Oh, my lady," said Gaheris in agonized tones, "has all our hard work been for naught? Have you absorbed none of our teachings?"

"And what *have* you done to this fabulous Paris gown, Your Majesty?" wailed Gawain, plucking at the queen's bloodstained sleeve.

"Oh, good God! I'm sorry I forgot," said the Queen through clenched teeth, "even for a short while, all your precious lessons about being useless, helpless, and brainless! But I was distracted by the task of saving this young man's life, if you please!"

All eyes turned to the stranger who had arrived with the queen.

A tall, good-looking fellow, he stared back at them with a blank, amiable expression.

Finally, Gaheris instructed, "Introduce yourself to His Majesty, King Arthur, sir."

"Huh?" The fellow blinked. "King ... Oh! The king? *Oh*. Pardon me! I didn't realize ..." He spoke with a foreign accent. "I am Sir Lanzelet von Lakzikoven, son of King Ban."

"Who's that?" asked Arthur.

"Apparently he's some Germanic king," said Guinevere.

"Bavarian," corrected Lanzelet.

"And King Melwas of the Summer Country kidnapped this fellow and held him for ransom."

"Good heavens!" said Arthur.

"But apparently Ban isn't that wealthy. Or maybe he just doesn't miss Lanzelet that much," the Queen continued.

"Papa does have a lot of sons," Lanzelet offered. "I'm not sure he even noticed I was missing until he received the ransom demand."

"So King Ban refused to pay the ransom. And after a couple of years of feeding and clothing Lanzelet," Guinevere continued, "Melwas evidently decided that the abduction was becoming too expensive and he'd better cut his losses."

"I beg you, Your Majesty," said Agravain, "not to use such a vulgar term as 'cut his l—' "

"So he decided to have Lanzelet killed," the queen continued. "And so half a dozen of Melwas' villains seized Lanzelet and dragged him out of the castle and into the forest."

"I was so scared I nearly wet myself," said Lanzelet.

The Quin Quart blinked in unison.

"But luckily," said Guinevere, "in an effort to escape the stifling effect of your makeover of my image, gentlemen, I was out riding in the Summer Country when those six rough fellows were dragging this unarmed, frightened knight out into the greenwood, where they planned to murder him and leave his body for carrion."

"Her Majesty was most bold and terrifying," Lanzelet said. "She came riding out of the greenery like a banshee from hell, screeching at the top of her lungs and shooting arrows at my captors."

"Oh, *no*," wailed Gaheris. "Screeching? A banshee? *Archery*?"

With a stern expression, Agravain said to Guinevere, "Is this true?"

"It seemed like a good idea at the time," Guinevere said stonily.

"Two of my captors were mortally wounded by her arrows," Lanzelet said. "A third rode away in terror."

"So I took out two more in hand-to-hand combat," said Guinevere. "Luckily, I had my dagger with me."

"This blood will *never* come out of this sleeve," Gawain said despairingly. "Couldn't you have been more careful?"

"And by the time I was finished with those two ruffians," said the queen, yanking her sleeve out of Gawain's grasp—

"Never *yank*," said Gaheris.

"—Lanzelet had dealt with the remaining villain."

The Bavarian beamed at this recognition of his valor.

Gareth groaned and held his head in his hands. "This is a disaster."

"If word of this gets out," said Gawain, "we're doomed."

"The polls will sink to a new all-time low." Forgetting his comportment, Gaheris slumped down onto a carved trunk and sat there brooding, his shoulders hunched.

"No!" said Agravain. "Look how far we've already come! I refuse to accept defeat now. There must be something we can do."

Distressed at seeing the morale of the Quin Quart at such a low ebb, Arthur tried to rally them. "Now fellows, let's look on the bright side. An abduction was ended and a foul murder plot thwarted. By God's grace, an innocent life was preserved because a brave soul happened along. Even if that soul was, alas, the queen."

"Oh, thank you very much," Guinevere said.

"I believe the Quin Quart has spoken to you about the evils of sarcasm in a lady," Arthur said pointedly.

"Oh, for the love of . . ." Guinevere sighed. "Never mind. I'm too tired to argue."

"For the love of . . . love of . . . *Love*." Agravain lifted his head. "Wait a moment. Wait just a *moment*!"

"What is it?" asked Gareth.

"Love . . . a brave soul . . . an innocent life saved . . ." Agravain's intent expression took on the glow of inspiration.

Gaheris gasped and leaped to his feet, his face animated now. "Of course!"

"Of course, what?" said Arthur.

"Ohmigawd!" said Gawain, looking at his brothers. "I think I see where you're going with this!"

"Going with what?" said Arthur.

Gareth slapped his forehead. "Ah-hah! It's so obvious!"

Gaheris clapped his hands and did a little hop. "It's what we've been missing!"

"It completes the makeover!" cried Gawain.

"*What* does?" asked Arthur.

Momentarily forgetting class consciousness in his enthusiasm, Agravain seized the King's hands. "*Courtly love*."

"Courtly love?" said the queen. "Oh, no. No, please. Not *that*."

"Oh, yes!" said Gareth. "The polls will shoot through the roof!"

"They will?" Arthur clapped his hands and did a little hop, too. "Er . . . how? Why?"

"We'll make hay out of today's unfortunate episode," explained Agravain. "We'll let it leak that King Melwas abducted the queen—"

"Oh, as if *I'd* ever be clumsy enough to let that dolt and his worthless minions capture me," Guinevere said in disgust. Then she glanced at Lanzelet. "Er, no offense intended."

"Huh?" Lanzelet said.

"Yes, the queen was captured, but fortunately," continued Agravain, "Sir Lanzelet von Lakzikoven . . ."

"Ouch!" said Gareth. "That *name*."

"Hmmm, yes, I agree," said Gaheris. "It's got to go."

"The whole Bavarian thing has got to go," said Gawain. "The hero of a love story should always be French."

"What hero?" said Guinevere.

"French . . ." Agravain pondered this. "Sir Lanzelet . . . Lanzel . . . Ah! Sir Lancelot?"

"Yes!" said Gawain. "And we can change 'von Lakzikoven' to. . . ." He thought about it for a moment and said, "How about 'du Lac?'"

Agravain tried it out. "Lancelot du Lac . . . Sir Lancelot du Lac. I like it!"

"So," said Gareth, "Sir Lancelot, the French knight, happens along as the queen's captors are preparing to murder her—"

"And saves her!" said Arthur, catching on now. "Defeating six ruffians in mortal combat!"

"Exactly!" said Gaheris. "And, naturally, the two of them fall madly in love."

"Yes!" cried Arthur. "The two of them fall madly in . . . Er, hang on."

"It'll be the greatest love story of the year!" said Gawain.

"Of the century!" said Gaheris.

"Of all time!" said Agravain.

"Let's just back up a step here," said Arthur.

"In love?" Guinevere said incredulously. "Have you lost your mind? I have spent all day with this fellow, and take it from me, he has all the intelligence and ingenuity of an acorn. Do you really think I'd fall in love with someone like him?" She added to Sir Lancelot du Lac, "Er, no offense intended."

"Huh?" said the formerly Bavarian knight.

"More to the point," said Arthur, "the queen is *my*

lady wife. She can't go around loving some French knight!"

"It's courtly love, sire," Agravain said soothingly. "Nothing happens. The lovers just act noble, write poetry, and sings songs."

"You're sure about this?"

"Absolutely."

"And it's all the rage," said Gawain. "Especially on the Continent."

"A heroic rescue followed by unconsummated love . . ." Gaheris nodded. "Oh, believe us, sire, it'll make the queen the most popular lady since the Virgin Mary."

"Excellent!"

"This will backfire," said Guinevere morosely. "Mark my words, gentlemen, this thing will go wrong in the end."

"Oh, nonsense," said Arthur, swayed by visions of soaring public opinion and a continentally fashionable court. "These are our image consultants, madam. We should trust their guidance."

The Queen sighed. "Fine. Whatever. But let's be clear about one thing. I'm not going to gaze longingly at Lanzelet—"

"Lancelot," corrected Agravain.

"—at jousts or in the banqueting hall."

"Of course you're not," said Gawain.

"Indeed, no," said Gaheris. "That wouldn't be seemly."

"You'll avoid his gaze, avoid speaking with him, and eschew his company. You'll try never even to mention him," instructed Agravain.

"Well, yes, I can do that," Guinevere said, glancing dismissively at the knight.

"And you will do the same, Sir Lancelot," instructed Gaheris.

"Huh?" said Lancelot.

"To gaze on the queen is too painful for you," explained Gareth.

"Oh, I don't mind it," said Lancelot. "It's true that

she's Welsh and sallow, but she's not a bad sort, really. And she did save my life."

"Which is something you will never mention again," Agravain said firmly.

"From now on, you will avoid looking at the queen, avoid even mentioning her," said Gaheris.

"Well, if you say so," Lancelot said amiably.

"In this way," continued Gaheris, "your actions will confirm that you are hopelessly, desperately—and above all, *purely*—in love with the King's wife."

"From time to time," Agravain continued, "you will absent yourself from Camelot, to escape the pain of your tragic and unconsummated love."

"A quest!" said Gareth as inspiration struck again. "He can occasionally go off on a quest of some kind."

"Ooooh," said Gawain "I like that!"

"Perhaps he could go in search of his abandoned dignity," Guinevere said with a smirk.

"*Never* smirk," Gaheris instructed.

"Gentlemen," said Arthur, "this is excellent work."

"Oh, good grief," said Guinevere.

"*Grief* is a word which scarcely describes my reaction to the depth of this latest depravity!" said Merlin, entering the chamber.

"What depravity?" asked Arthur. "What's amiss?"

Merlin sighed. "It's that verminlike upstart again: Mordred."

"Oh, no. What now?"

"He has convinced some of your vassals to side with him in his quarrel with you," said Merlin. "He's also spreading more rumors about, er, his supposedly incestuous parentage."

"What?" Arthur's face turned beat red. "As if I would *ever* have . . . um, you know."

"Never fear, sire!" said Agravain. "There's one key weapon that this Mordred fellow lacks in his ill-advised quarrel with you, and that's . . ."

"The Quin Quart!" cried Lot's sons in unison.

"Now that we've got the queen's image problems solved, sire," said Gareth, "we can focus on making *you* the most fabulous monarch in all the British isles!"

"All of Europe!" said Gawain.

"All of history!" said Gaheris.

"You really think you can help?" Arthur asked.

"Sire, consider your future secured," Agravain said warmly.

"Excellent!" said Arthur. "Where shall we start?"

"That's easy!" said Gareth. "Now that construction's nearly finished on the new hall, I was in there yesterday, since it will need decorating, of course. Well, you've got an immense round table in there. Very impressive. I've never seen its like anywhere."

"Indeed." Arthur said, "Hah! What did I tell you, Merlin?"

"And, sire," said Agravain, "we have some *fabulous* ideas about what can be done with that table . . ."

HOW JACK GOT HIS SELF A WIFE

John Alvin Pitts

John A. Pitts fled Kentucky for the Pacific Northwest over a decade ago but draws heavily from his
roots in the fiction he writes. He has sold stories to
anthologies like *Swordplay* and *Zombie Raccoons
and Killer Bunnies*, also from DAW. Other tales
can be found in great magazines like *Talebones*
and *Aeon*. He has a Masters in Library Science
from the University of Kentucky, and by day, he
works as an IT contractor in the aerospace industry. John lives in Bellevue, WA, with his wife, two
children, and a Jack Russell Terrier named Frodo.
He invites readers to contact him through *www.
japitts.net*.

Now, don't be thinking you know the littlest rind of
Jack's legend. There's more to the tale then many a
folk realize. I'll grant ya he's a handsome fella, but the
trouble with Jack is his tendency to high off on some
fool adventure. Don't get me wrong, he gives as good
as he's got, but sometimes the telling is a lot taller than
the deed.

But I do love him, the scoundrel, since the first time

I laid eyes on him. You shoulda seen him rollin' over the hill that fine spring morning, wrastlin' a bear for the sheer love of fightin'. I'd been sleeping under a tree when I heard what sounded like somebody swinging a sack full of polecats. You never heard such spitting and crying—and don't get me started on the cussin'. His momma would have been plum ashamed of the way that boy used the king's English. By the time he and the bear noticed me standing there under a tree with three loaded sacks at my feet, the sun had swung up over the horizon, flashing the pink and purple of her bloomers across thc sky.

Man and beast ceased their feuding long enough to look me up and down once or twice. Jack, well right away I can see he's sweet and funny, and a little bit on the lecherous side, by the grin that stole across his face. The bear didn't take as much notice of me, except for the fact I'd been recently dipped in honey by a giant before I'd made my escape.

"What're ya'll starin' at?" I asked the two of 'em.

The bear just let out a low rumble and licked his chops.

"Who might you be and why in blazes are you standing there drippin' honey all over my sleepin' clover?" Jack asked, puffing his chest out and hooking his thumbs in his suspenders.

"Name's Molly," I said with a brief curtsy. "I don't see no posting or notices that claim the ground under this oak tree belongs to you, nor mister bear," but I likely figured the bear had the greater claim.

"Name's Jack," Jack said, striding right up to me and holding his hand out like as to shake my own.

The bear grumbled again, raising up on his hind legs and showing off every inch of his eight foot length.

"Big bear," I said, impressed.

"Purt near a hundred stone," Jack said with a smile.

"So, why are you boys tearing across the greenness of God's good earth and depriving a tired girl a chance at some decent sleep?" I asked, giving him my best withering stare.

Jack, he just grinned like a fox in a hen house, all teeth and meanness. "Why, for the fun of it."

Typical answer from a man, I reckoned. "And what does the bear get out of it?"

The bear fell back down on all fours, pawed at the ground a couple times, and sorta roared in my general direction.

"See," he says to me.

I just shook my head. "You want to go acting all a fool, please do it someplace else. Killing giants and witches makes a girl tired. I need a bit of shut-eye."

Jack and the bear both fell to the ground laughing. I stood, showing the three bags at my feet, watching the two of them, rolling around in the first flashes of the brand spankin' new day.

When they finally were quit of their merriment, Jack stood again and faced me square. "I can see you've got three bags at your feet," he paced around me to the left. "What's in 'em?"

"Why, gold of course," I said as sassy as I could to cover the lie. "I just told you I killed a giant and a witch. Weren't you listening?"

I turned slightly, keeping him to my front, but trying to keep an eye out on that ole bear.

"But how do we know it ain't just full of laundry you were supposed to be taking down to the river to pound rocks with?"

The bear chuckled, which put me a little to the side of angry, cause of course he was mostly right—one small bag of gold, a sack with a crust of bread and a rind of cheese, and a large bag of laundry I was supposed to have washed for my mistress before that old witch snatched me up from the river. "And why is it any of your business, jack-n'ape?"

That sure knocked the grin off his face.

We stood there, eyeballing one another, waiting. The

light of the rising sun settled across the open ground, pushing the shadows off the grassy hillock and across the stony field below the oak.

"I believe you might want to be more polite to your betters," Jack snapped.

Then it was my turn to laugh. "Betters?" I asked. "Why, all I sees is a boy in short pants playing with a smelly old bear."

Both Jack and the bear stood up straight, heads back like I'd just slapped 'em, which I think they deserved at that point in the conversation.

"I'm tired and hungry. If you think you are so high-and-mighty, why don't you fetch me some breakfast?"

"Now, why in the whole wide world would I go and fetch vittles for an ornery girl who tells tales and insults strangers?"

"Oh, well," I said, shuffling my feet and glancing at my toes. "If you think it's too hard, I guess I'll just eat this here bag of gold instead."

They laughed a might until I reached down and pulled a bit of yellow cheese from the second bag, rattled a few coins in the smallest bag and popped the cheese into my mouth.

"Now wait one little minute," Jack said and strode up the hill. He and the bear put their heads together and talked for the longest time. When they was done, Jack looked down the hill at me and clasped his arm over the bear's broad back. "If we promise to go off and fetch you a bite, would you be willing to trade us for that bag of gold you was so willing to eat?"

"That's fair," I said sitting down under the oak again. "You run off and fetch me a roast goose with some plum sauce, a loaf of fine baked bread, and a bit of good sweet cream, I'll hand you this here sack of gold."

At the call for goose, Jack began to bristle and sputter. Just as he opened his mouth to protest, I nudged the smallest of the bags over and gold spilled out. The way the sunlight sparkled off all those shiny coins must've mesmerized Jack. He stood with his mouth open for the longest time, a bit of spittle rolling off his lower lip. The bear swatted him upside the head, sending Jack into a full somersault. When Jack got back on his feet, he rubbed his head and glared at the bear. "All right," he huffed. "You didn't have to whack me in the head."

The bear grunted, sat down on his back-side, and yawned.

"Goose it is," Jack said, stomping back to the bear. "Fresh-baked bread and sweet cream."

"Don't forget a knife and fork," I said as he and the bear ambled over the hill. He tossed back a look that set me to laughing.

I pushed the gold back into the sack, tucked the three bags deep into the roots of the oak, and curled up beside them to sleep. Three days and nights I slept under that oak, eating a bit of bread, and drinking from the nearby crick. Before you knew it, the sun was dipping toward the west of the fourth day when I heard the sound of bells.

I sat up, yawning and rubbed the honey out of my eyes. Across the hill came Jack leading a small wagon loaded with food. The bear was harnessed like a goat, pulling the contraption and as about as disgruntled about it as one could get.

The smell of roast goose flowed down the hillside and perked me right up.

"Why, Jack," I said, standing and stretching. "Time for a late lunch?"

"Time for you to give over one of those sacks of gold," he said sourly.

"What happed that it took you so long?" I asked, scooping a bag out from amongst the roots.

"That old fellah a ways back the road made me clean all his stables before he'd give me the first whiff of food. Spent two days di-verting a quick running stream into the stables, and out toward that yonder valley," he pointed to the west with pride. "Cleaned the stables and fertilized the land thereabouts at the same time."

The bear grunted and sat down. The cart nearly tipped over, and Jack blanched. "We woulda needed to cut all the hay in his fields to get the use of a pony," he grumbled. "But we worked it out." He unbuckled the bear from the wagon and bowed in my direction.

I strode up the hill to inspect Jack's work. The wagon was full of barrels and boxes, buckets and bags—each holding all kinds of good food, from goose and bread wrapped in brown paper to tubs of sweet cream, sacks of apples, salted pork, a barrel of pickles, and three types of cheeses. "Mighty nice work here," I said to him, slipping an apple from a sack and hefting in my hand. I set it back down in a puddle of honey.

"Better'n you asked for, I do believe," Jack said with a bit of pride in his voice. "So how about that gold?"

I thought about it for a moment, then shook my head walking away from the wagon. "I'm near drowned in honey, and that ain't no way for a woman to be."

The bear nodded and licked his jowls again.

"If you were any kind of gentlemen, you'd fetch me a kettle for a bath." I sighed heavily, swooning toward the side of the wagon. "I need a good hot bath before I can even think about eating a fine meal." I batted my sticky lashes at him. "You wouldn't want me to do a disservice to your fine deed?"

The bear moved to the cart and began snuffling around the spilt honey.

"Bath?" Jack asked, flummoxed.

"Yes," I said. "A nice hot bath, plenty of fire under a big kettle of water. You understand," I held my hands out in front of me, the honey dripping in great dollops.

"Where am I going to find a kettle big enough to put you in?"

I knew right where to get such a thing, as a matter of fact. That old giant I'd just killed, and the witch he lived with, had a kettle you coulda easily fit me inside, seeing as I was almost their supper a few days before.

"Run back over to the next holler away south," I said.

"Past that knobby hill that looks like a porcupine, you'll find a mean old house tucked in the shadow of the hill. In it you'll find a black pot big enough to suit a bath."

Jack looked up over the hills to the south. "How far?"

"No more than a night's walk," I said, striding back to the oak.

"A night's walk," Jack said, the anger rising up his neck to his cheeks. He was as cute as can be, that's for sure, but he tended to anger and rashness.

"A bath before I'll take a bite, it's the only ladylike thing to do."

The bear lapped at the honey pooling at my feet. I giggled when his great raspy tongue tickled my toes.

"And why wouldn't I just be taking my gold now, and going on about my business?" Jack said, watching the bear lick my left ankle.

"I'd surely add another of them sacks for you to have, if I could get a bath," I said.

At the thought of another sack—notice I never said gold—Jack began to pull all the food out of the back of the wagon. "Come on, fool bear. We gotta go get this here woman a bath." He spent the next while hooking that great big bear to that wagon again, climbed up on the buckboard and pulled it around to the south.

I blew a kiss off my palm toward Jack, who blushed all a sudden. "You may just save my life, young Jack."

"Come on, Bear," he called snapping the reigns. The bear snatched his head to the side, nearly pulling Jack from the wagon. No bit or bridle, but the reins led to the back of the halter.

"Thank you, mister bear," I said, holding my hand out toward the great beast.

The bear took a long swipe from my palm with his tongue, and he took off at a gallop. Jack had an odd look on his face as he rolled off the wagon and onto his back. He stood up, brushed the dust from his britches, smiled at me one bright time, and took off running after the bear.

They were gone for three days. I ate the crust and cheese from my pack, and drank the cold, sweet water from the crick that ran nearby. Each night I'd count the stars and think about Jack's sweet smile.

I was picking flowers on the west side of the hill when I heard the jangling of bells, and the halloo of Jack and the bear coming up out of the holler.

In the wagon was half a cord of wood and that giant's big stewpot.

He stopped the wagon at the bottom of the hill and stood with his arms spread wide. "You failed to mention the giant had a brother," he said, holding up a bloody sack. "Didn't know I'd have to take his head to take the pot. What say you now, honey-girl?"

I stood and clapped, tossing daisys into the wagon at Jack's feet. "You done fine, good Jack. Fine as can be. Toss that old thing over by the oak and let's get me a bath. My hero."

Jack beamed, chucked the bag with the giant's head to the base of the oak, and began to unload that big pot. He stacked the wood for a fire, but stopped when I coughed thrice in his direction.

He stiffened and stopped as he was striking a flint to the stack of wood. "Is there a problem, milady?"

I sighed at his sweet words. "As you are a gentleman," I said with a demure smile. "You'll understand that you need to build that fire atop the hill yonder."

Jack looked up the hill he and the bear had first tumbled down and swore under his breath. "And I'm sure you have a good reason why that's so," he said, a hint of bitter herb in his voice.

I blushed. "Why, it would be unseemly for you to be able to look down into my bath, now don't you think?"

He thought on that a moment, and it was Jack's turn to blush. Without nary a word he had a big fire going at the top of the hill and was carrying buckets of water up to pour into the big kettle. He carried one bucket, and the bear carried a second in his teeth. The bear must've been growing tired of the honey, or the game, because he growled and snapped at something Jack said. Jack dropped the bucket of water and launched into the bear. They both tumbled down the hillside and crashed into the stony field at the bottom. Both of them cracked their heads and sat dazed.

I fetched a large brown paper wrapping from the loaves of bread, soaked them in the vinegar brine from the cask of pickles and wrapped each of their heads. I carried the last pail of water up the hill, and brought the water to a near boil before banking the fire and slipping around to the back.

Jack and the bear watched the sunset, their heads in their hands, as I climbed into the hot bubbly water of the bath, clothes and all.

As I peeled each piece of clothing from my sugar crusted body, I flung it down the hill. After a bit, I was pink and clean as a whistle. Only I was naked as the day I was born.

"Jack," I called out. "For the final sack, I think I need you to fetch my clothes down to the crick and see them clear of honey."

"Once more into the breach," Jack said, standing and pressing the paper to his head. He picked up my honey drenched clothes and walked over to the crick.

The bear followed along, sullenly, and helped Jack wash out my clothes.

They brought them up the hill and draped them over rocks near the fire to dry.

"That's mighty fine, Jack," I smiled from the lip of the kettle. "You've certainly earned the three sacks."

"Have I also earned a kiss?" Jack asked edging toward the kettle.

I squealed and ducked down below the rim. "You stay back, you hooligan." A course, I only mostly wanted him to skedaddle.

Jack chuckled and reached his hands up on the rim of the kettle to lift himself up for a kiss, or a look, or both.

The bear, however, had had enough. It reared up, roaring and stamping in the last rays of the sun. He knocked Jack to the ground. I laughed as Jack rolled down the hill once more, the bear defending my dignity.

"You choosing her over me now?" Jack called out, scrambling to his feet.

I watched as the two of them began to fight again, fur and cuss words flying into the coming night.

With a sigh, I slipped deeper into my bath and waited.

Jack and the bear fought for seven hours, rolling east across into the wild lands and back west, over the fields he and the bear had fertilized days before.

Finally, they ended up rolling down the stream, each soaked through and battered. When the sun began to rise in the east, Jack strode up the hill, that bear's hide in his hands. The bear roared over the back side of the hill, naked as a jay-bird.

"My final gift to you, Molly fair. Will this bear skin earn me a kiss?"

I rose from the kettle, skin as wrinkled as a crone and kissed him on the end of his nose.

Jack did somersaults down the hill and picked up his three sacks. I slipped out of the kettle, pulling on my clothes and wrapping the bear's skin around me to ward off the cold.

Jack sat down under the oak and wept. The small sack of gold, being mostly stones, the empty cheese rind, and the sack of laundry hardly seemed fair.

But I slid down beside him, wrapping him in the bear skin and offered him a pickle. He brightened a bit and listened while I explained how the king over the holler where he'd cleaned out the stables would give us all the land to the west of his own for killing the giant.

Jack listened intently and scooted closer to me, resting his head on my shoulder.

"We can start a family," I said stroking his fine brown hair. "We can farm the land and raise a whole passel of children."

In that moment, wrapped in the fur of his friend the bear, I saw the wild gleam in his eye, the fear and the need to run off to the woods and battle the world.

But a kiss to the side of his mouth settled things, and we struck our final bargain.

Now Jack's a good man, when he's not sleeping in the barn or chasing after some tomfool adventure. He brings home a bit of gold, or cheese, or a goose now and again, but his claim about killing seven giants at a single blow and pulling the moon from the sky to taste a bit of green cheese, why, that ain't nothing more than fancy talk to impress the townies.

And it ain't like he forgets I'm a sittin' here, raising up his three daughters and keeping the farm. He recalls quick enough when I have to go down in the holler and cut him out of some ogre's stew pot or giant's gunnysack he's found himself caught up in. The trouble is, come spring, or a anytime a good load of firewood needs cutting, my man Jack will get a hankering to have some road under his feet and a open sky above his head.

That old bear is the one thing about this whole mess I worry about. I hung his skin outside our new house after the king had given us the land and all. Each night I put out a pot of honey and a jar of daisies, but he never came back.

When Jack is in his cups and running wild, I think of that bear and wonder if I had been rescued by the wrong one.

IF THE SHOE FITS

Dayle A. Dermatis

An interviewer once said of Dayle A. Dermatis that "she has so many aliases, you'd think she was a spy!" A dabbler in several genres (and with several coauthors), she's published novels with Virgin Books and short stories all over the place. She lives in southern California within scent of the ocean, and she and her husband spend their spare time following the band Styx around the country (and sometimes out of it), exploring the world via motorcycle, renovating their 1911 Craftsman home, doing historic recreation, and lounging in their hot tub. She loves music, cats, Wales, Joss Whedon, faeries, magic, laughter, and defying expectations. You can read more about Dayle and her pseudonyms at *www.cyvarwydd.com*.

When I heard the royal family would be holding a ball to find suitable wife material for the prince and heir, my mind went into overdrive.

But not in the way anyone would expect.

I didn't have specific information about how a royal household was run; I didn't know the number and skill sets of the servants, or even how many people would be invited to this shindig. But within ten minutes I had a pretty good sense of how much it would cost per person, even factoring in peacock meat (which seemed like a waste to me, what with chickens being that much cheaper per pound, but I also understood the art of entertaining sometimes meant being flashy to impress certain guests).

Not, mind you, that it was any of my business. Party planning wasn't really where I wanted to end up, but I loved the idea of it. Just the way my brain works: a challenge, a puzzle. I can put together a fundraising dinner and auction for 50 people without breaking a sweat. The concept of overseeing a royal ball made me go *squee* (on the inside).

Actually going to the ball? Meh. Marrying royalty didn't interest me in the least, and besides, I had finals coming up.

My aunt, Sheila, thought differently.

"It would be a good networking opportunity for you," she'd said.

"I'm not in the market for a husband," I'd said.

She'd rapped my knuckles with her spoon, not enough to hurt, but it got my attention. "Don't be an idiot," she said. "I'm talking about *business* networking. You're about to graduate with honors. All those other girls giggling around the prince? Their daddies will be there, and their daddies run corporations that have job openings for the right candidates."

Oh. Duh. I'd been so busy helping my sisters not lose their freaking minds over the ball that it hadn't even occurred to me that this could be all about the schmoozing. Bad future entrepreneur, no BMW.

There's a reason why Aunt Sheila runs a thriving chain of bakeries.

Around me, young women clumped together, giggling (just as Aunt Sheila had predicted) and craning their necks to get a glimpse of Rupert, Prince Royal and Most

Eligible Bachelor. I, on the other hand, had handed out a fair number of business cards and was feeling rather smug about myself.

Everybody says I work too hard. I just cannot abide a disorganized house. After my mother died, my father . . . well, he was grieving, plus he had his own business to run, so the household fell to me. I was still young, but I wasn't stupid. I could clip coupons and plan a week's worth of simple, nutritious meals.

When my dad remarried, bringing not only a new wife into the house but also two new stepsisters for me, I suggested a rota of chores. Seemed only fair. They all laughed and went on gadding about.

So I just went on managing things. Oh, it was a PITA, sure, but with more people in the house, *somebody* had to keep things running smoothly. Money was tight, but I was able to convince Dad to let me hire a weekly cleaning lady, so I had enough time to work on my degree in business management.

I was thinking about bailing and heading home to get some studying in when the crowd fell silent and parted, and there was Prince Rupert, handsome and dashing. He smiled, white teeth and dimples flashing, and the women around me gave a collective sigh.

Okay, he was a looker, I'll give him that. Piercing blue eyes, thick black hair, square jaw. Broad shoulders, slim hips. Almost a cliché.

He surveyed the people in this corner of the ballroom. I did my best to blend into the wallpaper. It would be the height of rudeness to sneak away, and I had a reputation to cultivate. With all the excitedly heaving bosoms around me, there was no way he'd notice . . .

Oh, *crap*. He was coming right for me.

He asked me to dance, and women who'd been planning their wedding invitations glared daggers at me as we walked away.

"Your Highness," I said as soon as we were out of

earshot of the crowd, "I'm honored by your interest, but I hope you'll allow me to speak plainly."

"Please," he said with a gracious nod of his head that struck me as a little too practiced.

Saying *I'm not interested in you* seemed a little blunt, so I explained that I didn't think I was princess material and that I had plans for a career and I was here largely to put those plans in motion. Only I said it much more politely and flowery.

"Well, I have to thank you for your honesty," he said. "When you first said you weren't princess material, it sounded like a line, but I think you really mean it. Believe me, that's refreshing. I've been desperate to talk to someone who has more on her mind than clinging to my every word and answering in a charming way that's designed to make me think she's The One."

It was quite a speech, let me tell you.

"If you want to find potential wives tonight, you probably ought to be dancing with them, not me," I said.

"Protocol states I must give you the full dance," he said, "and I appreciate the chance to talk to someone interesting. Plus, I've been dying to ask you: Where did you get your shoes?"

My . . . huh? What?

Aunt Sheila had lent them to me. She'd studied in Paris back in the day and had saved up her money for the one indulgence. I didn't know a shoe from a ship, but I knew these were exquisite, so-expensive-it-takes-your-breath-away pumps. They were, I knew, one of a kind, too—the burgundy silk and black lace were remnants, and no other pair had been made with the same fabrics.

I explained it all to Rupert (who was, I might mention, an incredibly good dancer).

"They really are fabulous," he said. "I wish I could get a better look at them. Would you like a drink?"

I blinked, recovered, and the next thing I knew we were in a private antechamber, and I was drinking the best damn champagne on earth, and he was turning one of my shoes over in his hands and examining the workmanship. He seemed to know what he was looking at.

He handed the pump back to me (I'd been afraid he'd gently replace it on my foot or something), and I slipped it on.

"You're so lucky," he said.

"Why?" I couldn't quite get that. He had the world at his fingertips, didn't he?

"You have choices," he said, "and the freedom to make those choices. My path is set: Marry a suitable woman, produce heirs, be the figurehead for a kingdom that already has a perfectly well-running government. The end."

Well . . . I'd never thought about that. "But there's so much you can do, with your connections and power. What about creating charities?"

"My future wife is expected to do that," he said. "Don't get me wrong, though—I do see those benefits. It's just that I'd give anything to have the freedom to pursue my own passions, live my own life." He waved a hand. "Oh, never mind."

I wanted to tell him to just go do whatever he bloody well wanted, because really, who was going to protest? Wasn't his decree practically law?

Then I thought about it. I could very well have moved out and left the chaos of my family home behind me, giving me tons more time to move ahead with my own plans. But I felt a responsibility to them—just as Rupert must feel toward the kingdom.

So we talked about that, and I have to say, he was pretty easy to talk to. I kinda liked him, in a "I've never had a brother" sort of way.

His counselor peeking in the door made us both realize how long ago we'd ditched the ball and made me realize just how late it was.

Crap.

There'd been no way in hell I could have driven

there; the traffic was beyond a gridlocked nightmare.
There wouldn't be any cabs. So if I didn't catch the last
train, which left Palace Station just after midnight, I'd
be stranded.

"Reallynicetalkingtoyou, gottago."

I grabbed my stuff from the coat check, laced on my
sneakers (there was no way I was going to commute
in those stilettos), and made a mad dash to the train
station.

It was only after I was sitting in the car and catching
my breath that I realized I'd dropped one of the shoes
somewhere along the way.

I said a word that *never* would have been appropriate
in front of royalty.

Thankfully Aunt Sheila was out of town, so I didn't
have to break the loss to her just yet. I was eyeballs-
deep in finals over the next few days, pulling all-nighters
at the library and crashing on a friend's sofa closer to
the university, so I didn't hear about the whole ruckus
until I stumbled home.

"Where have you been; I've left messages," my step-
mom said.

I pulled out my cell. Yep, there were messages. Who
knew?

"The palace has been looking for you." She twisted
her hands together. "We were hoping they were calling
about Genna or Clara."

"It's just about my shoe," I said. "I dropped it when I
was leaving. I'm sure they just want to return it."

But even I wondered why they couldn't have just
popped it into the mail, you know?

So I called back and was put on hold forever (royal
Muzak is no better than your local bank's, believe me)
before someone got back on the line and told me that
Prince Rupert would like to return the shoe to me personally, and was I free for a private dinner at the palace
tomorrow?

That just didn't bode well. I'd caught up on the news and knew that the prince hadn't selected a prospective wife (or even a short list of candidates) since the ball. I couldn't imagine Rupert taking the time to hang out with me when he had bigger fish to fry ... unless it was my fish he had an interest in.

Had I not made myself clear? Had *he* not made himself clear?

But I had to get that shoe back before Aunt Sheila got home.

I had a private audience with the prince in the "small" dining room, which was almost the size of my father's house. At least we weren't at opposite ends of the table that yawned the length of the room. If we had been, we'd've needed walkie-talkies.

We made small talk through the soup course, and then he leaned forward and said, "Ella."

His tone of voice made me vaguely itchy. I doubted I'd like what he had to say. "Your Highness."

"I have a business proposition for you."

Oh. Well, then. I sat forward. "I'm always interested in that."

"I need a wife."

I sat back. "I don't—"

"Please, hear me out." He looked almost as unhappy as I felt, so I let him continue. "I've met many fine women, so many who would be appropriate for the role of princess. But I ... have some special requirements, and I don't believe any of those women would understand or agree to them."

Great. He has a kinky streak.

"Those women are looking for a great romance, and that's something I can never give them," he continued.

Oh. A mistress, then, someone he could never put on the throne.

But no. He kept going. "You have other goals in life, ones that I can facilitate. I think we can both benefit from a joint venture."

He went on to detail what I'd get out of the deal, which included some pretty nifty corporate responsibilities. In return, I'd be his wife essentially in name only, and he'd be able to pursue his personal passions, as he'd called them.

The prenup included a confidentiality agreement, and when I read it, it was like a blinding light going off over my head. All of the signs had been there, but like everyone else, I just hadn't put them together.

His disinterest in the sea of heaving bosoms. His fascination with my fabulous shoes . . .

So there you have it. Rupert remains the country's figurehead and designs shoes and handbags (and occasionally hats) under a fake name. He's quite good; his latest line got a huge write-up in *Vogue*. We pay a private physician handsomely to keep quiet about the artificial insemination to get me pregnant. (Yeah, I've always focused on getting a career, but I never said kids were out of the question.)

And me? I get to be CFO of Rupert's design firm and manage the royal finances, and for fun I throw elaborate, glittering dinner parties and fundraisers for up to a thousand people.

Squee.

BIG MAN'S LITTLE WOMAN

Dory Crowe

Figment of an overactive imagination, Dory Crowe haunts the foggy bottom of make believe in Nobtucket—the quintessential Cape Cod, Massachusetts, town, second cousin to Lake Wobegon, Minnesota, and Cabot Cove, Maine. Any given day may find Dory hauling virtual lobster pots or raking cobbled clams, when not chronicling the adventures of restless Nobtucket neighbors—who fall in and out of love, solve murder and mayhem, and weather wash-ashores and tourists alike. For a taste of Dory's Olde Cape Cod, come visit the whole crew at *www. Nobtucket.com.*

A month and a day before Acacia Grimes' birth, five storks tried dropping Mrs. Bunyan's bouncing baby boy down the sandstone chimney next door. Paul got stuck so tight, Mr. Bunyan and Acacia's pa had to tear down that chimney stone by stone and dismantle half the house to get the boy free.

Some say it was the soot. Some say it was the lack of air. Some say his head got squeezed til his brains popped right out of his ears. Whatever the cause, Paul Bunyan grew up dumber than an ox and twice as big.

The storks were so busy the week Acacia came along—it being nine months after the snowiest December then on record—a hummingbird flew in with the baby girl slung from its beak. What she lacked in size, Acacia more than made up for in brains. At two months old, she could read, write and cipher to the rule of three.

Paul outgrew his pa's shirts and breeches at two weeks. Paul's ma took to sewing wagon wheel buttons on jeans and shirts she made from cloth she cut out of clipper ship sails. Acacia's ma fashioned yellow and black striped jumpers out of bumblebee hide and spider web thread.

Acacia's pa helped Paul's pa built a baby buggy out of a lumber wagon. They hitched it to a ten-ox team and fitted a walnut shell under the bonnet for Acacia. Townsfolk smiled and nodded and wished Mrs. Bunyan and Mrs. Grimes a good day whenever they drove Paul and Acacia to the general store in their custom-made buggies. Behind their backs, the townsfolk rolled their eyes and thanked their lucky stars little Johnny still fit into the blue sailor suit offered for sale in the display window of McGinty's Mercantile Emporium and little Suzie's toothless smile was big enough to see with the naked eye.

Now, a boy as large as Paul with a brain that small can become a worrisome thing, even in a town as big as Bangor, Maine. When Paul outgrew the wagon, the two neighbors built a raft; of course, they fitted a gimbaled milkweed pod on its mast for little Acacia. The raft floated down the Penobscot and into Penobscot Bay. Paul rocked and rolled in his new cradle, causing waves so big they sunk two clippers, three schooners and a newfangled paddle wheel steamer. Acacia, swinging free in her milkweed pod, never even got seasick.

On Paul's first birthday, when he'd long since clapped

and laughed all the window panes out of his house and the Grimes', his pa thought to distract his son with a pet: a baby blue calf named Babe.

Babe and Acacia hit it off right away. No bigger than a cricket, she sat in Babe's ear and watched Paul grow, and grow, and grow some more. She grew some, too, reaching her full height at the age of twelve—three and seven-eighths inches, give or take a sixteenth.

At breakfast Paul wolfed down forty bowls of porridge and a mile-high stack of flapjacks for every thimbleful Acacia's ma forced down her gullet. For lunch he picked seventeen turkeys clean. She filled up on two drops of broth. For dinner he devoured a side of beef, three sacks of potatoes and a bakery's worth of apple pie. She nibbled on celery strings and a lick of deviled ham.

You might say they growed up together, Paul and Acacia, if you could call Acacia growed. Round about the time a girl's head turns to dreams of boys and a boy's breeches fill with lust, Acacia moved from Babe's ear to Paul's. If it hadn't been for their tender ages and the difference in their sizes, they would have got married right then and there. To keep their parents happy, they settled for a long engagement, while they tried to figure out what to do about Paul's big . . . feet. You know what they say about the size of a man's feet.

Now, Paul, he had ideas as big as himself and twice as dumb. It took all Acacia's brains and the sugar-coated advice she whispered into his ear to keep Paul out of trouble. He would have been up that proverbial creek without a paddle if it weren't for his little woman. And that's a true fact.

Why, one cold night when Paul was logging the Pacific Northwest, a strong wind come a howling in off the ocean. Paul would have set the whole Cascade Range on fire, if Acacia hadn't made him pile rocks on top of his campfire. He kept piling and piling until he'd built Mount Hood. Took Acacia to make him stop.

Those 10,000 lakes in Minnesota? The storytellers got that one half right. It was Paul's big feet dug those lakes, but it was Acacia kept Paul from sinking like a stone into the bottomless muck. Wasn't til she fitted Babe and him out with snowshoes that he could keep the mud from sucking them down.

There are huge statues all over the north celebrating Paul and Babe. Not a one to the real brains of the outfit—Acacia.

There's the thirty-foot statue next to the Chamber of Commerce in Bangor, Maine, of course, and the slow-witted talker sitting in Brainerd, Minnesota. There's another talking Paul in Klamath, California, and the Canuck version in Ossineke, Minnesota. That's the one some dumb bastard took his pistol and shot Babe's blue balls clean off. But the strangest of all is the statue of Lucette, Paul's supposed girlfriend—some say wife—in Hackensack, Minnesota.

It all goes back to Paul's big . . . feet.

Despite their size difference, one day Paul propped Acacia in the crotch of an old oak tree, got down on one knee, and held out a 24K gold band.

"Will you marry me?"

He looked so shy and afraid Acacia almost laughed.

"Of course I will." She wrapped her arms around his pinky finger, failing to make them meet on the back side.

That very day, Ma Grimes started sewing a minuscule white satin dress with tatted neck and cuffs and a powder blue cummerbund to match her daughter's eyes. Acacia's hope chest brimmed over, as full as her heart.

They married in June under a fragrant canopy of white pine and oak in the Maine forest they both loved. Half the town turned out, and the other half watched from their rooftops.

For seven years they lived as man and wife, sharing their bed and their meals and their lives. Paul apprenticed to a lumberjack, and Acacia taught school. They seemed content.

Everything would have been just fine and dandy except for a certain large brunette from Trois Rivières, near Quebec City. Her name was Lucette.

On a hot July day in the middle of black fly season, she rode into town astride a three-legged, purple Guernsey cow. Paul clapped one eye on this buxom broad with the zee's and oui's and ooo-la-la's and lost what little mind he possessed, which, as previously mentioned, didn't amount to enough to fill a half a goober shell.

And Babe! Well, Babe himself turned a violent shade of purple whenever Lucy—for Lucette had named the cow after herself—drew near.

The trouble with heroes is that they are so easily distracted.

Especially from their marriage vows.

So it was no surprise to Acacia when she awoke one morning, rolled over on the pillow expecting to snuggled up to Paul's ear and found him gone. He'd taken his ax and the clothes on his back and Babe, with his appetite for thirty bales of hay a day, wire and all. No sign of Lucette or Lucy.

Acacia called on her friends the birds.

"I need to find Paul." She didn't tell them why, but somehow they already knew.

She climbed on the back of an osprey named Jake. It wasn't hard to guess the direction. Even through dense forest, from the air the fugitives' track wasn't hard to spot. Without Acacia to guide him, Paul had left a trail as wide as a highway and as deep as Moosehead Lake.

Paul hid in the lumber camps, moving from one to the next and slinking off whenever someone mentioned the word wife. Lucette concealed herself and her cow out in the forest, never far, but never near enough to keep Paul out of trouble—presupposing she had a brain in her head. Acacia had her doubts.

Acacia kept close on their heels, flying hawks by day and owls by night, resting only when her companions stopped to hunt. She lived on pine nuts and spring water, raw leg of mouse and juniper berries.

She tracked them over the White Mountains and into the Green, across New England and New York, following the swath of clear cut timber felled by Paul's two-bladed ax. The sight of so many trees lying prone, their branches stripped, their boles flayed free of bark, tied knots in Acacia's stomach.

Over Syracuse, huge unmistakable footprints—Paul's and Babe's, Lucette's and Lucy's—sunk deep in muck and filled with water to form the Finger Lakes.

At Oscoda, Michigan, Acacia came within a hair's breadth of catching up. Paul, claiming it as the place of his birth, had tried to set down roots. Flying low over a meandering river on the back of a swallow-tailed kite, she watched horror-struck as Paul strapped the river's foot to Babe's harness and slapped the reins. The giant blue ox strained and pawed the ground. Paul's voice shouted encouragement. Lucette led Lucy to the traces and hooked her up. With a mighty tug, the two great beasts pulled the river straight.

The kite swooped lower. Acacia's fingers tightened in the flesh under her feathers. She could already taste the sweet nectar of victory and the heady froth of revenge. Talons spread, the kite squawked her battle cry, swooping within inches of Lucette's face. The giantess ducked, turned aside, and hid her face on Paul's willing shoulder. He rubbed her back and shook his fist. But when the kite, sensing Acacia's triumph, swooped again, Paul and Lucette stooped and grabbed two barn-size burlap bags at their feet.

They flung them open. A blast of bitter air and stinging snow flew into Acacia's face. The wind howled. Thunder roared. Lightning forked down from sudden dark clouds.

In the moment's confusion, Paul and Lucette, Babe and Lucy jumped on a raft as large as Manhattan and sailed away on the lake behind a curtain of white snow.

It took the better part of two weeks, but Acacia picked up the scent on the other side of the lake in Michigan's Upper Peninsula. The trail led to Bemidji, Minnesota. Once again deep, telltale depressions were already filling with water and soon would be lakes.

She caught up with Lucette fifty miles southwest in Hackensack on the shores of Birch Lake.

"He's left me," Lucette said in a surprisingly soft and docile voice. She stood staring out at the lake, arms folded over her mounded cleavage, legs spread wide inside her gray striped skirt.

Acacia sent the kite aloft to check for any sign of her husband.

"He's not right for you, you know," Lucette said with more force.

"And I suppose you're just what the doctor ordered?"

"I have his body."

"Size isn't everything."

"I know." Lucette rubbed her belly and sighed. "You still have his heart. But I've got something else."

That look on her face, that glow a baby gives to its mother before it is born, melted the ice in Acacia's heart—and freed her mind.

"Dumped you, did he?"

"Oui. Told him he was going to be a papa, and he took off like he was being chased by angry swarms of white-faced hornets."

Acacia sighed. She and Lucette made a deal: Lucette would bear the child and together they would raise him, for there was no question in their minds it would be a boy—big and strong like his father.

While Paul and Babe wandered the north and west felling forests, digging the Grand Canyon with his axe, and running from the sound of the words "wife," "husband" and "father," Acacia and Lucette became the best of friends.

They lived happily together, raising their son to be a good man first and a hero second.

To this day, on the shores of Birch Lake in Hackensack stands the statue of a giant woman in a low-cut red top and gray striped skirt. She smiles at the six foot midget on the pedestal beside her. The memorial plaque reads: Lucette and Paul Bunyan, Jr. If you stand just so and squint and know what you're looking for, you can see something in Lucette's right ear. It stands three and seven-eighths inches tall—give or take a sixteenth.

Some claim Paul Sr. is buried nearby, if he's not in Kelliher under a stone reading,

"HERE LIES PAUL. AND THAT'S ALL."

BOLDLY REIMAGINED

J. Steven York

J. Steven York is the national best-selling author of a dozen novels and many short stories that have appeared in major magazines and anthologies. In his younger days he lived in Los Angeles, dabbled in scriptwriting, and narrowly ducked a career writing for television. These days his "sound stage" is a small workbench where he creates the weekly photo-illustrated web-comic, "Minions at Work," using action-figure "actors." He lives on the Oregon coast with his wife and fellow-author Christina F. York (who also writes mystery under the pen-name Christy Evans). They share a website at *www.YorkWriters.com*.

THE WRITER'S ROOM — DAY 1

"This has all happened before, and it will all happen again," said Todd the show-runner, staring at the big writer's room whiteboard like it was the source of all inspiration.

I wondered if Todd even knew he was ripping off *Battlestar Galatica*, not that it much mattered in this business, where borderline plagiarism is the sincerest form of flattery. I followed Todd's eyeline to the whiteboard, and all I could see there was a large, crudely drawn and vividly obscene drawing featuring a centaur and a big-boobed stick figure helpfully labeled "Paris Hilton."

It made a special impression on me, being the only woman (big surprise, she said sarcastically) on an otherwise male writing staff.

My name is Diana Mallock, and it was my first day as staff-writer on a vaguely defined new fantasy-drama series, a job I'd carefully chosen on the basis of how they were offering money and I needed work. But my agent told me that they desperately wanted somebody to give the show "weight" and were willing to sign me sight unseen. I only hoped they were talking about my awards and credentials, and not making cracks about my no-longer-so-youthful figure.

Actually, it was everyone's first day, except presumably for the show runner himself. Including Todd, there were five of us so far, with three others due to arrive in about a week.

By then it would be too late. In television, the first-in rule the roost. We'd already have set the show on course and roughed in half the season by the time they got here, or if we hadn't, the show would already be well on its course to becoming what the trades called "troubled."

Being basic-cable, this wasn't a big-budget show, not that writers in this business get the velvet and caviar treatment anyway. The writer's room, a double-wide temporary building installed next to a sound-stage in Vancouver, Canada, was still pretty pristine, probably having been hosed down after the last show had cleared out. There was a vague disinfectant smell that supported the notion. That wouldn't last either. I'd been in the business long enough to know that the shabby looking tables and desks would soon grow a rich patina of Starbucks cups, pizza boxes, Chinese food containers, and the multicolored pages of a million discarded script drafts.

Barry fiddled with his earring and tried unsuccessfully to look like a bad-ass.

I had Barry pegged as the "angry young artist" type. I was getting a bad vibe off Barry.

Barry sniffed contemptuously. "What the fluke does *that* mean?"

Todd ignored the meat of Barry's question, probably having already forgotten what he'd said. Instead, he squinted at him over the top of his wire-rimmed glasses and scowled. "What the heck is this *'fluke'* thing about?"

Josh, a skinny, prematurely bald guy with a studious demeanor spoke up. "Barry and I just came off that sci-fi show, *Wireworld.* On the planet where the show is set, everyone says 'fluke' as a curse word. Lets us get the *F-bomb* right past standards-and-practices."

"Must be convenient," said Marty, a moon-faced guy in a Darth Maul tee-shirt who looked like he's just wandered in from the local sci-fi club, and possibly had.

I realized that not only was I the only woman in the room, I was the oldest person in the room, I was possibly older than any two people in the room combined. I wondered if I was going to last on this show past the first episode. Part of me was looking forward to the severance check.

This was "one of those deals." After 23 years writing for television, two Emmys, a Golden Globe, and a WGA award, I had learned a thing or two. On a new show, the first 72 hours in the writer's room are the most important. In those three days, the direction of the show is set, its possibility for creative (if not ratings) success is determined, and, more important to me, the dominance positions in the writer's room are set. Often the show-runner would pick a right hand, or maybe two people that he closely depended on. Everyone else was down the totem pole, struggling to get anything recognizable onto the screen.

Now maybe I should have just trusted my talent, ex-

perience, and natural charm to rise to the top, but I'd
been around long enough to know that all that didn't
matter nearly as much in these situations as having a set
of externally mounted reproductive organs

There were at least one, maybe two too many bodies
in the room, and I suspect we all knew that.

Todd seemed distracted. "Wish we could get away
with that 'fluke' thing here. The suits want bold and edgy,
and it's hard to pull that off with togas and sandals."

"Fluking-A," said Barry nostalgically. "I'm gonna
miss 'shiz,' 'klok,' 'klunt,' and 'blue jeeb' too."

"Well," said Todd, "this isn't a sci-fi show, it's a bold
reimagining of 'Jason and the Argonauts' as a weekly
series, so, of course, everybody speaks English."

I suppressed a snicker and a snide comment about
English-speaking Grecks.

Barry looked Todd straight in the eye, and I sensed a
disturbance in the Force. "It's a bold reimagining. Who
says we can't make it a sci-fi show? 'Stargonauts.'"

"I like it," Marty said

Todd frowned, and for a second, I thought he was
going to buy it, which might have determined our little
power-struggle right there. Finally Todd shook his head.
"No, they want myths and sweaty, big-muscled heroes.
It's a fantasy."

Barry frowned, but he said nothing, obviously considering his next move. "So," I said, putting my toe ten-
tatively in the testosterone pool, "what have we got
beyond that? Is there a bible? I assume you at least sold
this on the basis of a presentation?"

Todd's face reddened slightly. "Actually, that's all I've
got. I went in to pitch a sitcom about two gay guys who
open a country-and-western bar in Utah, and it all went
horribly wrong. The network president's son had just pi-
rated *300* and *Beowulf* off the internet, and he was going
on about how much money they'd made, and how he
wanted something with 'swords and men and women
with big boobs.' I don't know squat about that stuff,

but I remembered 'Jason and the Argonauts' from high school. Nothing about it, just the title, so it just slipped out Next thing I know, somebody is on the phone, Ryan Roth was attached as our hot young Jason, and the project is on a fast track." He grinned as if he'd actually had something to do with it. "It was *so* fluking cool!"

Ryan Roth was the hottest young star in town, just off a five-year run on a hot teen show and rumored to be looking for his first adult project. Doubtless Todd had simply been in the right place at the right time and had talked his way through it on instinct alone.

That was the problem with this business. You don't succeed because you can write, you succeed because you can talk. It's all about the pitch: the sizzle rather than the steak. Some of us can do both pretty well, but lots of top people get by totally on the gab. Then they hire other people who can write and take the credit. I had a nervous feeling that old Todd was one of these. I looked around to see if any of the others, especially Barry, were going to take up his slack.

Josh nodded thoughtfully, though I could see he was drawing a total blank. "Jason," he said, slowly and carefully, as though it were the most profound statement in the world, "and the—*Argonauts.*"

A light-bulb seemed to go off over Marty's head. "Ooh, I remember all about it! There was a *boat,* right? And a quest for some golden fleas."

I sighed. "Fleece," I corrected him.

Todd looked at me curiously. "Is that another F-bomb substitute?"

"The Golden Fleece," I said, "like the wool from a sheep. The Argonauts were on the quest for Golden *Fleece.*"

Todd nodded thoughtfully. "A quest. I like it. Clearly you're our expert, Diana. Tell me more."

Barry scowled at me. Marty looked interested in what I had to say. Josh looked back and forth between Barry and me, trying to decide who would be his best alliance. Writer's rooms are very third grade.

Me, I was just trying to come up with a follow-up.

Expert? Hardly. I'd gone through a "heroes journey" period in college and had read a couple of mythology books from which I'd picked up a few nuggets before deciding that the ancient Greeks were misogynistic pedophiles. Of course, another thing I'd learned in television. It didn't take much to qualify as an "expert."

I rummaged around in the mental attic to see what else I could remember. "Jason was sent on an impossible quest by his evil brother to retrieve the Golden Fleece. He builds a ship, the Argo, and assembles a crew of the greatest Greek heroes of classical myth."

"Yo," said Marty, excitedly waving his hands in the air, "like an ancient version of the *Justice League,* or the *Avengers,* or *Survivor All-stars!*"

"Uh," I said, "yeah, basically. He has many adventures on the trip out, and on the trip back with the fleece, he fights harpies and a bronze giant named Talos, and this being a Greek story, pisses off the Gods and ends up dying tragically, crushed under the hulk of his own rotting ship."

"No shiz?" Marty looked amazed. "Crushed under his own ship?"

Todd rolled his eyes. "Don't worry, this is a bold reimagining. We can leave that part out." He looked over at Barry, who had been sitting quietly, rubbing the pretentious little soul-patch on his chin. "You got something, Barry?"

Barry sniffed, raised an eyebrow, and said simply, "Hercules was a cross-dresser."

Marty blinked. "What?"

Todd smiled. "Hercules was one of the Argonauts? Sweet. Name recognition. We can use that."

Marty still looked shocked. "Hercules was not a cross-dresser. Not in the comics, anyway."

"Technically," I said, "he was. By command of the gods, as punishment for something or another, he spent a year enslaved by a woman who dressed him as a female and made him do women's work."

Todd looked at me, eyebrows raised.

"I imagine," I said dryly, "we'll be boldly reimagining that part out."

THE WRITER'S ROOM—DAY 2

Despite our total lack of progress or direction on day one, Todd looked almost disturbingly pleased with himself. "Good news, everybody! I've had a breakthrough! It's a sci-fi show now! 'Jason and the Stargonauts!' I ran it past the suits in New York first thing this morning, and they love it!"

Barry's eyebrows went up, but he said nothing. Todd had appropriated his idea, but any sci-fi premise would seemingly favor him and his little buddy, Josh. Moreover, to his credit, Barry had been doing his homework. He'd put away his iPhone when he spotted me coming, but I'd seen enough to know he was cribbing Greek mythology off Wikipedia.

Of course, I'd spent the night reading actual *books* on mythology, but that wasn't as likely to be important now that we were headed in the sci-fi direction. Maybe I should have been studying the *Star Trek Technical Manual* instead.

"Okay," continued Todd, "we've got our bold new direction. Now, how many Argonauts—excuse me—*Stargonauts,* do we have to work with?"

Clearly, Todd hadn't wasted any of his valuable creative time doing research. I started to answer, but Barry cut me off.

"There are different accounts, and not all of them have the same players. There are nearly fifty possible names on the list." He smiled smugly, and glanced briefly in my direction.

Todd looked pained. "Well, fluke that. It's too many. We need to cut it down to about seven, for budget reasons if nothing else. We've got Jason, and *got* to have Hercules. Who else?"

Barry whipped out his iPhone again. "I just happen

to have prepared a list of candidates." He listed off Perseus, Nestor, Orpheus, Castor, and Pollux, and gave a brief case for each.

To his credit, it was a pretty good list, except for one thing, which I immediately noticed. So did Todd, though I didn't know it at the time, for completely different reasons.

"But those are all dudes, right?" He frowned. "We can't do a ship with nothing but guys. Weren't there any *women* in the Argonauts?"

Like I said, the Greeks weren't the most enlightened culture when it came to women, but I had looked into it. "Well, there was Atalanta, but a lot of scholars say that Jason wouldn't let her come precisely because she was a woman."

Todd shrugged. "This is just *inspired* by mythology. It's not like we're *tied* to it or anything. So, this Atlanta—"

"Atalanta," I corrected.

"Whatever, we'll probably want to change that name anyway. So, was she a babe?"

"Excuse me?"

"A looker. Not that she can't kick ass, but no reason she can't be hot too, in the Buffy/Sydney Bristow tradition."

Actually, according to myth she was a beautiful woman, but something in Todd's tone had set me off. "Hard to say. Her father wanted a boy, so he abandoned her in the woods, and she was raised by *bears.*"

"Eew," said Marty.

Josh snickered. "Probably doesn't shave her legs then."

"How about," said Marty, "that we boldly reimagine that she shaves her legs."

"Pits too," added Josh.

I squirmed as the testosterone level increased, but I knew better than to show weakness by protesting.

Barry grinned.

"Okay, so Atlantis is a possible. Who else we got?"

I signed. "The only other woman involved is Medea, kind of a witch or sorceress. She doesn't join them until they reach the fleece, but she falls in love with Jason, helps him get the fleece, and aids him on the way back, all for the promise that he'll marry her."

Todd nodded happily. "We can reimagine that marriage part about it, and have them just have hot, sweaty, Greek sex."

Marty sniggered at the word "Greek."

But then Todd frowned. "But that's not really enough. See, I had another phone call this morning, from Ryan Roth's agent. Ryan is going to be starting a TV movie here in Vancouver later this week. They want to look over what we've come up with by then, and he was really, really concerned that the show be—you know—*adult.*"

"Adult," I said, "as in sexy?"

"Adult as in soft-core porn, or as close as we can get on basic cable after 10 PM. He's looking to break hard— no pun intended—from his Disney Channel reputation. That's a deal breaker for him. We need three or four handy bedmates on the crew for him, plus the guest starlet of the week."

I sighed. "Three or four bedmates who can kick ass," I said.

Todd looked at me blankly. "Well—*sure.*"

Barry suddenly grinned. "I've got it. Remember, I said Hercules was a cross-dresser?"

Todd's brow furrowed. "Ryan wants to break from his image, yeah, but I doubt he'll go for a bisexual thing ..."

Barry shook his head. "No, no, no, that's not it. See, this is a bold reimagining! In this version, Hercules is a smoking-hot *babe!* Hercules is a *girl!*"

Marty looked appalled, but probably not half as much as I did.

Todd looked stunned for a minute. Then he smiled. "That's fluking *brilliant!*"

I could feel this whole thing slipping away from me,

swept away by a testosterone tsunami. I could also feel the show turning into crap. There was always the possibility that the bimbo-fest the guys were cooking up would be a surprise hit, but in a world full of lad-mags, pay cable, and internet porn, I sincerely doubted it could compete. Even if they didn't fire me, we'd be lucky to make it thirteen weeks.

Did I say I was looking forward to the severance check? That was a lie. Or rather, it was premature, because in my couple of days in Vancouver I had suddenly realized that I was starting to *like* it there. I'd lived in Los Angeles for almost thirty years, and I'd forgotten what it was like to live in a place where there were no wilting palm trees, where the sky wasn't muddy orange, and where ugly sun-baked sprawl didn't stretch scemingly off to infinity.

Vancouver had *real* trees, snowcapped mountains, water that wasn't pumped in through a pipe, crisp, clean air, green that didn't come in a graffiti artist's spray can, people who were sometimes actually *polite* on the freeway, and actual, honest-to-God *weather.* There was a ski slope within sight of downtown that I was dying to try, and I had a lead on a cute condo overlooking the bay. I suddenly realized that I was *so* ready for a change. I didn't *want* to go back to Los Angeles, and if this gig fell through, I'd probably have no choice.

I tuned back into the conversation just in time to hear Barry's suggestion that, instead of a captain's chair, the bridge of the *Argos* would have a big, round, bed.

THE WRITER'S ROOM — DAY 3

By lunch of the third day, the entire crew of the *Argo*, with the obvious exception of Jason, had gotten a sex change. To be more accurate, the *Argo* no longer *had* a crew, Jason had a harem.

And Todd had a new favorite son in the form of Barry, with Josh happily yapping at their feet. They were already well into outlining a two-hour pilot, where the crew was drawn together, in a series of seriocomic set pieces, by their common lust after the studly captain of the tramp space-freighter *Argo* (who was secretly an exiled prince). They eagerly join him in his quest for the Golden Pelt, an object of power that will restore Jason to his rightful place on the throne of planet Locus.

By the end of the second act, Jason had managed to bed all five women, including a big oil-wrestling scene with the gender-swapped Hercules and an extended three-way with twins Castora and Polluxia. There was also a big seduction scene with the Harpies. As a visual reference for the Harpies, Barry had pasted magazine cut-outs on the whiteboard, of Victoria's Secret lingerie models with little cherub wings strapped to their backs.

Like I said, crap.

Mentally, I was already checking out. To hell with waiting to get fired, I was ready to walk. Yet some stubborn part of me wasn't ready to do that. Instead, I decided to get away from the studio to clear my head.

I jumped into my rental car and asked the very polite guard at the gate for a dining recommendation. He directed me to a wonderful little sushi place a few blocks south, where the tuna was so fresh it hadn't had time to miss the ocean yet. The food was so good that I almost forgot about the train wreck *Jason and the Stargonauts* was turning into. I was half way through my assorted nigiri plate when I looked up and was shocked to see Ryan Roth walk through the door, trailed by an entourage of assorted assistants, agents, and a couple of bodyguards who looked like half-tamed gibbons stuffed in Italian suits. Jason was midtwenties, with wide shoulders, a narrow waist, a tight butt, dimples, and a thousand-watt smile that just wouldn't quit.

He was damned pretty. He was also nearly young enough to be my son, which didn't stop me from looking.

Did I say I was shocked? No, I was surprised, but not totally. After all, I knew he was coming into town, and we weren't that far from the studio, and Vancouver, after all, isn't *that* huge a city. No, I wasn't shocked until Roth looked my way, seemed to recognize me, and started walking toward my table.

He stopped in front of me and tilted his head curiously. "Your name is Diana, isn't it?"

I dropped one of my chopsticks, which speared itself into my wasabi and stood there like a drunken flag-pole. I finally found my voice. "Diana Mallock," I said. "I'm a writer."

He laughed. "I know. Look, I'm sure you wouldn't remember, but when I was a teenager, you were working on *Pentagon,* at Paramount, and I was shooting *Ricky Boomhower and the Rainbow* in the next stage over. My trailer was right across from the writing office, and well—" He actually blushed. "—I had kind of a crush on you."

I couldn't help but burst out in an explosive laugh. Ryan Roth had a crush on *me?*

He looked away and then back again. "I know that's silly. It was a *long* time ago. See, you kind of reminded me of my friend Dan's hot mom."

"Uh—Thanks—I think."

He continued. "But I'd see you out the window of my trailer, and I never had the courage to actually *talk* to you or anything. Really it was only a few weeks, I guess. *Pentagon* was canceled, and you moved on."

I chuckled at the memory. It was that kind of show. Sophisticated scripts about important issues. Critical darling. Lots of awards. No viewers. I'd been crushed when they announced the cancellation. I'd never have noticed some moon-eyed kid watching me out a trailer window. "You don't seem too afraid now."

He laughed. "It *was* a long time ago. Look, I'm not hitting on you or anything creepy. I just was always curious what your voice sounded like." He shuffled his feet nervously and looked back at his posse, who were now seated across the room, watching him curiously. Only the suit-gibbons remained, standing just out of earshot, poised to wrestle me to the ground if I attacked Roth with my remaining chopstick. "I'm sorry," he finally said. "Maybe this was a bad idea."

"No," I said, "it's okay. I'm flattered."

He grinned. "Let me pick up the check for your sushi. You here doing a show?"

"As I matter of a fact, I'm here doing your show, *Jason and the Stargonauts.*"

His smile faded. "Wish I was feeling better about this thing. My manager tells me I should hold out for a juicy movie role, maybe a romantic comedy. But I've got," he nodded toward the table across the room, "my little team of parasites there to feed." He considered. "Look, I could use some reassurance here. You would know. Is the show going to be any good?"

And there I was. He actually seemed sincere, a nice kid betting his career on this steaming pile of—shiz. Yet trashing the show was unprofessional, petty, and could come back to bite me. What to do?

My mother used to tell me, when you can't think of anything else to say, try the truth.

"Well," I said, "actually, I'm not that involved with it. In fact, I've been thinking about giving notice and heading back to LA. But the rest of the staff are really enthused. They're well into breaking the first episode. When I left, they were just working on your big sex scene with Hercules."

Roth's jaw dropped. There was a long moment of stunned silence, while the gibbons bobbed up and down, trying to decide if it was time to wrestle me to the floor yet. "Did you say me—my character—has sex with *Hercules?*"

"Yup. But first comes oil. And *wrestling.*"

He let out a gasp of exasperation. "Look, I'm as open-minded as the next guy, but we're not talking about an Ang Lee art film here, or even an HBO drama series. This is a stupid action-adventure sci-fi show for basic cable. Hercules? It would be career suicide. I'd be an instant punch line. It would start with Conan's monologue, and it would never end."

"You have a point," I said, not elaborating on anything I'd told him.

"Look, this is a shit-thing to do to you, but I don't think I can go through with this."

I shrugged. "Don't worry on my account," I said. "I'll be fine. I'm a survivor."

Roth went back to chew out his agent, and suddenly I wasn't hungry. I paid for my own sushi, and I was the first one back to the writer's room. Todd, on the other hand, was very, *very,* late.

He arrived forty minutes after I did, his face the color of ash. "Ryan Roth dropped out. I don't know why. I hear some rumors that he's up for the lead in the new Ang Lee movie. Our whole project is in limbo. The studio didn't buy the concept so much as the package. They're concerned that without star power, the show won't stand on its own. Being edgy just isn't enough to make the show stand out. It needs a *twist,* is what they told me."

Barry looked shell-shocked. He leaned back in his chair, and nearly fell over backward. "That's it then? We just got here, and already we're dead? What the shiz am I going to do? I just bought a houseboat!"

I felt a little bad for Todd, and especially for Marty. For Barry, not so much.

Todd shrugged. "I've got twenty-four hours to come back with a new proposal, 'two steps beyond edgy' is what they said. But I think they were just humoring me. I mean, with the gender swaps and the sex, how much farther can you go?"

Barry wasn't even listening. He stared at the wall and chewed all his fingernails at once.

So, I thought, that was it. I'd still have to leave Canada, but at least I wouldn't be leaving alone. Somehow that wasn't very satisfying. But Todd was right, given what the guys had come up with, how much farther could you go? A he-man hero and a ship full of beautiful, eager, sexy, women. They'd taken it just as far as though could go.

Then—and I don't mean this literally, though it would have been ironic—I received a visitation by the Muses. I blinked in surprise at my own idea. I knew what to do. Though in terms of exploitation, it might be a case of, "If you can't beat them, join them," I knew what to do.

The guys had gone as far as *they* could go. But I could see past that, to boldly take the show where no man had gone—*ever*.

THREE YEARS LATER

Todd left the show in the middle of last season, leaving me in charge. His new comedy-drama pilot, "Salt Lake Confidential" is drawing good buzz and has HBO and Showtime in a bidding war.

With Todd's encouragement, Josh held on for a year, but he never meshed well with the new staff or the new concept I came up with. He seems to have dropped totally out of the business. I heard a rumor he's working on a novel.

Marty has really matured, both as a person and as a writer. He's traded his Star Wars tee-shirts for cardigan sweaters, and he's got a fiancée that he didn't meet in an internet chat room. He's my number-one guy here on the show, and I don't know how I'd do it without him.

There are now three women out of eight writers in the writer's room. It's not parity, but it's an improvement.

Stargonauts premiered to solid, if not spectacular, numbers, which have continued to build every season. Even our repeats do well, a rarity in this day and age. And we're a critical darling. *The New York Times* called us "a smart, edgy, gender-bent take on Greek myth, with strong, heroic women and other women who love them." *Entertainment Weekly* said, "Every character is a gem, from the flawed and tragic Jasona, to her friend and sometimes lover Hercules, so uncertain of her femininity that she dresses in men's clothing, to the lone male character, loyal Medeas, who fiercely loves Jasona in a way he knows she can never return." *Femme Fatales* said, "muscular lesbian space hotties grinding groins in zero-gravity! It doesn't get much better than this!"

They love us. They really love us.

Oh, and Ryan Roth called me last week. He needs a date for the Academy Awards and wondered if I was available.

They'll probably just think he's brought his mom.

Still, I'm thinking about it.

Oh, and Barry didn't last much into the first season. He left to run another sci-fi show called *"Bender,"* about a company that perfects an instant sex-change machine. It lasted eight episodes on *Bravo* before they pulled the plug.

I hear he lives in Malibu now that he's come out of the closet and is headed for a sex change. And I know that probably, after the hormones and the operations, he—*she*—is going to want to return to writing for television. I wish her well. I really do.

But I have a warning for her:

This has all happened before, and it will all happen again!

ROXANE

Peter Orullian

Peter Orullian has recently been published in
other fine DAW anthologies, as well as *Orson Scott
Card's Intergalactic Medicine Show*. For grocery
money, he works at Microsoft in the Xbox division.
His other abiding passion is music; Peter recently
returned from a European tour with a successful
hard rock band. He has a New York agent currently shopping a few of his novels, which he hopes
will allow him to retire from Microsoft and sing
and write until everything bleeds.

She put on the red light.
 That's what you do when your stomach grumbles
and all that the poets are offering is flowery verse. Not
that there's anything wrong with a compliment or two.
Even a woman with flexible hips likes to hear something
sweet before the fleshy business (or so I've been told).
But I suspect by now she'd forgotten her girlhood, when
she still believed she would find someone to love. Someone who would love her. Before the red light.
 I hated being here myself.
 These days, the district was filled with gallants come

from Paris with their mousy mustaches and dreams of
finding love. Not a one (as I've heard) goes more than
ten strokes once the *love* begins. And never before a lot
of alley-side wooing.

Waste of time.

Still, it was the best I could do.

I was a French Army Cadet, soon to be dispatched
to Arras to fight the Spanish. Cyrano de Bergerac was
my name. I stood there, one hand resting comfortably
on my rapier, the other cupping something unseen (but
apparently important) in the air. I don't know how I got
into that pose. But it felt natural, nonetheless, for offering a verse.

So, I lifted my chin with my rhyme and wove it all
above the stench.

Which, given the size of my nose, surely came to me
in triple portions. Gutter-smell. All kinds of filth my
boots had never seen—on brushed leather, no less! But
I didn't mind. Instead, I went on about her charms and
wit and—

"My God, are you ever going to ask my price?" She
interjected, not mad, but edging with impatience.

I ignored her and went on about her eyes. As I did,
Roxane tried to draw in another "soldier of Satan,"
pointing to her red light. No good. I was wearing the
violet tabard of the military. No meager flesh-seeker was
going to compete with me for her bed tonight. She was
stuck until I either got on or got out.

"I've come to rescue you—"

"I don't need to be rescued, you arrogant bastard."
She said it politely. "What I need for you to do is stop
talking long enough for me quote a price."

No price. I wasn't here to hire Roxane. Pitiful as I'm
sure she'd think it, I was here for an open invitation, on
the merit of my true feelings for her.

"Poet, why don't you give her a poke with that pointy
nose of yours. That'll have her singing all right."

Roxane smiled at that, looking past me at the man

who'd offered the insult. The man came into the baleful
light, which was simply a thin red scarf wrapped around
her door lantern.

I dropped my raised hand. "I will ask you to with-
draw . . . but only once."

The man laughed out of the darkness. A coin flashed
across the alley and struck Roxane in the teat as the
man stopped in the dull gleam of the red light.

I caught a last glimpse of Roxane as I turned, a
strange look upon her face—did she know this man?
The scrape of my rapier being drawn free resounded
loud in the alley. I splashed through a puddle of piss
(you get to know such things) and rounded on a fellow
who stood a half foot taller than me and wore the cape
of the viscount.

I'd seen this little drama before, too. Men trying to
ennoble a woman by defending an insult aimed half at
themselves. But this time, it was me; this time, the viscount. I realized I would likely die one way or the other,
either here near a puddle of piss, or on a rack in some
sweltering dungeon if I out-dueled the noble.

"Oh, hell, come back, cadet, you can have this one at
two francs." Roxane tried to grab me. I shrugged her off
and took a challenger's stance.

"You should take her at that price," the viscount said.
"Though it's still a bit high, m'thinks. Last time I was
here, I took her from behind for two decimes."

"Apologize." My rapier rose. "To her and to me."

The viscount chuckled low, unthreatened. "I'll assume
you're drunk to lift your weapon toward me . . . and to
consider such a tired whore. Though, with that nose, I'll
guess this is your best option."

That was uncalled for. Roxane wasn't tired in the
least. Not like he meant, anyway.

"Kill him," she said. At last a charge directly from
her.

"Apologize," I repeated.

"My young man," the viscount began, still very calm,

"It is dark in this place, save for your tramp's little light. So, I'm going to inform you who I am before you tarnish the good name of the country whose uniform you wear—"

"I don't care who you are. The uniform I wear is a token of defense for *all* the citizens of France. And you have insulted a woman who gave you no cause. I will skewer your tongue for her pleasure unless you retract—"

"I am the viscount, cadet. You are now fairly warned."

"Draw," was all I said.

The viscount drew his own weapon, and we touched blades ceremonially, then crouched ready to duel.

In the dark and reddened alley, our rapiers began to ring and slap. Our feet shuffled over the stones, grinding dirt and grit beneath.

The viscount made a hard thrust, which drew a yelp from Roxane—it came hard near my side. But I side-stepped and parried the rapier away, slashing at the viscount's stomach. The noble drew back in time, resetting his feet. The rapiers twisted again, clanging loudly in the small alley.

Then the viscount feinted and lunged, trying to catch me off balance. But I didn't take the bait, and as the noble came forward, I dropped to one knee and thrust my rapier into the man's chest.

A gush of air came. Maybe from the viscount's mouth, perhaps from his pierced lung. And he fell to his side, groaning. His hands grasped my rapier as he shuddered over the filthy cobblestone, his head slapping the rock involuntarily.

The viscount's body stilled.

"I'll hold to what I said. Two francs." Roxane reiterated the bargain.

I looked up then, breaking my concentration on my victim. "What?" Then I focused on her. "But I meant what I said before."

"You mean all that poetry? I'm sorry, Cyrano, but

that's a laugh. We've had a fine friendship at The Drake, but not here." She pointed to the red light. "Besides, my heart leans elsewhere."

Wet, coughing laughter filled the alley. The viscount. Not quite dead. "You thought your poems were going to change the heart of a *whore*. My young man, have you *seen* yourself? What tenderness she doesn't sell will be given to some Adonis too dumb to know better than to fall in love with her."

I looked back at Roxane, uncertain, my poet's heart in conflict with the reality of the red-lit alley. She'd been a while in the sheets for her pay, but a touch of something better came down then, if you ask me. A poet-duelist wanting a little companionship. Standing, he hoped, for the honor of one in need of a champion. A viscount with a nasty tongue lay mortally wounded. The stink of the alley. And the red light.

She'd wanted a little nobility. *Wanted* that honorable defense. I felt sure of it.

That's about the time I retreated up the way. My feet smelling of piss.

But I'd bested the viscount in a duel. And though, ugly didn't *begin* to describe me, and a "ceiling watcher" wasn't interested in the compliments I tried to pay her, those pretty little couplets had surely made a tramp want to think of girlhood again.

I had to believe that.

I didn't want to go to The Drake for supper the day after killing the viscount.

Partly, I thought it smart to lay low. More importantly, that's where Roxane worked during the day. In fact, it's where I'd met her, and where I'd learned she laid up extra on the side with her red light. The Drake was a small hostel near my regiment's garrison. Roxane worked the kitchen in the back.

But Christian had insisted, saying he'd something to show me.

We sat in the corner, and I hoped someone else would get us our food today. But as we got involved in talk of the war, I lost my watchful eye.

"Potato pie or beef stew?" she asked.

My head snapped toward her. Roxane. Damn!

"Both," I said. And looked back at Christian, whose own gaze held a look I knew only too well—infatuation.

"Me, too," Christian said.

When she'd gone, I let out a long breath, unaware I'd been holding it in.

Christian watched Roxane go. Then turned back to me. "You know her?"

"Never mind. She's out of my life."

"Good. That's why we're here. I think I want her in mine." He smiled a bit devilishly.

"You're making a mockery of me. And it's not funny."

Christian looked genuinely confused. He gave Roxane a final glance as she disappeared inside the kitchen, then swung back around. "Truly, Cyrano, if you've no claim upon her, would you mind if I have a go?"

"Will cost you half a franc."

"What?" More confusion on Christian's face. He was simply too good to see the sin in her. And I'd already decided it would be a hell of a lot of fun to let him discover her evening affairs on his own. Besides, judging by the look Roxane had returned Christian, she held a spark of interest in him that my nose had undoubtedly squelched for me. The pair of them could discover together how equally ill-fitted they were all by themselves.

"You have to help me, though, Cyrano. I need your eloquence, since I have none." Christian's boyish face showed a repulsive sincerity.

"Son of a bitch."

"Me?"

I stared at Christian's delicate features. Of course she'd found him desirable. His nose didn't protrude off his face like a piece of fleshy fruit.

"I'll lend you my eloquence, if you lend me your con-
quering physical charm. Together we'll form a romantic
hero!"

To which Christian smiled in anticipation of winning
Roxane's affection.

For my part, I smiled too, anticipating the rare disap-
pointment my friend would find when he found the hue
of Roxane's door lamp. I chose to ignore the fact that
just yesterday I'd been willing to forgive her nighttime
romps if she'd forsake them and choose to love me. But
what the hell. A man with a face like mine has got to
exercise some ignorance.

"What's the plan, then?" Christian asked.

"We'll go by this evening. I happen to know where
she lives."

Christian cocked a funny look at my widening smile.
A smile half a result of the thought of Christian's up-
coming (rude) awakening, and half at the irony of going
back a second night to speak poetry to a tramp in hopes
of finding true love.

In the unseemly odor of the alley again, I looked up
at the cold door lantern. Maybe Roxane did her "back
business" somewhere else tonight. And I started away as
quickly as Christian and I had come.

"Wait," Christian said, putting a hand on my arm. "I
hear something."

"That'd be the rats in the garbage."

"No, it's someone singing. Quick." Christian began
running down the alley, cutting left to the backside.

When I caught up, Christian was looking up at a balcony on the lee side of the row of houses, which had
been built on a hill. Roxane's residence had a second
story from here. And her silhouette could be seen pass-
ing back and forth before the double doors. At least
she appeared to be alone tonight. And offering a few
phrases of song—something I'd never heard before. My
foolish heart ached a bit more for it.

If it were anyone but Christian, I couldn't possibly . . .

"We can talk to her from here. This will work." Christian pointed to a cluster of juniper shrubs beneath the balcony. "Stand in there. I'll call her out. You whisper the words I need to say to get myself invited in."

"And leave me here in the minty bushes while you climb up the balustrade and have a roll with Roxane, is that it?" I began desperately looking for a red light on this side of her apartment.

Nothing. The backyard had no external lamps that I could see.

"That's the basic idea. I think she's already interested. I just need your words to help convince her that I'm after more than sex. Women want to feel needed. So help me make her think there's more to me than just sex."

"I see. Quite a bargain for me, isn't it? Shall I wait for you here, too? In case you need me to talk you into a ménage-a-tois?"

But Christian was already throwing a small stone at Roxane's rear window. The brute had no idea of his own strength, however, and put the rock right through her glass. Though that did get her out onto the balcony in straight order.

"Who the hell are you?" she called down. "I'm going to call the police. You'd better get out of here."

Christian gave me a pleading look.

Here we go.

I whispered: "Wait, mademoiselle. I'm sorry for your window. I will pay to repair it. Any cost is worth it to have but a moment to gaze up at you in the light of this beautiful moon."

"Who is that?" Roxane asked again.

"Christian Duchamp, from the garrison. You served me today at The Drake. Do you not remember?"

"Ah, you sat with the Nose, right?"

"Yes. Cyrano. The Nose."

"Well, I don't care. Go away. I'll have it fixed myself.

Just leave me alone." Roxane looked down, avoiding the broken glass, and was almost inside when Christian demanded his next line.

"Your beauty surpasses every fine thing in the heavens this night."

"What was that?" She swiveled back.

"What now?" Christian whispered fiercely to me.

"I said yours is a surpassing beauty, Roxane. It lifts me when I'm tired. It calms me when I am in despair—"

"You really are Nose's friend. You even talk like him. Though you are far more pleasant to look at."

I whispered: "Tell her she's a horse's ass."

Christian shook his head violently.

"Yes, Mademoiselle. I really am his friend. But the words are mine, born from my deep feelings for you. Will you not let me stand here in the mild evening and feel your beauty cast its spell upon me a while longer."

I heard Roxane inch to the edge of the balcony, where she rested her weight on a creaking balustrade. "Tell me more."

The whore certainly likes attention when it comes from a pair of lips beneath a smaller nose. "Ask her where she works at night."

Christian ignored that one, trying something on his own. "You're hair is like straw in the harvest, your cheeks are like the soft fuzz of an apricot."

That'll be good for the courtship, I thought.

"Straw? Fuzz?" The balustrade creaked as Roxane pushed herself up.

"Quick, Cyrano, some words," Christian whispered.

"Tell her you want to hold her, caress her, keep her free from pain and doubt and worry."

Christian did.

Roxane sighed.

"Tell her you want to hold her safe, warm the chill on her skin, and kiss her clean, smooth brow until she falls asleep in your arms."

Christian did.

Roxane moaned.

"It's working. What else?" Christian adjusted himself, arousal straining in his trousers.

"Tell her that she'll know the merit of your love by the size of your nose."

Christian started to speak, stopping midway. "What? Cyrano. You said she was out of your life. Don't queer this for me."

So I didn't. Not right away.

Another hour I spoke to Roxane through Christian's smaller nose. The woman above me swayed and groaned in the moonlight like a love-starved schoolgirl rather than a callous-backed strumpet. It wasn't until she'd urged Christian to mount the balustrade that I stepped from the juniper bushes into the clear light of the evening stars.

I watched a few moments as the two embraced and began to share a tender kiss—one I'd always thought my words would earn *me*. Instead, I'd given them away to a friend, given Roxane away.

But I reminded myself that she hadn't wanted me. And felt some small generosity for giving her the words regardless.

Still, it hurt.

The whole thing was a bit ridiculous and comic.

And I couldn't watch anymore.

As I slid away, Roxane spotted me moving like a shadow over the grass. "Who's there?"

"Just a defender of harlot honor and the tongue that won her bed." I bowed extravagantly without turning or breaking my stride. "Congratulations on your evening's entertainment, m'lady. That'll be half a franc."

But then I did stop.

Turning, I produced the lantern I'd brought from the garrison. I lit it as Christian waved his hands at me to stop.

"No," my friend whispered, as though Roxane, standing beside him, wouldn't hear him if he whispered.

A smile crept onto my face as I wrapped a die-soaked sheet of paper around the lantern, which then cast a bloody hue over my chest and legs. "Maybe just five centimes, what do you say?"

But I did not wait for a response, instead leaving the red light on the lawn and disappearing into the fogs that had risen from the canal behind.

"Who was that?" I heard Roxane ask Christian.

"No one," my friend answered. "Do you want to have the sex? I can go many times. I'm very good at that part."

"Wait!" Roxane's voice cut the fog, stopping me in my tracks.

The strumpet scaled down from the balcony as though practiced at the art of getting out of places quickly, safely, and unseen. At the lawn, she broke into a sprint toward me. Coming close, she did not slow, but tackled me, driving us both to the ground.

"You jackass! You almost let me sleep with that guy, using your words to convince me I should."

I rubbed my head. "You convinced yourself, m'lady." And I gave a satiric smile. "He had the right words, the right shape, and the right nose. And none of it cost him a single coin."

Roxane stared at me a moment, her body pressing down. "The trouble with you is you're filled with self-doubt. Can't see past your own nose."

"The trouble with you," I fired back, "is that you think you know the trouble with me."

"Is that so?" She reached down and took my manhood in her hand, squeezing.

"Feels like *your* trouble is you haven't had a woman since your nose began to grow bigger than your face. That about right?" Roxane gave a wicked smile.

I started to speak, but Roxane caught my mouth in a kiss, smashing my great nose back in the process.

It hurt a bit, but not so much as to complain. And my

poet's heart believed she was right. I had my doubts. I also needed the sex.

But I also thought that those things had helped me see past the red light, all the way back to m'lady's girlhood. Something I was pleased to defend and give my best words to.

A LONG NIGHT IN JABBOK (OR, WHO, EXACTLY, IS IN CHARGE HERE?)

Janna Silverstein

When she realized that she'd been working as an editor for nearly twenty years, Janna Silverstein decided it was time to hop the fence and try to get some of her own work published. Her fiction and poetry have appeared in *Asimov's Science Fiction, Talebones, Marion Zimmer Bradley's Fantasy Magazine, Orson Scott Card's Intergalactic Medicine Show,* and the anthologies *Swashbuckling Editor Stories* and *Swordplay*. She lives in Seattle with two geriatric cats, a growing coin collection, a selection of antique porcelain hands, and many, many books.

Rachel finally soothed Yaakov to sleep. It had taken a lot of . . . work. He was so anxious about the meeting with Esau tomorrow, so concerned about the family. He hadn't slept in days and had been planning to spend this night in prayer. As far as Rachel was concerned, he'd prayed enough. They had a big day tomorrow. He needed rest. He also needed time to be with his people, his family, his wives, time to get to know them again.

She'd made sure, that night, that she and Yaakov had gotten thoroughly reacquainted.

And now, he was sleeping—fitfully, but he was asleep at last.

Once he'd drifted off, she'd heard a voice calling her. Was it a voice, really? She'd felt a pull out into the night air. She cleaned herself up, wrapped herself in a simple shift and two shawls against the desert night, and slipped outside.

Campfires crackled amongst the scattering of tents and filled the sky with columns of glowing, dancing cinders. Off in the distance, beyond the camp, sheep and goats bleated softly.

She stepped quietly through the temporary settlement. The scent of skewered, herbed, roasting lamb wafted past. She kept her head down as she walked and pulled her shawl close to her face; she didn't want to meet the uncertain gazes of her extended family. There in Jabbok, with Esau so close, they shouldn't be stopping; everyone knew it. She pulled her shawls tighter and walked on.

She headed toward the outer edge of the camp and nodded at the man standing sentry. A little relief in the middle of the night wasn't unusual, and he let her pass without comment.

Once beyond the circle of light emitted by the campfires, Rachel's eyes adjusted to the darkness. She made out the churned up evidence of their passage: feet and hooves in the hard, loose earth mixed up with scrubby, dry vegetation. Yaakov's blessing of wives and children and the growing tribe that El had promised was a burden, too. Sometimes gifts held secrets. Sometimes they held knives. In fact, Rachel realized, she'd never known a blessing that didn't carry a concealed weapon. Blessed by El or not, she and Yaakov both had to fight and lie to create the life they had.

Nothing had come easy.

She couldn't regret it. Maybe that was the way of things: Every gift has its price.

Rachel felt the pull again, a strange compulsion to continue on into the darkness.

Somewhere along the path they'd followed earlier that day, Rachel had seen an island of boulders perfect for leaning upon, for gazing up into the night sky and its spread of stars. She knew with a certainty that was the place drawing her on. She found it soon enough.

She mounted the low, surrounding rocks with short, sure-footed steps. Clear of the tents and smoke, the air was crisp and sweet.

As she sat down, a silhouetted movement caught the corner of her eye. Down by another, smaller island of rocks, Rachel saw what looked like someone crouched as if in prayer, facing east. The kneeling figure leaned to touch its head to the ground, then rose again. Rachel squinted as she tried to distinguish what moved in the moonlight. Hard to say; it seemed to change shape, man one moment, woman the next. Lion reclining? Then she could make out only a blurry glow. What was she seeing?

The figure moved, rising head and shoulders above hips, an unnatural, straight-backed motion.

Rachel had to hide. She rolled toward the edge of the rock and dropped to the ground behind it, breathing quiet and shallow. A spy perhaps? An advance scout sent by Esau to keep track of their movements?

She needed to get back to camp and warn Yaakov. She faced a challenge, she knew, with the boulders and the stranger between her and the way back.

She needed a weapon. Rachel looked about and found a fist-sized rock. She grabbed it up, hefted it to get a sense of its weight. She quietly edged toward one side of the boulders and looked toward the figure. It was gone.

"You don't know how to move in darkness."

She spun to face a man standing in the shadows of the rocks, perhaps two arm spans away, no more. He was taller than Rachel, but that was common; she was a tiny thing, even by her people's standards. He was broad and muscular beneath his pale, close-woven clothes. His face was obscured in the darkness. Her heart beat faster at his odd appearance. Light shone in his direction, but he seemed to absorb it; she couldn't make out a single feature.

"Who are you?" Rachel asked, softer than she meant to. "What are you doing here?"

"I've been looking for you. We have work to do together, you and I."

"Did Esau send you?"

"I am here."

"Who are you?"

"I will not tell you my name. Put down the rock," the man said.

Rachel looked at the rock and, without thought, dropped it.

"We have to wrestle," the man said. He stepped closer.

Rachel stepped backward, bumped into the boulder behind her. Wrestle indeed. She'd already wrestled enough for one night, and with a man far more suited to her taste than this stranger made of shadow.

"I just came here to sit and think," she said then. Try to buy time, she thought. Someone will notice you're gone. You have outwitted so many others; perhaps you can outwit this one, too.

"You came here to speak with El," he said.

"Why do you think that?" It wasn't true, but it might as well have been, given the route her thoughts had taken. Given a chance, she would have enjoyed having a word with El; He certainly had a lot to answer for.

"El knows. Anyway, it's all written already, so we have to wrestle."

"You lay a hand on me . . ."

"If I lay a hand on you, married woman, out here in the dark by ourselves, and we're discovered, you'll be stoned to death for an adulteress. Who would speak for you? But you have a higher calling—matriarch to Yaakov's brood—so you don't have anything to fear.

"Much."

The stranger sighed, put his hands on his hips. "Now, look, I'm just here because I'm supposed to be here." Then he stopped, looked toward the camp, then back at Rachel. Sounding peeved, he said, "You're really rude, by the way. Your camp's right over there and you haven't offered me anything to eat or drink. What would your husband say?"

Somehow, it seemed the most absurd question that Rachel had ever heard.

"*I'm* rude? You sneak up on me, threaten me, make me drop my rock" —Wait a minute. Is that what actually happened?— "and you won't tell me your name."

"Well, that's the way it's supposed to be," he said. "I don't make the rules."

"You keep talking about rules. Whose rules?"

"You're not very bright, are you?"

"And *I'm* rude?" Rachel wanted nothing more than to flatten this stranger right where he stood.

"Rachel?" A cry went up from the direction of the camp. Was that Yaakov? She didn't dare glance that way; she wanted to keep an eye on the stranger.

"Your man comes," the stranger said. "What will you tell him?"

What will I tell him? Rachel tried not to laugh. I don't have to tell him anything! He knows me. He trusts me. After all we've seen, all we've done . . . we've been through too much together for him ever to think that I would touch another man.

The idea made her want to laugh. This stranger knew nothing. He was guessing. She could use that. She had a few tricks up her sleeve. Tricks her father taught her. Tricks her husband taught her.

And as much as this stranger talked about wrestling, he hadn't tried anything yet. But he did take a step closer. She pressed back against the rock. To her left, more boulder. To her right, open ground where she could maneuver, maybe run back toward camp.

"Rachel!" That was definitely Yaakov, his voice closer than it had been before.

"What will *you* tell my man? If I tell him you're a spy, you'll have some explaining to do yourself."

"He will know me for what I am," the man said.

"And what's that, exactly?" Rachel asked, dropping her voice, low and seductive. He wanted to wrestle? Small she was, but she knew men. She pushed her chest out a bit. She just needed him a little closer.

He took another step toward her. She settled one hand onto his shoulder, a proposition in a gentle gesture, then she slammed her knee into his crotch.

He didn't move. "That's not a trick that will work on me," he said.

She was nonplussed only for a moment. Her father had taught her how to maintain her composure well.

"How about this?" she asked, and slammed her foot down on his. He cried out in pain. She grabbed his wrist hard and slipped to the right, twisting his arm as she moved. With two steps, she was behind him and pushed him against the boulder, his arm wrenched between them. Years of work had hardened her muscles, and Yaakov's training hadn't hurt. One thing about Yaakov: He knew she was smart, smarter than him, but he wanted to be sure she could take care of herself.

"Now, who are you exactly?" she asked, shaking her long brown hair, which had come undone in the tussle, out of her face.

"I am here," the stranger said, sounding surprised, straining against her hold.

"Rachel." To her left in the clearing, Yaakov limped up to where she stood with the stranger, his own long, dark hair tangled around his face and shoulders, eyes wide, beard disarranged. His knife was drawn and he looked shocked. "What's going on?"

"Why are you limping?" she asked, concerned. "What happened?"

"I ... um ... pulled a muscle earlier tonight ..."

Yaakov let the sentence trail off. His gaze was deliberate, and Rachel remembered one particular moment earlier that evening between them when things had gotten ... vigorous. She felt her cheeks warm, and she smiled. She nodded and made a mental note to apply a poultice later to help with the pain.

"Now," Yaakov said, "who is this man?"

"We have a visitor," Rachel said.

"Who is he?"

The visitor rested his forehead against the rock. "I. Am. Here," he said wearily. "Oh, God, I'm here, and I can't seem to get beyond this point in the conversation. *Please* kill me now."

"That can be arranged," Rachel said, and shoved him harder against the boulder. "Now, what do you want?"

The stranger lifted his head and gently knocked it against the rock again. "Haven't we talked about this already? Wrestle, remember? You, me? It's written and it must be done. I hate it that I can't say more than that, but those are the rules. There's a point to all this, if you'd only stop *talking!*"

"Will someone please tell me what's going on?" Yaakov interrupted. "Rachel, are you all right?"

It was her turn to have a moment of frustration. She'd worked so hard to get him to sleep, and here he was, awake again and all worked up. *And* he was injured. He'd never go back to bed now. Tomorrow was going to be hell.

"I'm fine. I've got this all under control," she said, and twisted the stranger's arm. He drew in a sharp breath.

"Why don't you let me take it from here?" Yaakov asked. "I'm stronger than you. I can handle it now."

"You're hurt. Let me take him back to camp and we'll question him properly," Rachel said. She liked the feel of this big man trapped against the rock wall; she liked that she'd out-maneuvered him so easily. Men—they never expected it.

Yaakov hadn't, on his first wedding day. Both he and

Rachel had suspected her father, Laban, wouldn't live up to the deal he'd made: that Yaakov would work for him seven years and receive in return Rachel's hand in marriage. They'd planned for Laban's deceit, inventing signs and signals to prove her identity behind the veils that would cover her face before they were bound to each other. When her father insisted that her elder sister, Leah, marry Yaakov first, Rachel rebelled . . . and then acquiesced, teaching her sister the signs she and Yaakov had conjured. No one had been more surprised than Yaakov when Leah revealed herself.

That had been hard. It had been the first of their trials together, the one time she had used his trust against him. It had never happened since. But she had learned from it, learned lessons her father hadn't been aware of teaching: where her loyalties lay, how people see what they want to see, what they expect to see, how they think they know all there is to know. She'd used that knowledge time and again.

What she never got used to was how proud of her Yaakov always was but also how surprised by her he always seemed to be, as if he forgot who she was and what she could do. Also, she never got used to how he kept insisting on playing the hero when she already had things under control, when she had proved once more that she was clever enough, strong enough, to do what needed to be done.

He stepped closer, took hold of the stranger's twisted-back arm. "Rachel, let me handle this."

She resisted rolling her eyes. "Yaakov, I have things under control already . . ."

"Hey!" the stranger interrupted. "Can you two save the domestic squabbles for another time? Can we just sit and talk like civilized people for a minute?" He twisted his head, still shrouded in shadow, toward Rachel. "And would you mind letting go of my arm? You're hurting me."

For a moment, so close to that dark, unnerving profile,

Rachel was nonplussed. Even now, she could make out no feature, only a profile that seemed to tremble like a branch of new leaves in the wind, there but not quite there. She tightened her grip.

"You, drop the knife," the stranger said. Yaakov complied without hesitation. He suddenly looked bewildered. Rachel knew that feeling. "Now, Rachel"—It was the first time the stranger had said her name, and the sound made her go cold inside—"let go please?"

Rachel loosened her grip. The stranger waited, didn't make a sudden move, which automatically made her feel a little less as though she were at risk. She released him and stepped back and away from him. Yaakov grabbed her and drew her behind him.

Such a hero. It was clear to her he hadn't realized that the dynamics among the three of them had changed.

"So you want to wrestle? For what?" Yaakov asked. Rachel was surprised. He was paying more attention than he usually did.

"*Thank* you," the stranger said. "I was sent to wrestle with Rachel. She is to be tested."

Rachel peered past Yaakov's arm. "Sent by whom?" she asked.

"Sent by whom?" Yaakov repeated. Rachel hated when he did that.

"I really need to talk to The Boss about this when I get back," the stranger muttered, but he didn't explain himself. "By the One Who Creates the Rules," he said louder, "and before you ask me why, I'll tell you again: because it's all already been written. And someday, long after you're both dead and gone, it will make sense. Your children's children's children will see the reason. I gotta tell ya, though, this job's already not what I signed up for."

"Wrestle me," Yaakov said. "You will not touch my wife."

"Yaakov, I've already wrestled him," Rachel pointed out. "Apparently neither one of you"—she glanced at

the stranger and then looked back to her husband—
"noticed. I won, and pretty quickly, too."

Neither of the men answered. Yaakov had that look
on his face that she knew so well. She loved him like
crazy, but sometimes he was a little slow to catch on.
As for the stranger, well, without a face, he was nearly
impossible to read, though she sensed surprise at how
she'd slipped that by him without his noticing.

"You do have a point," the stranger said.

"Where, exactly, will all this be written?" Yaakov
asked.

"I can't tell you that."

"Why not?"

The stranger put his hand on his hip, shifted his weight
to one leg. "Rachel?" he said.

She knew the answer. "It's the rules."

"It can't be Rachel," Yaakov said.

Both Rachel and the stranger turned to Yaakov.
"What?"

"It can't be Rachel. You can't write that Rachel wrestled with a strange man. Whoever reads it will wonder
why I let her live. They'll see the word 'wrestle' and assume it was more than an arm-twist. At the very least,
they'll wonder why I didn't send her away."

"So this is all about you?" Rachel said. And then realized she shouldn't really be surprised.

Yaakov looked down at the ground, then off into the
night.

"Well, if it's going to be written down . . ." he said.

Maybe I don't have to love him quite so much after
all . . .

"It's already written down," the stranger said.

"How? How is it written down?" Rachel asked. "Is it
in stone? Is it on parchment? How?"

The stranger paused. Rachel imagined that, though
she couldn't see his face because, well, he didn't really
have a face, he was wearing the same expression Yaakov
had worn just a moment before.

In a small voice, the stranger said, "I don't know."

"It can't be Rachel," Yaakov insisted again. He sounded like their young son.

"Now who's not very bright?" Rachel said under her breath. Men. She went on: "Stranger with No Name and No Face, how's this for a compromise? You and I have wrestled; you've done what you came to do, even though you won't tell us why. Your job is done." Rachel glanced at her husband with a sour look. "Since I can't be known to have wrestled with a man who's not my husband—even though you taught me to do it so I could protect myself—change the writing. Let it say that it was Yaakov whom you wrestled, for his honor's sake. Surely your scribe will be able to scratch out just a name here and there. I don't care if my name is written down somewhere. My children will carry on my name and my honor. Yaakov can have glory if he wants it; I'm not interested in such things. All will be satisfied."

Neither of the men immediately responded.

Finally Yaakov said, "We'll need proof. If I wrestled with a stranger, I'll need to prove it."

"Did anyone see you leave camp?" Rachel asked.

"No," Yaakov said a little too quickly. Hmm. If that's how he wants it.

"If that's the case, then you can tell anyone who asks that you're limping because of your mighty struggle," Rachel said. "We just don't have to be specific about what kind of struggle it was." She smiled again, remembering.

Then she turned her attention to the stranger again. "What do you think, stranger? Will the One Who Makes the Rules accept this arrangement?"

The stranger paused, then said, "I need a moment. I'll be right back."

He pushed passed Rachel and Yaakov, and walked about twenty paces away, then stopped. Rachel twined her arm about Yaakov's, and they watched the stranger together.

She'd managed the stranger well, she thought, though she had to admit that having Yaakov here, now, in the darkness, was a certain comfort. Even with all his child-ishness, she still loved his willingness to try to be more than he was, even if he was often late or not quite as quick as he might be. He was stalwart; he'd grown more honest with others and himself as he'd grown older. Here was a man worth loving, even if he was sometimes more child than adult.

The stranger descended to his knees in the moon-light, touched his head to the ground, just as Rachel had seen him do earlier in the night. His form wavered again: man, woman, lion, indistinct golden glow.

"Do you see that, Rachel? What's happening?" Yaa-kov asked.

Rachel took comfort in the fact that Yaakov, too, was seeing the stranger's peculiar transformation.

"I don't know," she responded.

The stranger rose again in that odd manner Rachel had witnessed earlier. He approached them.

"It's done," he said. "It's written that Yaakov wrestled a stranger in the desert— all night, as it happens, which makes him look pretty good. You won't be mentioned in this account at all, Rachel. Just as well, really. It'll all be redacted by your children's children's children later on. If you'd been mentioned, you would have been edited out anyway. Call it a sign of respect that the One Who Makes the Rules agreed to the change. She's not gener-ally interested in coauthorship, but you impressed Her.

"And She likes your cover story about his limp. Nice touch."

Rachel imagined the stranger smiled. She could hear it in his voice, somehow. She smiled, too.

"Now go," the stranger said. "Take your man to bed. I want to go home."

Rachel nodded to the stranger. His odd, trembly pro-file nodded back.

Rachel put her arm around Yaakov's waist; he leaned

on her shoulder, and they started back to the camp. His limp slowed them.

As they departed, she thought she heard the stranger say, "I'll see you again soon." She wasn't sure why his tone troubled her, but she couldn't help frowning at the sound. She glanced back, but the stranger was gone.

"Mighty struggle, eh?" Yaakov asked, drawing her attention back.

Rachel grinned. "Your mighty struggle," she agreed. "You heard him: You struggled all night long."

Yaakov grinned back. "I'm a changed man."

"That's it! You're a changed man. Let's give you a new name, shall we? Let us call you 'He Who Struggled.'"

"'He Who Struggled *with God,*'" Yaakov corrected her. "'Y'isra-el.' That's one way to interpret 'The One Who Makes the Rules,' isn't it?"

"*I* make the rules, my love, let's be clear."

"Y'isra-chel?" Yaakov asked. "He who struggles with Rachel?"

"Let's keep some things to ourselves, shall we?"

LOVE IN THE TIME
OF CAR ALARMS

Ken Scholes

Ken Scholes's quirky, speculative short fiction has been showing up over the last eight years in publications like *Realms of Fantasy*, *Weird Tales* and *Writers of the Future Volume XXI*. His five book series, *The Psalms of Isaak*, is forthcoming from Tor Books, with the first volume, *Lamentation*, debuting in Februrary 2009. His first collection, *Long Walks, Last Flights and Other Strange Journeys*, will be published by Fairwood Press in November 2008. Ken lives near Portland, Oregon, with his amazing wonder-wife Jen West Scholes. He invites folks to look him up through his website, *www. kenscholes.com*.

"Look, Bob," I told the empty chair, "I've been thinking a lot about it and I'm not sure we're right for each other."

The empty chair remained silent.

I sighed.

I'd met Bob Reynolds at a fire scene on the day after. I was helping the captain with his investigation, and Bob was there from CARECO insurance. We'd struck up a conversation, and I'd asked him out. He blushed, said yes, and here I was for Date Number Four.

Well, not a date exactly.

The trouble with insurance agents is that they take their jobs far too seriously. I put out fires. I face danger every day. But I still make time for my life.

Not Bob.

My cell phone rang, and I dug it out of my pocket. I hated purses and refused to carry one. I looked at the caller ID—it was my old college roommate, Sarah.

She didn't bother with pleasantries. "So," she said in a cheerful voice, "did you pull the trigger yet on Bob?"

"He didn't show up."

Sarah groaned. "Yikes. He's even late for the Break Up Coffee?"

"It's not a break up," I said. "We haven't technically started dating yet."

Sarah laughed, then coughed. "Sorry, Rachel."

I sighed again. "It's okay. He's a sweet guy. He just loves his work too much."

"Probably has deep-seated, intimacy issues," Sarah said. "And a wee little—"

There was a loud boom outside and the windows vibrated. Every car alarm in a five-block radius went off as paper from the trash cans and from the street were stirred up into a brief tornado.

"What was that?" Sarah asked.

"One of *them*," I said. Then, I looked up as Bob rushed in through the back door, fumbling with his briefcase and, of course, the roses. "Look, Sarah, he just showed up. I gotta go."

"Call me when you're done," she said. "I want details."

I hung up and put the phone back in my pocket.

Bob saw me and walked over quickly. He looked rumpled and worried but wasn't out of breath. "I'm so, *so* sorry," he said. "The bus and then the taxi and then there was this bicycle and—"

I raised my hand. "Don't worry about it, Bob. Sit down."

"These are for you." He extended the roses.

I shook my head. "I only have three vases," I told him.

Bob blushed as he sat. "I could get you another vase."

"I'm a three-vase girl, Bob. Four is too many." And then I pulled the trigger. "Look, Bob, you're a sweet guy. But this just isn't working."

"What's not working?" he asked. But the look in his eyes told me he'd heard this before. His shoulders slouched and his face took on that kicked-puppy look.

When his cell phone started to ring, I felt my blood pressure rising. "This—" I waved my hands in the air. "This *whatever* it is. I can't really call it dating because you're late every time and leave in the middle."

He nodded. His voice was heavy. "I know. It will slow down, I promise. Things are just really busy right now."

His phone continued to ring, then stopped abruptly.

I sipped my latte. "Things have been busy for the last three weeks, Bob."

He sighed. His phone started ringing again and his eyes went guiltily to his suit jacket pocket. "I'm sorry, Rachel," he said.

Then he answered it. "What is it?" He waited, turning away and cupping his hand over his mouth. "Can't you get NM on it?" He nodded while listening. "Okay."

I opened my mouth to speak and closed it when my own cell phone started to ring.

Bob was already standing. "Rachel," he said, "I am so, *so* sorry. Can we finish this later on? I'd really like to try again."

I looked at the caller ID; it was the fire station. "I don't think that's—"

But when I looked up from my phone, Bob was already gone.

"It's a big one," the chief said. "You'd better get down here."

Outside, the car alarms that were so recently silenced suddenly went off again and the windows rattled.

"I'm on my way," I said.

It was a high rise with a daycare and lots of families. The good news was that most people were at work. The bad news is that the traffic was even worse than usual.

I suited up and checked the flow to my OBA. "What's the situation?"

"Boy America is here. He's getting people out through the top."

"Great. Colonel Patriot." He was one of the oldest and probably the same one that kept setting off the car alarms and scattering trash all over the city in his mad hurry to interfere somewhere else. I rolled my eyes. "These guys just can't let us do our job, Chief."

His face was drawn. "We need it on this one, Tenner."

I looked at the building, flames rising from the middle section and licking the walls and windows, at least six stories and climbing. Maybe he's right, a voice inside nagged me.

"He's getting the upper stories. We're taking the ones beneath the fire." The chief pointed. "Take a crew in."

I looked and saw a blur of red, white, and blue and an old woman materialized on a gurney near the ambulances. A crowd of reporters shouted questions from a police line.

"I'm on it," I told him.

We worked our way in, and I lost track of time. My life was reduced to the sound of my heart in my ears and the sound of my breath in the regulator, louder even than the roar of the fire or the rush of the water. My eyes on the ground before me, my feet careful to find their way.

We'd finally gotten everyone out and were doing what we could to fight the fire.

We weren't winning.

An explosion above pushed us to the floor under a hot fist of wind and a cascade of burning debris.

"We need out," I yelled. "The building is going to come down on us." I looked around, saw a window down the smoky corridor and made for it.

Suddenly, the window was filled with a broad chest and an American flag. Colonel Patriot hovered outside, pulling the window frame out of the wall and tossing it into the river. "This way, ma'am," he said.

"Don't ma'am me, Freak Boy," I said. I turned to my men. "Go on," I shouted at them. "Get out of here."

He grabbed a man under each of his beefy arms and turned around so another could climb onto his back. "I'll be right back," he said to me over his shoulder.

Then he was gone.

That's when I heard the baby crying.

It was above me one floor, the sound drifting down from a window. I saw the green light of an Exit sign nearby and ran toward it. Dodging flames, I ducked inside the doorway and tried to control my breathing. My heart raced, and I felt my sweat drying from the heat.

I took the stairs two at a time, honing in on the baby's cry. There, in the middle of the hallway, lay a basinet and within it, my target. A beautiful little baby.

There was no time to say "Awwww!" I had a job to do.

I scooped it up and the baby stopped crying. Its eyes opened, and something shot out of its mouth—something like taffy—and it wrapped itself around my hands and torso. Then, baby, bassinet, and I were all tugged back down the hall, around a corner, and up an empty elevator shaft at a speed that made me see stars.

When we popped out onto the ceiling an armored man awaited us with a something like a fishing rod in his hands. I'd seen him in the papers before. Professor Something.

Question was, was he a hero or a villain? I tried to remember, but everything was a little fuzzy, what with the heat exhaustion and the smoke inhalation. I gasped for air, clutching the kid and trying to focus. Too hard. I lay down on the shingles, sat the baby next to me, and concentrated on breathing.

"Ah," he said. "Not what I was fishing for, but still . . ."

Then he had an enormous revolver in one hand. The bullets in the cylinder glowed purple.

Oh-oh. Villain.

While I lay panting on the rooftop, he snatched the baby from me.

I let him.

"Put down the baby, Professor Destructo," a new voice said.

I looked over and saw Colonel Patriot hovering at the roof's edge, his arms folded across his chest.

I crawled to my feet and forced myself to straighten. "Colonel Patriot, it's a trap. The baby is—"

But in that moment, Destructo hurled the baby at Colonel Patriot and raised his pistol. "Time," he chortled, "to test drive my Freakonium bullets. I named them after you."

I didn't even think about it, and it didn't matter that I didn't like him or his kind and their interfering ways. I threw myself between them as though they were any other citizens.

"Rachel," Colonel Patriot yelled, "don't!"

But it was too late. The power of the bullet caught my shoulder and tossed me back and over the edge. Above me, a pillar of smoke blotted out the sun.

I felt the hot wind rushing at me and felt my heart rate rising faster as adrenalin drowned my system.

I heard a boom. I heard car alarms going off and saw flaming debris stir up from the burning high-rise. Rocketing toward me, I saw Colonel Patriot with a look of terror and determination on his face like I have never seen, his hands outstretched and clutching for me. He caught me and I felt him shaking. "Are you okay?"

He slowed, then hovered, holding me to his chest.

"I'm bleeding, Cub Scout," I said.

Then I slipped away into fog.

I woke up in the hospital, my arm bandaged and in a sling.

I listened to the doctor drone on about keeping me under observation for a night, listened to the good news that in six to nine weeks I'd most likely be back to work. Then he left, and some nurse brought me what was supposed to be food and a shot of whatever they gave me to keep the pain at bay.

The food was terrible.

The drugs were outstanding.

I picked at my meal and watched television. The news was all that was on. Ann Marigold at Channel Three was reporting live outside the Medina Institute for the Criminally Gifted. I caught bits of it, but the pain medication kept me fuzzy headed. The gist of it was that Professor Destructo was behind bars again.

Then a picture of me came up—the horrible old one on file from the first time I managed to distinguish myself in the line of duty. It always felt awkward to see myself on the tube, in full uniform, looking as stiff and plastic as some kid's toy. It was even stranger to hear the announcer recite my record.

I heard a knock, but then I realized it was on the wrong side of the room—not at the door but on the opposite wall. I looked for what had made the sound and saw a familiar face outside my window. I tried to motion at him with my right hand, got it caught in the sling, and I nearly came unglued at the agony. I winced and raised my left hand in greeting instead.

He opened the window with one hand and poked his head in. He kept one hand behind his back. "How are you doing?" he asked.

"I'm fine," I said. "I'm going home tomorrow." I nodded to the television. "So it looks like you got old Destructo. And the Bogus Baby, too."

He nodded. "I did." He looked uncomfortable. "That bullet would've killed me," he added. "You saved my life."

I smiled. "You returned the favor. I'm not used to being rescued. I'm usually on the other side of that fence."

"Me, too," he said.

"Thanks," I said. "But I do have a question." Something had been bothering me for a while. Well, since I'd had time to process it, anyway. "Back on the roof," I said, "you called me by my name. How do you know my name?"

He shifted uncomfortably. "Uh," he said. "I've been keeping my eye on you."

I raised my eyebrows. "Really?"

He nodded. "I have."

"So when you're not fighting crime and fires, you're a stalker?" I asked. "Or do you have some kind of fire-fighter fetish?"

"Not exactly." He blushed. "Can I come in?"

I nodded. I watched him clamber through the window frame. There was something familiar about him but I couldn't place it.

I felt good. Maybe it was the morphine. I felt all warm and protected. But that still didn't answer my questions.

"Why are you keeping your eye on me?"

"It's complicated but I was hoping we could talk about that. Especially after today."

"Okay," I said. "So talk."

"I was hoping for another chance."

"Another chance at what?"

He pulled roses from behind his back. They were in a giant vase—a nice one made of crystal—decorated with satin ribbons and a bow. The card read, "I'm so, *so* sorry."

I just stared at the flowers.

He set them on the nightstand beside the bed and stepped back. "You did good work today, Rachel. You saved a lot of lives."

"So did you, Bob."

"You should call me Colonel Patriot in public."

I felt the drugs settling in like a fog, swallowing the pain that radiated out from my shoulder. "Okay, Colonel Patriot."

He leaned over and kissed my forehead. His mouth was cool against my skin.

Then I heard his cell phone ringing. "You going to get that?" I asked him.

He shook his head. "I have the night off."

"No," I said. "Save that for later, when I'm out of here and a bit more mobile."

He blinked at me. "Really?"

"Really," I said. "We have a date to finish." I was suddenly liking the way this guy made me feel—over and above the drugs . . .

He answered the phone. "Yes, NM?" He nodded. "I see." He nodded more. "Yes. I'll be right there."

He hung up and looked at me. "Lunatic the Clown has taken the President hostage."

"Go get him, Cub Scout," I said, yawning. "I'm sleepy. Taking bullets is hard work."

He kissed me again, this time on my mouth, and I felt it all the way down to my toes. "Okay. I'll be back soon."

"Shoo," I said.

He grinned. Then he was gone. A moment later, there was a boom and the car alarms went off again. The news had changed to a live feed from Washington, D. C., where Terry Barker reported that the President's kidnapper was now demanding fifteen truckloads of Twinkies, airdropped over West Africa.

The world was back to normal . . .

I looked back to the window and smiled. Chaos and pandemonium would undoubtedly bend to the red, white, and blue blur that streaked toward them.

As I absently listened to the news, I wondered what we'd do on Bob's next night off. I had at least a few things in mind.

"Maybe," I mumbled to the empty room, "he'll even wear his cape."

I sighed and looked back to the news. The camera had shakily panned the sky, following a streak that impacted solidly in the yard outside the White House.

I watched carefully. I wanted to stay awake until he wrapped this one up.

But my eyes were so heavy . . .

I figured he'd be back to check on me before he headed off to the next disaster.

The trouble with heroes is there's never enough of them to go around. The world needs them. What the heroes want doesn't really enter into it. They do what they have to, without thinking about it. They do it for anyone who needs to be saved.

The trouble with heroes is they belong to us all.

So I guess I'll have to learn how to share.

There's another boom outside my window and my heart skips. But this time it's just thunder. As the rain begins to slice downward across the night sky, I let myself drift into a light sleep.

Bob would come back soon, I told myself. The car alarms would wake me when he did.

THE PROBLEM WITH METAPHORS

Steven Mohan, Jr.

Steven Mohan, Jr. lives in Pueblo, Colorado with his wife and three children, and surprisingly, no cats. When not writing he works as a senior quality engineer for a major manufacturing company. His short fiction has appeared in *Interzone, Polyphony,* and *Paradox,* as well as several DAW original anthologics. His stories have won honorable mention in the *Year's Best Science Fiction* and the *Year's Best Fantasy and Horror;* his first novel, *A Bonfire of Worlds,* is duc out at thc cnd of 2009.

WHAT I DID FOR SUMMER VACATION

After it was all over, I ended up having this recurring nightmare. I'm in Mrs. Sherman's third-grade room in P.S. 142 standing next to her desk, my back to the big green chalkboard, facing the class.

I look over at Mrs. Sherman, who is sitting behind her oak desk. Mrs. Sherman is the most terrifying person I've ever known. To say she is a bit severe is like saying the ocean is a bit wet.

At five-ten, she towers over her small charges, an effect accentuated by her perfect posture. She is

improbably thin. Jimmy Hobart says she once went
to jail for murdering a kid who couldn't sit still during
fractions, but she escaped by turning sideways and slipping out between the bars. She wears her black hair in a
bun, and she favors the army-style work shirts common
among outdoor enthusiasts and the leaders of small
Latin American countries.

And as I stand there clutching a piece of notebook
paper in my hands, her gaze falls on me and she says,
"Enough of this tomfoolery, Megan Cranston." Her lips
thin. "Please. *Begin.*"

I turn to look at the class. Jimmy Hobart is there, and
so are my parents. My father looks angry. My mother
looks disappointed, which is worse.

The NASA brass is there. Director McNair is sitting
next to my mother. He has a sour look on his wrinkled
face. He never liked me.

Next to McNair is the President of the United States,
Bob Thompson. Apart from his politics, I don't really
like Thompson. He's a dirty old man. I know this because when we were standing shoulder to shoulder in
the Rose Garden for the photo op, he reached down and
goosed me. All his aides were huddled around us, so I'm
pretty sure no one saw it, but if you're wondering why I
look startled on the *Newsweek* cover, that's why.

Next to Thompson is Zeus, who is *king* of the dirty
old men. I never understood why Zeus is portrayed as a
hero in popular culture. Just look at his track record. If
he were alive today, he'd be talking to a prison psycholo-
gist about how his childhood poisoned his relationship
with women.

Maybe he gets a pass because he's so pretty. Zeus is
the very incarnation of male beauty, his beard thick and
dark, muscles rippling in his great arms, resplendent in
a white toga trimmed in gold, a crown of laurels in his
hair. He is also huge, dwarfing even the terrifying Mrs.
Sherman. Somehow he still manages to sit in one of
those little desks.

Sitting behind Zeus are all the people of the world. So, you know. No pressure.

Mrs. Sherman clears her throat, which sounds to my third-grade ears like the deep toll of impending doom.

Panicked, I look down at the paper clutched in my hands. It says:

THE PROBLEM WITH METAPHORS
What I did for Summer Vacation
By Megan Cranston
Grade Three
P.S. 142

And below that—
There is nothing else. The paper is absolutely and totally blank.

At this point I generally wake up screaming.

JUPITER

During the orbital insertion into the Jovian system, the ship decided it needed to have us awake. *Really* who it needed was Alexander Patoulidou, our pilot. If fancy flying was needed to save your life, then Alex was your man. I couldn't fly the *Minotaur*. Hell, I couldn't even drive a stick.

On the other hand, if the disaster could be solved by doing a quick Fourier transform of a harmonic waveform, I was your gal.

Anyway, *Minotaur* woke both of us. Alex was the first to come out of coldsleep. When I crawled out of my cryocoffin, shivering and weak, teeth chattering, my hair stinking of oxygenated perfluorocarbon, there he was, looking, I'm sure he thought, like a Greek god.

Alex possessed that superpower common among pilots, immunity to nausea, so he looked great even though he'd just detanked.

Me? I felt like I was about to vomit up my pancreas.

Alex was five eleven, wavy black hair cut short, bronze

skin. *Gorgeous.* He stood with hands on his hips (the better to show off his muscular physique), and since he'd just crawled out of his coffin, he wore nothing but a pair of white boxers that clung indecently to his, er, legs.

He leered at me. "See something you like, Megan?" His smile was a flash of white against his dark skin.

Apparently, The European Space Agency didn't have the same sexual harassment rules as NASA.

"Not if you were the last man on Earth," I said woozily.

He snorted. "The last man on Earth? Screw Earth. I'm the last man for 650 *million* kilometers."

At that precise moment the ship bucked, roiling my already unhappy stomach.

"So what do you say, baby?" he said. "I'll show you the stars."

I turned and threw up.

That might have been a nice moment, except right after that a jump tone sounded, shrill and high and panicked. *Computer failure.* I shrugged into a jumpsuit and followed Alex to *Minotaur*'s tiny bridge.

As he buckled in, a rapid gong sounded, joining the jump tone. *Collision alarm.* The ship shook as something bounced off the hull.

I settled into the seat next to him just as the bridge (more like a cockpit really) filled with sirens, wails, and shrieks.

"Cascading failures," I shouted above the din.

He jerked his head down in a tight nod. He hit a button, and the audible alarms suddenly cut out. A creepy silence filled the dark, cramped bridge.

Jupiter gleamed in the window. We were close enough that it didn't look like a planet. It looked like a vengeful god, a monstrous presence banded in orange and brick, rose and cream, a leviathan that watched us with a malevolent red eye. Flashes of lightning backlit clouds the size of a small moon.

I shivered. Looking at it made me feel like a bug.

"We've lost comms lock," I said. "We're tumbling relative to Earth."

"Our vector's shaping up all wrong." Alex's voice was cold and hard. Angry.

At my station I was scrolling through system logs. "We passed through Io's flux tube."

"That's not supposed to happen," Alex snarled.

Like it was my fault.

We were supposed to slingshot around volcanic Io and pick up Europa on the other side, running a science package as we passed. Somehow *Minotaur* had come in wrong—inside Io's orbit. We'd passed through the flux tube, the corridor of charged particles that linked Jupiter to the little moon it was killing.

And now Europa was nowhere to be seen.

I pointed at a graph on my screen. Ol' Jupiter was throwing thunderbolts at us. "We had lightning strikes here and here. It might've caused a hiccup in the nav program."

"Computer's supposed to be hardened against electrical discharge," he snapped.

"I'm just telling you what I got," I snapped back.

"Never mind. Just give me a vector."

The navigation program was already running in the background. I punched up a burn solution.

A cursor blinked thoughtfully on the screen for ten, fifteen seconds. And then the nav program offered us its best estimate of burn duration to get us back on course.

"Your pinky is a lemon wedge," said the screen.

For a good, long minute I just sat there, feeling the throb of my pulse in my wrists.

"Dammit, Cranston, I need that solution *now.*"

"Alex," I said. "We have a problem."

"What are you talking about?" he snarled, shouldering me aside and stabbing a button.

"I'm a very pretty little girl," claimed the computer.

Alex went pale. He shook his head. "I don't—Uh, did you try rebooting it?"

"No," I said. "Because *that* would be stupid."

His Adam's apple bobbed as he stared down at the screen.

I looked up at him. "You're going to have to eyeball it in, champ."

Alex's mouth opened but no words came out. We were off course with limited delta vee and a nav computer that was a little batty. And Alex was going to have to fix it.

Manually.

He settled into his chair and stared out the forward port.

The monstrous god masquerading as a world stared back.

Zeus was the first of the gods, the oldest child, lord of Olympus, thrower of thunderbolts. I know what you're probably thinking. Zeus? What happened to Jupiter?

Don't get thrown by the name—they're basically the same guy. The Greeks thought up Zeus and then the Romans came along, took him over, and renamed him Jupiter.

The Romans were always doing stuff like that. They were like all those 35-year-old new-money millionaires who'll buy a nice house that's a tasteful cream with sandalwood trim and paint it lime green just to prove they have enough money to spend it foolishly.

That, in a nutshell, is how Zeus became Jupiter.

EUROPA

Alex fought *Minotaur* all the way down. He used more fuel than he should have, and he missed our LZ by twelve klicks, but considering that when he was done, our vessel wasn't a line of smoldering debris arcing across a thousand kilometers of ice, I thought he did pretty good.

What did I say before: If fancy flying was needed to save your life, then Alex was your man.

He lay across the control panel, drenched in sweat and utterly spent. It almost looked as if he got a little action, after all.

I put my hand on his shoulder. I didn't mean anything by it except, thanks for not ending my life in a fireball half a billion miles from my home planet, but he got the wrong idea.

He turned and took my hand, tracing the skin of my palm softly with his fingers, a small smile quirking his lips.

I jerked my hand back. "Man, don't you ever give it a rest?"

His face hardened. "I need to get the antenna recalibrated," he said stiffly, turning back to his board. "We're never going to get computers back without Earth's help. Why don't you go work the probe?"

"I can help you with comms," I said angrily.

"That wasn't a request, Mission Specialist Cranston."

"Aye, aye, Captain," I snapped. I stormed off.

Nothing is more fragile or more infuriating than the male ego.

Certainly nothing is more dangerous.

So when I descended the ladder, I was angry. The descent wasn't going out live because of our comms problems, but strategically positioned cameras were recording my ponderous descent from six different angles. Unfortunately, I wasn't thinking about that, I was thinking about what an asshole Alex was.

And beneath that, maybe I was worrying a little about what would happen to us if we couldn't get the comms and the computer back.

So I wasn't really paying attention. My right boot got tangled up in one of the ladder's rungs, and I fell straight back.

That's why the first words of a human being to set foot on Europa were, "Oh, *shit.*"

More importantly, I jarred a system control module in my suit.

But I wouldn't find out about that until later.

I picked myself up and drove out to the probe site. I started out upset because of the fall, moved into excitement, because I'd spent the last nine years of my life readying myself for this mission. But it was a long drive.

I eventually settled into boredom.

Not much to do but sit on the crawler and watch the scenery roll by, and there wasn't much scenery. Europa was little more than the infinite intersection of white ice plains and black space.

Well, except for Jupiter, of course.

Jupiter actually looked bigger down here, because the landscape provided scale. Jupiter loomed over this little world like a dragon hoarding its treasure.

Which is pretty funny when you think about Europa's story.

Europa was a young beauty desired by Zeus. Getting her agreement was no problem—in fact it wasn't a consideration at all. Apparently, for Greek gods, rape was the equivalent of meeting a woman after work for drinks.

But Zeus's wife, ah, well that was a different matter.

You didn't want to mess with Hera—not if you were smart.

So to hide from Hera's jealous gaze, Zeus turned himself into a tame white bull and mingled with the herd of Europa's father. She saw the magnificent beast and became enamored of it.

(Does this kind of thing really happen on farms? Don't ask me—I grew up in New York City.)

Anyway, she climbed up on Zeus's back, whereupon he carried her across the sea to Crete, where she became queen, which just goes to show (1) the Greeks considered many different forms of government before they settled on democracy and (2) if you're a beautiful woman, Zeus could be anywhere.

I drove on in silence.

*   *   *

The crawler's little brain drove it (and me) unerringly to what looked like a red fireplug installed in the middle of barren ice. That little piece of technology represented untold mountains of wealth spent in the pursuit of this very moment.

Thirty-four years ago, the Chinese lander *New Day* had drilled down through the thick Europan ice and took readings that strongly suggested there was life on the little moon. Since that day the five space-faring nations had spent trillions of dollars, euros, rubles, yen, and yuan to launch a viable mission to the Jovian system. Fortunately, the US-European consortium had won that race.

I just hoped we didn't pass out before we crossed the finish line.

Beneath the fireplug-looking interface device was a nanofilament wire thirty kilometers long. And attached to *that* was a probe that swam in the sea at Europa's warm heart.

We were going to visit our neighbors.

I climbed down from the crawler and trudged over to the interface. Shielded inside one of the metal arms was a wire, which I extracted and plugged into a socket in my suit. A nanoglass wire snaked out from the socket and inserted itself into the cortical shunt behind my right ear, completing the connection.

For a moment nothing happened.

There might be a break in the connection anywhere along the thirty kilometers cable. I looked up at Jupiter in that black sky and thought, *This expedition was born under an evil star*.

Then everything suddenly went dark.

I/she drifts in the world, between the warmth of below and the cold of the sky. I/she floats near the sky's knife, a blade of coldness that appeared a generation's generation ago. I/she fanned the water lazily with a score of ribbons, tasting, tasting. The water tasted rich, thick with krillspawn where the knife's cold met the warmth of the world.

I/she fed.

Discord sliced through the water, arrowing toward me/her.

Male.

He is great and sleek, ribbons streamed along his bullet-shaped body, ready for speed.

I/she slowly withdraws her own ribbons, readying myself/herself for flight.

Sonar slashes between them. "You are not welcome," I/she says.

His tail twitches in anticipation. "You are beauty and grace."

"Not welcome," I/she says arching my/her back in aggressive posture. "I/she swims with another."

"There is no other, only me," he says, drifting toward her. "I am father of warmth, bringer of all life in this world and beyond, master of the slicing light—"

"Master of boasting," I/she intones.

"The part of you that belongs to beyond the world will not be released," he says, "until you swim with me."

But I/she do not believe his words.

I/she darts away.

He chases.

I/she races for the knife, hoping that he will blunder into the coldness of it and be turned away, but he is aware of this strange thing. He is powerful. He closes the distance, great jaws nipping at my/her tail.

In her panic, I/she races up and up toward the bitter cold of the world's sky, until at last he is forced to give way.

I/she waits at the very top of the sky, shivering against the little knives of cold that cut into her flesh.

I/she hopes he will depart, but he does not, only orbiting below me/her. In desperation I/she is ready to give myself/herself to him, but *no.*

He will not keep his promises.

And so I/she endures cold and fear until darkness sweeps over her.

Not me/her—just her.

Light returned. Alex stood over me, peering down. He looked worried. He had me laid out on one of the couches in the cockpit.

"Wha—" I croaked.

"You had a slow leak in your suit."

"No alarm," I managed.

He shook his head. "You killed a diagnostic module when you fell. Great job, by the way. Good thing *that* moment's going to be a part of history. Fortunately, your biomonitors were still working, so I knew to come and get you."

"Thank you," I said. "You're not a Greek god, Alex. You're not as good. Or as bad."

He frowned. Probably didn't understand it was a compliment. "I guess your ordeal was harder on you than I thought."

I closed my eyes and tried to make sense of all of it. I remembered the speed of water flowing over my gills, the cold of the ice, the fear of the male. "I was ... an alien."

Alex's pretty brow furrowed. "You must have picked up some of the probe's feed while you were out. We got some great recordings of exoorganisms."

"That's *probe* feed. I wasn't that ... distant. I was an *alien.*"

"Megan. You were hypoxic. Whatever you think you remember—" He shook his head. "It wasn't real."

I was silent for a moment, taking that in. It seemed reasonable enough.

But somehow I knew he wrong. What had the male said?

I am father of warmth—

Jupiter's tidal action kneaded the moon's core,

melting ice and creating an ocean safe from the cold death promised by hard vacuum.

—*bringer of all life in this world and beyond.*

Long had Jupiter stood sentinel in the solar system, protecting Earth from asteroid strikes.

—*master of the slicing light.*

Thrower of thunderbolts?

Jupiter?

Zeus.

Zeus had so desired Europa he had turned himself into a bull to accomplish his ends. Had Zeus wanted me enough to turn us both into Europans?

After all, it was the planet Jupiter itself that had knocked out our computer.

Our computer.

I looked up at Alex. "What happened with—"

"It's fixed. All I had to do was turn it off and then turn it on." He smiled smugly. "Just like I said."

Zeus had released us. Perhaps there was a grudging respect there because I'd refused him.

He was never so kind to the women that finally gave in.

I know it sounds strange. But could it be that a god's power might be imbued in the world that bears his name?

It's that question that wrecks my sleep and twists my dreams.

The problem with metaphors is sometimes they're *not* metaphors. Sometimes names mean exactly what they seem to mean. Sometimes the truth is right in front of you.

If you'll see it.

IF I DID IT

Allan Rousselle

For most of his adult life, Allan Rousselle has lived and worked at either one end of Interstate 90 (Boston) or the other (Seattle), but he grew up in one of the towns in between. In Buffalo, NY, local heroes tended to be celebrity athletes who had made their name there. Having been a former journalist when the story broke, Allan paid particular attention to the celebrity trial when one of Buffalo's hometown football heroes made national news as a murder suspect. He nonetheless denies any similarities between the "Trial of the Century" and the characters of his story included here. For more of Allan's writing, visit his personal website at *http://www.rousselle.com/allan*.

I want to tell you what really happened between Jason and me. I want to tell you about the truth and the lies, about the love and the loss. I want to tell you my side of the story.

First, everyone understand I had nothing to do with Glauce's murder. I am one hundred percent not guilty.

Those gossipmongers and Corinthian Palace Guards

don't have the slightest clue what they're talking about. I would never do anything to hurt my Jason. Ever.

Let me be perfectly clear about that. If anything, maybe I loved Jason too much. A lot of hurtful things have been said about me, but never doubt for one minute that I didn't love Jason with all my heart.

Like all couples, we've had our ups and downs. When we decided to part recently, it was a hard decision. But there had never been any doubt that we would remain close friends, if not something more, for the rest of our lives. His dalliance with the princess could never have changed that. She was nothing to him, whereas everything that Jason ever became, he owed to me.

Let me tell you about how we met.

Even before I laid eyes on Jason for the first time, I was already quite famous in my home country of Colchis. True, I was the king's daughter, but I was an accomplished healer in my own right, skilled in the ways of herbs and spells.

A few feared my power—I'd been called a witch, and worse, by the small-minded among our people—but for the most part I was the envy of my father's court and kingdom. My deeds were well known, and my prowess was sought throughout the land.

Some have said that Jason was a gold digger who was just using my position once he found me, but they don't understand. Jason had arrived in Colchis aboard the galley ship *Argo*, in search of the Golden Fleece of the Aries Ram. He had been promised the throne of Thessaly upon his return from this quest. Love pierced my heart the moment I first saw him; Eros himself couldn't have created a love this strong.

The point is, *I* sought *Jason* out, not the other way around. He was so beautiful, with his muscular shoulders and his wistful eyes, and yet so forlorn when he learned that my father would only grant him the Fleece if he accomplished three nigh-impossible tasks. His despondency broke my heart. How could I not help him?

Of course, it would be scandalous for one of my kind to fall in love with an adventurer such as he. The powers-that-be would certainly never have approved such a mixed-marriage as we would make. Nonetheless, I was in love and would not be restrained by social convention.

When I told him I could help him, he pledged to make me his wife. I knew we would be together forever.

My father had set Jason the task of plowing a field with fire-breathing bulls. So I prepared for my beloved an elixir that would protect him from the scorching flames as he yoked the oxen and set them to dig the deep furrows into the rich, brown earth.

Next, he was to sow the field with a dragon's teeth. I knew, however, that the teeth would become an army of attackers, so I had cleverly warned Jason and told him how to defeat them. He threw a rock into their midst before the fighting began, confusing them as to where the volley had come from. In the confusion, they fell upon each other, leaving Jason unscathed in the fray.

For the final task, Jason would have to defeat the sleepless dragon that guarded the Golden Fleece. I prepared an herbal sleeping potion, which Jason used on the dragon. With my help, the Golden Fleece was ultimately easy for Jason to win.

But this is a cruel world, and even the word of a king—and a father—is not to be trusted. Jason took me with him when he and his Argonauts set sail for Thessaly, just as he had promised. My father, however, was not so true. Instead of giving us leave, the king pursued.

People say that I killed my own brother and threw him overboard in an effort to distract my father's pursuit. This is absolutely, one hundred percent not true.

If I had done it, though, I would have chopped up his body and scattered the remains so that my father's ship would have to stop to gather up *all* the pieces for a proper burial—a custom important to my people. This would have slowed them down to the point of making any further chase fruitless.

What you need to realize is that I would never have had to do this. Even if my brother *was* a part of my father's treachery, stowing away on the *Argo* to sabotage our escape, there was no need to pay him back in kind. With Jason at its helm, the *Argo* had the finest crew the world has ever seen, and we had a long lead on our pursuers. To suggest that I would choose to kill my own brother to help us escape my father's poorer ship is spiteful, cruel, and untrue.

Our journey to Thessaly was difficult. We faced terrible winds. Some have said that Zeus sent the storms to push us off course, as a punishment for what had happened to my brother. To this, I say: mere coincidence. These things happen.

Some say that we then journeyed to the island of Circe, where I sought ritual purification for my brother's murder in an effort to earn a respite from the dangerous weather. Again, this is entirely false. Circe was my aunt, and we had simply stopped along the way so that I could visit and ask for her counsel. Why would I need purification for a murder that I absolutely did not commit?

Even after this stop, there were obstacles threatening our triumphant return. We had to get past the Sirens at Sirenum Scopuli. We had to defeat Talos, the bronze man of Crete. People don't appreciate the difficulties we faced. But after all we'd faced, after all I'd done, did Jason receive his well-deserved hero's welcome upon our return?

He did not.

When we arrived in Iolcus, Jason and I were again betrayed; this time, by the King of Thessaly. Jason had fulfilled his obligation to deliver the Golden Fleece, but King Pelias refused to abdicate his throne to Jason as he had promised.

I'm well aware that many of you think that in my

rage at how Jason was treated, I conspired to have Pelias murdered by his own daughters. This is simply a lie.

If I did it, however, it would not have been difficult.

Remember that my skills, of which so many people are jealous, include mastery of herbal potions. I could have tricked the king's adoring daughters into thinking I had command over the secret of youth. I could have dismembered an old ram, put the pieces into a cauldron with a boiling potion, and then revealed a young lamb in its place. Seeing this, the girls would have begged me to provide the same service by restoring their father's youth.

If I had done so, that could have been the reason the girls chopped up their father and threw him into a pot, where he died.

But I did not.

Even though I had nothing to do with the king's daughters' act of patricide, my beloved Jason and I were forced to flee to Corinth, when they accused me of deliberately not bringing the king back to life. Once again, we were punished for being the victims of someone else's treachery.

This is what you all seem to lose sight of. I left my home, my family, and my privileged position for foreign lands. I have made the world my enemy, all for Jason, although I never had a quarrel with any of them.

I know the meaning of devotion. I know the meaning of loyalty.

We came to Corinth, Jason and I, where we made our home. Even though we had not yet married, I bore him two children. And while I worked as a healer, Jason curried favor with the king.

People say that Jason was only ever after glory, that all he really wanted was power. But I know that's not true. He was devoted to us, and securing a good position with King Creon was the best way for him to protect me and our children.

But as should be very clear by now, I am also aware of the deceitfulness of kings. Creon poisoned my Jason's mind; he prevailed upon Jason to marry Glauce, his daughter, instead of fulfilling his promise to marry me. How could he not be confused, being put into a situation like this? To deny the king would give offense and again jeopardize us all; but to yield would still deny me and my sons our rightful place in society.

Faced with such a difficult choice, I certainly couldn't blame Jason for betraying me. For betraying his children. If it hadn't been for Creon and Glauce, Jason would never choose to abandon me.

But to say that I acted out on this unfaithfulness by killing Glauce, and her father the king as well, is an outrageous accusation.

They say that I bewitched my wedding gift to the young bride, that I caused it to set fire to her and the king. Nothing could be further from the truth. Yes, I did offer a gift to the princess, as a sign that I would be no further hindrance to her and my beloved Jason's marriage.

Does that mean I deliberately set a trap for her? Definitely, certainly not. But if I did it, here's what I would have done. I'd have used my skill with herbs to create a contact poison and bathed a pretty silk robe with it. I'd have scented the robe with lavender and vanilla, to cover any tell-tale smells from the wicked potion, and would have decorated the outer parts of the garment with frills and flower petals to distract from any stain.

The slinky fabric would of course be enticing, practically begging to be worn against bare skin. Glauce would naturally want to try it on right away. The poison would begin its work within seconds of making contact with the princess's cream-perfect skin. It would scorch her. She would writhe and shake and beat at herself, trying to slap away the burning sting. Flames? There would be no flames. But the sensation of fire would consume her all the same, and she'd pull and tear at the robe and her skin beneath.

Her father being there would have made him, quite simply, an unfortunate bystander. He would naturally rush to her aid. But as soon as his hands reached for her shoulders and touched the garment, he would have sealed his own doom. As he felt the fire on his own hands, he'd wipe them on his tunic, on his face, and perhaps press them against his bare knees as he doubled over in pain. The poison would spread, as would the pain, and he would follow the princess in a journey to death.

Creon was in the wrong place at the wrong time. But even though he was consumed by the trap that had been set for his daughter, he was not entirely blameless. He had, after all, set the events in motion that led up to Jason leaving me.

Fortunately for all involved, the servants who came upon the bodies had the good sense not to touch them. By using a heavy shroud to cover and then remove the bodies for burial, they ensured that if there were any criminal residue, it would be buried along with the bodies.

What happened to the king and his daughter is a tragedy, truly, but I had no part in it. My heart goes out to the royal family, despite their treatment of me; I know how their loss feels.

As for my two boys—the sons I bore Jason—words can never convey how deeply I feel their loss. I had nothing to do with their deaths. But if I had, I clearly would have done it out of love. They were spared a life of torment and slavery made certain by the king's decision to have us all exiled. A decision that followed Jason's agreeing to marry Glauce.

Jason blames me. Jason is hurt. But I am hurt, too. I, too, have suffered a profound loss, and I grieve deeply.

People who have never been in my position can never understand what it's like to be a powerful woman in these times. You could never understand what it's like to be loved so tenderly by so many in the public, while being despised and reviled by people of means. You have no idea what it's like to be tormented and threatened with punishment, while the guilty go free.

They said the robe with the contact poison that killed the princess came from me. But I never owned such a robe. If it doesn't fit, you must acquit.

The establishment fears a powerful woman with celebrity. My accusers are not interested in finding the real killers. They seek only to pin blame and disgrace upon me while they themselves escape any close scrutiny. In that, and in so much more, they share the blame for these terrible crimes.

You curse me, but never yourselves, for the events that have come to pass.

But I tell you again that I am one hundred percent not guilty. And I will not rest until the real killers have been brought to justice.

CLAY FEET

Kristine Kathryn Rusch

Kristine Kathryn Rusch is an award-winning mystery, romance, science fiction, and fantasy writer. She has written many novels under various names, including Kristine Grayson for romance, and Kris Nelscott for mystery. Her novels have made the bestseller lists—even in London–and have been published in fourteen countries and thirteen different languages. Her awards range from the Ellery Queen Readers Choice Award to the Romantic Times Book Reviews Reviewer's Choice Award. She is the only person in the history of the science fiction field to have won a Hugo award for editing and a Hugo award for fiction. Her short work has been reprinted in fifteen Year's Best collections. Her current novel, *Duplicate Effort*, is part of her Retrieval Artist series—stand-alone mystery novels set in a science fiction universe.

"I t's broken," Harper said. She still held the metal pry bar in her right hand. It took all of her discipline to keep from swinging the thing at the museum staff.

The crate's top lay on the storage room floor, straw and packing materials scattered everywhere.

But Harper wasn't looking at the packing materials or the crate itself. She was looking at the statue inside. Mercury's winged helmet tilted jauntily on his stone curls, looking more like Robin Hood's cap than the armor for the Messenger of the Gods.

"His helmet isn't supposed to be like that," she said, "and his feet! Look at his feet!"

The rest of the antiquities staff looked. Mercury's feet, which should have been stuffed in winged shoes, had melted onto the crate's bottom.

Harper dropped the pry bar onto the stone floor. The clatter did not make her feel better.

This ancient statue of Mercury was supposed to be the heart of their new antiquities collection. Harper had negotiated for it for the last decade. She'd even flown to Rome to meet with Italian authorities. Like so many other countries now, Italy wanted its precious antiquities inside its own borders.

Lately, cries of theft had reverberated all over the world—whether it was old thefts of Egyptian tombs (which benefited places like the British Museum) or Nazi thefts of Jewish art, which then got sold (without enough provenance) to newer museums throughout Europe and the United States.

Technically, Harper had gotten the Mercury on loan, but the loan was permanent, so long as the museum made annual lease payments that amounted to more than her entire salary.

The hat Harper could repair, but the feet—how was she going to explain the feet to the Italian government? How was she going to explain the feet to anyone? Marble didn't melt. Marble lasted centuries—*millennia*—buried underground, near rivers and streams.

"Have you ever seen anything like this?" she asked, more to herself than anyone else. She hadn't. Not with something that had such great bona fides. The provenance on the Mercury sculpture was the best she'd ever seen.

"Actually," said Malcolm Endicott, the senior curator, "I have seen something exactly like it."

She turned.

Endicott was an old man. He was old when she was hired out of college fifteen years before, and he was older now. His skin had mottled and loosened; his hair had thinned so much that it looked like ripped shirt covering his skull.

He wore bespoke suits to work every day, and at all times of year, he covered his wattled neck with a cravat instead of a tie.

His wife had died a few years before, and that seemed to give him permission to spend all of his time here.

Harper didn't mind. The old man had a wealth of knowledge that she hadn't sufficiently tapped yet, even though they'd worked side by side for most of her tenure.

"You've seen melting marble?" she asked him.

He smiled gently. He was sitting on a stool near one of the temporary walls. His back was straight, his expensively shod feet curled around the stool's rungs. If he fell, he'd break not only bones in his torso, but the bones in his legs as well.

"Darling," he said in a tone only he could use with her. "Marble doesn't melt."

His thoughts echoed hers, but she didn't say that. Instead, she swept her hand toward the statue and its ruined feet.

"Then what is this?"

His smile grew. "An elaborate forgery."

"You can tell that from over there?"

He nodded.

"The forgery fooled experts all over the world," she said.

"Then the forgery itself might be worth some money," he said.

"Only historical forgeries are worth money," she said.

Sometimes forgeries had a provenance too. Either they were completed by an artist who later made a reputation for himself, or they belonged to a moment in time, one that could be traced and reproduced just like the original.

For decades, the replica of the Venus de Milo was all that the art world had of that masterpiece. Many art historians believed a lot of the replicas were forgeries.

Then the original Venus was discovered, and the others lost value, but not as much as they would have without the provenance.

"I would wager," Endicott said, "this is a premier historical forgery."

"Wagering doesn't help us." Usually she wasn't that curt with the old man. But usually she wasn't faced with a forged treasure she had fought nearly a decade to receive.

"Did I ever tell you how I served after the war?" he asked.

"No," she said, trying to hide her impatience. She didn't have time for a story. Besides, she already knew about Endicott's past.

He had joined up late and served the last two years of World War II in combat. He then resigned for a tour to rebuild Europe. Occasional stories that leaked out from him or his late wife put him in Paris after liberation, Berlin after Hitler's death, and the Italian Alps after Mussolini's fall.

"I was on recovery duty." He put a hand on that false wall to brace himself as he untangled his feet from the stool. One of the younger staff members rushed to his side, but he waved the woman aside. The wall wobbled as he stood, but it didn't tumble the way Harper feared it would.

"Recovery duty," she repeated. She knew better than to ask a question. She didn't want to encourage the memory.

Endicott nodded as he walked toward her. His polished shoes slid on the straw, and she reached out in case he fell. He ignored her. Instead, he crouched and stared at the ruined feet.

"Plaster," he said softly. "Experts couldn't have been fooled by plaster."

She crouched beside him. Cautiously she reached inside the crate. The statue felt like marble on the surface, the way that fake marble countertops felt like marble. But fake marble countertops did not have the weight of marble.

This statue had the correct weight. Their normal delivery men would have noticed something lighter. She would have too as she helped them struggle the crate into the receiving part of the storage area.

Her finger brushed against the melted feet. The weight of this statue came not from the surface materials but from the materials used on the interior.

Endicott was right; it was plaster mixed with some kind of rock for heft.

"You've seen this before?" she asked.

He nodded. "At Carinhall, in a corner of the garden. My heart nearly stopped when we arrived to find *Nike of Samothrace* melting in the rain."

He left it there, waiting for her to ask questions.

But she didn't. She didn't have time.

Instead, she directed the staff members to take photographs and document the crate's arrival.

She had to check her own documentation, which she kept in her office.

But she couldn't stop thinking about *Nike of Samothrace*. It was one of the Louvre's most famous sculptures. Better known as *Winged Victory of Samothrace*, the sculpture anchored the wing between the Galerie d'Apollon and the Salon Carré with the new rooms built parallel to the Grande Galerie.

On her very first visit to the Louvre, Harper had run up the flight of stairs leading to *Winged Victory*, wanting to see both her and the Mona Lisa before her visit ended.

But Harper had spent most of her time gazing at *Winged Victory.* The huge statue, taller than most men, had been found in pieces on the island of Samothrace in 1863. It was reassembled into an imposing figure of a woman—Nike, the Greek Goddess of Victory—her wings extended behind her, body in motion, as she stood on the prow of a ship. The sculpture probably stood on a promontory overlooking the sea. The archeologists searched but never found the most important piece— her head—and yet the sculpture was impressive without it.

As Harper sat below it, she could almost hear the sea wind blow, and Nike's garments flapping in the breeze. No sculpture had taken her breath like that before; few had done so since.

Although the sculpture of Mercury, which the scholars believed to be as old as *Nike of Samothrace,* had taken her breath too when she saw it in a private collection near Rome. That was the day she decided to purchase it.

That was the day that started her on the long journey which brought her here.

Here, to her office, where she stared at the pile of documentation beside her. Provenance, insurance documents, down payments, and guarantees. Now she would face lawyers and legal challenges and headaches beyond imagining.

She needed to be back in the storage room, photographing the Mercury statue and the condition it arrived in. Her entire career rested on this sculpture now. Not dealing with the fraud directly would be disastrous, both to her and to the museum.

Still, she couldn't bring herself to go back downstairs. She had come up to her office to get all of the materials and to start downloading new copies of the email files from the past two months. She was supposed to print up the e-mails whenever they came in, but she was usually too busy.

Now she might pay for that as well. If any emails pertaining to the Mercury sculpture were lost, the trail might grow cold.

So she had electronically stored the files and now she was printing them, the printer queue backed up some 55 emails strong.

She should have looked through the documentation while she printed. Instead, she went to Google and typed in "Karenhall." She got some strange responses, most of which seemed to have nothing to do with Endicott or sculpture.

So she typed in "Karenhall" and "World War II" and got this message: *Did you mean Carinhall?* She hit that link, and discovered what Endicott meant.

Carinhall was Hermann Goering's country house, located fifty miles outside of Berlin. Goering had been a member of Hitler's inner circle. He had filled Carinhall with valuable artworks from all over Europe, then taken eleven traincars full of those artworks from the house just ahead of the Russian Army's arrival in early 1945.

Americans were not allowed on the site until the Russians had left in the fall of 1945, and then the only Americans who went there were part of an international group formed to return priceless artifacts to the countries the Nazis had stolen them from.

Harper found no mention of Endicott's name in connection to Carinhall, but she did finally understand why he had been in Paris and Berlin and in the Italian Alps. Anywhere the Germans stored priceless art, stolen from conquered nations, Endicott had been there, cataloging, discovering, saving.

She had no idea she was working with such a man. She wondered if anyone else in the museum did either.

She grabbed the stack of documentation for the Mercury sculpture, checked to make sure she had enough paper in her printer for the remaining emails, and then went back to the storage area.

Of course, Endicott was no longer there.

She found him in his office, a cloistered room in the very center of the museum. The room was hidden behind secret panels in the library wing. To get in, one had to know which panel hid the combination lock and what the combination was.

Staff members had told Endicott for years that the room was no longer safe for him to spend so much time in (if, indeed, it ever had been), but he didn't care.

If I die in there, he would respond, his faded blue eyes twinkling, *then eventually you'll smell me, and you'll know what happened.*

She hadn't liked that idea at all and checked on him twice a day—when she first arrived and just before she left.

She did understand why he spent so much time in his office, though. It was homey, in a cluttered Victorian kind of way.

Reproductions of bronzes and small Etruscan vases stood on various surfaces. Larger reproductions of some of the world's most treasured antiquities covered his floor.

Harper particularly liked the statue of Diana, which was a reproduction of another famous Louvre sculpture. One Christmas, Endicott had placed a wreath of mistletoe around Diana's head. The mistletoe remained all year. The next Christmas, he'd added a Santa cap to the stag that leapt beside her.

Even now, in June, the Christmas decorations looked appropriately festive.

His whimsy was apparent everywhere—in the lovely jacket he had placed over the reproduction of the Venus de Milo (the jacket had Anne Boleyn sleeves and did not button in the front, leaving Venus's greatest assets visible to the room), as well as in the placement of the screaming Harpies in front of a worried-looking statue of Zeus.

Most of the small jokes were beyond the newer curators and staff members, but Harper spent a lot of time noticing the details, and the details in Endicott's cluttered office all had meaning, most of it wry.

He was sitting behind his desk, another reproduction, this one of the desk Jack Kennedy used to use in the Oval Office. The statue of a small boy peered out of the opening near the feet, echoing the famous photograph of Kennedy's son, John, playing there when he was still a toddler.

"I thought I'd see you sooner," Endicott said. "Still worried about losing your job?"

"My job or any job," she said. "This is a drastic mistake. I'm not sure how I could have made it."

Endicott's smile was sad. "You didn't, my dear. Someone else did, either before the statue got crated or along the way. That's for insurance people and detectives to find out. You'll be vindicated. Somewhere there is a real statue."

"Like there was for *Nike of Samothrace*?" she asked.

"Ah, you looked it up," he said.

"Yes," she said. "There's even a documentary about the effort it took to take *Nike* from the Louvre shortly after the Germans invaded Poland. France didn't want its treasures stolen or destroyed."

"So," Endicott said, touching his fingertips together, "you think I lied about seeing *Winged Victory* in the gardens at Carinhall?"

"I'm assuming it was a reproduction," she said. "But I couldn't find confirmation in my very short search."

"It was," he said. "And not as good as the one you have in the storage area. The entire statue was made of plaster, not coated with some other substance like the one below. I have no idea what Goering was thinking when he placed it in the garden. He had to know it would melt."

She frowned at Endicott. "I didn't realize he reproduced a lot of art. I thought he confiscated it. The website

I found says he took everything from Jewish homes and museums and placed it in his various homes."

"He did." Endicott wasn't smiling any longer. "And he wasn't alone. It seemed half the German army was stealing art. And then the Allies stole art as well. It's a crime that we'll never recover from."

"So the reproductions?" she asked.

"Placeholders," Endicott said. "He commissioned them to fit into his designs until he found where the originals were hiding."

"Fortunately, he never found *Nike*," Harper said.

Endicott tapped his fingertips together. Then he slid his wheeled chair back and grabbed a large, thick book. It was covered in dust. He used a cloth to remove the dust, then he opened the book.

It was filled with yellowed clippings, photographs, and notations. He paged through it until he found some grainy pictures.

"I think he did find her," Endicott said. "I think he · replaced her with the reproduction, leaving the reproduction in Valençay."

"Tallyrand's estate?" she asked. "I thought Venus was there too."

She was an instant expert from her internet reading.

"And the French crown jewels, which I believe he left, expecting to come back for them."

"You have proof of this?" she asked.

He tapped the pictures. Harper leaned forward. She was wrong; they weren't grainy pictures. They were black-and-white pictures of the Carinhall garden in full flower, with sculptures everywhere. The reason the pictures seemed grainy was because whoever had taken them had done so in a downpour.

Nike of Samothrace stood in the center of the garden, water dripping off her majestic shoulders. Around her, water pooled, but the prow of the ship which was the sculpture's base, looked like it was intact. She saw no melting, no blurring of the sculpture's clean lines, which she should have seen with plaster in that kind of downpour.

"But the *Nike* in the Louvre is real," she said. "I've seen it."

"As has all of the art world for the past sixty years," he said.

"How did the sculptures get switched?"

"Ah, that's the question," he said. "It took special movers to get that statue to Valençay in the Loire Valley. Yet the Germans, with all of their very careful documentation, have no record of the work it would have taken to remove *Nike* from her storage spot at Valençay and take her to Carinhall—close to Berlin, no less."

"And then take her back," Harper said.

"Before the Russians arrived," Endicott said, "since she was majestically melting when I found her."

He grabbed another notebook. This one wasn't as dusty. He opened it to the middle, revealing photographs of the same garden, littered with rubble from the destroyed house. At the center of six shots stood the plaster *Nike of Samothrace*. The prow of the ship looked like a sunken bathtub, the grass covered with a whitish paste. The sculpture itself looked like a nude. The lines of the garment, which were designed to look like a Greek gown blowing backward in the wind, were gone, leaving only the sculpture's legs and torso. The magnificent wings dripped giant drops of plaster onto the plants behind them.

"My God," Harper said. "Who took the original photographs?"

Endicott shrugged. "We found these photographs in the house. I assume one of Goering's staff took the pictures, or perhaps his second wife, Emmy. It is one of those mysteries. We don't even know when they were taken, although we know it was before 1945, when the family fled the property."

Harper took a closer look at the original photographs. Then she grabbed one of the magnifying glasses that Endicott kept on his desk.

Behind a shrub, she saw the edge of a winged hat. Peeking through the leaves, she thought she saw winged shoes.

"Look at that," she said, pushing the photographs back to Endicott. He took a different magnifying glass.

"I don't think that's your Mercury," he said. "The body's position is different."

She stood, so that she could see it better. She wasn't sure. The body position might be accurate for her Mercury. It was hard to tell, now that the sculpture she had in the storage area was a reproduction. She had to trust her memory for forms.

She'd seen the original (and it had to be the original; she couldn't have been fooled by a fake) nearly a decade before. Her memory, while good, wasn't that good.

She scanned the other photographs. Their angle kept the statue hidden. They almost made Mercury seem as though he was hiding in the garden.

"I think it's just brilliant placement," she said. "Whoever designed this garden probably knew all of Mercury's identities."

"Perhaps," Endicott said, but he didn't sound convinced.

Harper set the magnifying glass down. "How much do you think a forgery with this kind of provenance would bring?"

"One of Goering's forgeries?" Endicott shrugged. "Hard to tell now. Maybe not so much in the art market, but in the historical markets, among collectors, quite a bit."

"Between that and the insurance, then, we might be able to make some of our investment back."

"Might," Endicott said, but he sounded dismissive, as if he didn't care about the insurance.

She did. She cared about the financial bath the museum would take because of her mistake.

"I'm not sure," Endicott said, "you're seeing what I see when I look at the original photographs."

"I'm sure I'm not," she said. "You were there. You know how they fit in context."

He shook his head. Obviously, he hadn't meant that either.

"What do you see when you look at the photographs?" she asked.

"Miracles," he said. "A garden full of miracles."

Usually, Harper appreciated Endicott's whimsy, but on this day, it irritated her. She felt she had lost precious time talking with him. He could have told her about the Mercury sculpture in the garden, the fakes that Gocring collected, and the possibility that one of them had found its way into her museum.

Instead, Endicott had played games, making her stare at old photographs until her eyes hurt, and talking of miracles.

Those photographs had no date on them. For all she knew, the *Nike of Samothrace* could have been the plaster reproduction, coated with something that held off the rain for a year or two.

She tried not to let her irritation blossom into anger because she knew she wasn't really angry with Endicott—he had provided her with a bit of salvation, after all—but with the so-called experts she'd hired to guide her Mercury statue on its journey from Rome to her storage room.

Someone had failed, and even if she didn't lose her job over it, she would lose time and honor and her spotless reputation.

Endicott wouldn't explain his "miracle" comment. He seemed almost hurt when she asked him to. Instead, he'd shrugged and mumbled something about the ramblings of an old man.

That was when she knew she had lost him. He had meant to explain something to her, and she had somehow offended him.

At the moment, she didn't care. He would get over his fit of pique. But she might not get over this blow to her reputation. She had to act now, with her own photographs and documentation. She needed to write up her own history of the purchase and call a lawyer, so that she was not only prepared when the time came to defend herself, but well represented.

She hurried out of Endicott's office and down the stairs. She hated taking the elevators after hours. The sound of the mechanisms in the empty museum always made her think of monster movies—something about to attack in the darkness.

Not that the museum was ever completely dark. Some of the collections had covers, protecting them from the lights, but each room had dim lighting. The museum had a single security guard, but mostly he monitored the security cameras. He only did a room-to-room visit once an hour, and even then what he did was a walk-through, not a thorough examination.

The main lights were off in the storage room. The staff had clearly finished up while she was talking to Endicott. Prints of digital photographs sat on one of the metal tables. The photos were good, but, as she feared, not good enough.

She looked around for the digital camera, thinking maybe someone had left it on the table. But she didn't see it. She would have to go back to her office to get her own camera, which made sense, because from now on, everything she did would be on her own.

As she turned, she saw a man sitting on the stool, his features hidden in shadow.

"For god's sake, Malcolm," she said to Endicott, "you're going to break every single bone in your body sitting on that thing."

He laughed. Only the laugh didn't sound like Endicott's. It was rich and warm and deep, almost as if it had its own built-in reverberation chamber.

"I've never broken a bone in my life," he said.

He was quite clearly not Endicott or anyone else she knew. She should have hit the lights when she came in, but she hadn't, and now they were by the door, which seemed very far away from her.

Because of a blackout years ago in which a security guard walked through a Vermeer canvas on loan from another museum, the directors insisted on flashlights at every corner. Since the storage room didn't have corners, it had flashlights on every table.

She moved slowly, so that she didn't seem like a woman panicked.

The flashlight leaned against a receipt book. She grabbed the light, flicked it on, and shone it at the man's face.

He didn't raise his hands to block the light. He didn't even squint. Instead, he looked vaguely amused. He had a stunningly handsome face—high cheekbones accenting a Roman nose. His eyes were so dark they looked black in the light. His hair curled around his forehead and down the side of his face like a small cap.

"Do I pass inspection?" he asked.

She didn't answer. His face looked oddly familiar, but the familiarity became something else as he moved. It was almost as if she'd seen one of the statues come alive.

And then she realized who he looked like.

She looked over her shoulder at the open crate. The assistants had moved it closer to the lights, which meant she could still see the features in the thin emergency lighting as well.

"Oh, by Zeus's throne," the man said. "Go turn on the overhead lights. I'll go stand by the stupid sculpture so that you can see definitively that I am the subject of the sculptor's vision. Then we can move on to other, more important things."

She almost didn't walk to the light switch, just because she didn't want to take orders from this strange man. But she did. And she also hit the silent alarm, so that the security guard would know there had been some kind of breach.

When she turned, she saw the man standing next to the sculpture. He was thin but heavily muscled—as a professional distance runner would be—and he looked exactly like the fake Mercury, except that he wasn't wearing a winged helmet, at a rakish angle or any other way.

"You made the forgery," she said.

"My dear," he said, "if I had made the forgery, it would have been a lot better than this one. I stole the forgery and had it sent to you."

"Excuse me?" she said. Did he just admit he was behind this whole mess? If so, why?

"You have no right to the statue," he said.

"I paid for it," she snapped.

"Ah, yes. American greed and arrogance. You're like so many other arrogant cultures. They all die, you know."

He was as irritating as he was pretty.

"The sculpture belongs to the museum," she said. "What did you do with it?"

"The original sculpture," he said, "belongs in a temple, where it can be properly worshiped."

"Worshiped?" She wanted to look at the door, to see if the security guard was anywhere close, but she didn't want to clue the crazy man that someone was coming.

"Worshiped," the man said. "All of these statues that you've pilfered are religious icons, you know."

"No one knows what this is," she said. "It was found in Greece nearly a century ago. There was no temple nearby, no clue as to why Mercury stood alone."

"Hermes," the man said.

"Excuse me?" she asked.

"The proper name is Hermes, although you've pilfered that name as well. And for a scarf. You have no idea how offended one god can feel."

The flashlight slipped in her hand. Her palms were sweating. This man was scaring her.

"Yes, yes," she said. "I know the Greek name for Mercury is Hermes. But—"

"But nothing," he said. "This is a Greek sculpture from a temple originally built to honor Hermes. It does not belong to you. Nor docs it belong to Rome. It belongs on its island, away from avid eyes that do not understand that gods were meant to be worshiped, not gawked at."

Hadn't the guard gotten her message? She was convinced she had sent it. So far this strange man didn't seem like a physical threat to her, although he might hurt the forgery. And that might be just as bad as losing the original in the first place.

She had to stall. Maybe the security guard, who wasn't the most courageous man, was waiting for backup.

"No one worships the Greek gods anymore," she said. "There are no active temples."

"And that," the crazy man said, "is a crime. But it is one we live with. Still, this image was stolen from its homeland. It must return there, to its proper place."

She swallowed. "Why?"

"Why?" he said. "To rebuild. We've let pale imitations of ourselves be studied for too long. We need to restore the temples and take our places as proper gods."

"Our places?" she asked, feeling even more confused than she had when the conversation started. "Yours and mine?"

He gave her a condescending smile. "I'm sorry, my dear. You are a minion, not a god."

She straightened. Of all the things people had called her throughout her life, minion was the absolute worst.

"Just because you look like a damn statue doesn't make you a god either," she snapped.

To her surprise, he smiled. "What came first, eh? The statue or the god?"

"The concept," she said, as if he were asking a really intelligent question instead of a facetious one. "And everyone knows that sculptors from Bernini to Michelangelo used real life models to represent made-up characters."

"Hermes is made up?" he asked.

"All gods are," she said.

His eyebrows rose. "A cynic."

"A realist."

"This sculpture," he said, "was not made by one of your late-model Italians. It dates from the era you call Before Christ."

"That statue," she said, "probably dates from last week."

"I am talking about the real sculpture," he said. "This one comes from sixty years ago. Your friend Endicott should have recognized it. His friend Goering had it made."

"Malcolm Endicott would not call Hermann Goering a friend," she snapped.

The crazy man held up his hands as if he were trying to calm her. "No, no, you're right," he said. "I simply meant—"

"That this is one of Goering's fakes," she said. "I already figured that out. Give me the original."

"I am the original," the man said.

"You are Hermes, Messenger of the Gods?" She couldn't keep the sarcasm from her voice.

He nodded slowly. "I have come to tell you and others like you that you may not keep our statues. It is long past time. We have put up with this long enough. We would like our temples rebuilt, our statues returned to their homelands and replaced."

He spoke as if he had been making a pronouncement. She glanced at the door.

"Why?" she asked, mostly to keep the crazy man talking.

"Why?" he said. "Because it is the right thing to do."

"All of you believe that?" she asked.

He nodded.

"That's the message?"

He nodded again.

She decided to humor his delusion. She wished the damn security guard would get here.

"You," she said, "the God of Commerce, are telling us to hurt our museum business and send one of our major draws away at no charge. That doesn't sound good to me. Does it sound good to you?"

His lovely eyes narrowed. "What do you mean?"

"This museum is a business. If you are Mercury or Hermes, as you seem to prefer, then you protect merchants and all commerce. They call you the God of Commerce. Are you going to deny the title?"

"I am also the Divine Herald," he said. "I lead people on their final journey, death. Are you asking me to respond in that capacity as well?"

She couldn't hide her shiver. But she straightened nonetheless. She wasn't going to let him know how much he intimidated her.

"Don't threaten me," she said.

"I'm not," he said. "I'm just amazed you're pulling out my resume to make me feel guilty. I am the messenger of the gods, and the message I bring is to let these statues return to their rightful place."

"Which would ruin my business."

"In the United States, a museum is not a business. It has protected status. That status is called a nonprofit, which makes it a charity." His eyes twinkled. "I am not the god of charities."

Whoever he was, he had a point. A museum was not a business. It got grants to supplement its income. It survived even if it didn't make a dime.

"You've done this before," she said. "You took *Nike of Samothrace* and returned her to the Louvre."

She expected him to deny it or to be surprised by the question, not understanding it at all.

Instead, he smiled again. "You are smarter than you look. But I did not return her to the Louvre. I sent her to a protected place in the Loire Valley, while I searched for the remains of her temple. I have not yet found it."

"You sent her to Valençay. And now she is in the Louvre, where she started out."

"She will be returned to her homeland," he said, "when a place is prepared."

"Do you have a place prepared for my statue?" Harper waved her hand at the dissolving reproduction.

"No," the crazy man said softly. "I am just tired of my image being set up on a pedestal to be gawked at by ignorant tourists."

"You would rather have your image in hiding?" she asked.

"I would rather be worshiped," he said.

Of course he would. What man wouldn't?

"Would you rather be worshiped as the God of Commerce or the messenger for the others? Doesn't that make you an errand boy instead of a god?"

"I am not that," he snapped.

"That's how you're acting," she said.

"I am not," he said, straightening.

"Then tell me," she said, trying to keep the smile off her face, "why the God of Thieves is angry that someone has stolen a statue made from his image."

The crazy man's chin rose. His eyes narrowed, and for the first time, he looked formidable.

He might come at her. The only way she could prevent it was to keep talking—and maybe find that metal pry bar.

"You're right," she said, her throat suddenly dry. "Museums are not a business. And many museums, many *famous* museums, have stolen artifacts inside our

walls. Some have paid hefty fines to keep precious artifacts. Others have had to return those artifacts to their
home country."

"So?" the crazy man asked. She had his attention
now.

"So," she said. "If you are who you say you are, you
claim you want your image in a place of worship. What
better place to worship the God of Thieves than in the
antiquities section of a well-known museum?"

It was her last gambit. She had probably offended him
so deeply that he would lunge at her, hurt her, maybe
even do damage down here.

She clutched the flashlight like a club, ready to use it
if she had to.

But he didn't look like a man about to lunge. Instead,
he was frowning slightly, as if he were thinking.

"Thievery and commerce both," he said slowly. "For
museums make people pay to see the things you've
stolen."

"Yes," she said, her heart pounding.

"And often, these things you've stolen have been stolen from the dead, whom I have led to their final resting
places."

She nodded, afraid to interrupt his reverie.

"And yet, people come here. They look in awe at
the treasures you've assembled. The treasures you've
stolen."

"Well, someone has stolen them," she said. She wasn't
going to admit to theft. So far as she knew, she hadn't
committed any.

So far as she knew.

He nodded. Then he bowed slightly.

"I have misrepresented you," he said. "You are not
a minion. You are a high priestess. The high priestess of
the museum."

Her cheeks flushed. "Thank you," she said. "I think."

He touched the crate. "I cannot speak for the others.
I am their messenger, not the one who makes decisions

for all of Olympus. But I can speak for myself. I am sorry to have misjudged you and your kind. And I am sorry that I disturbed you."

"You didn't . . ." she said, and then she let her voice trail off.

Because he had disappeared.

Literally vanished, right in front of her.

One moment, he had been standing there. The next, he was gone.

She walked toward the crate, and waved a hand where he had been. Nothing. No one stood there.

Then her gaze went to the statue. It looked different.

The winged helmet was on straight—and the winged boots were back on the feet. She touched the legs. Marble. They hadn't melted at all.

Had she dreamed all of this?

She went back to the table.

No. The pictures were still there, with the missing shoes, the melting plaster, everything.

The doors burst open. The guard and Endicott hurried into the storage room.

"Something wrong?" the guard asked.

"Yeah," Harper said. "I pressed the alarm at least a half an hour ago. What took you so long?"

"Three minutes, ma'am," the guard said. "It's only been three minutes. I have it all in my log."

"I heard it too," Endicott said, "and I came running."

Three minutes? How was that possible? That was the longest three minutes of her life.

"What's wrong?" the guard asked.

"Someone was here," she said. "Do you have video in this room?"

"Only of the doors, ma'am," he said.

"Check it," she said. "But first, make sure we're alone."

"Yes, ma'am." He put a hand on his gun, and walked around the edges of the storeroom.

Endicott peered at her. "What's going on?"

She waved her hand toward the crate, without looking at it. "Tell me what you see."

He put his hands behind his back and walked to the crate. Then he peered at it for the longest time.

She didn't look at him. She watched the guard shine his own flashlight in the corners, making sure nothing lurked there.

He wouldn't find anything. She knew that now.

"My God," Endicott whispered.

"The statue is real now, isn't it?" she asked.

He did exactly as she had. He went for the photographs.

"It's been replaced," he said.

She nodded.

"How?" he asked.

She took the photographs from him. "That," she said, "is a very long story."

"I have time," Endicott said.

He did. So did she. And she had to tell someone.

She looped her arm in his, still clutching the photographs, and walked him toward the door. They would have dinner. Then they would come back and reassess.

"The story," he urged.

She smiled. "You know the photograph of Mercury in the garden at Carinhall?"

"Yes," he said.

"You were right. That wasn't my statue back hiding behind the plants."

"What was it?" Endicott asked.

"A miracle," Harper said. "An annoying little miracle."

ABOUT THE EDITOR

Denise Little has been involved in nearly every facet of the book business in the past twenty-five years. She worked for Barnes & Noble/B. Dalton Bookseller for ten years as a bookstore manager, then for four more years as their national book buyer for science fiction, fantasy, and romance. She then joined Kensington Publishing, where she founded and ran her own imprint, *Denise Little Presents.* Since 1997, she's been executive editor at Tekno Books, working for Dr. Martin H. Greenberg. She's edited twenty anthologies for DAW, including her most recent: *Front Lines, Mystery Date, Enchantment Place, Swordplay, Witch High,* and *Cosmic Cocktails.* She's also an award-winning writer of fiction and nonfiction, including the national bestseller *The Official Nora Roberts Companion.* Her short fiction has appeared in DAW's *Civil War Fantastic* and *Alternate Gettysburgs.*

There is an old story...

...you might have heard it—about a
young mermaid, the daughter of a king, who
saved the life of a human prince
and fell in love.

So innocent was her love, so pure her
devotion, that she would pay any price for the
chance to be with her prince. She gave up her
voice, her family, and the sea, and became
human. But the prince had fallen in love with
another woman.

The tales say the little mermaid sacrificed her
own life so that her beloved prince could find
happiness with his bride.

The tales lie.

Danielle, Talia, and Snow return in

The Mermaid's Madness
by Jim C. Hines

Coming in October 2009

"Do we *look* like we need to be rescued?"

DAW 109

Fiona Patton

The Warriors of Estavia

"In this bold first of a new fantasy series... Court intrigues enrich the story, as do many made-up words that lend color. The smashing climax neatly sets up events for volume two." —*Publishers Weekly*

"The best aspect of this explosive series opener is Patton's take on relations between gods and men."
—*Booklist*

"Fresh and interesting...I look forward to the next."
—*Science Fiction Chronicle*

THE SILVER LAKE

978-0-7564-0366-9 $7.99

THE GOLDEN TOWER

978-0-7564-0577-9 $7.99

To Order Call: 1-800-788-6262

www.dawbooks.com

DAW 55

MERCEDES LACKEY

Gwenhwyfar

The White Spirit

A classic tale of King Arthur's legendary queen. Gwenhwyfar moves in a world where gods walk among their pagan worshipers, where nebulous visions warn of future perils, and where there are two paths for a woman: the path of the Blessing, or the rarer path of the Warrior. Gwenhwyfar chosses the latter, giving up the power she is born to. But the daugther of a king is never truly free to follow her own calling...

978-0-7564-0585-4
hardcover

To Order Call: 1-800-788-6262
www.dawbooks.com

Patrick Rothfuss
THE NAME OF THE WIND
The Kingkiller Chronicle: Day One

"It is a rare and great pleasure to come on somebody writing not only with the kind of accuracy
of language that seems to me absolutely essential to fantasy-making, but with real music in the
words as well.... Oh, joy!"   —Ursula K. Le Guin

"Amazon.com's Best of the Year...So Far Pick for
2007: Full of music, magic, love, and loss, Patrick
Rothfuss's vivid and engaging debut fantasy
knocked our socks off."   —Amazon.com

"One of the best stories told in any medium in a
decade. Shelve it beside *The Lord of the Rings*
…and look forward to the day when it's
mentioned in the same breath, perhaps as
first among equals."   —*The Onion*

"[Rothfuss is] the great new fantasy writer we've
been waiting for, and this is an astonishing
book."   —Orson Scott Card

0-7564-0474-1

To Order Call: 1-800-788-6262
www.dawbooks.com

DAW 111

[9]